P9-DGX-414

ALSO BY JAMES HAN MATTSON

The Lost Prayers of Ricky Graves

Reprieve

A Novel

James Han Mattson

HARPER LARGE PRINT
An Imprint of HarperCollins*Publishers*

This is a work of fiction. Names, characters, places, and incidents are products of the author's imagination or are used fictitiously and are not to be construed as real. Any resemblance to actual events, locales, organizations, or persons, living or dead, is entirely coincidental.

HarperCollins books may be purchased for educational, business, or sales promotional use. For information, please e-mail the Special Markets Department at SPsales@harpercollins.com.

FIRST HARPER LARGE PRINT EDITION

ISBN: 978-0-06-311748-8

Library of Congress Cataloging-in-Publication Data is available upon request.

21 22 23 24 25 LSC 10 9 8 7 6 5 4 3 2 1

For my parents, Ronald Robert Mattson
and Donna Marie Mattson

PART I
Witnesses

Witness:
Cory Stout

Cross-Examination Excerpt
September 16, 1997

Q. When you got to Cell Five, what did you see?

A. The defendant was holding a knife to Bryan Douglas's throat and screaming for John.

Q. Just to clarify, he was screaming for John Forrester, the owner of the Quigley House?

A. Yep.

Q. Was John there that night?

A. Nope.

Q. Did you recognize the man with the knife?

A. Recognized his voice. Dude was on our blacklist.

Q. Can you clarify, please, your blacklist?

A. It's a list of people who've threatened us.

Q. Is this list reserved for people who live in Lincoln, Nebraska?

A. Not at all. It's got people from all over the world, but mostly from Nebraska, I guess, since the biggest pains are usually local.

Q. Is the list long?

A. Yep. Hundreds.

Q. But let me get this straight, you recognized his *voice*? You'd never actually met my client in person.

A. Yeah. I knew his voice well. He left messages almost every day all crazed.

Q. Okay, so you saw the defendant with a knife to Bryan's throat, then what?

A. Everyone rushed down to Cell Five—the crew, the cast, people in the control room, everyone. Nuts. I didn't want 'em to crowd like that, but sometimes people aren't too bright.

Q. So the entire cast and crew witnessed the defendant holding a knife to Bryan's throat?

A. Yeah. And the other contestants, they witnessed it too. They'd been competing in that cell.

Q. And who were the other contestants?

A. Victor Dunlap, Jane Roth, and Jaidee Charoensuk.

Q. And Kendra Brown, the one who'd initially CB'd you, was she there?

A. No, not in the cell. She was in the control room.

Q. Why was she there?

A. She'd been in the parking lot, 'cause that's where . . .

She'd run to the house for help. She thought I'd be in the control room, but I wasn't. I was in Cell Five, like I said. So, she saw it.

Q. Saw what?

A. Well, she saw what happened.

Q. And what exactly did she see?

Kendra

After her father's funeral, in a bright, green-carpeted reception hall, Kendra Brown, age fifteen, sat in a corner by herself, flipping quickly through the pages of *Pet Sematary.* She was at the part where Louis Creed, protagonist and ideal father, witnesses his child's death-by-truck, noticing, sickeningly, that his son's baseball cap is filled with blood. *Filled with blood.* That's what it said. *Filled with blood.* Kendra shook her head, thought: How would a baseball cap, presumably cloth, *fill* with blood? Wouldn't the blood just soak in? Wouldn't the cap deflate? Wouldn't there have to be a *ton* of blood for the cap to *fill*? If so: gross! She looked up.

In the center of the room, her extended family—most from the D.C. metro, but a few from elsewhere—mingled. They carried baked goods held upright by red and yellow napkins. Some nibbled; others devoured. Her cousin Iris, whom she hadn't seen in five years, stuffed half a chocolate-chip cookie in her mouth, chewed vigorously. Her jaw dislocated left, then right, then left, then right. She slouched, her free arm reaching for the floor, her stomach flowing over her pants, her breasts free and pendulous against her rib cage. Kendra swallowed. Look at her, crying like that, she thought. Like she was close to him.

Kendra opened her book again. The words ran into one another. *Filled with blood.* She blinked. She closed the book, sighed.

"Kendra, baby, come over here," her mother, Lynette, called from behind the food table.

Kendra set her book down, went to her. Her mother had been furiously rearranging the dishes, making sure the baked goods, the fried goods, the desserts were all in their proper places. She set down a plate of brownies, strode around to the front of the table, met her daughter.

"Mom," Kendra said.

"What a mess," Lynette said, unwrapping a mint, popping it into her mouth. "I told them to keep it orderly." The harsh light enlarged her weariness. Her cheeks were drawn, her forehead deeply grooved. Kendra had always found her mother striking—long-limbed, large-eyed, smooth-faced, a direct contrast to her own short-limbed, small-eyed, freckled self—but there, in front of all that food, she looked rabid and ancient, a woman in need of a month of hot meals and warm showers. She wore a pair of rumpled black pants, creased and bunched in odd places, and a flowy red button-down that opened slightly at the top, exposing a dark, rigid clavicle. Kendra reached out, grabbed the collar, pulled it closer to her mother's neck. "All of this," Lynette said, shaking her head. "A mess."

"Mom," Kendra said.

"I know," Lynette said. "I know. But why are you over there by yourself? Don't do that. Don't you do that to me today."

"What do you want?"

"Kendra," Lynette said. "We talked about this."

"We did?" Kendra said.

"For one damn day," Lynette said.

"Fine, fine, fine," Kendra said, feeling prickly, turning slowly toward the clump of family in the middle of the room. "Fine, fine, fine," she said. She walked.

It wasn't that she actively disliked her family. For the most part, they amused her. Her cousins, her aunts, her uncles, they'd all, at some point, helped her mother out, and individually they were great conversationalists: for instance, Kendra could sit and listen for hours to her uncle Howard talk about how, when he was young, he'd nearly died on a yacht in the Bahamas. Something about a rotten mango. Something about a high-speed car chase. Something about a white man mistaking him for a seaside restaurant employee. Anyway. As a collective, and especially at major functions, her family all talked over one another so that together they became this buzzing, barking mass, and Kendra found this extremely irritating. Packed together in one room, they overwhelmed her with their intense animation, and so she withdrew.

But this was a different kind of day. And she'd told her mother that she would engage. So she walked to the center of the mass and allowed them to descend, their funereal breath mixing, fluttering. They said: *Kendra, how* are *you? Kendra, I'm sorry. Kendra, I've been prayin' for you. Kendra, what you need, hon? Kendra, come here, let me look at you. Kendra, you need food? Kendra Kendra Kendra Kendra Kendra Kendra Kendra*

"Kendra." Her uncle Nestor—all 325 pounds of him—stood in front of her, put his hand on her shoulder, tilted his head, said, "You okay?"

Kendra looked away. Around her, condolences weighted the air, constricted her throat. She wasn't quite ready to receive them. She wasn't quite ready to understand that her dad had become permanently erased. She looked up. The ceiling seemed impossibly far, all glaring white fluorescence. She looked to her left, to the wall, to a painting of Jesus praying in Gethsemane, his head haloed gold, his eyes beseeching and sad.

"Hey," Nestor said. "I was just thinking. You remember how your dad used to lift you over his head and run around the house? You were like, 'I can fly, I can fly, I can fly!'" He chuckled. "You'd giggle so much you'd *cry*! Whole buckets of tears and you, all cute, goin' on about flying. He'd put you down and you'd say, 'More, more, more!'"

"Hmm," Kendra said, blinking hard, still looking at Jesus.

"Whenever you two were in a room together you were smiling broad as ever," Nestor said.

She looked at him, focused on the mole in the center of his forehead. "When did you see me—"

"He cherished you completely, K. *Completely.*"

Kendra stuffed her hands into her pockets, looked longingly at the chair in the corner. How full was that baseball cap? she thought. A tablespoon? A cup? A pint? She imagined Louis Creed picking it up, letting the blood spill out all over the road.

"Greg's at peace now," Nestor said, nodding. "He's smilin' down on you."

Kendra smiled, turned, shoved her way to the outskirts of the group, nodded, embraced, nodded, embraced. *Kendra, I'm sorry. Kendra, you come visit anytime. Kendra, you try the brownies? Kendra Kendra Kendra.*

She thought: *And what exactly am I supposed to do with all these fucking sorrys?*

She found her cousin Bryan, the only family member without food, standing at the perimeter of the group with his hands clasped in front of him, solemnly observing. She reached up and hugged him, felt warmth.

"You look weird in a suit," Kendra said.

"I wanted to come over and say hi before," he said, pulling back, "but you seemed busy with your book." He smiled. His teeth gleamed.

"I guess," she said.

"I'm sorry about your dad," he said.

"Yeah," she said.

Standing next to her cousin made her feel tiny. He was six-foot-two; she was barely five feet. He was athletic, lithe, confident, the type of guy who endlessly frustrated women. She was inward, clumsy, sullen, a girl who roamed invisible down school hallways. For some reason, though, they got along best: it was him she'd called directly after the accident, saying: *I think this is shock?* Though he lived in Nebraska with her mother's sister Rae, she saw him the most out of all her cousins. Rae and Lynette were exceptionally close.

"Don't know why you'd wanna read books when you're not in school," Bryan said. "And that? Here? Now? Stephen King, man. He's fucked up."

"What do you know," Kendra said, her vision clouding.

"I know enough."

"I can't deal with all this," she said, staring once again at Iris, who was still chewing.

He sniffed. "I dunno. You're what they call . . . what is it? Someone who doesn't fit into normal life?"

"Fuck off, Bryan."

"No, I don't mean it negative. All the brilliant people are like that."

"A misanthrope?"

"Maybe."

They stood in silence for a while. Gray light from the window fell over her cousin, shadowing his eyes. Outside, traffic rumbled and screeched down Rhode Island Avenue. Kendra winced. Since her father's accident, she couldn't stop envisioning loud, clamorous impacts. Every honk, engine rev, or shriek of rubber on asphalt signaled a grave, untimely death, and though nobody had been in the car with her dad, whenever she closed her eyes she envisioned everything: the white truck edging closer and closer to her father's lane, her father's horn blaring, her father shouting, *Get in your lane!*, the car ahead not accelerating, the car behind not decelerating, the middle-aged truck driver growing sleepier and sleepier, his head bobbing up and down, the truck careening over the line, her father grabbing the steering wheel so tight his hands shook, the spray of dirt, the small hill, the sudden shouts of the truck driver, who still, impossibly, raced beside him, the fumbling brakes, the choking seat belt, and finally, the wide, wide trunk of the scarlet oak tree.

"You okay?" Bryan said.

Kendra breathed in through her nose, out through her mouth. "Uncle Nestor told me how my dad used to lift me over his head and pretend I was flying," she said.

"So?" Bryan said.

"My dad never did that."

"When you were little—"

"He never did that."

"I think I remember something . . ."

"No, Bryan."

He shifted his weight from his left to his right leg, stuffed his hands in his pockets. "Hey, when you gonna get out of this all-black phase?" he said, looking her up and down. "Haven't you heard? Goth shit is a white loser thing. Black people got *enough* problems—we don't wear them for show, you know?"

"Whatever," Kendra said. "It's a fucking funeral."

Bryan said, "Well, I guess."

Kendra thought of the last time she'd seen Bryan. He'd been at her house talking to her dad, who, as per usual, sat poring over paperwork in his starched white shirt and solid blue tie. Bryan had been discussing his new girlfriend, gesticulating wildly, trying, Kendra supposed, to make up for her father's cool rigidity. Bryan told Greg, her father, how this girl, Simone, was different from all the others, how she challenged him, made him think. "I've never felt this way before," Bryan said. "I'm serious."

Kendra had walked in on them, looking first at her dad, then at her cousin. She'd thought: *Bryan, no. Haven't you learned anything?* but said nothing, letting her cousin continue speaking to the stone structure that was Greg Brown, and when Bryan was finished, after he'd briefed her father on all the particulars of Simone's wondrousness, Greg removed his glasses, rubbed his eyes, sighed, and said, "I'm sorry, Bryan. I'm just not interested in this right now."

In the reception hall, Bryan wrung his hands by his sides. There was a nervousness to him that Kendra had never witnessed before. She didn't understand it.

It wasn't like he and Greg had been close. "Are *you* okay?" Kendra said.

"Your mom's gonna need your help," Bryan said. "She's not good."

"Nobody's *good*," Kendra said.

"I'm just saying," Bryan said.

"You know he was a fucking jerk," she said. "You understand that, right?"

"Kendra," Bryan said.

"What."

She closed her mouth. Part of her stoicism was an act, she knew. Part of her wanted to cry, or race around like her mom, or spill memories like everyone else in the reception hall. Part of her felt like falling into the grief, letting it consume her, displaying the displays that everyone expected, but another part, a stronger part, remembered too much, remembered the nights her mother had called Greg at eleven P.M., midnight, one A.M., pleading for him to come home. *Your clients will be there in the morning,* she'd said. *But we're here now.* Kendra remembered how he'd missed her last three birthdays without so much as a card, how he ate fancy dinners with clients while Lynette slathered jelly on toast, how, when he *was* home, he walked around without speaking, grunting hellos, then retreating to his study. Could she properly grieve a man who'd tried so badly to be missing? She didn't know.

"I'm just saying," Bryan said, "Lynette, she's gonna need you more now. So stop sulking in your room, reading those books. You're gonna have to seriously work together, figure shit out."

"What do you know," Kendra said.

"I know enough," Bryan said.

"Okay," Kendra said. "Whatever." She touched her cousin's arm, squeezed, then went back to her chair.

After the reception, Lynette said she needed a few things from Greg's office in Alexandria, and though Kendra protested, the idea of metroing alone that day horrified her, so she hopped in her mother's Ford Escort and looked out the window as Lynette raced across town to the Fourteenth Street Bridge.

Kendra had been across the bridge hundreds of times, of course, and it usually gnawed at her, knowing she'd soon be spending time at her dad's boring workplace. But today, with her mother's distress constricting the car, her father dead, Nestor's words ringing in her head (*He cherished you completely, K*), everything seemed different, everything seemed *new.* The dying sun lit the clouds, and the pink wisps danced down the black water. The lights of Pentagon City dotted the edges of the river, and though she'd always found the Potomac somewhat boring, a river that native D.C. people often avoided recreationally, on that day, it seemed strangely beautiful, a natural insertion plopped between two hubris-laden cityscapes. It's pretty here sometimes, she thought. I should remember that.

It was late, and the office was empty. She followed her mom through the front door, the dark lobby, past the marble reception desk, down a small hall, to the third door on the right.

"Why do we have to be here again?" Kendra said, feeling suddenly hungry. She hadn't eaten any of the food at the reception.

"You don't have to whisper," Lynette said.

"What do you actually need?"

"Kendra," Lynette said. She pushed the door open, turned on the light.

Every time Kendra saw her father's office, she was struck by its orderliness. The law books stood neatly against the shelves behind the desk, the framed degrees hung perfectly on the north wall, the file folders and notebooks stacked tidily atop the oak desk, the pictures, the typewriter, the clock, even the window that looked out on South Fairfax Street, all of it utterly in place, as if forever unused, forever stationary. Despite the twinkly sanitization, however, she'd always found the neatness an affront: why would her father spend so much time curating such bald-faced organization here when at home he rushed through everything, leaving clothes on the floor, food on the counter, dishes in the sink? His home life, it seemed, had been something he needed to barrel through and zip past so he could get back to his actual life, his meaningful life, his *office*. It angered Kendra; even with him gone now, she still felt his professional urgency everywhere, diminishing and minimizing her, filling her with a profound sense of neglect.

And then there was her mother, who'd just let it all happen. Kendra looked at her, frowned. Lynette sat at Greg's desk, spreading her hands out on the wood. She drummed her fingers against the shiny top. "It's amazing," she said. "I've never sat here. Not once since we've been married."

"Mom."

Lynette leaned back in the chair, looked up at the lights, crossed her hands behind her head. "I couldn't go home yet, Kendra," she said. "Just not yet." She blinked hard, lifted her long, toned legs, put them on the desk, crossed her feet. If she hadn't looked so depleted, she might've looked powerful. She closed her eyes. "Our lives are going to change," she said. "Vastly."

"They're already changed," Kendra said.

"I'm not sure I can do this," Lynette said. "I'm not sure."

Kendra shook her head. She'd never understood why her mother had put up with her father's continued absences. On the phone with Greg, Lynette had always sounded weak, succumbing to his sternness without mustering any of her own. There was no *reason* Lynette couldn't have demanded his presence. Kendra's friends' mothers did it all the time. In fact, her best friend Camille's mother ordered Camille's stepfather around so much that she—Camille's mother—sometimes *begged* her husband to make a decision.

Lynette opened her eyes, blinked up at the white light. "We were together so long," she said. "Like an appendage."

Kendra sat on the chair opposite her mother, leaned back. "But we're gonna be okay, right?" she said. "I mean, you're okay financially?"

Lynette folded her legs, sat upright in the chair, looked at Kendra with red, slitted eyes. "Really? That's what you're caring about now? That's what you're thinking about?"

Kendra shrugged. "Is it a bad thing to think about?"

"I'm gonna get a job," Lynette said, smirking. "Don't you worry about that."

"It's not such a weird question," Kendra said.

Lynette shook her head. "Why don't you just wait in reception for a minute, okay?" she said. "I wanna be alone here."

"In the waiting room?" Kendra said.

Lynette pursed her lips. "Or outside. Or go home. I just need a minute, okay?"

"But, Mom—"

"Please, Kendra," Lynette said, her voice sharp. Kendra stood up, backed away.

"I don't *wanna* just sit out there," she said.

"Then go home!" Lynette said.

"What?"

"Just a few minutes, okay?"

Kendra fumed, balled her hands into fists. "I mean, this is happening to me, too, you know."

Lynette went cold. She sat back in the chair, looked at her reflection in the window. Kendra stood for a while in the doorway, willing her mother to say something more, but Lynette stayed silent, and after a few minutes of suffocating quiet, Kendra left the office and took a seat in the dark outer room.

A few weeks later, Kendra sat listlessly in geometry class, listening to her teacher, Mr. Blaisdell, drone on about parallelograms. He drew a slanted box on the board, adding numbers, letters, symbols, and Kendra, feeling exceptionally tired and ornery, wondered why it was that he never came to class in anything but wrinkly khakis and faded polos. Teachers made okay money, she thought, right? Certainly he could afford new clothes. She rapped her pencil against her book, loud. Blaisdell turned around, put his hands on his hips, tilted his head.

"Miss Brown?" Mr. Blaisdell said.

She didn't look at him, just stared at her textbook.

"Miss Brown, is everything okay?"

She looked up, choked. Replacing Mr. Blaisdell's squishy face was the lean face of her father.

"Oh my god," she said.

"Miss Brown?"

She blinked; Blaisdell's face returned, but her father still staggered about in her mind's eye. She shook her head.

"Miss Brown," Mr. Blaisdell repeated.

She grabbed her bag, stood up, walked. Thirty eyes burned into her. Still, she kept going, out of the room, into the hallway, past the restrooms, past the principal's office, past the long row of gray lockers, to the front doors. She pushed, breathed in clean autumnal air, and walked some more, down the steps, across the street. She sat on the curb, hugging her knees, watching as the cars on N Street stopped, flashed their blinkers, waited.

Memories fell upon her in one enormous flood—her dad eating silently, grinning down at her, him at a park, she a young girl, her mother's face shiny with promise, reflecting the sun—and each of these images reminded her that her father hadn't always retreated into work, that there had been times when he was fully present, such as the day he'd made her sit and watch the Rodney King video, the one where a group of white cops beat Mr. King with batons. She'd been in fifth grade—impressionable, not yet jaded—and her father had rewound, repeated, rewound, repeated. When she'd finally said, "Stop, Daddy!" he'd grabbed her by the shoulders, stared her down, pointed at the screen, and said, "You watch this, Kendra. This is the world we live in." A little over a year later, riots broke out; people were shot, killed; stores in Los Angeles demolished, set aflame; and he came home that day drunk and sweaty, dropping his briefcase at the door, stumbling helplessly into her mother's embrace. He'd sobbed and shook, and Kendra had watched, horror-stricken, thinking that the fires of L.A. were headed for her neighborhood.

Why else would her father be crying so hard? Why else would he look so defeated?

On the curb, Kendra exhaled a long, ragged breath, blinked back tears. In front of her, Dunbar High School rose like an asylum, a boxy, seven-story brown monolith, housing for the city's adolescent leftovers. She clutched her knees tighter. Beside her was a tree whose branches curved perfectly up and out like a big, leafy, inverted umbrella. She moved a few feet to the right, catching its shade.

I didn't even really know you, she thought. *So just leave me alone.*

She looked across the street at the school. Students trickled outside. Some went to cars. Some walked. Some crossed the street and surrounded her on the sidewalk. A few snickered. She didn't stand up. They left her alone. She was now the girl whose dad had died in a freak car accident, which was better, she guessed, than being Tasha Vance, the girl whose dad died with a prostitute, or Koreesha Simonson, the girl whose dad shot her mother, but still, she hated that people kept such a wide berth: it wasn't like she'd contracted some contagious disease. She pulled her knees closer, shivered, watched all the kids, wondered if her mind would ever take a rest. *I don't want to think about you,* she thought. *Please just go away. Please, please, please—*

A person was hovering. She looked up. Her friend Shawn Sims stood above her, playing with his fingers. Kendra squinted.

"Hey," he said.

"Shawn, I'm not in the mood, okay?" she said. She brought her hand to her forehead. He looked impossibly tall.

"I know you're going through a lot, but—"

"Shawn, no," she said.

"Movies might help you take your mind off things," he said.

"No," she said. "No."

He was gangly and thin, his plain white T-shirt oversized and loose. When she stood, dusted herself off, he immediately looked away, as if the death of her father had reconstructed her face into something foreign. They'd known each other for two years now, had started an unofficial horror-lovers club at school, which, at first, had boasted fifteen members. The group had convened once a week in one of the English classrooms. They'd exchanged novels, traded videotapes, discussed the merits and demerits of things they'd watched and read, even talked about filming a movie up in Rock Creek Park, a slasher that they'd tentatively titled *President Death.* The movie never got made, of course: nobody had equipment, nobody knew how to *get* equipment, and the few pages of script that Shawn had written were, according to him, so bad they literally smelled. Eventually, without the movie serving as an anchor for the group, membership dwindled to only Kendra and Shawn: the others cited increased extracurricular obligations, schoolwork, or just general disinterest.

"Things aren't good at home," Kendra said, zipping her bag, running her arms through the straps. "My mom's a mess." Around them, clusters of students passed. Vanessa Harrison, a girl she'd known since the first grade, looked at her, arched her stenciled eyebrows, then turned swiftly toward Breanna Davis, whispering. Walking behind Vanessa was Jeremy Hortense, a football player, a boy Kendra had crushed on for years. He said, "Shake it, V!" Vanessa ignored him, laced her arm into Breanna's, started skipping.

Kendra turned back to Shawn, tilted her head. People sometimes made fun of him, mainly because his forehead was enormous. It sped over half of his face, his eyes, cheeks, lips, and chin seemingly squashed together to prevent further extension. They also called him "Oreo," which annoyed Kendra. There was no such thing as *white on the inside*. That would mean there's only one way to be Black. "Our group is done with anyway," she said.

“No, it’s not,” he said. “There’s us. And we can get more. But until then . . .”

“Until then?” she said.

“Come on,” he said. “Let me come over. Please. We can watch *Hellraiser.*”

She sighed. “My dad just died, Shawn. You really think I wanna watch *Hellraiser*?”

“But *Lord of Illusions* is coming out on video soon,” he said. “Don’t you wanna do a Clive Barker marathon before we see it?”

“Didn’t that movie *just* come out in theaters?”

Shawn shrugged. “It doesn’t take that long . . .”

She tightened her backpack straps, looked over at the school. Only a few students trickled out now. She glanced at her watch. “Shit,” she said. She turned around and walked quickly down the sidewalk. Shawn followed her. “I’ll bring popcorn,” he said.

“No,” she said.

“Come *on,* Kendra,” he said, panting. “You know I can’t watch these by myself.”

She smiled. Shawn, horror lover that he was, was also a big ’fraidy cat. During the hospital scene in *Jacob’s Ladder* he’d bitten his knuckles so hard that he’d left indentations. She’d had to treat him with antibiotic ointment and a Band-Aid afterward. *Big fucking baby,* she’d said, laughing.

"Okay," he said, "maybe not *Hellraiser,* but how about something dumb? *C.H.U.D.*? *Ghoulies*? I haven't seen *C.H.U.D. II* yet. You wanna?"

She stopped, turned. "*C.H.U.D. II*?" she said. "Seriously? Who watches *C.H.U.D.* anymore?" And yet: as silly as the idea was, watching a low-budget '80s horror movie sounded, at that moment, incredible. She shook her head.

"Fine," she said, pulling her hair behind her ear. "Fine. Saturday. Regular time."

Shawn's forehead creased: five long squiggles in a sea of skin. "Really?"

"Fine," she said.

"But what do you want me to bring? Do you want *Hellraiser*? Or . . ."

"I gotta go," she said. "See you Saturday."

"Kendra. What do you want—"

But she was already across the street, running home as fast as she could.

Three days later, on a bright, crisp Saturday, Kendra sat on her couch with her friend Camille Brennan, eating Fritos and bologna sandwiches and watching *The Bugs Bunny & Tweety Show.* Camille—skinny, brace-faced, light-skinned—usually let Kendra talk only when she, Camille, literally couldn't—like if her mouth was full or she had laryngitis. Her outpourings had gotten so bad that by the eighth grade, Kendra started timing her friend's chewing and swallowing habits, knowing that if she wanted to get a word in she'd have to interrupt, or insert herself when Camille's risk of choking was highest.

On this day, as per usual, Camille commented extensively on the TV show, saying things like, "What is a *rascally rabbit* anyway? I've never *heard* of anyone calling anything *rascally*" and "I don't think some old grandma could move fast enough to clobber a cat like that" and "What's a *roadrunner*? Are they actual animals that live in the desert or something?" Knowing that Camille loved Fritos and ate them nearly every day, Kendra had bought two bags, replenishing the bowl as soon as it was half-empty. Kendra had things she needed to talk about, and if she could manage to get a word in, she could direct Camille's focus.

She set the bowl of Fritos on Camille's lap. Camille looked at her, shrugged, and said, "You trying to get me fat or something? Doesn't matter. I've been exercising. Sorta like 8-Minute Abs but I add exercises that work the sides and chest and stuff—you should try it." She took a handful of Fritos, shoved them in her mouth.

They'd known each other forever, or at least that's how it seemed to Kendra. In elementary school, Camille, scrappy and loud, had pushed Paul LaFleur to the ground when he'd yanked on Kendra's hair at recess. Camille had shouted, "Get used to being down there, you stupid lowlife." And Kendra had felt so grateful, so cared for, that she'd followed Camille around until Camille had finally turned to her and said, "So what *is* this? You want to be best friends? Well, fine."

Eyeing the bowl of chips, Kendra said, "Shawn Sims is coming over this afternoon and I want you to stay here with us, but you *can't talk* during the movie, okay? You *can't talk*. I don't wanna be alone with him, at least not now."

Camille swallowed. "I don't know *why* you hang out with him. He's such a weirdo and his face is, like, so creepy."

"He's not that bad."

"I mean, I'm really sorry about your dad and everything, Kendra, I've said that a hundred times. I'm sure you're feeling a bit messed up, but that doesn't mean you should just try to lose your virginity to help calm things down. It doesn't work, believe me."

"What? I'm not gonna have sex with him. I'm not *you*."

Camille shrugged. "I mean, maybe he's good? Maybe he's got all the right moves 'cause he's so funny-looking? I hear that's a thing. You know, weird-looking dudes being fucking *amazing* at sex. Like they're so grateful for anyone even paying any attention to them that they'll just make sure that you're totally pleased in every possible way. But anyway, you want me to stay? Fuck no. Sorry, K. You two can have your own little love-gore fest. I'm not any part of that shit. I don't wanna—"

"He hasn't been over since my dad died. I've blown him off. And now I feel a little weird, like he's my friend and I just ignored him. I thought it'd be good for all three of us to be here. Like—"

"But then," Camille said, "who knows? You like this guy, I can tell. Sure, you do. He's like . . . I mean, you're both sorta . . . I don't wanna be hateful. But—chemistry is chemistry, I guess. Maybe he's the one."

Camille scooped another handful of Fritos. Kendra said, "This isn't a date. I just think it'd be good for all of us to watch together, and my mom, she basically spends weekends in her room, so she won't be a big deal—"

"Kendra! I'm *not* staying. This is your life and your date, and you need to do this by your*self*." She chewed. A crumb sprang from her lips, fell onto the floor. "He'd probably get one of those embarrassing boners around me anyhow." She ran her nails along the couch. "I'm gonna go now," she said. "You'll have to tell me all about it."

"It's not what you think," Kendra said.

"It's good, Kendra. Nerds are more your style. I'll be honest, and don't take this the wrong way, okay, because you know that I think you're cool but you're also real smart and I think guys like Jeremy Hortense will most likely fall short for you in the intellectual department if you know what I mean. But anyway, your first matters. So, think about it real hard. I'm gonna get outta here now." She stood, beamed down at her.

"Camille," Kendra said. "No, please—"

"Go put something cute on. Like something that shows your boobs. I mean, look at you. A date in a *Pixies* T-shirt? I seriously don't know about you, Kendra." She walked to the front door.

"Camille, wait—"

"Call me later, okay? Call me and fill me in. I'll be waiting by my phone. Ha."

"But Camille. Can you just wait—"

"Have a good time! Bye!"

And then she was gone.

Kendra pouted, crossed her arms over her chest. She'd thought for sure that Camille would've stayed—she liked eavesdropping on every minor happenstance in Kendra's life—but Camille had been seeing a boy herself recently, an older guy who called himself

"Special D" and whose entire wardrobe seemed comprised of NWA T-shirts and gray sweatpants, so she figured her meeting with Shawn gave Camille an excuse to go see him. Kendra had only met Special D once, and had told Camille afterward that she could do so much better, that she didn't need to date a guy that chewed with his mouth open and guzzled beer like it was water, but Camille had just looked at Kendra, shook her head, and said, "Someday you'll understand, baby K."

On the couch, Kendra closed her eyes, thought of Shawn's forehead, his close-set eyes, his spindly arms, his tiny waist. She'd distanced herself from him not just because of her dad but because she'd thought he was getting too close, too comfortable, too much like a *boyfriend.* And did she want that? With him? She didn't actually think she was attracted to him—mostly, she fantasized about guys like Jeremy Hortense, big athletic types—but since the horror club had devolved to just the two of them, she'd found herself oddly nervous when Shawn was close, and one time, during the hobbling scene in *Misery,* she'd put her hand on his leg and left it there for a while. He'd been wearing khaki shorts; her fingers prickled against his leg hair. She moved her palm around in small circles, reveling in the scratchiness, wondering what it'd be like to just let hair grow wherever. When he glanced at her, she recoiled, withdrew her hand, looked away, felt her face heat.

"You know," she said, moving farther down the couch, "in the book Annie Wilkes actually cuts his feet off."

They spent the rest of the movie silent, and afterward, he'd left without saying goodbye.

He arrived at her house at 2:10 P.M., two videotapes in one hand, a single bag of uncooked microwave popcorn in the other.

"I figured we should start with *Hellraiser*," he said.

"Shawn—"

"I know, I know. I brought *C.H.U.D. II* as well, but we can *start* with Pinhead, can't we?"

He walked in, placed the tapes and the popcorn on the coffee table, sat down. Kendra thought he looked remarkably comfortable sitting there—his legs splayed wide, his shoulders slouched, his head tilted slightly to the side. Kendra looked down at the videotape.

"Your brothers okay?" Kendra said.

"Well, you know," he said. They always watched at her place because he had four loud siblings who seemingly never left the house, and strangely, though

Shawn was second oldest, he wielded almost no power over them. In fact, the last time Kendra was over to his place, Fenton, his thirteen-year-old brother, had walked into the room as soon as they'd put the movie in. He'd flopped on the couch between them, watched for five minutes, said, *Nah,* got up, ejected the video, took the remote, and turned it to MTV. Kendra sat up, said, *Excuse you,* and turned expectantly to Shawn, certain he wouldn't stand for such incorrigible behavior from an underling. But Shawn stayed still, watching silently as his little brother flipped through channel after channel after channel, and when it was clear that Fenton was now lord of the living room, Kendra stood and went home.

When she'd asked him about it later, Shawn told her that it'd always been that way, that the more he stood up for himself, the more his brothers acted out. He'd learned to let things go: nobody, it seemed—no sibling, parent, or friend—ever came to his defense.

"I think they all think of me as some sort of freak," he told her. "Like I'm so different than all of them, like maybe I was a mistake."

"The world is ass-backwards," she said, thinking of a few of her own extended family members, how they chided her for reading books. "Like people tell you that you need to do one thing to better yourself, then make fun of you when you actually do it. I don't get it."

"Well, I guess that makes us the rebels, huh," he said.

"Ha," she said. "Yeah, something like that."

At her house, Kendra sat on the couch, a safe distance from Shawn but not so far as to be impolite. She said, "My mom's in her room, right down the hall."

"Will it be okay?" Shawn said.

"Yeah," she said, fidgeting with the bottom of her T-shirt. "She doesn't come out much. Just to use the bathroom, sometimes to get food, but she'll leave us alone." Kendra thought about her mother that morning, hair mangled, cheeks wrinkly, her robe stained with what looked like spaghetti sauce. She'd moved around the kitchen without speaking, grabbing a box of cereal and a spoon before retreating to her room. Must be nice to just give up like that, Kendra had thought. To not have to interact, go to school, whatever. To just sit in there and rot.

"It's gotta be difficult for you two right now," Shawn said.

"Some days," she said.

"I don't know if I told you, but my grandma died a couple years ago."

Kendra pursed her lips. "So, I guess *Hellraiser* first?"

"Save the laughs for last," Shawn said, smiling.

"Fine," Kendra said. "Put it in."

The reason Kendra didn't like *Hellraiser* was because she thought it relied too much on gore. She read a lot of horror novels—particularly Stephen King—not because she liked being scared but because at the center of many of these books was a love story, a torrid, or sweet, or newfangled romance that endured tremendous, often supernatural, strain. She read these books to see whether the couples made it through the strain, whether the most harrowing of circumstances was enough to tear them apart. In this way, she categorized good versus bad books. For instance: *Carrie,* bad. *Pet Sematary,* bad. *The Stand,* good! *It,* good! *The Shining,* so, so, *soooo* bad!

But after this viewing, as the credits rolled, she felt strangely solemn, almost transformed. How hadn't she seen it before? *Hellraiser* was a love story! A twisted, bloody, crazy one, but a love story nonetheless. Julia was deeply in love with Frank, so much so that she was willing to make sacrifice after sacrifice to restore him to humanity! It was *tender.* It was *romantic.* It was *beautiful.* She turned to Shawn, grinned, and wondered what her father would think of this scenario, her on the couch alone with this boy. Her dad had never directly spoken to her about the opposite sex but had once discussed it succinctly via Lynette. Her mother had been on the phone with her father, laughing, and when she'd hung up, her eyes dancing, Lynette had looked down at Kendra and said, "I'm supposed to write it down." She raced to the kitchen, scribbled on a piece of paper, then handed the folded scrap to Kendra. Still chuckling, she said, "A message from your brilliant father. He thought it was *very* urgent." Kendra opened the note. It read: KENDRA, ALWAYS REMEMBER: BOYS LUST. GIRLS TRUST. THIS IS THE MAIN PROBLEM.

"You wanna take a break before *C.H.U.D.*?" Shawn said, eyeing the uncooked bag of popcorn.

Kendra didn't answer, just stared at the blank screen. Outside, near-dusk cast hectic shadows onto the living-room floor. Beside Shawn's left foot, on top of the red-green oriental rug, sat a rogue Frito, half-pulverized.

"Hello?" Shawn said.

"Shawn," Kendra said, turning to him, feeling warm, grabbing his hand. "Did you think that movie was sort of romantic?"

"Romantic? *Hellraiser?*" he said, looking down at her hand over his.

"I mean, obviously not the bloody stuff and the Cenobites," she said.

Shawn shook his head. "There's nothing really *romantic* about it, Kendra," he said.

"But I remember once in horror club you saying that you loved horror because it tested human limits. Like, wouldn't this have been an ultimate test of loyalty?"

"I guess," he said. "But is loyalty the same as romance?"

She leaned back, let go of his hand, sighed. The conversation in question had happened early on. Shawn, self-appointed president, had asked everyone to state why they'd wanted to join the club, what drew them to the genre. When they'd finished, he'd cleared his throat and said, "Horror tests limits. Horror shows who we are. When we're faced with a monster, or a ghost, or a serial killer, what we're actually made of comes forth. I like to see what people are made of. Therefore, I like horror."

Kendra had found his small speech inspiring—it'd propelled her to really examine why she was drawn to the macabre. And now, thinking about Julia and Frank and the lengths they went to love each other, and thinking of Shawn in that classroom, talking about limits, about what they were made of, she felt a sudden, overwhelming sense of serenity, and her father's face, though still ever-present, blurred around the edges. She turned to Shawn, drew in a deep breath.

"Shawn," she said, her forehead hot.

"Hey," he said.

Without thinking, she mashed her face against his. His lips tightened at first, a surprised blockade, but then they opened, and his top lip massaged her bottom one, and she tasted lemonade. She reached inside his shirt, felt the smooth curve of his lower back, pulled him toward her. Though he was skinny, his weight felt substantial and sheltering, his arms wrapping around her like insulation. On her thigh, she felt his cock pressing through his jeans, insistent, and she understood then that he *would* be her first, that she *wanted* him to be her first. At some point—not today, maybe not even in the next year, but someday—she would be ready, and it would be remarkable. She'd see fireworks, as Camille had claimed. She'd be transformed.

No limits, she thought.

She closed her eyes, allowed his lips to consume hers, and for the first time since his death, her father was nowhere to be found.

In late March, the winter winds finally subsiding, Lynette, breaking from hibernation, sat down with

Kendra on the living-room couch. Lynette looked near-normal, her red blouse unstained, her black pants creased in the right places, and the puffiness that'd defined the top part of her face had been replaced with smooth, unblemished skin. It was a Sunday, and Kendra had a geometry quiz the next day. She sat with her math book open in her lap. She hadn't done any problems, had just been looking at the numbers till they fuzzed.

"I got a call from Mrs. Witmer," Lynette said, her eyebrows sinking. "She's worried about you."

"She always worries," Kendra said, thinking about her principal, wondering why she'd call her mom. It's not like she was failing any of her classes.

"She said you sometimes leave class early."

Kendra shrugged. "I'm not failing," she said. "Isn't that enough?"

Lynette sighed, ran a hand through her hair. "I think we should talk," she said.

"I'm fine," Kendra said.

"We haven't really discussed your dad. Not directly."

"I'm *fine*," Kendra said. She looked down at her book, saw a bunch of triangles and numbers.

"Well," Lynette said, smoothing down her shirt, "I know this has been a tough school year."

Kendra shook her head, looked out the window.

Her neighbor, Raynelle Parsons, an old, single widow, walked by with her cane. She stopped, glanced up at the sky, then hobbled along. She always took walks in the afternoon, rain or shine.

"I'm glad you have a good friend," Lynette said.

"Huh?" Kendra said.

"Shawn Sims? I'm glad you're able to—"

"He's not a *friend*, Mom," she said, though as the words came out, Kendra wondered: what *was* he? Outside of Saturdays, to her dismay, she didn't have much of a relationship with Shawn. She saw him in class, and in the halls, and she always smiled, said hi, but they rarely spoke, the school environment with its jocks and cheerleaders and broad, imperious administrators somehow negating their more personal weekend association, the times when they watched movies and made out. They hadn't progressed to more than kissing—she hadn't felt the moment was right yet—but their make-out sessions were intense, and she'd allowed him to touch her everywhere above the clothes.

"I'm just saying that I'm glad you have someone to talk to," Lynette said, grimacing.

"I talk to Camille," Kendra said. "I talk to tons of people."

"I haven't seen Camille much these days," Lynette said.

“That’s ’cause you barely come out of your room,” Kendra said.

“Kendra, please,” Lynette said.

“What?” Kendra said.

“Just . . .”

“What do you want?”

“Why are you being difficult?”

“I’m not being *difficult,*” she said, folding her arms over her chest. “I have a *test* tomorrow.”

“I’m checking in,” Lynette said. “I’m acknowledging that this hasn’t been easy for either of us. I’m also . . .”

“You’re also what?”

Lynette turned fully toward Kendra. She reached out, grabbed her daughter’s hand. Kendra withdrew, said, “Jesus, what?”

“You know, I really love the relationship you have with Bryan,” Lynette said, stumbling. “I never had cousins that I was close to. What you two have is special.”

“*Bryan?*” Kendra said.

“I always wished I were closer to my extended family, but we never really gelled.”

“Why are you talking about Bryan?”

Lynette breathed in deep, closed her eyes. “I think we should be closer to them,” she said. “I think it’d be good for both of us.”

"But they're in Nebraska," Kendra said, feeling her chest tighten.

Lynette closed her mouth, looked down, fiddled with a button on her shirt.

Kendra's heart raced. "No," she said. "No."

"I'm having a hard time getting work here," Lynette said, talking to the floor now. "Rae said she could line me up with a receptionist job. You remember when she worked at Paw Pediatrics? Well, it turns out they actually *remember* me from the last time I was out there. And the current receptionist is leaving in a few months, so the timing's perfect. Anyway, she thinks it'd be good for us to be away from here, this house. I agree with her."

"But you haven't even *tried* to get a job here," Kendra said, sitting up, her vision blurring. "You've just been—"

"Bryan's moving out of their apartment, going to college," Lynette said. "You'll have your own room."

"I have my own room *now*!"

She thought, then, of Shawn, of how his face tightened right before a jump-scare, how he noticeably relaxed at the end, how he turned to her after he'd pressed Stop on the remote, burrowing his gaze into hers, gauging her reaction through sustained eye contact. She thought about his tongue, that slithery-soft slab that probed and investigated and explored not only her mouth but her neck, shoulders, and arms. She thought about their movies, how on the screen, some killer would be decapitating or stabbing or chainsawing and they'd be lip-locked, saliva passing freely, hands everywhere, legs intertwined. She thought about all the times they'd shared a popcorn bag, how their fingers touched, how even that small gesture sent a bolt of warmth up her spine. Saturdays were an absolute reprieve from her zombified mother, her boring teachers, her self-absorbed best friend, and her caustic, raging, dead dead dead father, the man whose face threatened to hurtle back at her full-force should her Shawn Sims Saturdays be taken from her.

"It'll be temporary," Lynette said.

"I can't live there," Kendra said. "I can't. You can't *make* me move there."

"I'm sorry, baby," Lynette said, putting her hand on Kendra's cheek. "We'll be back to visit all the time. I promise, okay?"

"No," Kendra said, brushing her mother's hand away. "It's *not* okay." She grabbed her math book, ran up the stairs, slammed her bedroom door. "It's not okay!" she shouted.

Later that night, she called Camille, told her the news.

"*Nebraska?*" Camille said. "What *is* that?" She sounded out of breath.

"It's where my cousin and aunt live," Kendra said, feeling dread. "It's out—"

"Oh wait, I just saw it on a map. Kendra, you *can't* live there. Does your mom even know anything about it? Kendra, you *must* tell her. It's shaped like a fucking *cannon.* That and Oklahoma, like two states down, they're *cannons.* Like they wanna shoot you further west, like to California. Kendra! You can*not* move to a state that's shaped like a goddamn cannon! This is the worst. And—what's that, baby? Yeah, she's moving to Nebraska! I know! I told her . . ."

"Who're you talking to?" Kendra said.

"Who do you *think* I'm talking to? He said that there's no such thing as Black people in Nebraska because they're all lynched. Anyone who moves there and is Black, the KKK just hang 'em up."

"That's ridiculous. My cousin—"

"You think there's not a *reason* that state is shaped like a cannon? D says during Civil War days they made those state lines for a purpose, to tell Black people who's boss. Like Southerners wanted everyone to know—"

"Nebraska was *not* part of the Confederacy," Kendra said, rolling her eyes.

"Listen, I'm just saying that it's very suspicious that it looks like that, and even if you *don't* get lynched, how're you gonna manage all that white? It's white *everywhere.* Swear. Like, I've been to Minnesota once, like Minneapolis. I was like: Where the fuck am I? How the fuck did this happen?"

"It can't be *all* white."

"Are you listening to anything I'm saying?" Camille said.

Kendra sighed. The girl was so difficult to talk to; just once she'd like to be able to speak without having to wait through a long-winded Camille retort. She wondered sometimes why she even remained in such a one-sided friendship: she wasn't really getting much out of it. Certainly there were other more generous girls around in whom she could confide.

And yet: with Camille there'd always been that fierce loyalty, that protective quality that Kendra had rarely received from either of her parents. Camille said it came from constantly defending her little brother Reggie, who'd been born with a hearing deficiency and wore a large gray hearing aid on his right ear.

"People are so dumb," she'd once told Kendra. "I mean, why would anyone ever make fun of someone for something they couldn't control? It's not like Reggie's using that thing as a *fashion* statement."

On the phone, Kendra said, "I'm listening."

"Have you told Shawn?" Camille said. "You just gonna leave him with his creepy slasher flicks? Boy'll probably turn into some raging serial killer without you, I swear."

"You're being stupid," Kendra said.

"Whatever," Camille said. "You'll see."

"I'm gonna call him now."

"Good luck. He's gonna freak."

Kendra hung up the phone, stared at it on its cradle, willed herself to pick it back up. She didn't want to hear his voice, didn't want to feel that tight urgency flood her body the way it did every time he spoke. Should she get the sex part over with? she wondered. Invite him to her house, tell him she was ready? If she didn't, it'd be too late, right? She'd be more than a thousand miles away. And on the visits her mother claimed they'd make—would there ever be enough time? Would it be right if she waited?

Slowly, she dialed his number. When he picked up, he sounded groggy, like he'd just awoken from a nap.

"Nebraska," he said once she told him. "Wow."

There was a long silence. "Yeah," she finally said. "I think she wants to leave after the school year is done."

"But that's in a couple months," Shawn said.

"I know," Kendra said. She sat on her bed, pushed her right palm beneath her thigh. "Hey, I was thinking . . ."

"Yeah?"

"I was thinking about you and me. I was thinking, and I'm not, like, one of those types of girls who get all clingy, seriously, I'm not, but I was wondering, like, what *are* we? Like are we, you know, going out?"

There was a long pause. Kendra's entire body tensed, her bottom teeth pushing hard against her top. Fuck, she thought. Fuck, fuck, fuck.

"It's okay," she said. "I don't even know why I asked."

"Yeah," Shawn said.

"Yeah?" she said, her voice a hideous squeak. "What do you mean, yeah?"

He hesitated. Kendra heard churning water, either a dishwasher or a washing machine. "Maybe we can talk about that later," he said.

"Later," Kendra said. "Yeah, sure."

More silence. Kendra wondered if she should hang up. She looked out her window. Pink rays of dusk settled comfortably along the street. A streetlight flickered on.

"So," Shawn said. "Nebraska."

"Yep," she said.

"You know that's where the Quigley House is, right?"

"Huh?"

"You haven't heard of it?"

"No," Kendra said, irritated, wanting only to talk about that *yeah* he'd uttered seconds before. "Why would I have?"

"Because it's amazing," he said. "Because you'd love it."

In a soft, measured voice, he filled her in.

Witness
Victor Dunlap

Cross-Examination Excerpt
September 16, 1997

Q. Mr. Dunlap, how did you get involved with the Quigley House?

A. I work at Calderon Bank in Des Moines. John Forrester was doing a promotion that involved area banks. We were one of them.

Q. What sort of promotion?

A. We were going to help him advertise. He was going to give us a free tour. We thought it'd be good publicity on both ends, given that he had so many devout followers.

We talked to local news, got the word out. We were Team Calderon.

Q. And you got the free tour?

A. Yes. I was one of the contestants.

Q. And who were the other contestants from Calderon?

A. Just one other. Jane Roth, my fiancée.

Q. But a team needs to have four contestants, is that correct?

A. Yes. I roped Jaidee into joining.

Q. And how did you know Jaidee? Was he involved with the bank somehow?

A. No, he was a student at UNL. I'd been his English teacher in Thailand. We met again sort of coincidentally, I guess.

Q. And what about the fourth?

A. Quigley supplied Bryan.

Q. Meaning what, exactly?

A. Meaning if a group wasn't able to round up a full team of four but had three people, the Quigley House had reserves of contestants.

Q. And you weren't able to get four. You weren't even able to get three? Why is that?

A. Quigley isn't everyone's cup of tea.

Q. How many people at the bank did you ask to be a part of your team?

A. Almost everyone.

Q. And how many is "almost everyone"?

A. Twenty-five?

Q. You approached twenty-five people and they all declined. What were their reasons?

A. They didn't give any. Like I said, it's just not everyone's cup of tea.

Q. And you? Was it *your* cup of tea?

A. I'm the branch manager.

Q. That's not what I asked.

A. I don't know. Maybe it's not my cup of tea. But it's not *not* my cup of tea, if that makes sense.

Q. Why did you go, then? Just because you felt obligated as the manager?

A. Well, that and Jane.

Q. What about her?

A. She was ecstatic. She was so excited.

Q. So you went because of her.

A. Partly.

Q. Interesting. So what you're saying is that out of twenty-seven employees, only *one,* your fiancée, was excited to take the tour?

A. I suppose. But I got excited later on. Just not right away.

Q. So the four of you—you, Jane, Jaidee, and Bryan—went through the house, made it through four cells together, is that correct?

A. Yes.

Q. Did anyone take the lead?

A. Excuse me?

Q. Did anyone become the natural leader in these cells?

A. We worked as a team.

Q. Yes, I understand, but did anyone emerge as a team *leader*?

A. Bryan, I guess.

Q. Why do you think that was the case?

A. I don't know. His cousin worked there, so we all assumed he had some information we didn't.

Q. That, and he was one of the *reserves.*

A. Yes.

Q. And were you aware of how these reserves were picked?

A. No.

Q. So you didn't know ahead of time that Bryan was related to one of the employees?

A. I didn't know that until a few days before I went.

Q. And how did you find out?

A. Jaidee called and told me.

Q. And what was your reaction to hearing that information?

A. I guess I thought it was weird, like maybe he was joining to sabotage us? But Jaidee convinced me that wasn't the case. He said Bryan was in it to win. He said Bryan could be a big help.

Q. I see. Mr. Dunlap, let's fast-forward to Cell Five, okay?

The defendant is behind Bryan with a knife, and you, Jaidee, and Jane are in front of them, watching. Put yourself in that moment, please. Try to remember Bryan's face. Does he look genuinely frightened to you?

A. Yes.

Q. Genuinely frightened.

A. Yes. But I thought he was faking.

Q. I'm confused. He looked genuinely frightened but was faking?

A. Yes. I thought he was being a really good actor.

Q. An actor who could fake sincere terror?

A. Man, I don't know. I just thought he was faking, okay?

Q. So you thought he was acting?

A. Yes.

Q. But why would you think that? Wasn't he on your team? Hadn't Jaidee convinced you that he was legitimate?

A. Yeah, but he'd been chosen by Quigley.

Q. And you thought he was in on it right up till the moment he was killed?

A. Yes.

Q. Even though he looked *genuinely* frightened?

A. Yes. No. Dammit. I don't know. It's all so confusing now.

Q. You thought the defendant was also an actor?

A. Yes.

Q. And when you witnessed him standing behind your teammate with a knife, how did he, the defendant, look to you?

A. He was acting like a maniac.

Q. How so?

A. He kept calling John's name. Over and over.

Q. He was acting like a maniac but you still thought he was an actor?

A. Yes. All the actors in that place acted like maniacs. I just figured he was another one.

Q. Interesting. So he was acting like one of the *actors*?

A. Yeah, I guess.

Q. Was he wearing a costume? A mask?

A. No.

Q. But you still thought he might be an actor.

A. Yes! How would I know differently?

Q. Mr. Dunlap, you said that you thought Bryan was faking his fear, that he was playing you. Did you discuss this with the other contestants?

A. Yes.

Q. With whom did you discuss this?

A. Jane and Jaidee.

Q. And what was their response?

A. They thought he was playing us too.

Q. So they thought what was happening was a production. That both my client and the victim were actors.

A. Yes.

Q. You're timed in each cell, right?

A. Yes.

Q. So while everything was going on down there in Cell Five, you thought you were running out of time?

A. Yes. The clock was still running.

Q. And the next cell, Cell Six, was the last cell?

A. Yes.

Q. And what happens if you make it to the last cell?

A. There's a chance to win money.

Q. And you'd made it so far. You were almost there. You just had to get through this one obstacle.

A. That's what we thought.

Q. So even though all the actors were there, and the production crew, and Cory Stout was trying to get Leonard to put down his knife, and the lights were on, you thought it was all still part of the game?

A. It was the last cell, like I said. Who wouldn't think that?

Q. And the clock was ticking.

A. Yes.

Q. So what did you do?

A. Jaidee and I made a plan.

Q. *You* made a plan? Or Jaidee made a plan?

A. We both did.

Q. Whose idea was it? Who initiated discussion of the plan?

A. Me, but . . .

Q. Please describe this plan for the jury, Mr. Dunlap. Be as specific as possible.

Jaidee

Jaidee Charoensuk, age ten, crouched behind a tall, wispy bush just outside the Kanchanaburi city limits while his best friend, Aran, tied the neighbor boy, Narong, to the trunk of a tree. The rope was frayed. Jaidee imagined it itched and chafed, but Narong didn't complain; he stood still with his arms against his sides, his forehead slick with sweat, his hands balled into fists. As Aran coiled the rope around and around the tree trunk, Narong stared out at the vast rolling greenery.

"Who's going to save you now?" Aran said after he finished tying. "Your prince is in jail. He's going to be killed by our master."

It was late afternoon, hot. Around them, insects wheezed. Jaidee batted away a grasshopper, peeked above the bush. Though it was a good mile away, he thought he could see spokes of the River Kwai bridge poking through the trees. He wiped his forehead.

"I'll be saved!" Narong said, shouting his lines to the sky. "Just you wait."

"Nobody's here!" Aran said, arm outstretched. "Nobody knows this place *exists,* princess."

"I'll be saved!" Narong repeated. "I'll be saved!"

"No matter how loud you shout, nobody can hear," Aran said.

Jaidee bit his lip. On this day, he played the hero and Aran the villain and Narong the damsel: this was how it usually went.

"He'll come for me!" Narong shouted. "You just wait, he'll come!"

"Nobody can save you now, princess!" Aran said. "Nobody!" He wandered around, picked up a long branch, dangled it close to Narong's throat. "You know that I'm an expert swordsman, yes?" His eyes narrowed. "I have defeated thousands of men all on my own, some of them high-ranking people of the king's court. Your hero, your Belly-Kos, is no match for someone like me. Renounce him and his family at once. Call me master and I may allow you to live."

"Never!"

"Well then. Prepare to die, princess. You've made your choice."

Jaidee's knees ached. He hated crouching for so long—it was the worst part of the scene. He put his hands behind him, sat cross-legged. His right knee was now visible, but he didn't care. He rested a hand on his cheek, thought about Teacher Halverson, his pasty, obese farang English instructor who'd asked him, one day, why he'd felt the need to be so bellicose. Jaidee hadn't understood the word, of course, but he'd liked its sound—*belly* like happiness when full and *kos* like "kill on sight," something he'd heard on *American Blademan.*

"Belly-Kos, Belly-Kos!" Narong shouted. "I know you hear me. Save me save me save me!" He wrinkled his face. "Please, Belly-Kos! I need your help!"

"Quiet now," Aran said. "I hate it when women die screaming."

They'd come up with the idea of writing and acting out stories in Halverson's English class. The teacher, who panted and smelled like day-old meat, had broken the class into groups and assigned each to write and perform a play. Jaidee and Aran's group wrote about a twenty-fingered alien that journeyed to Earth on a spaceship shaped like a teapot. When Earthlings threatened to destroy the alien, the alien snapped his fingers and the teapot-spaceship poured boiling tea over all the world, killing everything. The class cheered so loudly that Halverson shouted at them to stop. Jaidee and Aran, it seemed, had found their calling.

They met weekly at Jaidee's apartment, scratching together scripts that detailed Belly-Kos the Great's life. A story crystallized: Belly-Kos had been born in an emerald cave and raised by three-legged, two-faced creatures called Kos-Koses; he'd developed superpowers at age three, and thought often about his absent mother, who, Jaidee determined, had fraternized in some devious way with the teapot alien; his main enemy was Villain, an ugly, malodorous, deformed man who kidnapped members of the royal family and resembled Teacher Halverson; and he, Belly-Kos, symbolized goodness and freedom, while Villain symbolized tyranny and mayhem. It was all very serious to Jaidee and Aran, and many late afternoons were spent poring over stacks of papers that contained dialogue for hundreds of different scenes.

Narong—two years younger than the boys—lived next to Aran. Whenever possible, the younger boy inserted himself into the older boys' projects, tagging along like a pesky gnat, and though he mostly irritated Jaidee with his high-pitched obsequiousness, Jaidee also found him necessary: Narong idolized Jaidee and Aran, so he filled all the ancillary and undesirable roles perfectly and without complaint.

"Belly-Kos!" Narong screamed again, "Save me, please! I know you're out there. Save me, please!"

Jaidee, hearing his cue, sprang from the bushes, grinned, raised his stick in the air. "Not so fast, Villain!" he said.

"I told you he'd come!" Narong said. "I told you."

Aran sneered, took his stick off Narong's throat. "Well, well, well. Belly-Kos. I thought I'd locked you up forever."

"Give her to me!" Jaidee said, pointing his stick at Aran's heart.

"I don't give anything away for free," Aran said, looking down at the stick.

"Okay, then, prepare to die!"

Aran raised his stick, knocked it against Jaidee's, and they fought. Their eyes dimmed; their breathing leveled. Jaidee feinted right. Aran lunged. Aran feinted left. Jaidee leaped back. The sticks clapped against each other in crowded bursts. Around them, heavy air dampened their shirts. They maintained eye contact.

"Kill him, Belly-Kos!" Narong shouted. "Kill him kill him kill him!"

Belly-Kos wore a simple black T-shirt, white shorts, and a mask made from a long banana leaf. Villain wore the same outfit, except his banana leaf was painted black. Jaidee wiped his free hand on his shirt.

"This is your last chance to save yourself!" Jaidee said.

"It's you who needs saving!" Aran replied.

The fight went on. Left, right, back, lunge. Right, left, back, lunge. Jaidee twisted, turned, raised his stick behind his back, horizontal across his forehead. He danced, shook, flicked, bounced. On and on and on. Behind them, Narong yawned. Jaidee whapped his stick as hard as he could against Aran's and Aran let go right at that moment. The stick flew.

"You were saying?" Jaidee said, panting, pointing his stick at Aran's heart. "You don't need saving, huh?"

Aran fell to his knees. "Please," he said. "Spare me."

"And why should I spare you, after all you've done?"

"I can change," Aran said. "I can be good."

"You will never be good."

"I will. I can show you."

"Prepare to die, Villain."

"Please. I—"

Before he could finish, Jaidee plunged his stick deep into Aran's armpit. Aran gasped, coughed, and finally fell over on his face.

"My hero," Narong said, trying to wiggle a mosquito off his face.

Jaidee beamed over at Narong, ran to him, began untying. "But you know he'll be back," he said. "Villain never dies. He just re-forms."

"But you'll be there again, to save whoever needs it," Narong said.

"Of course I will," Jaidee said. "I will forever protect this world because this world deserves protection."

"You are such a hero, Belly-Kos," Narong said.

"I am just a man," Jaidee said. "That's all I am."

Jaidee took his normal circuitous route home that afternoon, biking up and down parallel streets, dodging the middle-aged ladies with their faux-designer purses, racing with the tuk-tuk drivers, circling around a few blocks, stopping at a food cart, buying some mango, eating it, then reluctantly pedaling to his parents' apartment building. When he opened the door, he felt momentarily irritated, his family a reminder of the unreachable landscape of his other world.

Outside, dusk filtered through the windows, casting long shadows across the white tile floor. The pillows against the wall sat in perfect order, as if they'd gone untouched all day. The dining table was full of food, and everyone was around it, eating noodles and vegetables, their mouths *smat-smat-smat*-ing as they chewed.

"Jaidee," his mother said, "hurry and eat."

Jaidee sat down, began eating, and listened to his mother berate their upstairs neighbor for throwing his cigarette butts out the window. Instead of confronting him, she'd collected the butts that fell on her porch, put them in an envelope along with pictures of dead Thai TV stars, and slid them under his door. It was supposed to be a warning, she said, but the incorrigible neighbor didn't seem to catch on: the more envelopes she slid, the more he smoked.

"I'm running out of pictures," she said, her mouth full of noodles. "At this rate, I'll have to wait until someone dies before I can give him his next envelope."

"Perhaps you can find famous TV animals," his father said.

"That's not the same," his mother said. "He's not an animal."

"But if you run out of people . . ."

"Why don't you just call the building owner?" Jaidee said.

His mother shook her head, closed her eyes. "You're too young to understand these things."

His mother liked saying he was too young for everything, but Jaidee, on many days, felt much older than her. She was petty and bored, and though she spent a great amount of time cooking, cleaning, praying, he couldn't help but think that this whole fiasco with their neighbor concealed the fact that she simply wanted something else to do, a job. Before she'd met his father, before they'd had him, she'd been a secretary to one of the top military figures in town, and she often talked about how, during that time, she'd learned government secrets that she couldn't even tell her family.

"Maybe I'll find children? Children who have died?" she said.

"That's too strange," his father said.

"But it'll get the message across."

"Maybe you should give him some of those foreign bootlegged tapes in your closet," Jaidee said.

"How would that change anything?" his mother said, frowning. "He'd just get free entertainment."

"There's lots of violence in American movies," Jaidee said. "Maybe he'd understand."

She sighed, looked at the far wall. "You know those tapes are special, nok," she said. "You know most people don't have access to those shows. But you do because of me. You do because of my *connections*." She turned to her son. "Anyway, you must stop being late for dinner. You must stop that play nonsense you do with Aran and his neighbor friend."

"What?" Jaidee said.

"It's silly. You need to concentrate on your studies. This whole acting madness is not what you're meant to do."

Besides citing how young he was for everything, she also enjoyed telling him the things he "wasn't meant to do," these things completely dependent on her mood. One day he wasn't meant to bike so much, another, to shower so little. A few days he wasn't meant to eat in the evenings, another, to watch television in the dark. Some days he wasn't meant to read paperback books, write with his right hand, hum on the balcony, carry his backpack like a briefcase.

"I don't want to be an actor for real," he said. "It's just fun."

"Well, you have too much fun. You're not meant to have so much fun." His mother was stout, broad, with a face that looked constantly swollen and extremities that looked inches too short. When she spoke, her eyes hardened.

"We practice our English," Jaidee told his mother. "Through the acting."

"Pfft," she said. "You're playing—that's that. Don't make it seem educational, nok. It isn't."

"We're going to sell our stories someday," he said. "It's going to be a big hit. Wait and see."

His mother groaned, cleared her plate from the table.

"Focus on studies," she called out from the kitchen. "That is your only way to happiness. All this play will pass. You'll see."

* * *

Years passed, and as his mother had predicted, Jaidee's commitment to Belly-Kos the Great waned: puberty and hormonal unruliness replaced his interest in the hero of his childhood imagination. In his bedroom, with his best friend Aran, he noted how all the scripts they'd written amounted to nothing, how nobody but complaining family members attended their performances—what they'd considered masterpieces were simply childish amusements, he said, and it was all starting to seem a little silly to him.

"I don't agree," Aran said.

They were both fifteen now. Aran had grown taller than Jaidee, his hair chopped in the usual crew cut, his cheekbones strong, his face assertive and symmetrical. He'd become boisterous and outspoken, a more dominant presence in the classroom, and during their script-writing sessions, he'd gripped the reins where Jaidee had slacked, sometimes working alone while Jaidee did homework or watched TV.

"What is there to disagree with, yai?" Jaidee said. "This is all just make-believe. What good is it?" He sat cross-legged on the floor, looking out the window. Aran sat at the rolltop desk, poring over a stack of papers, the contents of which held the penultimate scene between Belly-Kos the Great and Villain. In this scene, Villain would die for real—Belly-Kos had finally discovered the one thing that would destroy his archenemy: a rare Amazonian wood containing pink emeralds.

"What's wrong with you?" Aran said.

Jaidee shook his head. "This is kid stuff. I started it when I didn't know what 'bellicose' meant. Now I do. So it's all just stupid. Why do we keep on?"

Aran smarted. Over the years, the two boys had drifted apart: Jaidee had become withdrawn, hypercritical, ornery. While Jaidee still excelled at school, he often slunk down in his desk at the back of the classroom, arms crossed, eyes glazed, silent. He found fault with his friends, and he often made these faults known, deepening the already considerable rifts between them. Slowly, one by one, each friend drifted away, leaving Jaidee to his solitary misery. Only Aran stuck around: though the script meetings had become biweekly instead of weekly, he still consistently attended, and even when Jaidee emitted his trademark grouchiness, Aran stayed and worked, dedicated as he was to finishing the Belly-Kos saga.

As time passed, however, Jaidee's investment declined so sizably that by this day, he hadn't written a thing, had just sat in the room watching Aran write, occasionally looking out the window.

"We're older now," Jaidee said. "Continuing this is foolish."

Aran shook his head. "We've worked on this story for six years, nok. You can't just abandon it."

"We fight with little sticks," Jaidee said. "We memorize dumb lines. Nobody cares about this story. Even Narong won't allow himself to be tossed around anymore. It's time to grow up."

"Narong is an idiot."

"I don't know why you keep coming over here," Jaidee said.

"What does that mean?"

"I don't ask for your help on this, but you insist."

"I insist?"

"Yes. You insist on coming over here and pretending we're still children. Isn't that why you love the Belly-Kos story so much? So you can pretend we're still little?"

Aran looked hard at the papers. "Why would I want to be little again, nok? You make no sense."

Jaidee sighed. "I abandoned this project long ago. It's clear. But still, week after week, here you are."

"It's not *your* project," Aran said, turning around, glaring. "We started this together."

"Oh, it's not *my* project?" Jaidee said. "I'm not the one who came up with the whole idea? I'm not the one who secured all our practice locations? I'm not the one who named Belly-Kos and all his enemies? I'm not the one who roped Narong into joining us? Please. If it weren't for me, you wouldn't be sitting there right now."

"I wouldn't?" Aran said.

"You wouldn't."

"Are you sure about that?" Aran said.

"I'm sure."

"Well," Aran said, inhaling deeply. "If that's how you feel, I suppose I should go."

Jaidee shrugged. "Do what you want."

Aran sniffed, stood up, walked to the bedroom door. "So this is done?" he said. "For real?"

"It was done a long time ago," Jaidee said, not looking up.

"Well, okay then. Goodbye, nok."

Jaidee didn't reply.

With Belly-Kos essentially defunct, Jaidee turned further inward, and much to the chagrin of his mother, he watched hours on end of the pirated American VHS tapes she kept in her closet. His favorite was *American Blademan*, a series about a man named Xavier Klein who'd been born with metal fingers, toes, knees, and elbows. Klein had initially hated his condition, had gone through high school a bullied mess, but once adolescence retreated, he transformed. A video montage, accompanied by sufficiently upbeat music, outlined his renewal—Klein lifting weights, Klein running marathons, Klein molding his fingers, toes, knees, and elbows into sharp, masculine weaponry—and in the end, he emerged a six-packed American superhero, vowing to fight all enemies, foreign and domestic, his body now a fortress, an armament, a sculpted work of art.

Jaidee watched breathlessly. At night, he envisioned Xavier shirtless, gleaming, unbreakable, his thick chest hair matted to his swollen pecs; his neck, arms, legs, veiny and bulging; his granite jaw, nose, ears, eyes an exercise in graceful symmetry. While his friends at school talked and giggled about girls, Jaidee thought about this actor, Chad Mirseth, a native of Chicago, a star who'd risen to fame after a series of car commercials in which he, only twelve at the time, had played a mischievous son who tried to drive his father's truck down the driveway.

After Jaidee finished the series, he came upon a realization: because he'd had such deep feelings for Xavier Klein/Chad Mirseth, an American boy was undoubtedly in his future. This boy would be very much like Xavier Klein—tortured but beautiful, blond, strong, considerate, caring; a boy who put the welfare of others before his own, moved effortlessly in his body, and treated his family like royalty. This boy and he would eat together, sing together, meet at each other's apartments, sleep together, and happiness would accumulate from days spent as a couple, touching. It was just a matter of time before this boy happened, he thought. He was out there waiting.

Time happened and the boy didn't come. As Jaidee neared the end of his secondary school career, he became despondent, thinking that perhaps he'd have to seek out the boy after graduation, that he wouldn't simply appear one day. But then, his last year of school, an English teacher named Victor Dunlap—tall, broad-shouldered, twenty-five years old, from Nebraska—joined the faculty. When Jaidee saw him, his body tingled, his heart hammered in monstrous beats, and his head bounced erratically above his body.

It happened, he thought. It actually happened.

Mr. Dunlap was blond, athletic, poised. He had a deep, throaty voice, reminiscent of Xavier Klein's, and he instructed with confidence: he wasn't like so many of the foreigners who came to Thailand and knew nothing about their discipline; he could tell a participle from a gerund, a colon from a semicolon, and it was clear that he actually cared about his students' progress. Jaidee swooned.

One day early in the term, Jaidee stayed after class, stood hesitantly in front of Victor's desk, rocked back and forth from foot to foot. His heart clapped in his chest. He put his hands in his pockets.

"Teacher," he said, his mouth dry. "Do you know Chad Mirseth?"

"The *American Blademan* actor?" Victor said, looking up.

"Yes."

"Like, do I know him personally?"

"I don't know. No."

Victor leaned back in his chair, grinned. "That was one of the best shows."

"I can't believe it was only three seasons."

"You've seen it? I wouldn't think you could here. You remember the episode with Phantasma? She was in it for, like, one minute but I heard they're making a spin-off show for her. Crazy, huh?"

"But why?" Jaidee said. "Why not just keep Blademan? That's what everyone wants."

"I heard they want more women viewers, but let's be honest, right? Dudes are gonna watch her, and probably not women. I mean, it's Pamela Anderson."

"They shouldn't have canceled the show."

"I agree." Victor paused, narrowed his eyes. "Say, Jaidee, your English—it's good."

"Thank you, Teacher."

"It's actually the best in the class."

Jaidee flushed. "I can say Chad Mirseth taught me a lot."

Victor chuckled. "Well, then."

"You know, Teacher," Jaidee said, breathing deep, "you look like him. You look like Chad Mirseth."

"Ha-ha, nah. That handsome dude?"

"You are very handsome."

"Well, Jaidee. I appreciate it." He looked at the clock. "But listen, I've got to get going. I'll see you tomorrow, okay?"

"You have similar faces and bodies."

"You're too kind," Victor said, shuffling some papers, looking down. "Someday we'll have to talk more about *Blademan.* That show was incredible."

"Yes. I'd like that."

"I'll see you tomorrow," Victor said, not looking up.

"Okay," Jaidee said. He stood for a moment longer, waiting for something to happen, then walked to the door, his head light, his face hot. "I like this class the best," he said before he left.

"I'm glad," Victor said, still shuffling papers. "Thanks, Jaidee."

From then on, Jaidee searched for signs of interest—every time Dunlap called on him, every time he aced a quiz, every time Dunlap said, "Good job," every time they made eye contact. The hints were subtle, he thought, but they were there: the surreptitious smiles, the pats on the shoulder, the longer-than-normal gazes, the overly encouraging written commentary. At home, Jaidee greedily scanned his corrected homework assignments, looking for clues of amorous intent, something hidden that would impart Dunlap's true feelings. He didn't find anything at first—only cursory comments, cursory praise—but then, one day, he noticed small black smudges at the bottom of each vocabulary quiz. Could it be? he wondered. The spots floated in the center of the page, blemishing each sheet with tiny imperfection, and the closer he examined, the more he saw that each spot looked vaguely heart-shaped, two curves delineated by a central break. This is it! he thought. This must be it! His chest felt puffy and light, his stomach lurched upward. I knew he'd send me a sign! I knew it! He put the assignments in a folder, stuffed them in his desk, and went to the front room to watch TV.

The next day in class, Victor split the students into groups. He asked the group members to arrange a series of sentences in the order they deemed most appropriate—*Watch for transitions,* he said. *Pay close attention to every word.* Jaidee thought the task relatively elementary, but no matter: He'd seen the hearts. His entire world was now different. He would do anything Victor asked of him.

It was a group assignment, however, so he couldn't simply do the exercise alone, couldn't hand it in to receive more hearts, so he snapped at his classmates: they were impediments, he thought, and they were so unabashedly stupid.

"I don't think 'consequently' should go after a sentence that doesn't have a command," said a girl named Malee.

"What?" Jaidee said.

"Because it is cause and effect. Command and action is cause and effect."

"You're an idiot," Jaidee said. He leaned back in his chair and shook his head. That school year, because of Victor, he'd read voraciously—mostly the Stephen King and Danielle Steel novels that were sold at the nearby used bookstore—and had spent hours at home practicing his writing and speaking skills. His mother, while happy with her son's diligence, told him that he needed to pay attention to all his subjects, that he wasn't meant to focus so hard on one.

Malee's face reddened. "You don't need to be terrible," she said.

Jaidee sighed. "Do what you want. We'll just get bad points."

The group pored over their sentences while Jaidee slouched, crossed his arms over his chest. After a few minutes, Victor came to the group, sat next to Jaidee. Jaidee sat up, moved his chair closer to Victor's.

"How's it going here?" Victor said.

"We're doing good," said Malee. She was round-faced, pockmarked, chubby. "We're understanding. But this word 'consequently.'"

"'Consequently' infers cause and effect," Jaidee said. His groupmates turned to him, glared. "It means something happens as a consequence of something else. It clearly goes after sentence three." Jaidee leaned closer to Victor, smelled cologne.

"Jaidee," Victor said. "I'm impressed."

"I've already said this," Malee said.

"My group thinks that a sentence that infers effect must come after a sentence that is a command. I don't understand this logic, Mr. Dunlap." Jaidee looked away, smiled.

"Just look at the word," Victor told the group members. "Notice that there's a 'seq' in the middle. What other word can you think of that has that arrangement of letters?"

The group looked back, blinked.

"Come on," Victor said. "Think. That arrangement of letters isn't that common in most English words, so it must mean something."

"Sequin?" Malee said.

Victor smiled. "Well, that word has that arrangement for sure."

"Sequo?" said a boy named Anurak.

"I don't think that's a word," Victor said. "But—"

"It's clearly 'sequence,'" Jaidee said.

"Yes," Victor said. "It *is* sequence. And when you think of sequence, then what?"

"You think of things in order. So it makes sense that it would be cause and effect because one thing follows another."

"Awesome, Jaidee," Victor said.

"But again, my group doesn't seem to understand cause and effect. Because they think it must come after a command."

Victor looked at Malee. "After a command?" he said.

"Yes," Malee said, her face near broken. "Isn't that . . . because you command and then an action happens or doesn't happen."

"I suppose," Victor said, stroking his chin. "But

there are many instances of cause and effect that don't involve a command. I can say something like, 'He dropped a book. Consequently, there was a loud thud.' It just means one thing causes the other. That's all. The book dropping causes the thud."

Jaidee beamed. His groupmates didn't look at him; they returned to the paper. Jaidee looked at Victor, grinned. Victor stood up, went to the next group.

On the last day of school, Dunlap brought everyone an American treat—a spongy yellow log-shaped candy called a Twinkie. Most of the students loved it, gobbled it down in seconds, but Jaidee felt sick and only ate half before putting the rest on his desk. Stomach rumbling, he excused himself to the bathroom and cried into his hands for five minutes: It had been announced, the week before, that Victor would not be staying for another school year. He'd loved his time in Thailand, he said, but it was time to return to America and resume his life.

"It's been such an honor to teach you," he'd told the class. "It's been so much fun." The class replied with smiles—all except Jaidee.

Two days prior, Jaidee had gathered all his courage and once again lingered after class. He went to Victor's desk, put his hand on the wood. Victor smiled up at him with brilliantly aligned teeth, and Jaidee thought that he'd never seen a man so happy.

"Jaidee," Victor said. "How can I help you?"

Jaidee's mouth filled with salty sand. He moved his lips and his tongue, but nothing came out.

"Thank you for speaking up today during the writing exercise," Dunlap said. "You had some great things to say."

The sand moistened, disappeared. Jaidee said, "I don't want you to leave, Teacher."

Dunlap smiled. "That's kind of you," he said.

"Please don't."

"Ah. You'll be fine."

Jaidee hesitated. "I found the hearts."

"Excuse me?"

"I found . . . at the bottom of the assignments."

"I'm not sure—"

"I know . . . secret, but you're going away, so . . ."

Victor stood, gathered his file folders and textbooks. "Hey man, sorry. I have to get going. I'll see you tomorrow, okay? Again, great contributions today. I appreciate it."

"Mr. Dunlap—"

"Gotta run, Jaidee. Have a great afternoon."

"But—" Jaidee said.

"Good job again," Victor said. Then he left.

In the bathroom, crying that last day of class, Jaidee thought how hatefully unfair everything was—Victor embodied everything that was good and necessary, and it seemed that Jaidee's time with him had been cut short. When he heard the door open, he wiped his nose, breathed deep, splashed cold water on his face.

"What's wrong with *you*?"

Standing before him was, of all people, Aran, looking too tall, too self-possessed, too sure of himself. Jaidee looked in the mirror, breathed. Aran went to the toilet, unzipped, peed.

"Almost finished with school, huh," Aran said. He zipped, turned around, and looked at Jaidee. "Hey, you look unwell."

Jaidee shook his head. "I'm fine."

"Look at us. Almost men." Aran looked at his face in the mirror, moved a few strands of hair around. "Will you study at Chulalongkorn?"

"I will work with my father for a while," Jaidee said. "I plan on studying in America."

"I thought you might do that," Aran said.

They fell silent. Jaidee wanted his old friend to leave, to let him be alone with his sorrow, but Aran lingered, studying his reflection in the mirror. He's grown incredibly vain, Jaidee thought. Just because he's so tall.

Just because the girls giggle around him. Just because his skin is smooth and unblemished. But he's only a boy, he thought. Probably still thinking about all that Belly-Kos nonsense.

"I wish you luck, my friend," Aran said.

"Thank you," Jaidee said. "You as well."

Aran half smiled, waved limply. His eyes, Jaidee saw, implored more conversation: they shimmered around the edges, hesitant and sad.

"You should go to America too," Jaidee said, knowing full well that Aran's family couldn't afford it even if he were admitted somewhere. "The land of promise."

"I wish you good luck," Aran repeated, turning around.

"The path to opportunity," Jaidee said. Then, in English: "The land of the free, home of the brave."

"Goodbye, nok," Aran said, opening the door. "Nice to see you."

"Goodbye, yai," Jaidee said, but the door had already closed.

Jaidee splashed more water on his face, closed his eyes, and thought about what he'd said. America, he thought. Yes, that's it. America. He hadn't actually known he was going until he'd said it aloud, but once he had, once the word "America" had breezed past his lips, he knew, unequivocally, that the land of Hollywood and hamburgers and New York City was in his future. And why not? His family would approve. His uncle would bankroll. In fact, they'd all be thrilled: his father had studied there for two years, repeatedly recounting it as the most inspiring time of his life, and though he hadn't pressured Jaidee to apply, he knew that he'd be happy to have a son with a college degree from abroad.

So Jaidee strode out of the bathroom with his head up, his face dry. In the classroom, Victor laughed with a group of students. Jaidee watched, smiling, remembering something Blademan had said during the second season. He'd just revealed who he was to Becky Thatcher; he'd come to her in his Blademan outfit but had taken it off, exposing himself as a very mortal man. She'd been shocked, horrified even, but had, in the end, fallen into his arms. After their kiss, Blademan had said, *Love takes work, and any love that doesn't isn't worth a damn.*

Jaidee thought, *Of course. Love takes work.*

So, he would find a way for this love to work. Because surely, undeniably, Victor Dunlap was worth a thousand damns.

EXHIBIT 3A:
The Knife

Summary:

- 10" chef's knife from Coralax, Inc.
- Brown wooden handle, scratched
- Jagged bloodstains crossing both handle and blade
- Letters inscribed on the blade: TLB
- Fingerprint ID: Leonard Grandton

Leonard

Leonard Grandton met Mary Kenilworth in the canned-foods aisle of the West Lincoln Hyvee: she was crouched down, inspecting a tin of peaches, when Leonard, contemplating the music above, pushed his cart directly into her. Mary yelped, fell onto her side, dropped the can of peaches. Leonard gasped, rushed to her, extended his hand. She didn't take it; she shook her head, propped herself up, wiped her hands on her thighs, and said, "Don't worry about it." She grabbed her can of peaches and went to her cart.

"Are you okay?" Leonard said, rolling up next to her.

She didn't look at him. "Yes, of course," she said.

"I'm so sorry," he said.

"No worries, really," she said, and pushed off.

Neither Leonard nor Mary was a planner: their

grocery-store visits relied on impulse and recall. Neither brought a list. They strolled down each aisle hoping the products themselves would trigger a memory. Because of this, they passed each other in the coffee and tea aisle, the cereal aisle, the snack-food aisle, the frozen-food aisle, the seasoning aisle, the beverage aisle. They avoided eye contact, looking quickly away when the other appeared, but their routes synced so completely, and the store was so feebly populated, that the other's presence became enormous, and by the time they reached the perimeter—the deli, the dairy, the produce, the bakery—they stopped pretending and started playing. Mary, bagging broccoli, saw Leonard, bagging apples, and coolly walked by, nicking his foot with her grocery cart. She turned around, shrugged, mouthed *I'm sorry!*, giggled. And Leonard, checking eggs, saw Mary, examining yogurt, and with much dispassion, walked by and grazed her knee. *I'm so sorry!*, he mouthed. She laughed. Versions of this flirtation occurred in the bakery and the deli, and by the time they made it to the checkout, they were both thoroughly delighted.

"Those look like some *great* peaches," Leonard said, tapping his cart against hers.

"How offensive," she said.

"Sensitive, huh," he said.

She turned away.

"Didn't mean to offend."

"Is this your process with women?" She still faced forward.

"Yes," he said. "My process."

"It's a lame process."

"Well, it's mine, so."

They paused. Ahead, the cashier said, "Hello, Mrs. Wilson."

"Maybe tomorrow?" Leonard said, feeling a sudden wave of confidence. "We could talk about how lame it is? I could tell you otherwise?"

She smiled. "Tomorrow's bad."

"Next week, then?"

"Next week next week next week."

"That's what I said."

She shook her head, loaded her groceries onto the conveyor belt.

They met next week. Then they met the week after. Within two months they were cohabitating, and Leonard, a lifelong opponent of marital domesticity, thought, for the first time, that a life shared was a life expanded, that love was a worthy and admirable goal. He'd had girlfriends before—a straight line of divisive, prolonged entanglements—but had found their companionship utterly dispensable: he always faded, unwilling to even humor the idea of something perennial and warranting classification. He thought of these women as somewhat interchangeable: staid, middle-aged Midwestern women who understood their prime man-catching years to be historical. Sometimes they were divorced, sometimes single, but in all cases, they were willing to settle for someone like him: a balding, thirty-seven-year-old hotel manager with a soft belly and a lopsided smile. Mary Kenilworth, however, was different: she'd traveled, for one—Kenya, Morocco, Spain, Australia, Belgium, Belize, Japan, Vietnam, etc., etc.—and spoke in a way that emphasized these travels, not necessarily referring directly to these exotic lands but syntactically underscoring a sophistication that proclaimed worldly eminence. Instead of "really" or "so" or "very" she'd say "quite," as in: It's quite warm out today, isn't it? She also used multisyllabic words like "palliative" and "ostentatious" and "incendiary," and sometimes, after they talked, he looked up her vocabulary in the dictionary, partly to discover the exact meaning, and partly because he wanted to know if she'd used it correctly. In one hundred percent of the cases, she had.

They shopped together. Though Leonard had rudimentary bed-, bath-, and kitchenware, enough, he said, to get by just fine, Mary required a few more elevated items.

"Like a knife set," she said. "How have you gone through your entire life without a knife set?"

He shrugged. "I have a knife," he said.

"That rusty one in the silverware drawer?"

"I mean. It works."

They bought a new knife set. It wasn't until after they opened the box, removed the wood block, inspected each blade, threw away the cardboard, that they noticed, engraved shakily on the steel of the chef's knife, the small letters *TLB*.

"That's weird," Mary said, tracing the letters. "None of the other knives have it."

"These are Coralax knives," Leonard said. "I wonder what TLB stands for."

"The longest blade?" Mary said.

"The largest beauty?" Leonard said.

"The lengthiest breast," Mary said.

"The littlest butt," Leonard said.

For weeks afterward, this became a running joke. "Could you hand me the luckiest butthole?" Mary would say. "I'm gonna chop up this celery for the dip."

"The last bitch still needs washing," Leonard would reply. "It still has some cilantro on its blade from last night."

They never discovered the meaning of TLB, but they concocted stories and told them to each other before bed.

"See, there's this sweatshop," Mary said one night. "And all they do is make knives, and one day, some guy, let's call him Albert Lee, decides that he wants to add his own flair to one of the blades because he's tired of so much monotony, so much boring steel, so one night he sneaks into the sweatshop and takes one and engraves the initials of his secret gay lover into the steel—Trenton Lyle Borschadt."

"Trenton Lyle Borschadt?" Leonard said. "That doesn't sound very Chinese."

"I never said it was in China. Racist much?"

"Would sweatshops even have engraving equipment?"

"This one does."

"I'm not buying it. I'll tell you what actually happened," Leonard said.

"Huh. Sure."

"Well, this box of knives sat in one of Coralax's warehouses forever and for some reason it would never get shipped off to Target or Walmart or wherever, and one of the warehouse employees noticed this, that this lonely box was just sitting there forever, so he stole it, brought it home, knowing nobody would ever really miss it. Well, he put this knife block on the counter, and his wife, who just used a perfectly good *single* knife for everything, one that she kept in the silverware drawer, she thought that this was a hint about her cooking, so she got pissed off and chased him around the house with the knife screaming, 'I'll skin you alive!'"

"This is a stupid story," Mary said, grinning.

"Well, she finally calmed down and grew to love the assortment of knives, and this warehouse worker, partly out of love and partly out of fear of his wife, engraved her initials into the knife—Theresa Lynn Bootyman—so if they ever found his body hacked up, they'd know exactly who had done it. He told her, of course, that it was a dedication."

"Bootyman? Really?"

"Better than Trenton Lyle Borschadt."

"Hardly."

He laughed, draped himself around her, peppered her neck with kisses. He felt, then, inordinately happy, inordinately lucky; he'd never met a woman who'd lifted his spirits so constantly, and he wondered how he'd gone through four decades of life without experiencing such bliss: it seemed that if everyone felt this way all the time, if everyone understood this sort of unbridled joy, that nobody would ever fight, and nobody would ever die.

Their sex, at first, was timid: he hadn't witnessed many taut bodies unclothed except in magazines, and in her presence, he felt obscenely unworthy, refusing to take off his shirt during their first bout of frenzied lovemaking. As it happened, though, after a couple rounds, she confided that she preferred men like him, men who didn't preen and sculpt and obsess about body-fat percentages and protein shakes. She said she liked to be the woman, meaning, in her words, that she was the pretty one and he was the man.

"Well, clearly you *are* the pretty one," he said, rubbing his belly.

"I wouldn't call myself traditional in any sense, Leonard. But in this sense, perhaps."

Leonard's confidence soared: he not only removed his shirt during sex but also allowed lights to be on, daylight to filter through. He found this newfound body-acceptance exposed an entirely new world, a world of *sex wherever*, and so, in a public place, overcome by this newly minted swagger, he'd take her to the nearest bathroom, shut the stall door, hold her against the wall, and examine her pores, her hairline, the small creases around her eyes all while thrusting, panting, fucking. He memorized her face—the Massachusetts-shaped sunspot on her left cheek, the small flecks of gold dotting her right iris, the slow, gentle curve of her lips when she pressed them together—and at work, he would sometimes draw her, stashing each coarse portrait into his desk drawer, starting over the next day.

He asked about her life. He wanted to know everything. She said:

"I've only lived in Lincoln for a little while. I moved to town to take care of my mother; she's undergoing chemo and radiation for metastatic breast cancer. Before Lincoln, I was in Hartford, Connecticut. I was a travel writer. I worked for a magazine called *Tarmac*, the official magazine of Eastjet Airlines, and while they mostly had me write about the food, nightlife, and culture of various domestic cities, once in a while I'd be sent abroad, thus my impressive international résumé."

Leonard found her previous life utterly unapproachable—he'd barely left his home state, had been born and raised in Omaha, and moved to Lincoln for two years of college before dropping out, had started working at the Claymont Hotel, had stayed—and one day early in their relationship, he asked her, earnestly and reticently, what someone like her was doing with someone like him.

They were sitting in his living room, both on the couch turned toward each other. She curled up her left leg so her foot sank behind her right knee. It was a Saturday afternoon. The sun peeked through the blinds, lighting one side of her face, the sun-spotted side.

"You're beautiful and worldly and smart and, really," he said, "I'm telling you now, you can do a lot better. I mean, look at me."

She sighed, smiled, brushed her hair off her shoulder. "Oh, Leonard," she said. "Really, you're a lot more than you think you are."

"But I'm sure in all those places you've been you've met more *interesting* people, more accomplished, more handsome people, right?"

"Why would you compare yourself to projections?" she said. "These people you're thinking about are not real and therefore irrelevant."

"Meaning you *haven't* met more interesting, accomplished, and handsome people?"

"Meaning if I have, they're not sitting with me now."

"I don't want to be your charity case."

She laughed, dimpling her forehead. "Is it terrible to say that I enjoy how much you like me?" she said.

"But do *you* like *me*?"

"I do," she said. "I like you very much."

"But why?"

"Well," she said, "if you must know, you make me laugh, and laughter, really, is my primary aphrodisiac."

She moved her hand up his leg to his thigh, winked. "And you're kind. And you're thoughtful. And none of my past matters at all because this is the present and we're together here now so let's not talk about the why and just be, okay?"

But Leonard, as time went on, found that he couldn't just *be*, that her reasons for liking him, while seemingly legitimate, would never stand the test of time, that eventually she would grow tired of his coarseness, his squishiness, his lack of ambition. Lincoln was no cosmopolis, he knew, but even in his town there were much more distinguished gentlemen, men who knew their way around books and films and plays, men discerning about scotch and wine, men whom Leonard assumed Mary would one day leave him for.

"I don't get it," he said, leaning into her, kissing her cheek. "But I'll take it. I'll take it however I can get it."

Time marched, and Leonard's insecurities grew: every comment Mary made about his work, his dress, his diet—mostly insignificant, quotidian, entirely commonplace in a healthy domestic situation—Leonard took as a slight to his character, assuming that in their aggregate they would result in her realizing his ineptitude as a man, and since he loved her more than he'd loved anyone else, he thought the only way to hold on to her was to improve his livelihood: if he demonstrated real ability, if he was able to provide her with a more comfortable living arrangement, if he proved to her that he was just as capable of success as anyone she'd met in her previous life, his fear of her swift exit would vanish and he could finally just *be,* as she'd so simply put it. So he devised a plan: he would consult with the one person he thought might talk to him, his most successful consort, and get advice on opening his own hotel, one in direct competition with his current workplace. This associate had significant experience both nationally and internationally, and though the idea of approaching someone who'd been on television fluttered his stomach and frenzied his fingers (every interaction they'd had had been curt, official, short-lived), he understood that it was possibly the only way to legitimize the pursuit.

He told Mary about the plan one evening in May. He sat at the kitchen counter bent over a sheet of paper, top teeth biting his lower lip, while she stood at the stove, stirring.

"Think about it," he said. "I've been at the Claymont for fifteen years. I have so much experience. It seems like the next logical step, right?"

"I thought you *liked* working at the Claymont," Mary said.

"I do, I mean, it's like a second home. But I need to

move on with my life, don't I? I'm thirty-eight. I need to take a risk. I can't just work there till I die."

"Well, not till you die, but maybe until your retirement kicks in. Plenty of people do that."

"But what kind of people are those?" he said.

"Normal," she said.

Mary, over that year, hadn't worked: she had savings from her previous job and a small inheritance from her deceased father. Instead of actively looking for work (she was in between careers, she told Leonard, and needed time to think), she went to her mother's house, busying herself by reading cookbooks and experimenting in both her mother's and Leonard's kitchens. On this day, she was cooking a vegetarian stew, stirring the broth while Leonard wrote notes on his paper.

"I need to make this list," he said. "I need to be methodical. I need to be *strategic.* I need to figure out everything step by step."

"Starting a business is a huge endeavor," she said. She stopped stirring, brought the wooden spoon to her mouth, sipped. "Hmm," she said. "Taste this."

"I know vendors, I know staff," he said. He leaned over, sipped at her spoon. "More salt," he said.

"Well, it's expensive," she said. She pinched salt into the pot, stirred.

"I'll get a loan."

"Mmm."

"I really can do this, Mary," he said.

She turned from the stove, looked at him, frowned. "I know you *can,* but is it really what you *want* to do? It's a big responsibility. A lot of time."

He scratched his chin, hesitated. "You know," he said. "I have someone at my disposal. An extremely successful someone. I could get professional advice. Maybe he'd even become an investor?"

"Oh yeah?" she said. "And who is this wildly profitable entrepreneur?"

He swallowed. "John Forrester."

Her mouth fell open.

"He runs a hugely successful business," Leonard said.

"What?"

"He's made a lot of money."

She shook her head. "Nope," she said. "No. No. No."

"Why not?"

"His hugely successful business has caused irreparable *damage* to people."

"Oh, come off it."

"Really?"

"Damage?"

"Yes, damage."

"It's a haunted house! It's smoke and mirrors. People in masks."

"You know it's more than that."

"No matter what it is, it's successful, and I communicate with Quigley House all the time. I don't talk to John that much, but I could, I know I could."

"Well," she said, turning back to the stove.

"This could be good for us too," he said.

"Mmm," she said.

"I've got a great feeling about this, Mary."

"John Forrester is a creep," she said, stirring hard. "He's a bona fide creep. I hate that you're even associated with all of Quigley's disgusting nonsense, but working directly with that sadistic crazy?"

"Mary."

"He's a wretched man. A commonplace swindler. A person who revels in suffering. He's filth."

"*Mary.*"

"But you do what you want, okay?" she said. "You do what you want."

"Please. Don't be upset. I have a good feeling . . ."

"Good. Now, let's move on, okay? Food's done. You ready to eat?"

* * *

The Claymont Hotel, Leonard's employer for fifteen years, had, for nearly a decade, partnered professionally with the Quigley House, John Forrester's extreme haunted-house attraction. The Claymont offered free accommodations for contestants who traveled from afar, direct-billing John, and Leonard, being the most senior manager at the hotel, oversaw all the transactions. Because of this arrangement, Leonard made frequent contact with the Quigley's office staff, and sometimes, if he asked particularly taxing questions, got patched through to John. The day after he talked to Mary about his proposed venture, he told Quigley's accounts-payable clerk that he needed to talk directly to the owner, and though there was hesitation on her part (she didn't like disturbing him, she said; he was just so busy), she eventually forwarded the call.

As the ringtone buzzed, Leonard's hands sweated and shook. He didn't have any sort of formal business proposal for John Forrester, and he wasn't even certain what he'd say (though he'd brought, for confidence's sake, the cheat sheet he'd written the evening before), but he knew, in his heart, that this was the way to go: if Forrester helped him out, plans would be expedited, things would get done—it'd only be a matter of time.

John picked up on the third ring. "Leonard," he said. "Nice of you to call."

Leonard choked, grabbed his cheat sheet. Though he'd talked to John on numerous occasions, he still felt nervous every time he heard the man's rich, even voice.

John was a real celebrity, had done all the major talk shows, made cameos on prime-time television, had even had a documentary focused on him and his haunt, and whenever they talked, Leonard's heart fluttered.

"My weekend contestants aren't causing a row, are they?" John said.

"What? No, nothing like that," Leonard said. He breathed, let the moment pass. "Hi, John, it's Leonard Grandton from the Claymont!"

"Well, yes," John said. "I think we've established that."

"If you are willing," Leonard said, feeling his heart in his throat, "I would like to get some advice from a world-renowned entrepreneur."

"Leonard," John said, "are you *reading* something?"

"No, well, I mean." He pushed his paper aside. "I was just hoping that . . . it's about hotels, but—I'm sorry. I can start over."

John coughed. "Veronica says you have some sort of proposal for me?"

"Yes. Well, not a proposal, not like an official proposal. Just something I'm thinking about. I'd like your advice if you'd give it." Leonard bit his lip, shook his head. He wanted to hang up.

Silence. Leonard imagined John on the other end, stifling a laugh. *This idiot,* John probably thought.

"Sorry," Leonard said. "I was just—"

"Listen," John said. "What are you doing tomorrow night?"

"Tomorrow night? What?"

"Yeah. You know Pete's in Havelock?"

"Pete's? Like, the biker bar?"

"Yeah. It's a dive. But I go there, you know, to unwind. Nobody bothers me there."

"Okay?"

"I was thinking I'd go tomorrow. You wanna come?"

"Go to Pete's? With you?"

"Yeah, sure. We can talk about whatever it is you want to talk about over a few whiskeys. Sorry so abrupt. And if you have plans . . . it's just a thought that came to my head just now."

"Are you serious?"

"Of course."

"Well, yeah. Yeah, I'd love to go."

"Terrific. Okay, meet me there around eight P.M. tomorrow. I gotta run now, okay? But I'll see you then."

"Okay then. See—"

But John had already hung up.

That night, after work, as Mary stirred yet another vegetarian concoction (she'd told Leonard that meatlessness wouldn't be every day, but maybe three times per week?), this time in the form of stir-fry, Leonard talked about his conversation with John as if it'd been the most pivotal moment of his life. He said, "He wants to meet up with me socially! Can you believe that? Totally out of the blue!"

Mary, having had an awful day with a mother who refused to eat and a television that refused to turn on, didn't respond. She batted at the broccoli, the cauliflower, the pea pods and peppers and mushrooms. She added salt.

"This is crazy," Leonard said. "You know I've only met him in person once? Like, in the whole time I've worked with him I've only met him once, and that was like a decade ago, like before he was as famous as he is, before he became this multimillionaire. And now he wants to meet at *Pete's* of all places."

"Pete's?" Mary said. "That shithole out in Havelock? That place where that guy got knifed a few weeks ago?"

"Yeah, I was as surprised as you, but you know, him being famous, he has to keep a low profile."

"Pete's is *not* low-profile. Those are his people."

Leonard squinted. "What does *that* mean, his people?"

"Oh, you know *exactly* what I mean."

"I don't."

"Must I spell it out for you?"

"Please do."

She turned, put her hands on the counter. "The people who love the Quigley House are the same people who go to a place like Pete's. That's his element."

"And what type of people are those?"

"Please, Leonard. Use your imagination."

"Trashy people. That's what you're saying."

"I didn't use those words, but sure. Yes. Trashy people." She added oil to the wok. The wok hissed. She stirred.

"That's a bit snobbish, wouldn't you say?"

"Well. I'm an insufferable snob, so."

"Listen. I don't want to argue about this. I just wanted to tell you that this is happening. In one day, I made something happen. I had a plan, I had a goal, I stuck to it, and it's happening. Tomorrow I'm meeting with one of the richest men in Nebraska. I'm going to ask him for advice. I'm going to sit there across from him and have a few drinks and talk about my future. And maybe he and I can collaborate, what do you think of that? Maybe in the future—the near future—he'll help me get this thing started. We'll have a totally different life!"

"Well, be careful. Don't get knifed."

"Mary, Jesus."

"Everything's fine. I'm happy for you. Now, are you ready to eat?"

Leonard had never been in Pete's and wasn't prepared for its rancidness. As he stepped inside, a gust of cheap beer and wet rags made him cough. Layered above this stench was the definitive odor of sweat and urine. His eyes adjusted. He looked around, saw destitution in the form of grizzled, sweaty men who looked like they hadn't moved from their stools or booths for years. The light was dim, yellow, seedy. Above the bar were two large-screen TVs to which the men on the stools remained transfixed, even during the commercials, only talking when their drink was empty. Behind the bar, scrawled in black pen on white paper, were the beer specials: *PBR Tap $1.75. Old Mil Tap $2. Lots of cans just ask!*

John Forrester was perched on one of the stools, watching the TV with the others. Leonard approached.

"Leonard!" John said, extending his hand. Leonard shook it. "Hey, let's get a booth, huh? What do you want to drink?"

"Whiskey, neat," Leonard said.

John smiled. "Perfect. Ray, give this guy a whiskey neat. Put it on my tab."

In the booth, Leonard felt momentarily claustrophobic, like the darkness of Pete's would suffocate him if he stayed still, so he moved his shoulders, his legs, his arms, his head.

"Hey, bud, you okay?" John said.

On the table was a small black lamp, the kind one might find in a library. It seemed incongruous to the rest of the place, a source of light meant for a place of interesting and incisive thought backed by scholarly articles. The table itself was scratched and dirty. A straw wrapper lay crumpled in the corner of the booth. From above came the screeching voice of Steven Tyler.

"Great place, huh," John said.

"Yeah," Leonard said.

In the dim light, John looked ghoulish. His pockmarked cheeks narrowed to a strong, pronounced chin, and his eyes were shifty slits, unchanging even when he laughed. His mouth was tiny, his lips dry, and when he smiled, it seemed that he was missing a feature, that there was too much skin around the lower part of his face.

"It's, like, one of the only places in town where people are totally genuine with me, you know?" John said, leaning in.

"I can't imagine what it must be like," Leonard said.

Leonard had only met John once before: he'd gone to the Quigley House to deliver a large binder containing papers that needed signatures. As instructed, he'd entered at the west entrance of the mansion, the administrative entrance, and inside, instead of a maze of horrors he found a maze of cubicles, each staffed by a middle-aged woman. He roamed around the maze before coming to a private office with a glass door. Beside the door, a plaque read VERONICA HALL, ACCOUNT MANAGER. He knocked, opened the door, said, "Guess who?" but stopped when he saw not a curly-haired, bespectacled woman but a small-mouthed man with close-cut graying hair sitting behind a computer, squinting so hard it looked like his eyes were closed. Leonard stood awkwardly in the doorway. John looked up.

"Oh, Veronica's out right now," he said.

"I just have this packet," Leonard said, holding the binder out dumbly.

"A packet for what?"

"I'm from the Claymont? We've chatted before, on the phone. I'm sorry for intruding. I just thought Veronica—"

"Oh, the Claymont. Yes, Leonard, right? Please, just set the binder on the desk there. It's great to meet you."

John stood up, and Leonard felt, suddenly, like he was witnessing a monolith rise from the dirt. The man was tall—six-foot-three—but more than that he was imperious, his face, strange as it was, conforming into something utterly confident, precisely intimidating. As they shook hands, Leonard felt he was touching a personification of brilliance, a prodigy so virtuosic that nobody for years had been able to come close to comparing. Leonard had no interest in horror or haunted houses or anything of the sort, but that didn't matter: the man had created something legendary, and respect was always due where respect was always due.

In Pete's, however, with all its heavy scents, it was difficult to be in awe of anything; everything, including John, seemed supremely dilapidated. Still, Leonard thought, perhaps that was part of John's genius, to surround himself outside of the Quigley House with a sort of pervasive wretchedness. He did, after all, run a house that fed on people's desire for terror.

They drank whiskey and talked about the Claymont. John seemed unduly interested in the inner workings of the hotel, which surprised Leonard: to him, his job seemed unexceptional. But John kept on: How many rooms? How much staff? Were the complimentary breakfasts made from scratch? Did the staff ever screw in the empty rooms? To this last question, Leonard laughed, said, "Probably."

At the end of the night, Leonard, feeling brave from the whiskey, asked John if he'd like to meet again, told him that it'd been a while since he'd had a drinking buddy.

John looked at him, eyebrows arched. "A regular thing, huh?" John said.

"I mean, I know you're busy," Leonard said.

"I'm here this time, every week," John said. "If you want, you can be too."

"Yeah?" Leonard said.

"Yup," John said.

And Leonard felt the keen sense of things coming together.

The next time the two men met, they sat in the same booth. The light, it seemed, shone brighter this time around, and when Leonard mentioned it, John laughed and said, *Ray finally replaced a few bulbs.* The increase in attempted cheer, however, did nothing for the despondent men atop their stools. One man, a paunchy, wide-faced farmer-type with a tangled gray beard and dirt-clad boots, squinted forever out at the bottles, his beer glass held right next to his lips. Once in a while, the bartender waved his hand in front of the bearded man's face, startling him.

"The regulars here are a trip," John said. "Fascinating lives, all of them."

Leonard looked past the bearded man, up to the

TV, which showed Hillary Clinton in a soft pink blouse fielding questions from the press, denying some sort of wrongdoing called Whitewater.

"They put C-SPAN on in a bar like this?" Leonard said.

John looked up at the TV, grimaced, then looked back at Leonard. He shook his head, sipped his whiskey. "I don't know about this country sometimes," he said. "How someone like that . . ."

"You're political?" Leonard said.

John stared at Leonard for a while, then softened his eyes. "Leonard," he said, "'political' isn't a dirty word. It's a necessary way of life for guys like us, okay?"

"Guys like us?" Leonard said, feeling warm.

"Let me ask you something," John said.

"Sure," Leonard said, smiling.

"What do your parents do?"

"My parents?" he said. "Sure. Mom's dead, Dad's retired, but in a past life, Dad was a foreman, and my mom helped out at her church. Mostly, though, she just raised me and my brother."

"And look at you now," John said, leaning back.

"What's that?" Leonard said, looking down at his glass.

"Look at you now," John repeated.

"I mean, I'm not successful like you or anything, but I'm okay."

"Okay?" John said. "You run one of the most well-known hotels in this town! All their profits? That's *your* doing. Without you, they'd sink. Why do you think I chose to partner with the Claymont?" He paused, licked his lips. "Reputation, Leonard. It matters. And your place has a stellar one."

"I guess," Leonard said. "If you put it that way, we do okay."

"You're too modest. You think I got where I am by being *modest*? You do *more* than okay. You *outshine*. Remember that."

Leonard said nothing. It was strange, having such a successful man talk about *his* success, as if Leonard's managerial skills had ever gotten him anything but talkings-to from Corporate. *You need to motivate your staff better,* they said. *You need to be innovative with your advertising,* they said. *The breakfast is free, but food cost is real; you need to keep tabs on this,* they said.

"What I'm saying, Leonard," John said, "is that your parents did a good job. They split duties very simply: a breadwinner and a child-rearer."

"Is this political?" Leonard said, looking back at

C-SPAN. Hillary Clinton was talking about the death of her father, blinking hard. "Like the split duties? Does that have to do with politics? I'll be honest. I don't pay much attention. I should, though. I know."

John shook his head. "There's a natural order to everything," he said. "And that woman, up there in her pink blouse, well, it seems to be her mission to dismantle that order, you know?"

"Hillary Clinton?" Leonard said. "But she's just the First Lady."

"Exactly," John said. He breathed out. "*Just* is the key word there. But look, I could go on. I don't mean to. All I'm saying is that you turned out pretty good. You've got your parents to thank for that."

Leonard shrugged. "They were okay," he said, sipping. "Just normal. Average."

John smiled. "You kidding? You and your family, that solid unit, your foreman dad, your churchgoing mother, you're what makes everything great, you know that? You're what makes this country *run*."

"Well, if you insist," Leonard said, grinning, lifting his glass.

Before this meeting, Leonard had coached himself in front of the mirror, had stared at himself while practicing his lines. "I have fifteen years' experience in the hotel industry," he told his reflection. "I know I can turn a major profit if given a chance. It's a dream of mine to have my own chain of hotels. If you helped me out, believe me, I wouldn't let you down." At the "dream of mine" part, his left cheek twitched. He practiced again. Another twitch. He performed in front of Mary, asked if she noticed the twitch.

"It always happens when I say 'dream.' Maybe I should say a different word?"

"Why would it twitch because of a word?" she said.

"It's always been my *goal* to own a—"

"Nope. It twitched again."

"Dammit."

"This is clearly a sign," Mary said.

"I could say 'ambition.' I'll try that out."

At Pete's, however, he found it difficult to insert himself this way into the conversation. He'd never really asked for favors from anyone, and while John seemed amenable to nearly everything Leonard said (especially, it seemed, to the most mundane things), he feared that bringing their friendship to this other level, this professional level, might sour John, might make him less likely to sit and chat. Surely *tons* of people asked him for things: he couldn't be bothered with yet another leech, right? Leonard needed to be different, gain John's trust before suggesting any sort of business partnership.

Time passed, however, and Leonard's apprehension didn't dissipate. In fact, as the weather cooled, then froze, then thawed, he forgot completely about his initial intent, the combination of alcohol and ardor and validation materializing into something strong and pleasant and pulsing and utterly, remarkably sufficient. Instead of working on his business proposal, he began watching the news, reading articles about the Clintons, finding faults, pointing fingers, and soon, as spring pollen speckled the air and closed his sinuses, he found himself aligning with his new friend, who seethingly described the first couple as "the Great American Disgrace."

"She's power-hungry," John told Leonard one evening. "And she mocks women who aren't. She's so full of hate for people like me, people like you, the average dude just trying to make a living. We need to watch out," he said. "If we don't, she'll weasel her way into the presidency."

"I agree," Leonard said.

John continued on, telling Leonard all the crooked things he'd heard about her, about her misuse of travel funds, her shady land deals, her insistence on having a stake in lawmaking, how she'd strong-armed her husband into putting her on a task force for health care, how even as a simple woman figurehead, a woman whom nobody had voted for, she'd slithered her way into White House politics.

"But I could go on," John said. He had a habit of saying this every time he talked about the First Lady. "And in the end, it doesn't matter. In the end, it's you, and people like you, who matter." He leaned back, smiled. From above, Three Dog Night belted "Mama Told Me (Not to Come)." "Great song," he said, rapping his thumb and forefinger against the wood. "Simpler times, right?"

At home, Leonard found himself insecure and confused. Talking to Mary directly after talking to John was muddy and disorienting. One the one hand, he loved her. He adored her. He smiled every time she smiled. He lived for her happiness. On the other hand, however, she often embodied the things that John (and now he) purported to loathe. When he spoke to her about politics, which was seldom, she sided with the Clintons, especially Hillary, saying that she was proud to have a strong woman in office, wasn't he?

"But don't you think she's going a little too far?" Leonard said.

"Too *far*?" Mary said. "What does that even *mean*?"

About a year and a half into their relationship, she brought up the idea of starting her own business. Once her mother wasn't an issue, she said, she could take out a loan, rent out that empty space on Eleventh Avenue, turn it into a health-food store.

"I might not even *need* a loan," she said. "Since I'm an only child, I'm pretty sure I'm getting everything."

Leonard's head instantly went hot. He assumed that she'd suggested this because his enterprise seemed forever locked up in endless whiskey meetings with John Forrester. He assumed that she was taking the reins, so to speak, was trying to show him up.

"What about kids?" he said. "Who'll take care of them?"

They were once again in the kitchen. She was once again cooking. This seemed to be the context for all of their interactions. At first he'd liked it—her food, while healthy and full of ingredients he couldn't pronounce, was, for the most part, delicious, and since dating her, he'd happily witnessed his waist size decrease. But now, watching her stir, shake, cut, sprinkle, he saw this cooking for what it was: an exercise in control. He didn't *like* vegetarian food. He'd *never* liked vegetarian food. But look, there she was, dictating not only what they ate, but *how* they ate. And now she was going to start her own business? Was he even relevant anymore?

"Kids?" she said, side-eyeing him as she tasted her broth. "What's *that* all about?"

"Simple question," he said.

"Leonard, we don't *have* kids."

"And that means we'll never have kids?" he said. "Is that your decree?"

She turned around, glared. "What's gotten into you?"

He didn't respond, just stared back at her.

"We haven't had this conversation," she said, turning back to the stove. "You can't just assume without having the conversation."

"Okay," Leonard said. "Let's say we have the conversation. Let's say, just for argument's sake, that we decide to have a kid. Don't you agree that it's best that the child's mother is there for him?"

"Him?" she said. "Really?"

"Well, don't you?"

"In this scenario, I'm raising this kid," she said, her voice even. "In this scenario, *I'm* the one changing the diapers, feeding, putting to bed, bathing, all that. In this scenario, *you* have a career, is that it?"

"That's not an unusual scenario."

"And in this scenario, *you* have your own hotel, or chain of hotels?"

"I don't know," he said.

"But that's the thing!" she said, wiping her hands

on her jeans. "You've had *months* now to get on with this thing. Months to ask John Forrester for whatever you were going to ask him for."

"I'm cultivating a relationship," he said.

"Bullshit. You're going out drinking. That's it." She pursed her lips, shook her head.

"I just asked a simple question," he said.

"You're asking who'd take care of an imaginary child because I deigned to suggest that I'd develop a new career. That's what happened here. It wasn't a simple question." She paused. "This is John Forrester getting to you," she said.

"He has nothing to do with this."

"Please. Everyone knows he's a raging sexist."

"They do, huh?" Leonard said, smirking. "Everyone."

"People talk. When there's someone like that in town, people talk."

"I see," Leonard said.

"The way he staffs his haunt. The way he only deals with male vendors. It's not a secret. I just never thought you'd give in to that shit. But now?"

"You're way off track."

"Well," she said, stirring brusquely. "Maybe you should lay off those meetings for a while, huh?"

"Oh really," he said.

"Yeah. I told you. That man's poison."

"So you're telling me, right now, what I should do with my life. You're telling me who I should have as friends."

She sighed. "Jesus," she said.

"You know," he said, "I'm really not that hungry. I think I'm gonna go out."

"Are you serious?" She turned toward him, folded her arms across her chest. "I told you about this dinner, like, weeks ago. I told you I was gonna try—"

"Yeah," he said. "You *told* me. You never *asked* me. But whatever. I don't have an appetite. I'm going out."

"Fine," she said, opening a cupboard, closing it. "Fine."

"Don't wait up," he said. He took his beer, walked to the front door, and slammed it behind him.

From then on, their relationship ruptured, bled, flattened. Week after week after week Leonard came home stinking of Pete's, and on these evenings, he slept on the couch, too wound up to face Mary's distance. He hated her detachment—her silent, downturned face, the way she turned every time he entered the room—and he'd almost, on a few occasions, caved and apologized, vowing he wouldn't see John again if that's what she wanted. Every time he came close, however, he caught her perusing a stack of bank papers, or a book on entrepreneurship, or a health-food pamphlet, and he'd fill with a rage so intense that he'd need to leave the room.

Finally, one day in June, two years into their relationship, she told him that she was moving in with her mother. She had a spare bedroom, she said. It'd be easier that way. Take care of yourself, okay Leonard? she said. Maybe we can be friends one day.

Leonard didn't respond.

When she left, when she was physically gone from his apartment, he found he couldn't bear the cloudy, suffocating absence that filled every room. He'd never experienced such an abrupt halving before, and it demanded so much from him mentally, emotionally, and physically (memories everywhere, future-imaginings everywhere) that for a few days after the breakup, he slept in his office at the Claymont.

At Pete's, Leonard confided in John. He said, "She's gone."

John said, "Man, I'm sorry. That's tough. Next round's on me. Let's get you nice and hammered."

They drank while Leonard talked about Mary—her pretentiousness, her control issues, her indecisiveness—and John intermittently broke in, offered generic words or support, told Leonard about the only woman he'd ever loved, a woman who'd started the Quigley House with him, a beautiful blue-eyed siren named Charity.

"You could probably say that the Quigley House is around because of her," he said, grinning. "She encouraged me from the beginning. She supported me. But then the support just stopped. I said I wanted to do full-contact, and she became indignant and self-righteous. So that was that." He shot his entire whiskey in one gulp, shivered, exhaled. His eyes, glassy and warm, settled on Leonard's and Leonard felt momentarily safe. "Sometimes," John said, "women don't understand the expansiveness of men's ambition, you understand? They're limited in their own, so don't understand that men know no bounds. It can cause massive destruction, this ambition, but it's ultimately what propels society forward. A good woman knows this. A good woman steps back, lets us do our work." He smiled.

"So now," Leonard said, "you don't date. Not at all?"

"Oh. I have outlets. Or rather: *had.* Not so much anymore. Busy, busy, busy."

"What do you mean?"

"Leonard," John said, leaning forward. "Have you ever been abroad?"

"Like overseas? No."

"There are other worlds," John said. "Places that understand men. Places that understand the unique needs of *American* men."

"What places?"

"I used to go to Thailand twice a year. It's magic. You can have whatever you want whenever you want."

"*Thailand?*"

"It's a place to reenergize," John said. "Lose yourself. It's wonderful."

"Are you talking about the sex-tourism stuff?"

"Oh, it's more than that, Leonard," John said, looking at the table. "It's the people. It's the respect. It's the food. It's the culture. It's the foreignness. It's all intoxicating."

"You're not afraid of AIDS?"

"Don't be naïve," John said, frowning.

"And you don't go anymore?"

"No, unfortunately. Like I said: busy." He paused. "But Leonard, you should go. You should definitely . . . do you want to? I have contacts. I can get you deals. I'd be happy to arrange it."

"What?"

"Yeah, Leonard. Let me do something for you. Let me arrange this trip for you. You have some vacation days built up, I'm sure. And everything there is so cheap. So what do you say? I'll give you some general information—where to go, what to see—and I guarantee when you get back you'll feel like a new guy. You'll feel *amazing*."

"I'm not sure."

"Let me give you my travel agent's number, okay? You just tell him you know me, and he'll set you all up, find you the best flights. It'll be good. I promise, you'll have a terrific time."

"Well," Leonard said.

"I'll give you something for the plane ride, two pills and you're zonked. Seriously. This'll be good."

"Well."

"I'm going to call my agent tomorrow, tell him to be expecting a ring from you. I'll set things up, call you at work with the details."

"Can I think about it for a bit?"

"Sure," John said. "You have till tomorrow."

Leonard stewed. At the Claymont the next day, he thought about the one vacation he'd taken with Mary, a week in San Francisco. She'd never been there, she'd told him—could he believe that? A travel writer who'd never been to the Golden Gate Bridge. It seemed preposterous. So they'd gone, and it'd been January—damp, windy, cloudy—and the boutique hotel that'd promised "ultimate relaxation and pampering" had experienced electrical issues, making their room oscillate between hot and cold. Still, their laughter during this week was generous and easy, and at night, despite the damp, they clung to each other—clawing, scratching, thrusting—until they both fell swiftly asleep.

On one of their last evenings in the Bay Area, they dressed up (which, for Leonard, meant wearing a shirt with buttons and pants that weren't jeans), took a cab to Sausalito, and had dinner by the ocean at a restaurant called Eventide. At the table, candlelight caressed Mary's face, chiming her eyes, relaxing her cheeks, and as he looked at her, a spongy pressure built in his chest, a velvety-soft constriction that crept up toward his neck and rested at the bottom of his throat. It wasn't that she looked beautiful—she did, but she often did, lighting only amplified it—but there, in that moment, she looked utterly taken, utterly swept, utterly *his.* Every time she looked at him, her face slackened: her eyes retreated to half-sleepiness, her forehead smoothed, her cheeks, flush with wine, glowed, anticipatory. She was in love, he could tell. And as the sky dimmed, the gray-white waves changing from violent outbursts to mere background noise, as they chewed their seafood, drank their wine, smiled coyly at each other, he thought how strange it was that true happiness could arise from the dreariest of circumstances, that a simple look, a tiny flicker of the eyes, a momentary vision of love, could erase any overly complex environment, could simplify a setting so completely that the world itself could dissolve into one remarkably enormous hoax, flattening and funneling around a singular entity: this person who genuinely, authentically wanted to be a part of your life.

After dinner, though it was cold and drizzly and dark, they walked outside by the ocean. At times, they held hands, but mostly they just walked side by side, listening to the smashing of water against land. At a bench, they sat, Leonard wrapping his coat around Mary's shoulders. To their right, yellow lights of houses rose against a steep cliff. Mary looked out at them, then out at the black water. She hugged Leonard's coat to her shoulders.

"Are you cold?" he said.

"Yes," she said.

"We should go back."

"Not yet," she said. She laid her head on his shoulder. "It's so cliché, right? To sit by the ocean and ruminate. With or without a loved one. It's a completely unsurprising thing to do."

"You think too hard," he said. He inhaled deeply, smelled a clean, wet wind.

"But it's a cliché because it's so lovely," she said.

"People want to do lovely things. That's why they become popular. We need more loveliness."

"This has been a great trip," he said, leaning into her, kissing her forehead. "The greatest I've ever had."

She sighed, burrowed her head into the crook of his arm. "I think we should stay for another five minutes."

"Okay," he said, wrapping his arm around her shoulder. "Five minutes."

The wind burned his temples, the damp pierced his bones, and around him, the world darkened, the voices of tourists braving the weather retreating elsewhere, the lights of the seaside houses blinking, then dimming, then blackening, and soon, though the elements still raged around him, he felt cocooned in a deep, buzzing satisfaction, and five minutes turned to ten, which turned to fifteen, which turned to twenty. By the time they got up, in fact, the restaurants behind them had shuttered their windows and their clothes were soaked, their hair matted, their hands wrinkled and white. Mary looked at him and let out a chuckle, as if just realizing that they'd sat by the sea in a minor storm. She threaded her arm through his, bit her lip, and walked.

At the Claymont Hotel, Leonard felt an enormous weight in his stomach. Over the last week, he'd tried drink, he'd tried sleep, he'd tried overworking himself, but the image of Mary remained always, even in his dreams, and often these dreams were violent, horrific, and he'd wake covered in sweat and wonder, for a small moment, if the warmth on his sheets was blood.

So he called John. He said, "Okay." He said, "I'll go." He said, "A break from everything will be good. Just tell me what to do."

And John did.

PART II
The House

Cell One

They walk in single file—Jaidee, Jane, Victor, Bryan—and spill into a room that's red and in-flamed. A scoreboard illuminates one wall. It reads:

- # Envelopes Total: 8
- # Envelopes Needed to Proceed: 5
- CONTESTANTS WHO ATTACK WILL BE DISQUALIFIED
- FIRST-AID KIT BEHIND CLOCK

On the scoreboard is a time clock. It counts down from fifteen minutes.

Bryan's eyes adjust. He looks around.

Spaced evenly in two rows are eight cages, each containing an angry, roving humanoid. Some monsters growl, throw themselves against the bars; some scream, gush black; some brandish weapons—axes, knives, torches, saws, swords; some wield sticks crackling blue electricity. From somewhere impossibly above, dusty tubes of pale strawberry light crash into the prisons. The light slinks across the cement floor like a slow-spreading disease.

Holy shit, Victor says.

Bryan walks, surveys the cages. They're tall, wide, rusty, with interiors large enough to comfortably fit two people. At the top of each, twisted rods unite to form a small metal doughnut; at the bottom there's a name plaque, black and gold. His name is attached to three cages: one containing a squat man whose face—disorganized, squashed, bulging in odd places—erupts blood from a mouth attached to the bottom of his chin, one containing a giant man in a diaper, and one containing two actors: an ax-wielding executioner and a witch bearing a shock wand.

Fucking Christ, Bryan says.

Sheets of plastic surround each cage, holding back two feet of blood-spattered confetti. On the south side of each one sits a small door—three feet tall, two feet wide.

We only need five envelopes, Jaidee says, standing next to him.

Bryan stares at the blood-spewing man. The man zigzags his arms, claws upward. *The envelopes,* he says. *They're under all that shit they're walking through.* He turns, looks at his group, thinks: We're dead. Victor and Jane look destined for L.L.Bean-model stardom, the type of people who endorse lake life and soy milk, and Jaidee, well.

So we pick the calmest monsters, right? Jane says, running a hand through her hair. *This one doesn't look so bad.*

Look down, Bryan says. *You've been assigned.*

Oh, she says.

The group huddles. *We agreed to follow the rules,* Bryan says. Everyone nods. Bryan blinks hard. Jane shivers. *Just dig. Ignore what the actors do. Remember: they're just people, okay? Remember that.*

They separate. They unlock and enter the cages of a seven-foot wolfman, an eyeless woman, the man erupting blood, and a tiny, skittering insect-girl. Bryan wades through the confetti, sweat prickling his back. He doesn't look behind him.

Dig! Bryan shouts, plowing through the confetti. Everyone shouts back. It becomes incantatory. *Dig! Dig! Dig!*

Machinery squawks above. *Ignore it!* Bryan says. From somewhere distant, Jaidee yells. *Hey! Hey!*

The machinery grows louder. Soon, three cages—everyone's but Bryan's—shake; the shaking cages rise into the air. Jane, Victor, and Jaidee scream. *Shit!* they say. *Fuck, fuck, fuck!* They suspend twenty feet above; the cages become unsteady, precarious. The airborne three dig, but they also fall; still: the eyeless woman, the wolfman, and the skittering girl balance perfectly, pouncing, scratching, and punching before withdrawing, cackling, pouncing again.

Bryan's cage stays on the ground. He continues digging, doesn't look up at his teammates. From behind him, he hears grunts, moans, groans, then suddenly, forcefully, he's doused in hot, syrupy blood. *Fuck!* he says. The bloody freak laughs, waddles around the cage, says, *Dum-de-dum-dum-dum.*

Bryan digs, tries to focus. This isn't bad, he thinks. I can do this. The blood is sticky, heavy, but it's not too terrible. He's endured worse. He digs, bent over, feels for floor, pats around for something pointy and square. From above, he hears his teammates shout. He thinks: *Don't say it. Don't any of you dare say it.*

He wonders, as he digs, why he cares. The money? Maybe. 15k would be nice. Like Kendra said, he could take Simone somewhere, on vacation. She'd like that. She talked about Hawaii, said she'd never seen palm trees.

You don't have to go all the way to Hawaii to see palm trees, he'd said.

But that's where they're the best, she'd replied, smiling.

He'd said okay, vowed to take her one day. Simone liked travel, seeing new places, eating new foods. Him? Not so much.

The short man waddles up behind him again, chuckles—*Huh-huh-huh*—retches, heaves, and Bryan's covered again, head to toe. The goo slides down his cheeks, his neck, his arms. Bryan moves away, tries another part of the cage, but the man follows him, vomits up another fresh batch.

Go the fuck away! Bryan says. This time the liquid seems hotter, like candle wax. It burns and dries all over him, making his movements crackly. He digs.

Yes, he thinks, ignoring the guttural chortles behind him, tossing confetti, fifteen grand would be impressive. Simone hadn't liked that he was doing this, especially that he was doing this with his ass of a roommate Jaidee, but when he'd told her he was going to win, that it was almost guaranteed, her eyes had changed, become glossier.

How can it be guaranteed? she'd said.

There are ways, he'd replied.

And though she'd never fully supported him—

neither encouraged nor discouraged—after this conversation, he'd known she was okay with it. She was thinking of the money too. She was thinking of palm trees and big waves and coconut rum and seaside breezes. They'd fuck five times a day, he thought. At least.

Above, Jaidee, Victor, and Jane try to balance and dig. Bryan looks up at them. Mistake. Blood-vomit man gets him right in the face. *You fuck!* he says, rubbing at his eyes. It burns.

From above, he hears Jane's needling voice: *Got mine!* she shouts, triumphant, waving a red envelope. The eyeless woman engulfs her with screams. *Now what?*

Keep digging! Bryan says. *There might be more than one in a cage!*

Jane grabs the bars, shakes them. The eyeless woman grabs her shoulders, shrieks in her ear.

Jaidee, next to her, is being thrown around the cage. Well, maybe not *thrown.* But it seems that way. The wolfman grabs him, lifts him up, shakes him, sets him down in a different corner. The wolfman has claws; Bryan imagines he's leaving marks.

Who'd have thought? Bryan thinks.

He'd approached Jaidee in their dorm room, told him about his alternate status. *My cousin, she practically begged,* he'd said. At first, Jaidee had been repulsed. *You?* he'd said, his face a mess of wiggling lines. But then—strangely, magically—Jaidee's face had softened, his attitude abruptly changed.

I'm sorry about what I said, Jaidee had said. *I really don't think those things. We must do Quigley House. We must.*

Above, Victor is struggling to keep his balance. The skittering girl—her legs impossibly thin, eyes impossibly large—keeps rushing him, and while small, she's fast, and each rush throws him into the bloody confetti. *Stop!* he shouts at her. She giggles, skitters away, rushes again, giggles. *How do you not fall down?* he says. She giggles, continues on.

Focus! Bryan shouts from below. *Victor, focus!*

On the ground, Bryan has found his envelope. He stuffs it in his pocket. His legs ache. The blood makes movement slow. He scrambles out of the cage. *Fuck you,* he calls back to the deformed man. He looks up at the swaying cages. *Only Jane?* he shouts. *Either of you—*

I got mine! Jaidee shouts. He waves his envelope in the air just as the wolfman picks him up, snarls in his face.

Bryan looks at the clock. Seven minutes left. They've only acquired three envelopes. They need two more.

He rushes to the next cage bearing his name, grabs the key, crawls inside. This one holds a man-sized baby, his eyes gleaming and anticipatory. He's wearing a diaper, his belly smooth, pink, and protruding. On first glance he appears harmless—some weirdo in a bad Halloween costume. Bryan ignores him and starts digging.

The man reveals a knife, a ten-inch blade, and Bryan's heart drops. Instead of attacking Bryan, however, the man slices himself. Blood trickles from his wounds, drips onto the confetti. He dances around the cage, trickling—*plip, plip, plip*—and some of it trickles onto Bryan and Bryan smells and tastes real blood. The man slices again, this time his left forearm, and the trickle comes again, and Bryan can't look away.

Bryan! Jaidee screams from above. *Hurry up!*

Bryan looks away from the man-baby and continues to dig. The baby slices again and again and again. His smile is ludicrous. He hums something happy. A lullaby? He dances and dances, staining the confetti slowly. *Plip, plip, plip.* Bryan breathes. He finds the envelope—easier this time. He rushes out of the cage, the baby's lullaby ringing in his ears.

So we have four? he shouts to the dangling cages.

Yeah! Jaidee says. *Victor hasn't gotten his yet.*

Okay, Bryan says.

Machinery grinds.

Bryan runs to his next cage, unlocks the door, crawls in. There are two monsters. One: an executioner—not too inventive, a muscular man in black carrying an ax. Two: a witch, a slender woman with long, stringy dark hair, a powdered face deeply wrinkled, a beak nose, an impossibly long chin, warts. She holds a glowing stick, presumably electric. The cage is bigger than the others, fits three comfortably, and as soon as Bryan enters, the executioner waves his ax and chases the witch. The witch dodges the blows, scurries away, shocks the executioner in the back. The executioner jerks, regains composure, swings. Bryan thinks it's mesmerizing, almost balletic, their movements, and if he didn't have to find the envelope, he'd sit and watch for a while, putting dibs on the witch—her grace would surely outmatch the lumbering muscleman. Though maybe, with just brute force, the executioner—

But no. He doesn't have time to waste. He breathes in, scampers around them, tries to dig where they're not, but they take up space, and he feels the whoosh of the ax near his body, the crackling of the wand near his face. He digs while the executioner hulks and the witch scuttles. Twice, the witch's wand strikes Bryan, and Bryan feels white heat scatter up his body, paralyzing him. He can't breathe. He remains still. Eventually, he composes. His blood-drenched body weighs him down, fatigues him. He scratches at it. A few hard, waxy flecks fall to the floor. No time, he thinks. He digs. She jabs him again, and he's stunned.

He stands, enervated. Is this for love? he thinks. Simone had been insistent on categorizing them as buddies (she was too proper to insert the word "fuck"), and at first, he'd been okay with that. They'd tried the relationship thing, and he'd fucked up, sort of. But she still liked him. She still wanted to sleep with him, she still wanted to be his friend, no matter how big of an ass he was, so they'd be buddies—no commitment, all casual.

Seems complicated, he'd said.

Casual is the opposite of that, she'd replied.

So they were casual. But not? He stayed over at her place more often than not. She did his laundry; he cooked her breakfast. They held each other at night, and when he went down on her, she squirmed just like she'd squirmed when they *hadn't* been complicated.

But I can fuck whoever, he'd said.

Whomever, she'd replied.

And do I tell you? he'd said.

Why would you do that? she'd replied.

He digs. There's nothing. He's so intent on avoiding the wand that he digs in the same place multiple times. He looks at the clock. Three minutes, twelve seconds.

He thinks of Simone's face. How embarrassing would it be if they didn't make it past Cell One?

He senses another person with him, cramping the cage. He whips around. An arm wraps around his waist, dragging him. He struggles, punches the air.

Jesus, calm down, Victor says. *I'm getting you out.*

The arm lets go, and Bryan stands straight, sees his dimpled teammate.

What? Bryan says, heaving.

Come on, Victor says.

They rush to the cage door, exit. Outside, his three fellow contestants, secure on the ground, look at him, grinning. Bryan wipes his brow. *What,* he says.

We made it through! Jane says.

What? Bryan says.

The cages lowered after you left the last one, Jane says. *We got the other envelope. I mean, Victor got it.* Victor looks stunned. He's been shocked by a wand, Bryan can tell. His hands are still trembling. Those things are no joke.

Victor points to a cage holding a red, spiky minotaur bearing a red, spiky saw. The minotaur throws the saw to the floor, bellows, rushes the bars.

Shit, Bryan says.

Look. Jane points to a door at the edge of the room. It's open, spilling white light. Bryan looks at the time screen. The clock is still counting down: 2 minutes, 33 seconds.

We still have two and a half minutes left, Jaidee says. *We could get all eight. Our chances . . .*

Forget it, Bryan said. *Let's just keep going.*

But—

Come on.

Below the clock these words flash: YOU MAY PROCEED.

Kendra

"So you said this was temporary," Kendra said, looking out the car window as her mother drove into Lincoln's city limits. "Right?"

It was early summer, sticky. Outside, gas stations flanked by fast-food joints flanked by dilapidated motels whizzed past. The sky was gray, coating each building in dense, hazy film. The few people on the streets looked puffy and fatigued and alarmingly white, walking without purpose, wearing clothing that hung from their bodies like bedsheets.

"I know what I said," Lynette said, her face drawn and severe.

"Just making sure," Kendra said.

"Well."

Lynette drove around the downtown area toward an enormous phallus-shaped building. She pulled over, squinted up at it. "Now, why the hell," she said.

"That's the penis of the prairie," Kendra said. "I looked it up."

Lynette shook her head, muttered, "It's just a building." She put her car into drive, drove.

They passed more gas stations, a record store, an adult video store, some restaurants. On the corner of Twelfth and O, a young white couple stood waiting for the light to change. The boy wore khaki cargo shorts and a blue Oasis T-shirt. The girl wore pink shorts and a button-down flamingo-print blouse. Kendra shook her head. They looked extremely Nebraskan; she repressed an urge to yell obscenities out her window.

"You know," Lynette said, "the university here is top-rate."

"Maybe in farming," Kendra said, staring at the couple.

"Bryan's going in the fall," she said.

"I know. Good for him."

"Kendra," Lynette said.

"What?"

"We need this to work."

Kendra opened her mouth, closed it again. She was

tired of arguing with her mother. It was all they'd done the last month. She pulled her knees to her chest, made herself small.

"There are worse places," Lynette said.

"There are *better* places," Kendra said.

Her mother didn't answer, just drove toward Kendra's new home.

Rae and Bryan greeted them with overindulgent grins. Rae commented on Kendra's height, which, to her credit, had changed quite a bit since the funeral—Kendra was still short, but less so, five-foot-two now, a late growth spurt—and Bryan wrapped his cousin up in a big bear hug, said, "Good to see you." Kendra lingered in his embrace.

"I'm so glad you're both here," Rae said, cupping her hands by her chest. "This feels *right*."

Kendra forced a smile, played with the collar of her shirt. Rae looked larger than the last time she'd seen her, her gray T-shirt puffing against the lower part of her abdomen. She'd sat next to Kendra at her dad's funeral, and at one point, Rae had leaned in and whispered, apropos of nothing, "Your daddy loved my cookies." For the rest of the service, Kendra wondered if "cookies" meant something other than the burnt chocolate chip and walnut monstrosities Rae sometimes baked during the holidays. The thought repulsed her.

"Still wearing black in the summer?" Bryan said, grinning down at Kendra.

"It's just a damn shirt," Kendra said.

"Just sayin'," Bryan said.

"Oh, look at the college boy," Lynette said, moving in to hug her nephew. "I'm so proud of you."

"Gonna read as many books as Kendra," Bryan said.

"Ha," Kendra said. She looked at Bryan, then her mother, then her aunt, grabbed her suitcase, and wheeled it down the hall.

Bryan's old room, the room where she was to stay, smelled like sweat and cheap cologne. It was markedly smaller than her room in D.C., and in each corner sat a different mountain of clothes.

"There's such thing as a hamper," Kendra said.

"I'm organizing," Bryan said, coming up behind her.

On the walls were various posters of hip-hop artists—Redman, Snoop, Nas—and on the ceiling, staring down onto the bed, a life-sized portrait of Lauryn Hill, her eyes looking shifty and seductive, her hair big and braided. She wore blue overalls over a plain white shirt, one strap undone, and Kendra wondered if someday, as an adult, she could pull off such plain clothes and still look so beautiful.

"Why would you put her on your *ceiling*?" Kendra said.

"Goddess," Bryan said, kissing his fingers, blowing the kiss upward. "Fucking goddess."

"Gross," she said. She rolled her suitcase to the closet. "I mean, I don't even think there's enough space here for *half* my clothes."

"Don't worry," Bryan said. "I'm getting all my shit out soon."

"But school doesn't start for another few months," Kendra said, turning around.

"I got places," he said. "Don't worry. And look at you. Don't you just wear the same thing all the time? Black T-shirts with band names on them? I mean, who even listens to Bad Religion? Bunch of whiny white dudes who shout a lot."

Kendra scoffed. "And I suppose 2 Live Crew *doesn't* shout a lot?" she said. "Why are you so obsessed with my clothes anyway? You wanna borrow some?"

"And those earrings?" Bryan said. "They're, what, spiderwebs?"

"Ugh," Kendra said.

He shrugged. "Listen," he said, "I'll get my shit

out ASAP. You'll have plenty of room for your suicide wardrobe."

She looked at his desk, frowned. "I can't believe you're going to college."

"It's not that weird," Bryan said.

"Yes," she said, "it is."

She walked over to the desk. Stacked neatly on top were a small pile of textbooks—his first semester's classes ready for review: astronomy, college algebra, English composition, sociology, philosophy. She imagined her cousin hunched over these books, writing notes, highlighting, making flash cards. The image was odd, contradictory to how she'd always pictured him. He'd barely gotten through high school, spending more time arranging parties than doing homework, and when, after high school, he'd gotten a job driving the city bus, everyone had thought he'd found a stable, reasonable calling. He'd seemed happy, even met a few women on his route, and nobody, not even Rae, expected him to quit, at least not for a decade or so. But then, a month after her dad died, Bryan had called and said he was going to UNL, that Greg's accident had made him really contemplate his life. *I've got a lot more in me than driving a bus,* he'd said. *A shit ton more.*

In the bedroom, Kendra felt suddenly sick. She went to the window, opened it.

"The air's on," he said.

"I know," she said.

He went to her, put a hand on her shoulder. "It's not so bad here, you know? You'll get used to it."

She shook her head. "It's just temporary," she said.

"Yeah," he said, removing his hand. "Sure."

They spent a lot of time together her first month there, him acquainting her with her surroundings, introducing her to the bus route, easing her into a situation she'd already deemed fatal. They ate ice cream and talked about life with his mother, which, it turned out, didn't scar as much as she'd thought it would. They often biked to Holmes Lake, a man-made stretch of water about a mile from their apartment. Kendra loved this lake, reveled in its straw-smell placidity. Whenever they went, they encountered few people, and this, she thought, was why people moved to places like Nebraska: here was nature unencumbered by human trampling. Here was an *actual* place of quiet.

She'd never been to a lake before, she told her cousin—wasn't that weird?

"Nah," he said. "You have a river, and you're close to an ocean. You don't *need* a lake."

"It's funny," she said, "how people always gravitate

towards water. Like for all their recreation, water's always important."

They stood under the shade of a small brown shelter, taking swigs from plastic water bottles, holding their bikes. Kendra didn't like the bike she'd been given: it'd belonged, once upon a time, to Rae, and it looked terribly outdated—the red crossbar screamed "Schwinn" in bright-white letters; the seat was wide and flat, made for a person much larger than Kendra; and the handlebars curved awkwardly toward her in a U shape, making sharp turns near-impossible. Bryan's bike, on the other hand, was sleek, blue, modern, with thick new tires and spongy black handlebars. He often raced ahead of her, even when she screamed at him to stop, and when she'd finally catch up, he'd laugh and say, "Get on, old woman!"

"I still don't know how you lived here your whole life," Kendra said. "Everything's so boring."

"Boring isn't bad," Bryan said. "I mean, look at this. I guess it's all boring as shit. But it's nice, right? It's pleasant."

Kendra shrugged. "I guess." She drank. It was morning—nine thirty A.M.—and the sun threw small, golden dots on the water. When everything was calm, the lake looked like a dark-blue mirror cutting straight through the hills, and it seemed, if she were careful, she could walk out on it and not get wet.

She imagined sitting out there with Shawn, his arm wrapped tightly around her, his lips nuzzling her neck. Would he appreciate the calm? Would he be okay with the endless green? He'd probably love it, she thought. He'd probably concoct stories about cannibal serial killers who lived in the park and lurked behind trees, waiting to taste young girl flesh. On the phone back in D.C. he'd said that Nebraska sounded *beautifully ominous*—all that land, those farms. She'd said, *Are you kidding? There's nothing* beautiful *about being stuck in the middle of the country.*

"Did I tell you my roommate's gonna be some dude from Thailand?" Bryan said. "How crazy is *that*."

Kendra looked at him, saw the dreamy anticipation in his eyes. "You know that already?" she said. "It's only June."

"It's not that early, Kendra. Summer's gonna zip by."

"Why didn't you pick your roommate?" she said.

"I wanted to expand my horizons."

"Well, they're expanded, I guess."

"Ha-ha. Yeah."

She was nervous about school, about roaming the halls of Lincoln High by herself, a Black girl surrounded by heaps of white. Though she'd been assured both by her school and by Rae (*You're going to the most diverse school in Lincoln,* she'd said. *I made sure of that*), she didn't believe that a town with a 3 percent Black population could ever lay claim to any sort of diversity.

"I mean, people live like this all the time," she said, gripping her water bottle tight. "*You* did."

Bryan frowned. "Kendra," he said. "Look at me."

She looked at him. His face was suddenly stormy. "I'm here. My mom's here. Your mom's here. Even if we were the only Black people in this town, we've got each other at least, right? And you're always gonna have us."

"Hmm," Kendra said.

"We're always gonna be here," he said. "No matter what."

"Okay," she said. "Okay."

They biked.

As summer pressed on, however, Bryan decidedly *wasn't* there. He spent more time with friends, on campus, at his ex-girlfriend Simone's house. (How she was "ex" was beyond Kendra—she didn't know anyone who regularly spent the night with *former* lovers.) And Kendra, knowing this would happen at some point, tried doing things on her own—biking to Holmes Lake, biking to the ice-cream shop, biking downtown.

These solitary excursions, however, eventually became too depressing, so she stopped, telling herself that she'd start again once school began. Maybe she'd make a friend? Stranger things had happened.

One steamy day in July, Kendra sat in her bedroom, rereading *Carrie,* trying to determine if she sympathized with the telekinetic murderess or if she was just pathetic, when Rae knocked on her door, opened it, and in her meaty, disapproving voice, said, "Phone's for you. It's a *boy.*" Kendra's heart jumped into her throat. She grabbed the phone and tried to shut the door. Rae stuck her arm out. "I'm waiting for a call from the electric company," she said.

"Okay?" Kendra said.

"Keep it short."

"Don't we have call waiting?"

"*I* have call waiting," Rae said. "*I* pay the phone bill."

Kendra stared at her for a bit, put the phone to her ear, then politely nudged the door closed.

She hadn't talked to Shawn Sims since that phone call where she'd embarrassingly demanded to know their relationship status. He'd evaded, of course, and had commandeered the conversation by shifting the subject to a place called the Quigley House. She'd listened, albeit tensely, both aggravated by and understanding of his pivot, and at the end, when he'd told her for the fifth time how amazing this haunt was, she'd had to lie down, her body seemingly giving out on all ends. I can't just ask him to come over for sex now, she'd thought. I've totally blown it.

"Hi, Kendra," he said.

Her breath caught in her throat. His voice! How she missed his voice! She missed his deep sound and his gingery smell and his wiry body and his curly hair. Shawn was *familiarity.* Shawn was *ease.* Shawn was *home.* And there he was, calling her, giving her another chance.

"I'd meant to call earlier," he said.

"Shawn," she said, relishing his name on her lips.

"How are you?" he asked.

"I'm doing okay," she responded.

They talked for a bit about Nebraska, the vast expanses, the corn, the whiteness, the red, red barns. After a while, Shawn asked about the Quigley House, asked if she'd had a chance to check it out.

"I don't think it's, like, right in town," Kendra said. "It's in the country."

"But isn't everything out there country?" Shawn said.

"Um, no," Kendra said. "It's an actual town with

things. It's not, like, some prairie with a few houses." She giggled.

"But even so, you're literally a few miles away from it now, Kendra."

"So?" she said.

"I did some research," he said, "and I found this other article in *The Horror Monthly* and I got one of the Quigley managers' names—Cory Stout. You could look him up? Like, in the phone book?"

"Like, *now*?"

"Maybe?"

"But why would I—"

"It's the only contact name I've found. I mean, there's John Forrester, of course, the owner, but he's not gonna show up in the phone book. But this Cory dude, his *address* will probably be in there."

"I mean, is this place as cool as you say it is? It sounds a little weird." She felt suddenly paranoid. Like was he *using* her? He'd obviously not called to pick up where they left off, so maybe? But then: Why *wouldn't* he use her when she was in a place that contained something he loved? Wouldn't she have done the same?

"I think you have to be eighteen to be an actor," Shawn said. "But they probably have other things you could do? It'd be amazing, you working there."

"Wait. Working there?"

"I'm not saying you have to."

"Of course I don't have to. Are you high?"

"I'm getting way ahead of myself," he said. "Sorry. I just can't stop thinking about it."

But can you stop thinking about me*?* she wanted to say.

"They're already this huge deal," he said.

"And if I worked there, like if I had some sort of part-time job, you'd want to hear about it all the time."

"Well, obviously."

Kendra drew in a deep breath, stood up. She went to Bryan's desk, sat down. "Like, you'd maybe visit?" she said.

"Holy shit, I wish," he said.

"Hold on," Kendra said, her head buzzing. She stood, paced for a few seconds, set the phone down, then went out to the kitchen, where she found Rae whisking an egg wash, her rapid wrist movements flapping her arm fat.

"You done?" Rae said.

"Do you have a phone book here?" Kendra said.

"I said, '*Are you done?*'"

"Almost! Just need a phone book," Kendra said.

"You're *on* the phone," Rae said. "What you need a phone book for?"

Kendra put her hands on her hips. "Do you have one or not?"

Rae groaned, stopped whisking. She opened a drawer, brought out the book, handed it to Kendra without looking at her. "You finish soon," she said. "The electric company's probably trying to call."

"You have call waiting!" Kendra said, and retreated to her room. "Okay," she said once she picked up the phone. "I have the phone book. What did you say this guy's name was?"

She didn't, at that point, know if she actually cared about the Quigley House—it sounded interesting, for sure, but it also sounded gross. A haunted-house attraction where the actors could touch you? No way. She could tell, however, that if she stopped talking about Quigley, Shawn might stop talking altogether, and she couldn't have that. She couldn't. So she flipped through the book, looked up "Stout," found "Cory," said, "He's here. He's in the book."

"And his address?" Shawn said.

"Listed," Kendra said.

"Holy shit," Shawn said.

"I can't just *call*," Kendra said. "Like out of the blue, that'd be weird."

"Why not? You just say that you saw an ad."

"There was an ad?"

"Not really. In this interview I read, this dude just said that they're always looking for talent. So not really.

Not an actual ad. But those were his words, and this magazine isn't that old, like a few months, so I'm sure they're still looking." He paused. "Summer's definitely the best time. Like, they're preparing for the season, getting everything organized. They're probably *actively* looking for people."

"I don't know," Kendra said, chewing her lip. "I just moved here."

"So?"

"Shouldn't I start school before I get a job?"

"Why?" he said. "I mean, shit. You said before you left that you're gonna hate it, and you probably will, you know? So why not have a fun job to take your mind off how much you hate everything?"

"You're so *excited.*"

"Yeah, I'm excited. It's a big deal. Honestly, I'd switch places with you if you got to work there."

"If I worked there, I'd show you around. You'd visit and I could show you around."

"Total wet dream," he said.

"Ha-ha," she said. "Well."

"I mean, you don't *have* to call him," he said, his voice suddenly hard and distant. "I just thought you'd like it."

Kendra swallowed. She blinked hard. "Are you mad?"

"What? Why would I be mad?" he said.

"You just sounded—"

"I just thought it'd be a fun distraction for you. That's it. But if you don't want to do it, don't do it. Simple."

Kendra walked over to her window, which looked down on a wide patch of grass dotted with conifers. Her mother had enthusiastically called this area a "park," though to Kendra it looked more like an intensely sad scrap of land that'd tried—and failed—to be revitalized into a number of useless things: it contained a crumbling shed, a rotting bench, a rusty swing set, and a small weed-ridden garden, all situated around a cracked sidewalk weaving through identically coiffed cone-shaped trees. Kendra shook her head.

"You're right," she said. "A fun distraction would be good."

"So you'll call?"

"I'll call," she said. "Why not."

"Holy shit," Shawn said. "Holy shit, holy shit!"

"I'll call today, like right now," she said, feeling his energy soar. "Like, right after we hang up, how about that?"

"Yeah? Holy shit!"

"It'll be fun," she said.

"It'll be fucking *amazing*," he said. "Seriously, you'll

have to call me *every day*, and I mean it, tell me everything."

"Of course," she said, smiling. "Yeah, of course."

"Every day, Kendra. I mean it."

"Every day," Kendra said, her chest light, her head spinning. "No problem."

The call with Cory Stout was short. The raspy voice on the other end simply said that he needed to see her, that he could do nothing on the phone. He could meet that day, if she wanted. Did she know where the Willow Green Apartments were? No, she said. What about Antelope Park? Normal Boulevard? I just moved here, she said. But I know the bus route.

"Bus?" he said. "You know you'd need wheels to get to Quigley."

"I could find rides," she said.

"Eh," he said. "Fine." Luckily, he said, Willow Green was right next to the 30 bus line, so he'd see her in about an hour? She said yes. About an hour. Depends on the weekend schedule.

She arrived in forty-five minutes, holding a small scrap of paper with the address and apartment number in front of her like a guide. Willow Green was significantly nicer than her complex (which, to her, looked like a series of large, hastily erected three-story office buildings with cheap siding), with a glimmering fountain in the center courtyard and a small convenience store by the main office. She thought, then, that maybe Quigley House was more high-end than she'd assumed—she certainly hadn't thought an employee of such a place could afford these amenities. She found his building (3) and buzzed his apartment (212), and a few minutes later, she stood in front of a long-jawed white man with a short beard and two sleeves of fiery tattoos. She didn't move for a moment, paralyzed, realizing, for the first time, that she was about to enter the home of some random stranger.

"You just gonna stand there?" the man said.

Kendra willed her legs to move, wondering how Shawn would react to her dismembered body on the news.

His apartment was impeccably clean, a bright contrast from the cluttered claustrophobia of Rae's place. It was roughly the same size—three bedrooms, two baths—but housed only one person, so looked more spacious, less worn. On his kitchen table—round, wooden, polished—sat neat stacks of bills, each marked with a Post-it: to pay, paid, to file. In the living room was a large, sleek entertainment center and three CD towers—Metallica, Sepultura, Skid Row, Mötley Crüe—surrounded by three enormous bean bags and a leather recliner.

Cory grabbed an open beer from the table, asked Kendra if she wanted anything. He flopped himself down on the recliner, raised the footrest up. "Lazy day for me," he said, motioning her toward one of the bean bags.

She sat on the black one, the farthest away from him. Her ass sank nearly to the floor.

"Not a predator," he said. "Don't have to sit so far."

She didn't say anything, just moved uncomfortably in the bag.

"Well, have it your way," he said, and took a long swig. "As you can see, I'm a bit informal about these things. I hope that doesn't freak you out. That's just the way we are at Quigley. We don't do things the normal way, 'cause none of us are fuckin' normal." He paused, looked at her, squinted. "So why don't you tell me. What exactly do you know about our little house of horrors?"

Her mouth went dry. Shawn had told her so much back in D.C., but she'd been so preoccupied with leaving, with leaving *him*, that none of it had actually registered. The only thing she knew was that it was a big house in the country where people went to compete for a cash prize. She squeezed the edge of the bean bag, made a nipple. The air conditioner kicked on, hummed. "I don't know," she said.

"You don't *know*?" Cory said.

"I should maybe go . . ."

"How did you know to contact me if you didn't know?"

"My friend, I just moved, and I was thinking of work and . . ."

"So your *friend* knows about us," he said.

"Yeah," she said, looking at her fingers, thinking of Shawn's excitement after she'd told him she'd call. "I know a little."

"Well, we're not for everyone," Cory said, leaning back. "You can think of us as this big, fucked-up family, you know?"

Kendra wondered, then, what her aunt Rae would think if she knew where she was. Rae—perennially bloated, flatulent, and ornery—had, over the weeks, experienced these sudden, unexpected spells of exasperation. Though she wasn't as difficult as Kendra had thought she'd be, Kendra still caught her looking at her from time to time, her brow furrowed, lips pinched.

Kendra leaned back, imagined the look on her aunt's face if she could see her now, alone with a man twice her age, a man who, she thought, looked like he regularly used heroin and played in some bad alternative rock band when he wasn't operating the Tilt-A-Whirl. She settled into her bean bag, said, "Can you tell me a bit more about the house?"

He smiled at her, exposing a row of surprisingly straight teeth. "Owner's name is John," he said, "but you must've known that. Everyone knows that."

She nodded. "People have actually gotten hurt there?" Kendra said.

"Nobody hurts anyone."

"But they can actually touch people in there, right?"

"It's a big game. That's all. It's fun. And if you win? You make money. What could be better?"

The whole point of the "big game," he said, was to collect as many red envelopes as possible in the hopes that if you made it to Cell Six—the final cell—you'd have found the envelope whose contents matched those of Martha Quigley's.

"Martha Quigley?" Kendra said.

"Some batshit broad we made up," he said.

Martha Quigley, he said, was this witchy, crazy fuck of a woman who, at night, had prowled around the neighboring towns in black, sneaking through windows, kidnapping children, chaining them up in her basement. Every day she'd cut off a child's body part—sometimes small like the tip of a finger, other times big like a foot. She'd bandage the child up as best she could, and then keep cutting until he or she died. In the backyard, the cops found the remains of fifty-five children, and in the master bedroom all the severed limbs hanging on the walls. Next to the limbs were dates of extraction, written in black marker, and next to the dates were Polaroids of each appendage's owner.

"Gross," Kendra said.

"It's just a story," Cory said. "It's not real."

"But people think it is?"

He shrugged. "People believe what they want."

"And what about the game?" she said, leaning forward.

"Simple, really," he said.

In Cell Six, contestants met the ghost of Martha Quigley, who handed them two red envelopes, one containing a picture of a child, one containing a picture of an appendage. If the contestants got to Cell Six without calling the safe word, and held envelopes that matched hers exactly, they won $60,000. They also got a T-shirt.

"It's simple?" Kendra said.

"The game is. The rules are. But getting through? That's different."

Most people didn't make it to Cell Six, he said. Most called out the safe word—*reprieve*—after the first cell. It was that intense.

Only one group had ever made it through and won the money, he said, a group who called themselves the Ferocious Four. They were UCLA students—two

Asian men, two Asian women—and they were a *shock* because they looked so regular: skinny, approachable, smiley, whatever. They definitely didn't look like the guys who usually competed. But they did it, and said they made it through because they worked as a team the whole time. They were a unit. They didn't waver.

"Now, people say shit—all media hype," Cory said. "They call them plants, say they're acquaintances of John Forrester, you know, typical bull, but I was there, and I saw it: they did it fair and square. People talk 'cause they have nothing better to do. And if you work for us, you gotta get used to that."

"What do they say?"

"Oh, you know, the usual. Actors block the envelopes. There aren't as many envelopes as the screens suggest. The clock skips numbers. Any sort of conspiracy to downgrade us. But I've been there a long time. We're legit. John's legit. We deserve the attention we've gotten."

Cory finished his beer, climbed out of his chair, went to his fridge, grabbed another one. "Sure you don't want anything?" he called out. "Water? Kool-Aid? I got some chocolate milk too."

"I'm fine," she said.

He went back to his chair, set his beer down on the table. "Some of those haters are my neighbors here, ya know? I think there's even a petition to kick me out of this complex. But I pay my rent. I'm no nuisance." He picked up his beer, chugged, wiped his lips. "Here," he said, reaching into his back pocket. "I'll show you the house." He pulled out a wrinkled picture, handed it to Kendra. She looked. Against a gray sky filled with cloudy menace stood a three-story white-brick mansion. Gnarled trees paraded in twos and threes across a long, winding driveway, partially obscuring a flat, weedy yard; yellowing curtains bowed each yawning window, revealing an interior of ritual dark; the white brick looked unsteady and unbalanced, tilting the structure slightly to the right. At the top of the house, jutting skyward, was an open-air belfry, where, according to legend, they'd eventually found Martha Quigley dangling from a noose, so emaciated that the wind banged her body against the bell over and over and over.

"Creepy, huh," Cory said. "You can keep that pic if you want. I have plenty of others."

"You keep a picture of it in your pocket?"

"No," he said, laughing. "I knew you were coming, though."

They sat for a while. Kendra felt chilled. She tried sinking further into the bean bag. "I'm sixteen," she said.

"You said," Cory said. "I mean, I'm not looking

for actors, you know that, right? We're all stocked up there, have a list a mile long. People wait in *lines* to try out for us, you know that? But I do got a parking-lot position."

"Parking lot?"

"Yeah," he said. "You know. Attendant?"

"Like, I take money?"

"No. We don't charge for parking. You'd just be directing."

"Like, standing outside?"

He shrugged. "Well, that's where parking lots are." He drank, finished his beer. "Thought I was all staffed up there, too, but then one girl bowed out a couple days ago. Guess her parents didn't like the hours. But they aren't bad for a high school kid. Thursday, Friday, Saturday night. Full week during Halloween. We close in November, open again in March, though spring is different, more relaxed. I was gonna call up a few girls I knew, but then you called, and I thought what the hell. Don't get cold calls for these things that often, you know?" He looked at her, his eyes softer now, tempered by alcohol. "It's a pretty cush gig. Only minimum wage, but you just point, and when you're not pointing, you get to hang out in the shed and eat doughnuts. The girls out there are great too. Christy and Sarah. This is their second year. You'll like them."

"So I'd just stand and point?"

"You'd be in costume too. It's all fun, you know?"

"Okay," she said, wondering if Shawn would be disappointed by this limited-capacity job.

"Okay? Meaning you wanna continue?"

"Continue?"

"Yeah," he said, "you'd have to talk to John a bit. Nothing huge. He just likes to meet all his new employees." He squinted. "You said you didn't have a car?"

"I have a way to get there," she said.

"Well, okay," he said. "So is that a yes? You wanna continue?"

She scheduled a "talk" with John Forrester through Cory during the second week of July. She didn't tell her mother or her aunt—she knew they'd disapprove—but she needed a ride, so one day she revealed everything to her cousin in a long, excited monologue.

"Hey now," Bryan said. "Slow down."

They were in her room, the door shut. Though it was still summer and Bryan wouldn't move into the dorms until the end of August, she'd been hesitant to make the room her own, but he'd assured her, a few weeks after her move, after he'd put his stuff in the garage, that he didn't mind how she decorated. *It's your place,* he'd said. *Put up your death posters. It's cool.* And so, little by little, she'd unpacked her stuff, plastering the walls with the weird, macabre blacklight posters she'd bought at the Crazy Arts store in Adams Morgan back home. Her favorite, the one that she put directly above the desk, showed the Grim Reaper with his scythe standing alone on top of a big hill, the wind billowing his cloak. Below him, instead of the usual screaming, begging, tortured masses, was the lone image of a young Black girl, chewing a fingernail suggestively, looking away from him at a house made of bones, the top of which contained a blood-drenched flag that said, in small print, *unnecessary.*

"It sounds crazy, I know," Kendra said.

"So you went over to that guy's *apartment*?"

"He's a decent guy," she said, scratching her leg. "It's not like that."

"He's a dude. It's *always* like that."

"I just need a ride," she said.

"And what then? What about when you get the job? You'll be needing a ride all the time. You can't hide this stuff from my mom. She'll find out. And your mom too."

"I'll figure that out later."

She hadn't thought about how she would broach the topic with her mother and her aunt. Neither of them had ever said anything about the Quigley House, though they were certain to disapprove: if she *did* get the job, she'd have to sneak, at least for a little bit. It might be difficult, especially given Aunt Rae's overbearing presence. But then: Rae went to bed so early every night—never up past nine P.M.—and during the half hour or so before she slept, she became completely incoherent, like a bad drunk: slurring, sighing, staring. Lynette, who'd gotten the receptionist job at the veterinary clinic, worked long hours and sometimes didn't get home until after seven P.M., so given this, and that her mother also went to bed early, Kendra thought she could figure something out. Perhaps she could say she'd made a friend at school? They'd like that.

"I don't like this," Bryan said. "Gives me a bad feeling." He paced in front of her bed. "I mean, Quigley House? You know about that place, right? You know how fucked up it is."

"That's all media hype," Kendra said, mimicking Cory.

"What do you know about media hype?"

"People talk shit about things they don't understand," she said. "And really, I just need a ride."

He shook his head. "I can't believe you went over to that dude's *apartment*."

"Please, Bryan. *Please*."

"Really living out your goth identity, huh," Bryan said, shaking his head. "Fucking *Quigley* House."

"Yeah," she said, "that's it. My goth identity." She looked at her closet, saw mostly black, vowed to buy a multicolored shirt.

"You're a real freak, huh," he said. "Like for *real*."

"I just need a ride," she said.

"Lemme think," Bryan said. "When do you need to go?"

They drove to the Quigley House that Friday night, late, around nine. Kendra had thought it a very strange time for an interview, but Cory had only shrugged.

"John's not like normal people," he said. "But I'm sure you know that."

It rained hard, in spurts, leaving ponds around the streets. The sky had darkened early, effecting the beginning of some slasher flick where people were stranded, then fake-comforted, and then slaughtered. They turned into the Quigley House's dirt driveway, and Kendra felt something wet slither in her stomach, a gnawing, greasy dread. The headlights speared the rain; the windshield wipers whipped back and forth. Along the driveway, the tall, barren trees leaned toward them, smothering. They passed a sign that said QUIGLEY HOUSE PARKING HERE. A green arrow pointed right. She thought of standing out there, next to that sign, pointing dumbly.

Bryan said, “I park here?”

“No,” she said, kneading her stomach, “Cory told me to keep going, to park in front of the house. John’s expecting us.”

They continued driving. After about a thousand feet, the trees parted, and the house loomed, pressing aggressively against the dark, an enormous slab of storybook terror. The first-floor windows blazed orange, highlighting a series of knotted, twisty trees in the front yard, and the edges of the house, racing out to an empty field, clawed so far skyward that Kendra wondered how the house was only three floors. One of the upper windows was illuminated, and though it at first looked empty, Kendra swore, just as she looked away, that she saw the silhouette of an old woman walk past. *Martha Quigley,* she thought.

“Wow,” she said.

Bryan turned off the car, and they sat for a while, listening to the rain attack the roof.

“Well,” Bryan said.

Kendra sat paralyzed, her breath coming out in small gasps.

A shadow emerged on the porch: a man. He put his hand in the air, left it there, frozen.

"We can go back," Bryan said.

"No," Kendra said. She opened her door to the rain.

John greeted them on the porch, ushered them quickly inside. He led them to a mahogany table stacked with papers and file folders. He offered them drinks. They declined.

"Well, okay then," he said.

He wasn't what she expected—more subdued, perhaps, straighter teeth, cleaner hair. She'd seen images of him on the library computers, and in them he looked unbalanced, his eyes too small, his face too narrow. But here, in person, he seemed utterly respectable: he dressed dapperly—white shirt, gray-patched coat, slacks, brown-and-gray flat cap—and secreted a warm hospitality she hadn't yet encountered in Nebraska. He looked like an ordinary man, one who read books and played chess. He pushed a stack of papers to the side, stared at them both silently for a while. They sat. He raised a cup, sipped some tea.

"Kendra Brown," he said, putting his cup in his saucer. "Great to meet you. And this is?"

"Bryan Douglas," Bryan said, sitting forward, extending his hand. "I'm her cousin."

"Well," John said, giving him a quick once-over, shaking his hand, "we're all family here, aren't we?"

From somewhere, Kendra heard a soft ticking; she looked around but found no clock. Directly above them was a chandelier: gaudy and glassy and twinkling. It hung from the ceiling by a cord that threatened to snap. She put her hands on the table, willed her leg to stop bouncing. She thought of Shawn, how happy he'd sound once she told him about this meeting. She wished she had a camera.

"I always start by filling my new employees in on some of the basics," John said, smiling. "But really, it's just me being boastful of my little enterprise."

He leaned forward, smiled. Kendra noticed one of his incisors came to a sharp point, like it'd been purposely filed down to look animal.

"So, let me start with the bragging," he said. "Let me start with all the stuff that makes us phenomenal."

"Sure," Bryan said, looking down at the table. "Whatever."

"Okay then," John said. He drew in a deep breath, let it out, then discussed how Quigley had been featured on national television shows, how it'd won international Scare Awards, how it'd frightened and amused (and, according to many, harmed) thousands and thousands of tourists. Even celebrities made appearances, he said. Stephen King called it "by far the freakiest place [he'd] ever been" and Wes Craven said, "You need a stronger disposition than mine to make it through even one cell at Quigley." The application for admission was ten pages long, mostly questions about allergies, past medical procedures, current medical concerns, anything that might flag a participant as a health risk.

"We've had exactly zero problems health-wise," John said. "We have a medical professional on-site during all tours. We take safety seriously." He sipped his tea. "Everyone who works here is family," he said. "I'm sure Cory told you that." He placed his hands on the table, in front of his teacup. He stared hard at Bryan. Bryan looked away.

He motioned to the wall behind him, upon which hung three framed black-and-white photos, descending diagonally. One showed a man, maybe twenty-five, standing alone in a field of dirt, looking out into the horizon, hands on hips, muscles straining against a stained white T-shirt, boots and jeans striped with soil. The middle showed a curly-haired woman, around the same age as the man, seated on the front stoop of the house, caught mid-laugh, her eyes, inflated with joy, staring straight at the camera, her milky legs marching out from a pair of shorts. The final picture showed the man and woman together in front of the house, the man's arm around the woman's shoulder, the woman leaning into the man, her head resting squarely on his left pectoral, both of them looking confidently out on the horizon—a staged picture, but beautiful nonetheless, a definitive snapshot of pioneer tenderness. John identified these people as his great-grandparents.

"This house," John said. "They worked so hard."

"They look happy," Bryan said.

"They were," John said.

He told them about the house, the changes it'd undergone, how he'd started with nothing—no staff, no infrastructure, no money—but had had a vision for the place, a lucrative vision, and he'd pieced together the haunt slowly, the first opening just him and six of his friends in the basement, boom boxes everywhere, painted plywood, dollar-store streamers, dollar-store masks, dollar-store Halloween décor, his first visitors comprised mostly of friends and family, screaming out of politeness, telling them what a wonderful place it was, how *absolutely terrifying* their tour had been. Martha Quigley lore hadn't existed back then, and neither had the "big game"; all that had existed was a bunch of dudes in masks popping out from behind random places, pretending they didn't know almost everyone who came through.

"We all knew we could do more," he said. "So we did. Over the years. Slowly."

But even after the haunt started gaining some local

popularity, the six friends, and his girlfriend at the time, a woman named Charity, quickly tired of the extra volunteer work, so they dispersed, got married, had children, moved away. John, however, because it was his house, his vision, his dream, continued on, hiring managers, designers, electricians, plumbers, sound people, light people, the whole works. Every penny he earned from his day job (in a past life, he said, he'd been an insurance agent) he fed to the Quigley House, and when that wasn't enough, he borrowed, went into massive debt; soon, collectors called him every day, and he had to forgo opening for three consecutive years because he'd grown so poor he'd become malnourished, sometimes subsisting on oatmeal and toast. But then things changed, seemingly overnight. A journalist with the *Washington Post*, visiting his alma mater over homecoming, played the Quigley game, loved it, and called John after he returned home, told him that he was doing a special feature on nationwide haunts—would he be interested in an interview? John was interested. And from that article sprang an entirely new subset of people, a national subset: men, women, teenagers, all obsessed with horror, all looking for the next best thing.

"Quigley was, and still is, the next best thing," John said.

"Just one article?" Bryan said. "That's all it took?"

"Just one little article. Isn't it weird how one seemingly small thing can change your life forever?"

"Yeah," Kendra said, thinking about her dad.

She looked past the dining-room table to the wide living room. It was strange, she thought, so livable. It was comfy, even: antique everything—rugs, lamps, furniture—and the art, well, it definitely wasn't horror; it was that mess on canvas that rich people propped up as high-end that looked done by a five-year-old. But outside there'd been chipped paint, uneven steps, weeds, old, pathetic trees. A façade. She turned back to John, her stomach unknotting.

"Fear is the purest emotion," John was saying, maintaining strong eye contact with her cousin. "It's what's left when everything else is stripped away."

"But aren't other emotions pure?" Bryan said.

"In their own way," John said. "But not in the way fear is." He scratched his leg. "Fear reminds us that life is an illusion. If you're afraid enough, you'll do and say things you never thought you'd do or say. All the things we're taught about respect, ambition, loyalty, honesty, love—fear takes all those teachings and gorges on them, then spits out the bones. And in my observation, there's only one thing that can triumph over fear, at least temporarily."

"What's that?" Bryan asked.

"Well," John said, "greed, of course."

Bryan asked if they could see the haunt itself, and John looked down, shook his head. "Only contestants and employees can see that," he said. "But if you want, I'll show you upstairs."

He took them up a flight of stairs, down a dim hallway to an airy room filled with monitors, keyboards, microphones. The gray faces of each screen stared back at them accusingly. "This," he said, grinning, "is the control room." He looked at Kendra. "You see, this is all an illusion, just an illusion taken one step further."

Kendra didn't think actual assaults with shock wands and dowels could be categorized as an illusion, but she stayed quiet: she had an uneasy sense, walking through this house with this man, that it wouldn't be wise to ask too many questions, at least not yet. John, while less explicitly foreboding than she'd expected, still commanded a deep authority, and she didn't want to annoy him on their first meeting.

She looked around the room. A Jason hockey mask stared down at her from a shelf above the monitors. Above the mask, mounted on the wall, a machete gleamed.

"Those were my first ever props," John said, following her gaze. "That machete is plastic, but you can't tell, can you. Even in the light."

Kendra walked to the row of monitors, still staring up at the mask. She'd watched *Friday the 13th* I, II, and III with Shawn, and while unnerved, she'd been even less scared of Jason than she'd been of Pinhead. Jason wasn't *frightening*, just big and dumb, but he didn't talk, and that was freaky, because if a serial killer didn't speak, they *could* be something other than human, like a wild beast. And the mask without a human behind it? Just hovering above a bunch of monitors and keyboards? Well, that looked sinister, like some disembodied ghoul that watched over all the normal people, directing and controlling them. She shivered.

"Does anybody wear it anymore?" she said.

"The Jason mask?" John said. "No. Things have evolved since then. Our contestants—they expect a little more."

"So what do they wear?" Bryan asked.

"Well," John said. "Let me show you."

They exited the control room and walked two doors down. Inside, John switched on a light. Kendra gasped. It was a department store: rack after rack of clothing extended every which way, some splattered with color, others crunchy and black. Mirrors lined every wall—spotless, brilliant—and in one corner of the room were seven green dentist chairs, each illuminated by a series of lightbulbs surrounding a mirror. On the shelves by the mirrors were cases and cases of lipstick, rouge, powder, foundation, and tubs and tubs of stuff simply marked BLOOD.

"You wouldn't believe how much fake blood we go through," John said, coming up behind Kendra. "I mean, you expect it, but it's really crazy how messy we are actually."

"Shit, what *is* some of this stuff?" Bryan said. He was at a rack, riffling through costumes. "A gigantic *ladybug*? Who'd be scared of *that*?"

"You'd be surprised," John said.

"I don't think you'd *ever* get me to be scared of a damn *ladybug*," Bryan said.

"Well," John said, putting his hand on a rack, petting a gorilla costume, "admittedly, that's not the number one choice for actors."

"They get to choose?" Kendra said.

"I'm no dictator," John said.

"And all those masks?" Kendra said. She pointed to the perimeter of the room, which was lined with an assortment of severed monster heads.

"Yeah. Mostly, they can choose."

"Mostly?" Kendra said.

"Within reason."

They walked about a bit more. Kendra touched as many costumes as she could. Here was a spider. Here was a ghost. Here was a bloody clown. Here was a plain pair of jeans, splattered in blood. She remembered one year, for Halloween, her father took her to a costume shop in Dupont Circle. It'd been small, cramped, and the costumes had been chaotically placed—it'd taken them an hour just to find the young person's section. She'd gone that year as a princess, not because she liked the idea of waving a wand and dressing in glittery pink but because everything else she'd wanted—the skeleton, the mummy, the devil—hadn't fit her. To make up for the girliness of the costume, she'd insisted that her father let her wear horns and circle her eyes with heavy shadow: She'd be a demonic princess, she'd told him. She'd cast spells of treachery. Her father laughed, and despite protests from her mother, gave in.

"So the parking-lot people," Kendra said, running her hands along the fabric. "They can wear—"

"They can wear anything," John said. "They're uninhibited. Out there, no restrictions."

Kendra smiled. She thought of taking pictures, sending them to Shawn. *Rate them,* she'd say. *Tell me your favorite.* If he chose the more revealing ones, she'd know he at least *thought* about her from time to time.

"This is awesome," she said.

Outside, on the porch, after John had said goodbye and told them Cory would be in touch, Bryan said, "Damn, what's *up* with that dude?" They stood looking out at the dark. The rain had stopped. Moths batted against the porch light. *Fft. Fft. Fft.*

"I like him," Kendra said, still thinking of Shawn's reactions to her outfits. *You're a sexy freak!* he'd say. *Wish I could be there to show you off.*

"What *was* that?" Bryan said.

"This'll be fun," she said.

"*What* will be fun? Damn, Kendra, that dude is *weird.* He kept looking at me. Seriously."

"He's fine," she said, blinking away the mist. "He's just running a business. He has to put out that weird vibe. I mean, that's his whole thing. But he's smart. He's successful. He knows what he's doing. You can just tell."

"He's weird as fuck. This place creeps me out."

"It's *supposed* to." In the distance, thunder growled.

"People just come into his house? Like, through the front door here? Where's all the boogeyman shit?"

"The main entrance is on the side of the house. Didn't you see? It leads to the basement where everything happens."

"I didn't notice," he said.

A moth flapped around her face. She waved it away. She felt hot, itchy. "Let's check it out," she said.

"Now?"

"Why not?" she said, suddenly irritated.

He looked at her for a moment, his face half-lit by the porch lights. He looked back at the front door, shook his head. "Let's go," he said.

"Come *on,*" she said, walking off the porch. "I'm sure it's locked anyway. Come *on.*"

Without looking back, she trudged through weeds, across the gravel driveway. Around her, everywhere, crickets hollered. She walked slowly, her hands out in front of her. The porch light wasn't effective on the side of the house. It was dark. She stood still, waiting for her eyes to adjust.

"Bryan," she whispered. "Come *on.*" In the distance, she heard footsteps. "Hurry up."

She stood in front of something enormous, a man-made creature guarding the haunt entrance. She walked closer, her arms still outstretched. The creature crystallized, the painted wooden planks cohering into the skeleton of a fifteen-foot child with bleeding eyes. Draped over the child was a shock of black cloth, dangling from shoulder to leg. It fluttered in the breeze, hitting the child's thigh with an insistent *whap.* To her right was a door: the entrance. It loomed tall, steel with a large, glistening handle, like a vault. She wrapped her fingers around the handle, felt its prickly cold. She pulled. Nothing. She pulled harder.

Suddenly, her father appeared in her head, his face taking up her entire field of vision. She was moving, floating—no, *flying*—and he was there below, grinning up at her, his thick, toned arms straining against a red T-shirt, his deep-set brown eyes with their dark flecks just outside the iris, the whites dull, webbed with red. He panted as he whizzed around their house, and from some distance, she heard herself scream in delight.

"Shit," she said, letting go of the vault door.

"Hey."

She turned around. Bryan's silhouette stood next to her.

"It's locked," she said.

"Obviously."

"I thought maybe . . ."

"That thing is fucked up," Bryan said, looking at the giant bleeding baby. "Really, let's get out of here."

"Bryan," Kendra said. "Tell me the truth."

"Come on. Walk. He's gonna come out here, I can feel it."

"Tell me the truth," Kendra repeated. "Do you think my dad was a good guy?"

Bryan didn't answer.

"Tell me the truth," Kendra said.

Bryan sighed. "I don't know. I didn't know him all that good. Anyway, this isn't the place for a conversation like this, okay? Let's go."

"I was just wondering what you thought."

"I know." They walked. "And we'll talk more later, but right now, I just want to get out of here."

As they turned out of the driveway, a shadow appeared on the porch. It was John, the house a blaze of orange-yellow light behind him. His face was hidden, a black outline, but Kendra could tell, as they rolled away, that he was smiling. She looked out the back window. He raised his hand and froze, his fingers spread against the light of the house, his arm a beautiful ninety-degree angle, his body stretched and tall; he was reaching for the sky, she thought, laying claim to his synthetic asylum, concocting, brooding, creating: he was, forever, harvesting the night.

Cell Two

A bedroom. Two king beds with musty floral cheap-motel comforters, damp, brown, stained. Ten different bureaus surrounding the beds—brown, cracked, covered in thorny vines. The bureaus and vines crawl up the walls, fifteen feet; the bureaus contain hundreds of small drawers: an enormous card catalog. A small bathroom off the bedroom, the tub, sink, and toilet filled with blood. Smell of mold. Bryan turns, coughs. The fake blood on him continues to dry, harden. *This can't be good for you,* he says.

The scoreboard reads:

- # Envelopes Total: 8
- # Envelopes Needed to Proceed: 6

- CONTESTANTS WHO ATTACK WILL BE DISQUALIFIED

- FIRST-AID KIT BEHIND CLOCK

The time clock counts down from 10 minutes.

They huddle. Bryan says: *Jane, you're the shortest so you'll open the lower drawers. Jaidee, you'll help her. Victor, you're gonna get the top drawers, and unless you wanna get all torn up, you're gonna have to jump from the bed as high as you can, grab a drawer, pull it out. I'll help you out after I search the bathroom.* Bryan stares hard at Victor. *You ready for this?* he says. Victor nods.

A door opens and in walk three people, presumably triplets—disfigured, older, male. The men look straight from the swamp. Bulging, mismatched eyes, blood-stained overalls, abnormally large mouths upturned into exaggerated grins. Each of them holds a different type of stick—one a long dowel, one a blue wand, and one a simple tree branch. Bryan watches as they wander aimlessly, sluggishly, as if half-blind. He inches toward the bathroom.

A deafening alarm rings—EEEEEE-RRRR-EEEEE-RRRRR. The lights fall red, and the inbred men, triggered, chase everyone except Bryan. Jaidee zips by (*whoosh*), Jane zips by (*whoosh*), Victor zips by (*whoosh*), and Bryan stares out at it all, feeling momentarily disconnected from himself. From somewhere far away he hears his teammates' shouts mixed with demonic laughter, but nothing specific registers. His head, for a moment, is simply a cloud.

And then: *BRYAN! MOVE!*

It's Jaidee, his roommate, shouting in his face. Behind him, a man is hitting Jaidee with a branch.

Bryan rushes to the bathroom, shoves his hand down the blood-filled toilet. He moves his fingers all over the interior, searching. Somewhere above, a chain jerks and an enormous gush of wind plasters his shirt to his skin. His arm sticks in the toilet. He screams, and longs, briefly, for a few moments of detachment. Just a few more. But he's not gonna get them. He's here, alone. And time's ticking.

Blood sprays his face. His hand is lodged in the hole, pulled in by a colossal current. *Fffffsshhhhhhh.* He wiggles his fingers, feels only three of them—ring, index, middle. Are the others still attached? He screams again. The wind abates. He pulls his arm out. It's all gore, but still intact. He sighs. There's no envelope. He goes to the bathtub. He holds his breath and puts his hand into the tub. Nothing happens—nothing sharp, nothing sucking, nothing grabbing, just red-black syrup. He exhales, moves his hand all over the bottom, finds a plastic bag. He grabs it, pulls it out—

EEEE-RRRR-EEEE-RRRR!

He drops the bag. *Plop.* Behind him, one of the demon trio has slugged him with a wooden dowel. It's not painful, really, but it's shocking enough, will leave a mark. He looks behind him, comes face-to-face with a grinning triplet. The man smells of rot—dirt, sulfur, compost. Bryan looks closer, sees that the face is not a face at all, but a mask painted onto a face. It's very good. It looks real. Kudos to them. He wonders, for a moment, what the face beneath looks like. Disfigured? Handsome? Nervous? The demon-man hits him three more times—*whap, whap, whap*—then straightens up, walks out of the bathroom, joins the others. Bryan dives back for the plastic bag, brings it out. Inside is an envelope. *Score.*

In the bedroom, Jane, Jaidee, and Victor are scrambling, opening drawers, feeling inside them. The clock reads: 5 min, 42 sec. Jane and Jaidee have one envelope each. Victor has two. The demon triplets are clumped in the corner of the room, seemingly dazed, waiting for their alarm. Once in a while, they chuckle dumbly. When they do, their lips hit their ears.

Bryan shakes his head. What a mess, he thinks. What a fucked-up chaos.

A fucked-up chaos.

A fucked-up chaos.

Simone had used that phrase a lot. *A fucked-up chaos.* For a while, she'd worked as a server at the Spaghetti Shack downtown, slinging bowl after bowl of pasta (unlimited refills!), and when she'd gotten in the weeds, when she'd been double, triple, quadruple sat, when the kitchen was slow, or the printers weren't working, or the manager followed her around, making sure she was taking plates away and pouring refills quickly, she'd come back to her apartment, flop on the couch, and say, *Work was such a fucked-up chaos.*

When Bryan cheated, when she'd come home from work early one day to find him with his tongue down Leslie Hemming's throat, she'd told him, later that night, that her head wouldn't stop spinning, that everything going on inside was some serious fucked-up chaos.

Why her? she'd said. *Why the fuck her?*

Thing was: he hadn't even liked Leslie that much, but he'd just been hanging out at Simone's, waiting for her shift to end, and Leslie had come over. She'd asked for Simone, and when Bryan said she wasn't home, that she was at work—didn't she know that?—Leslie had pushed her way in, asked if Bryan had any beer, sat on the couch. She said, *Can I just stay a bit before I go to work? I've got, like, an hour to kill.* He said yes. She downed her beer, asked for another. He gave. And then they made out.

We just kissed, Bryan said.

I almost wish you'd been fucking, Simone said.

What?

That kiss . . .

It'd been just a kiss, but it'd been an honest kiss, an urgent kiss, a kiss that'd surely lead elsewhere. Bryan knew this. But still.

You really wanna trade me in for some skinny white chick? Simone said. *Is that it?*

No, he replied. *Of course not.*

Are you a cliché? she said. *Is that what you are? Just some tired cliché?*

I don't know what that means.

She shook her head, mumbled, *What a fucked-up chaos.*

They'd talked and talked—that evening and many evenings afterward—but Simone couldn't get the kissing image out of her head: Bryan's head tilted, tongue sliding, eyes closed, hand running through Leslie's blond hair, and Leslie's arms folded near her chest, shrinking herself, making herself vulnerable, leaning into his strength. Simone had eventually kicked him out, and he'd moved back in with his mother, calling Simone every night, receiving dial tone. The few times

Simone answered, she asked why: Why would he sacrifice everything they'd built for some inconsequential romp with her coworker? Why would he choose Leslie of all people, the prototypical white girl? Why didn't he just push her away, remind her of Simone? Was she that powerful that she could cow him into submission like that? Her petite frame and blond hair and small tits, was that all it took? At these questions, he blanked, partly because they came as a full-on barrage, but mostly because he didn't know the answers. Leslie had been nothing to him—then, now, forever—but something had happened, and he couldn't take it back, and moments like those, moments where behaviors effectively erased purported values, were forever defining, he knew, and there was nothing he could say or do now to make it go away.

In the motel room, they have only three envelopes left to find.

Victor's arms are streaked red—he has jumped and jumped and jumped. He tells Bryan that he'd thought the drawers would fully detach, that he'd just need to pull and hold on, but that wasn't the case: he and Bryan not only have to jump but they must brush away the brambles, pull the drawer open, and reach inside in the second before gravity tosses them to the ground. A few times Victor's held on to the drawer, dangling, opening drawers beside the one from which he dangles, but his arms weaken quickly, and the falls burn his legs.

Bryan, strangely, has grown softer to Victor. The guy has proven himself willing to do shit Bryan didn't think he'd do. There was something in every person, Bryan thought. Something remarkable beneath the surface.

And Victor's been lucky so far. In his first fifteen tries, he's found two envelopes, one on his second jump. But now it seems the battles with the skittering woman and the minotaur from Cell One have fuzzied his mind.

EEEE-RRRR-EEEEE-RRRR!

And then there are the freaks, seething in their corner. Their awful unison cry every twenty seconds—animating, racing around the room, striking with their ridiculous sticks.

The blue-stick man comes after Jane, who screams and runs toward the bathroom. She's trapped but somewhat safe: the blue-stick man abruptly turns, runs for Bryan. Jane edges out, but the dowel-man blocks her way. She stares at him for a second. His mouth is full of saliva. He moves his lips up and down, fishlike. Each time he does, threads of spit form a miniature prison in his mouth. She shakes her head, manic.

Remember, Bryan calls to Jane, leaping onto the bed, jumping. *He's just a person.*

3 min, 25 sec.

Bryan's sweat rains down on the green shag carpet. He jumps, opens, finds nothing, drops. He does this five times, realizes that if he wants to reach the drawers at the very top, he'll have to climb. Each of those drawers, he knows, contains an envelope. They have to.

But those vines and those man-made thorns! Imagine his hands and arms! What if one of those razors hits something vital? What then?

And yet: climbing is the only way to stop all this fucked-up chaos. So he goes to one of the bureaus, kicks away some brambles, puts his foot gingerly on one of the drawer handles, tests his weight. It holds. He looks up, grabs a handle wrapped in vine. A thorn pokes into his middle finger. He breathes, ignores the sting. He moves his other foot, his other hand, and slowly, gracefully ascends. Behind him, the shouts of his fellow contestants are muted. Halfway up, he feels a wooden dowel hit his ankle. *If I fall, land on my neck, what then?* He continues up. By the time he reaches the top, his legs, cheeks, hands, and arms are latticed with scratches, some long, some short. His body burns, but he's thinking of envelopes. He's also thinking how strange it is that he's actually connected to this very real, very dangerous game, that he's sat at the owner's dinner table, that his cousin is a parking-lot girl, that all of this exists just a few miles from where he grew up.

He opens a drawer at the top, reaches in. *Envelope.* He reaches across, opens another top drawer: *Envelope.* He reaches for a third drawer: *Envelope.* He looks down. If he falls, he'll break a leg. The Quigley House will not be responsible. He signed a goddamn contract. How valid? Who knows. But he can't chance it. *Careful now,* he thinks. *Careful, careful, careful.* He descends.

1 min, 22 sec.

Bleeding, he shows his comrades his arms, the envelopes.

Oh my god, Bryan, Jane says.

You did it, Victor says.

Damn, Jaidee says, panting.

The men in masks huddle in their corner. In unison, the contestants look to the scoreboard.

Below the clock, these words: YOU MAY PROCEED.

Jaidee

On dorm move-in day, after Jaidee and his new roommate had both settled in, Jaidee stood awkwardly in the middle of the room, looking everywhere but his dorm-mate's eyes. It'd taken four years of collegiate rejection for him to get here, four years of working for his dad at the bank—licking envelopes, folding letters, punching numbers on a small calculator—four years of revising his personal statement, inserting phrases like "rich cultural heritage" and "diversity of experience" and "self-motivated toward success," four years of mindless American television and American novels and English language exchange, and now, after all that waiting, he stood in a room the size of a jail cell. Jaidee frowned. The brochure pictures had connoted spaciousness, but there was hardly any space at all; indeed, after his roommate, Bryan, had moved his loveseat in—pushing it beneath his raised bed, propping a TV tray next to it—the room seemed unreasonably truncated. Given the vastness of the land outside the room, this smallness seemed an affront.

And then there was his roommate.

Jaidee excused himself to the bathroom, sat in the stall. He thought perhaps he could go to the housing office, tell them he wanted a single, or that he wanted to be moved to a different hall. Bryan was not what he had expected—he didn't know if he'd be able to acclimate.

It's not that he's Black, he would tell the housing office, *it's just that I'm not used to—*

To what? He had nothing.

He left the stall, splashed water on his face, and returned to the dorm room. Bryan was hanging shirts up in the closet, running his hands over the length of each one, smoothing them out.

"So you're from Thailand, huh," Bryan said, standing back from the closet, taking inventory.

"Yes," Jaidee said.

"Huh," Bryan said. "That's cool."

"Yes."

"Come a long way from there," Bryan said, looking over at him.

"Yes. A long way."

"Well, welcome to America."

"I like it here. So much space."

Bryan laughed. "Maybe too much."

They ate dinner together in the student union—Bryan got pizza, Jaidee a burger—and after they'd opened their respective cardboard containers, Bryan asked about Thailand—what's the food like? What's the weather? Is it true, the sex tourism? How long was the flight? Jaidee, surprisingly, warmed to Bryan's earnestness, and thought, during that first dinner, that perhaps he'd wait a while before going to the housing office. After all, if he'd been roommates with someone he felt attraction toward, how would that affect his studies? School needed to be his primary concern: his parents would require frequent grade reports, and if he was caught lying . . .

Bryan's questions dissipated, and Jaidee felt compelled to ask some of his own: Was he from Lincoln? What's the weather like? Where was the nearest mall? What kind of music did he listen to? When his questions dried up, they sat silently, paying close attention to their food. After a few minutes of this, two men—one tall, one short, both Black and athletically built—came up to the table and clapped Bryan on the back.

"Look at the *geezer*," the short one said. "Midlife crisis, huh?"

Bryan looked over at him, smiled. "Hey, man, still wearing your baby sister's hand-me-downs, I see."

"Nah. She outgrown my ass."

They all laughed. Jaidee picked at his bun. He'd never understood the allure of the hamburger. It seemed almost offensively simple—just bread and a slab of meat. Still, he was hungry. He took a bite.

"Hey, this is my roommate," Bryan said.

"Oh yeah, you're in the fuckin' *dorms*," the tall guy said. "You *are* a freshman."

"Hey, dude," the short man said, extending his arm. "I'm Terrence. And I'm sorry."

"Sorry?" Jaidee said.

"Yeah, sorry they put you in the geriatric wing."

Jaidee chuckled. "He's not old," he said. "I'm older than him, I'm sure."

"Seriously?" the taller one said. "You look like you're fifteen, no offense."

"I'm twenty-three."

"Damn," Terrence said. "You two are *ancient*."

"Terrence's brother's my good friend," Bryan said, smiling at Jaidee. "I've known this kid since he was shitting in diapers."

"Dude," the taller guy said. "He's *still* shitting in diapers. You see that bulge in his ass?"

"That *is* my ass," Terrence said. "It's just that I *got* an ass, see?"

"Yeah, an ass that emits radiation. My whole body's singed just from standing next to you."

"And I've also known this kid since diapers," Bryan said. "Except he grew a bit more since then."

"Cheap shot," Terrence said.

The taller guy extended his arm. "Eli," he said. "Nice to meet you." They shook. "You keeping this guy in line?"

"We just met," Jaidee said.

Both Eli and Terrence laughed. "Hey, what're you guys doing later?" Terrence said. "There's a party out at the Bottoms. Lots of girls—Kappa girls, ya know? Jaidee, has Bryan told you about Kappas yet? No? Well, he should. Kappas are—how would you explain 'em, Eli?"

"What did Joe Brighton say the other day? Studious and playful? Playful and studious? Anyway. They're real nice."

"I still have to unpack," Jaidee said. "What's the Bottoms?"

The two men stared at him. "Unpack?" Terrence said.

"Yeah. I have clothes still in my suitcases and—"

"Dude," Eli said. "You're in college now. Haven't you seen any American movies? We don't *unpack* when we get here. And the Bottoms is where we hang, where everyone hangs."

"Hey," Bryan said. "If he's gotta unpack, he's gotta unpack. And there won't be any Kappas there. You know that. They don't go anywhere but the frat houses. And really. I might have to unpack a bit myself. Still need to shop too. Preparation, gentlemen. Can't do it hungover."

"You *are* ancient," Eli said. "You gonna get in your jammies at eight P.M. too? Set your alarm? Drink some herbal tea and read a book?"

Bryan shrugged. "Nothing wrong with that."

"Well," Eli said, "if you change your mind, give me a shout. Hopefully I'll be finished unpacking by then."

"Welcome to UNL, bud," Terrence said, walking away. Jaidee didn't know if he was talking to him or his new roommate. "Catch you later."

After they'd gone, Bryan turned to Jaidee and smiled. "Don't mind them," he said. "They're good guys overall. Jokesters, you know? But good guys. I was Eli's babysitter when he was a kid. The guy wouldn't sit still. I lost him, like, five times. Seriously. Him and his sister would just run out of the house late at night and scare me to death. I'd be chasing them and yelling at them and they'd just be hollering and waking people up. But then as a teenager he changed, joined this band, really got into the saxophone. And he's in the marching band here. I think he's even won some awards."

"He seems good," Jaidee said. He'd eaten his burger. His stomach bulged. He felt slightly nauseous.

Bryan leaned over, put his elbows on the table. "You really have to unpack?" he said.

The house was crowded by the time they arrived, the rooms trembling with synth pop and top forty, each space fashioned with a different, elaborate sound system. There was a keg in the kitchen, and students huddled around it, filling their red cups with cheap beer, pumping the handle, laughing. Bryan zeroed in on a tall Black girl with wavy hair and sparkly eye shadow. "My ex," he said in Jaidee's ear. Jaidee nodded. "You wanna meet her?" Jaidee shrugged.

After pouring a couple beers, Bryan and Jaidee went up to the girl, who stood alone, surveying the room. She looked unamused, her face a series of sharp, unforgiving angles. Jaidee thought she was a strange pairing for his new roommate.

"Hey, Simone," Bryan said. The girl looked at them both, her face unmoving. "How you been?"

She didn't answer, just looked at Jaidee. Jaidee looked away.

"This guy is my roommate," Bryan said. "He's from *Thailand.*"

"Thailand?" Simone said.

"The kid comes all the way from across the globe to Nebraska. That's fuckin' *nuts.*"

For a moment, Simone's face relaxed. "One of my group members in my finance class last semester was from Korea," she said. "Really, really smart."

"Why *did* you come here anyway?" Bryan said, turning to Jaidee.

"What?" Jaidee said.

"I mean, it just seems like they'd have tons of universities over there, right? So why come here? Just 'cause it's America?"

Jaidee shrugged. "I wanted to study abroad. Many people in America go abroad to study too."

"Yeah, for like one *semester.* They don't pack up for, like, four *years.*"

"Bryan," Simone said, her eyes narrowing, "everyone wants to study here, don't you know that? It's well known."

Bryan shook his head, tipped his red cup, swallowed. "Well, I'd never want to go to college in a place where

I didn't know the language. Can you imagine? How would that even work?"

"I know the language," Jaidee said.

"Well, you know what I mean."

Jaidee's temples burned.

"He speaks fine to me," Simone said. "I think the accent's cute."

Jaidee smiled. "*You* have the accent," he said. "You realize that, right?"

As the night went on, the state of Jaidee's face seemed to be the only thing anyone wanted to talk to him about. People'd shuffle by him and say, "Yo, you're like a fucking *beet*," or "Jesus, dude, your face," then go about their way. His roommate mingled, and Eli and Terrence hadn't come after all, so after four beers, Jaidee gathered his courage and approached a group of four floppy-haired white guys laughing and slapping one another's backs. He smiled, said, "What's so funny?" and a couple of them turned, looked at him amusedly, then went back to their friends. One of them whispered in another's ear while looking at Jaidee. The whisper recipient looked at Jaidee, then back at his friend, then burst out laughing. "I'm a freshman here," Jaidee said. More roars of laughter. "What are you guys up to?" Jaidee felt suddenly conscious of his face. He'd heard of Asian flush before, and he knew he got it bad, but he assumed that Westerners had something similar, that it wouldn't be noteworthy, certainly not warranting all these chortles and guffaws. He shook his head, left the group.

He tried to find Bryan, but the crowd had become so thick, and the house was bigger than he thought, and soon, feeling the alcohol tugging at his head, he felt that if he didn't go outside, he might fall over. So he pushed his way through as best he could, beer sloshing on his arms, his shoulders, his cheeks. A few girls screamed as he passed, said, "Where ya goin? Where ya goooooin?" A few feet before the door he inhaled marijuana fumes. He coughed, looked up, saw a skinny, dark-haired guy with a joint sticking out of his mouth, bopping his head. The guy smiled at Jaidee. Jaidee reached for the doorknob.

Outside, the air felt expansively breathable. A group of women stood on the stoop, three of them trying to console one, the one in the middle sobbing into her hands.

"He's such a fucking asshole," the sobbing girl said. The others agreed by way of back pats. "I wasted a whole year of my life on him!"

Jaidee walked past them.

On the sidewalk, just a few feet from the house, a hand shot out of the dark. "Hey, man!"

It was Eli, Bryan's friend, the taller of the two. Jaidee reached for his hand, shook it. "Hi," he said.

"Where you going?" Eli said. In a pink polo and khaki shorts, he looked bright against the wide panel of night. His eyes were happy, altered, no doubt, from liquor.

"I'm heading back," he said.

Eli looked at his watch. "It's only eleven."

"I'm just tired," Jaidee said. "Long day."

"All right," he said. "I hear you."

They stood awkwardly for a moment. Jaidee waited for a comment about his face.

"I hope you like it here," Eli said. "I know it can take some adjusting, but it's a cool enough place."

"I think I'll be okay," Jaidee said, though something in his stomach betrayed these words. He felt suddenly helpless.

"Bryan's a good guy," Eli said. "You couldn't ask for a better roomie."

"I think I'll be okay," Jaidee repeated.

"We go way back, and I'll tell you, I haven't always been the most stand-up dude, but him, he has been, just saying. He'll help you navigate all this shit." He paused, scratched his cheek. "I'll tell you this: One time—this was when I was in middle school—I got caught shoplifting. Dumb stuff, really, some action-figure toys I wanted to give my little cousin for his birthday. Anyway, I went on probation and did some community service and got a tongue-lashing from my mom, but Bryan—he was in high school at the time—when he heard about it, he just looked at me and asked what specific toys they were, then he went out and bought them and wrapped them and signed my name and shipped them to my cousin in the mail even though my cousin only lived, like, a mile away from me. I didn't know anything about it until my cousin called and screamed *Thank you, thank you!* and I didn't know what to say, was confused, but then remembered Bryan asking me the specific toys and I put two and two together. Bryan never mentioned it because that's just how he is. I'm telling you: you got the cream of the crop as far as roommates."

Eli's forehead glistened. He wiped it. Jaidee looked down the sidewalk. Three guys emerged from the dark under a streetlight. One said, "Dude, the house is over *there*."

"I think things'll be okay," Jaidee said.

"You'll be more than okay with that dude," he said.

"Have a good time at the party," Jaidee said. "Bryan's inside somewhere."

"You'll be more than okay!" Eli said, walking toward the house. "Just remember that!"

Back in his dorm room, Jaidee felt, for the first time, that maybe coming to this university across the world might not have been the best idea. The entire time Eli had been talking, a thorny homesickness had writhed in his chest, and as he laid his head on his pillow and closed his eyes, he smelled curry, heard the dull roar of motorcycle taxis, heard his mother cursing their neighbor, his father comforting a client, his friend chirping about school. He thought about Aran, about that last meeting in the bathroom—how smug he'd been! Aran had just been being friendly, and he, Jaidee, had taken that friendliness and smashed it, haughtily discussing America and all its potential. The four years between high school and college he hadn't seen Aran at all—his former friend had enrolled at Chulalongkorn and moved to Bangkok, but Jaidee knew he was back in Kanchanaburi every weekend. Jaidee could've gone to see him, damn his pride.

Anyway.

In Thailand, he'd envisioned Lincoln as a city like Bangkok—alive and breathing, an entity of its own with a real, human pulse, but here now, surrounded by these gently rolling hills, these straight, paved roads, these large Westerners, these square, sterile buildings,

Jaidee wondered what sort of life flourished—it seemed too automated, too robotic, a bit too slothful.

"But it's early," he said aloud in Thai. "I just got here."

He thought of Victor Dunlap, his pale blue eyes, the muscles on his forearms jumping when he wrote on the board, his deep, gentle voice, his shirt hugging his chest. He'd seen other attractive boys around campus, and at the party, but compared to Victor Dunlap, they looked small. He'd brought to Nebraska a picture they'd taken on the last day of class: in it, all his classmates huddled around Victor, and he, Jaidee, stood closest to the beautiful teacher, smelling Victor's slightly meaty sweat, putting his hand on Victor's lower back, feeling a small ridge of muscle. Victor had moved away, and Jaidee had moved closer, the physical contact electric and necessary and beautiful, and if he could, he would've fused skin to skin, making it impossible for Victor to ever leave his sight.

"Hey, man."

Jaidee started, sat up. He hadn't heard Bryan come in. He looked over at Bryan's bed, saw that he was rubbing his eyes, kneading his forehead. "Oh dude," he said, "I shouldn't have had that last one. *Man.*"

"Drink some water," Jaidee said.

Bryan got up slowly, went to their mini-fridge,

pulled out a bottle. Instead of drinking it, he held the cool plastic to his forehead. "Were you sleeping?" he asked, sitting back down.

"Nothing," Jaidee said.

"Hmm?"

"Oh," Jaidee said.

"You have fun at the party?" Bryan said. "You left early."

"It was okay."

"Sorry about Simone. She's a bit wacky sometimes."

"Everything was okay."

"Those parties can get old so quick, you know? Sorry if you were disappointed. I mean, just thought since you're new, you'd wanna see—"

"It was okay."

"But Simone, man, she can be pretty rough. She's so *distant,* you know? All the time we were together, it was like this wall. I mean, I know that's like what chicks say about dudes, but it's almost like she was a dude like that and that made me uncomfortable. But we're cool now." He unscrewed the water bottle, took a long swig. "Dude, your face gets red as *shit* when you drink. That normal?"

Jaidee didn't answer, just turned around and breathed heavily, pretended to sleep.

"I think that's an Asian thing, right? But man, yours . . . yours is something else, I gotta tell you."

Jaidee closed his eyes and willed himself to dream of Victor Dunlap. Instead, however, he dreamed of a big stretch of green field that ended in a bouncing red balloon. The balloon, after a while, became his face. And his face laughed at him for hours and hours.

* * *

The first semester was punishing. For a month it seemed like Jaidee lived in the library, looking for books on Kant (philosophy), John Muir (environmental science), gun control (composition), operant conditioning (psychology). When he wasn't looking for research material, he was writing page after page of trigonometry, dutifully showing his work, checking the back of the book for answers. All around him was talk of parties, bar-hops, late-night boozing, and this astounded him. When did they have time? How could they possibly keep up with school and engage in so many alcoholic extracurriculars? At night, he'd lie exhausted in his bed, running everything for the next day through his mind—was he ready for the discussion? Had he read the right chapter?—but his roommate would distract him, talking on the phone into the early hours of the morning. Jaidee bought earplugs, but they didn't work: he could still hear Bryan's voice, muffled or not.

On the night before his first psychology exam, he sat up in bed, took out his earplugs, and said, "Hey. I have a test tomorrow. I have to sleep."

Bryan looked at him, blinked. "Just a minute, Kendra," he said. He put a hand over the receiver. "What's that?" he said, looking over at Jaidee. "A test?"

"Yes," Jaidee said, feeling suddenly warm. "I have a test."

Bryan looked at his watch. "It's eight o'clock, Jaidee."

"My test is at eight thirty A.M."

"You need twelve hours of sleep?"

"It's not like I'll wake up right before the exam."

Bryan sighed. "I think you need to relax a bit. Maybe get some air. Clear your head."

"I need to sleep."

"Dude," Bryan said, "you've got to chill about all the school stuff. It's not like a B is gonna kill you."

"Can you please just let me sleep?"

Bryan shook his head. "This is important, okay? Sorry." He took his hand off the receiver. "You there?" he said.

Jaidee flopped back on the bed, put his earplugs back in. As Eli had said that first night, Bryan had been a good roommate—he'd left Jaidee alone for the most part—but these late-night phone calls were wearing on Jaidee. Sometimes he'd fall asleep only to wake up at midnight and still hear his voice. Sometimes he even dreamed of Bryan, mostly Bryan on the phone in various locations—ice caves, Bangkok, mystical villages surrounded by sheets of lavender, lopsided dorm rooms, farmhouses—and in his dreams, he, Jaidee, would say, politely, "Are you nearly finished?" Bryan would simply hush him and continue talking on his phone among the wildlife or the fairies or the farm machinery or the villagers. On this day, however, the day before his psychology exam, Jaidee didn't want to stand for it, so he sat up, huffed, threw on some clothes, and walked out of the dorm.

It just so happened that on this evening, the campus gay and lesbian group was meeting in the student union—there'd been flyers posted around the university, some of them ripped, a few of them with doodles of erect penises. He'd noticed them as he'd gone from class to class, telling himself that when he got a minute, he'd join, see what it was all about, perhaps meet a boy with whom he could practice kissing. As he walked around the buzzing student union that evening, he remembered the flyers. He found one and noted the location. When he got to the designated room, the meeting was nearly over. The leader, a round, curly-haired woman named Hayley Wells, turned to him, smiled, and waved him in. He looked at the group: there were ten women, five of whom had visible facial piercings, and nine men. The men, Jaidee thought, looked mostly unremarkable, though there was a group of three who sat toward the back and smirked, their arms identically crossed over their chests, their hair coiffed, their skin bronzed. Two were blond, one was dark-haired, and when Jaidee sat next to the dark-haired boy, the boy looked immediately to his right, at his friends, then at Jaidee.

"Remember," Hayley was saying, "we have a Pride Committee meeting next week. We need to try to make our float structurally sound this year. We can't have another—"

"That wasn't my fault!" came a squeaky voice from the front. It was one of the women with piercings, this one a small hoop in her lip.

"Nobody was saying it was your fault, Katie," Hayley said.

"You looked right at me!"

"I was looking everywhere," Hayley said.

The boy next to Jaidee sighed. He leaned back in his chair, yawned. He was wearing shorts, though it was

October and only fifty degrees outside. His knees were knobby, covered in fine, dark hair.

"I'm not going to argue this," Hayley said. "We can talk later if you want."

The boy in the middle leaned over to the dark-haired boy, whispered, "It *was* her fucking fault."

"What was?" Jaidee asked.

The boy looked at him, his eyes small and suspicious. He had blond hair, spiked, and his forehead collapsed into a surprisingly meaty face. The face shouldn't have been attractive—each component part was too exaggerated or wide or beady or plump, but it all cohered into something startlingly mischievous and sexy, and as the boy spoke, Jaidee had focused on the lips—thin, dry, pink—thinking they would be good lips to practice kissing on.

The boy didn't answer, just leaned back in his chair, crossed his arms again.

"I'm new here," Jaidee said.

"Yeah, no shit," the dark-haired boy mumbled.

The other two chuckled. Jaidee looked away.

Afterward, Hayley, the group leader, came up to him, smiled, asked him his name. She told him about the meetings, how they usually had a topic to discuss but that this time everyone had been consumed by this Pride float gone awry—apparently Katie, the protesting girl in front, had managed to flub the float so it made a high-pitched whine as it moved.

"We go out afterwards as a group," she said. "If you're interested."

Jaidee looked at the door, where the three boys he'd sat next to huddled. They snickered and sneered and tried hard to look as aloof as possible.

"Ugh," Hayley said. "Those guys are ridiculous. I don't even know why they keep coming to the meetings."

"Ridiculous?" Jaidee said.

She leaned in. "It's like they think they're in some sort of TV show."

"They're actors?"

She looked at him, squinted, then shrugged. "I guess. In a way."

"They seem okay."

"Probably best not to think about them too much, you know?" she said. "So what do you say? You wanna come with us to the bar?"

Jaidee didn't go with them to the bar that night, but instead went back home and found Bryan in bed, facing away, headphones on, looking at a book. When Jaidee came in, Bryan glanced over his shoulder, grunted a greeting, then returned to his textbook. Jaidee undressed, climbed into bed. He tried to run through famous names in psychology—Freud, Jung, Piaget, Skinner—then tried to match them to their area of expertise—dreams, animus, development, conditioning—but his thoughts kept racing to visions of the blond boy's lips. What would lips that thin feel like when pressed against his own? Like tough skin kneading his face? Or maybe surprisingly soft, the slight jut of the lower one transforming into a sort of plush cushion once it made contact with his mouth. For years, he'd imagined Victor Dunlap's lips, the prickly stubble scratching beneath his nose, the hot breath filling his throat, but Victor's lips were wide and substantial—very different from the blond boy's. Was it worth it even to try, then?

Of course.

Jaidee went back to the group the next week, and the week after that, and the week after that, and he sat with the boys in the back, learned their names—Nick, Chris, Jared—and tried as best he could to enter their conversation. Their barriers, however, were seemingly impenetrable: every time Jaidee leaned in, contributed, they shot him a half-bewildered, half-irritated look, then went back to talking among themselves. They sometimes wore caps, backward, and they almost always wore brand names, the type that loudly advertised themselves in reds and blues: Abercrombie, Gap, Banana Republic. Jaidee called his uncle, told him he needed new clothes, that he—his uncle—should expect a few more charges on his credit card because Jaidee had grown out of all the clothes he had.

"Are you becoming fat?" his uncle said.

Jaidee assured his uncle that he wasn't, that actually the opposite was true: he'd lost weight and his clothes were much too baggy.

"How is it possible to lose weight when you go to America?" his uncle said.

Jaidee went to the mall. He changed his wardrobe. He got a haircut, showed the stylist pictures of movie stars, said, "I want to look like this." He bought a cap. He wore it backward. He watched lots and lots and lots of TV. He studied American idioms. He started saying "dude."

Nick, Chris, and Jared watched his transformation with amusement. Sometimes Jaidee would show up to group wearing the same shirt as one of the boys. The boys would remark on it, unkindly, then turn back to their threesome. "Dude, that shirt," they'd say.

From the other international students around campus Jaidee kept a distance. He now found them distasteful. The floppy hair! The ethnic clothing! The groups huddled together, not speaking English! He was different, he knew. Even having been in the country one semester, he had assimilated. He'd adapted to his surroundings, he thought. He shopped at Abercrombie & Fitch.

One evening, in the student union, munching on Doritos and watching a *Friends* episode, he noticed a guy sitting on the leather chair a few feet away. In his lap was a sandwich wrapped in paper. The boy opened it carefully, took a bite. Some of the sandwich's contents—lettuce, cheese, ham—fell back into the paper. Jaidee stared.

The boy was cute—brown hair cut Caesar-style, a five o'clock shadow, broad shoulders, arms that pressed tight against the sleeves of his white T-shirt. Jaidee assumed the boy had sat next to him for a reason. There were other places to sit—why sit so close? Jaidee stared some more. The boy didn't look away from his sandwich or the TV, however, and Jaidee attributed this to shyness, so he got up, moved to a chair that was directly across from the boy, thinking that maybe he'd be less bashful if Jaidee was in his direct line of sight. He stared some more, but still the boy only paid attention to his sandwich and the TV. Canned laughter came from the screen. The boy chuckled.

"That was funny, huh," Jaidee said.

The boy stopped mid-chew, looked at Jaidee. Jaidee saw that his eyes were green.

"Uh, I guess," the boy said.

"So what is your major?" Jaidee asked.

The boy didn't answer, just continued to watch.

"What is your major?" Jaidee asked again, thinking maybe he hadn't heard.

"Finance," the boy mumbled, chewing.

"Oh, that's a good major," Jaidee said.

The boy stared intently at the screen. It was a commercial for an auto dealer.

"You have a car? Or are you buying a new car?" Jaidee asked.

"What?" the boy said.

"You are interested in buying a new car?"

"Dude," the boy said, "what's your problem?"

"My problem?"

"Jesus," the boy said, shaking his head, wrapping the rest of his sandwich in the paper, putting it in his backpack.

Jaidee felt a wave of heat course down his spine. "I would like to talk to you more," Jaidee said.

The boy stood up, looked down at Jaidee, his brow wrinkling. "Dude," he said, "I know you're from, like, an Oriental country, but you're kinda coming across as a homo."

"What?" Jaidee said.

"Later," the boy said, and left.

Jaidee went through the rest of his day with gray cumuli roiling above his head, noting how everyone on campus looked happy and content, hating them all for this happiness and contentment. He noticed, then, how people *didn't* notice him, how they looked through him, passed by without a second glance. He was an *Oriental homo*, he thought—whatever was he doing in white America?

And yet, at the group that evening, he still sat next to Nick, Chris, and Jared. He still wore his brand names. He still leaned into their discussion. Nick, Chris, and Jared still ignored him, though once in a while Chris—the thin-lipped leader, the spiky-haired communications major—would look at Jaidee and smile, and one day, a bitingly cold day in early November, Chris's comrades, Nick and Jared, had to go home right after the group, had tests to study for, and Chris wanted to stay out, so Chris told Hayley that yes, he'd be going to Brewsky's that night, that he was hungry and thirsty and it sounded lovely. After his friends had left, Chris smiled once again at Jaidee and said, "Hey, man, you coming?"

The music was loud, and the bar was smoky. They found a long table, sat on uncomfortable stools.

Chris sat across from Jaidee. In the bluish light, his face looked friendly. "I mean, in this day and age," he said. "It's the fucking *nineties* and people are still calling people faggot? God."

"No, not faggot. Homo."

On the way over, Jaidee had told him about his incident at the student union, eliminating, of course, the fact that Jaidee had been unable to control his stare. "Seriously," Chris said, "it's Nebraska shit. Believe me, I've lived here my whole life. Lincoln seems all liberal but it's just like everywhere else in this fucking state—redneck heaven. Everyone here's lame. Seriously. All they talk about is the Huskers and the Quigley House. You heard of that shit? People pay to get beat up there. It's all just messed up—tons of protests, as you can imagine. Anyway, I swear, when I graduate, I'm getting out. Probably go to Chicago. Maybe New York."

"Paid to get beat up?" Jaidee said.

"At the Quigley? Yeah. It's what they call a 'full-contact' haunted house. You haven't heard of it? It's, like, all anyone ever talks about besides football."

"That sounds really weird."

"It is, man," he said. "But everything in this town is weird. Screwed up. Husker Suckers is what I call people."

He had a raspy voice, a voice that reeked of years of

cigarette use, though as far as Jaidee knew, Chris didn't smoke. Jaidee didn't particularly love the voice, but it did lend Chris a sort of masculine quality that some of the others didn't have. Jaidee hummed a bit, tried to make his throat vibrate. The server came over. She looked at him and cocked her head. "You okay?" she said. She was chewing gum. Jaidee could smell watermelon.

"I'm seriously outta here when I graduate," Chris repeated after they'd ordered. "All these lowlifes. Bottom-feeders. And the gay guys, man. They're so ridiculous." He shook his head. "All of 'em thinking they're so great. They're nothing, you know? Nothing."

Jaidee looked away. Though he found Chris nominally attractive, he realized, then, that his allure was directly attached to his association, that without the other two, he lost some of his luster.

"I think maybe I'll go backpacking through Europe," Chris said. "Like, right after I graduate. Just take off, go through all those European countries."

The food came. Jaidee picked at it. He felt scratchy. He wanted to sleep.

"So what's your deal, Jaidee? You came all the way over here from—where? China? What a place to come! You must have a ton of culture shock."

"Thailand," Jaidee said, chewing on a fry.

"What's that?" Chris said.

"You said China. I'm from Thailand."

"Oh," Chris said, winking. "Well, it's Asian all the same, right?"

Jaidee shrugged. He'd found it difficult to impart to Americans just how different Asian countries were from one another. Americans seemed to see them as one big cultural mass, all with the same history, the same geography, the same government. People in America said "Africa" and "Asia" like they were countries, not continents, and yet when you talked about their state, their small land mass in the middle of an enormous country, they became self-righteous, indignant, inflamed: How dare you not know Nebraska! How dare you not know Iowa! How dare you not know Kansas! My state is *the* state.

The gay guys, interestingly, were the opposite, deriding Nebraska, praising the coasts, wistfully planning on one day being in a city, able to look down on the simpletons of their youth.

The server came back, checked on them. Chris ordered a beer—it was his fourth. Jaidee also ordered a beer—it was his first. He'd tempered himself since the party. In America, it was best not to be red.

"Nick and Jared couldn't come?" Jaidee asked.

Chris shook his head. His eyes were small, distant.

He leaned in, smiled. "Hey, man," he said. "Why are you drinking so slow? You're nursing that beer like a girl."

"I just don't want—"

"Drink up, man. It's Thursday night. Thirsty, thirsty Thursday."

Jaidee smiled hesitantly, brought the mug to his lips. When he did, Chris reached over and pushed on the bottom, forcing beer down the sides of Jaidee's mouth.

"There ya go," Chris said. "Put some hair on your chest. Or—is that okay to say to an Asian dude? You don't got hair, I assume." Chris reached out, rubbed his hand swiftly across Jaidee's chest. "Nah, you don't. I can tell. Look here." He unbuttoned his shirt. "Look at all that fuckin' hair, man. It's like a forest there. A hairy, hairy forest. Go ahead, man, you can touch it. It's all me. All me, and all hair." He chuckled. "You can touch, seriously. You know you wanna."

Next to Jaidee sat Katie, the ruiner of Pride floats. She looked over at Chris and rolled her eyes.

"What's that, Katie?" Chris said. "You want some of this too?"

"You're such a douche," she said.

"Yeah, well," he said.

Chris looked over at Jaidee and winked, buttoned up his shirt. Jaidee wondered what the wink meant. The beer buzzed in his head. He could feel his face getting hot. He wanted more to drink but knew what he'd look like. Still.

"You know," Chris said, "you could be cute. I mean. Yeah, there are dudes who go for the whole Asian thing, right? I think there are dudes who *only* go for the whole Asian thing. You should try to hook up with one of them."

"What?"

"Hell yeah. I mean, people all got their tastes, right? Take Nick, for instance. He, like, *only* goes for guys twice his age. It's weird. Like some hot guy will wanna get with him, some twenty-two-year-old or something, and Nick won't even give him the time of day, won't even say *hi*, you know? Will only talk to guys who are, like, our dads' age. Kinda gross, but, well, to each his own, I guess. Anyway, works out for him 'cause those guys go fuckin' *bananas* over him; like, buy him things, take him places, just go nuts. So I guess it works out. It'd be cool to be into old dudes, I think. But me, you know, I just can't stomach the thought. Grosses me out." He chugged the rest of his beer, raised his hand in the air, signaling the server. "Another!" he said. "And for my friend here too. Put it on my tab, please."

Jaidee looked at his beer. It was still half-full. He was certain his face was turning. Everything felt warm. He looked at Chris and wished he'd touched his chest hair when he'd had the chance. In Thailand, he'd obsessed over Victor's body hair, the dark puff that sometimes escaped his shirts, the soft golden padding on his forearms, the curled bristles on his legs. He'd seen body hair, of course, but only rarely, and it was never the flax coloring of Victor's. At home, he'd sometimes stand in front of the mirror naked, wondering what it'd be like to have a body covered in hair, if it'd be itchy. Victor, he remembered, sweated a lot, darkening the pits of his shirts, streaking the front of his clothes, and Jaidee assumed all that sweat was because of the hair—that extra layer had to be warm. Maybe that layer toughened you, though, he thought. Maybe because you were in this constant state of heated discomfort, you went through life ready to take on any challenge because movement itself was a challenge.

"I just don't get him, you know? Going for those old dudes. There are plenty of guys who'd love to be with him. Normal guys our age." Chris smiled, reached over, touched Jaidee's cheek. "Look at you. You look like you're, like, fifteen, but you're what, like, twenty-five or something? You're older, right?"

"Twenty-three," Jaidee said.

"So you're like a *double* nontraditional student. Like, from Asia *and* older. That's nuts."

They stayed for two hours. The rest of the group paid their checks and left the table without saying goodbye. They didn't like Chris, Jaidee knew, thought him and his cohort insufferable in their idle, superficial chitchat, but Jaidee wondered if beneath that dislike was also envy. Chris and his friends moved through gay circles easily, were accepted, and often welcomed, in gay male environments, and had a cadre of attractive female friends who adored them. Others in the group moped through their lives, bemoaning their weight, their height, their relative unattractiveness. Chris and his friends did this as well, but in a different way, in a way meant to elicit scoffs from others, like: "Oh my god, I'm so fat" (scoff) "Oh my god, I feel so ugly" (scoff) "Oh my god, my skin is so dry" (scoff) (girl, please).

Three beers later, Chris and Jaidee stumbled out of Brewsky's. The cold air sobered Jaidee for a second, enough for him to realize that the night might not be so good, that he was likely to be sick, that his face was certainly beet red. He walked quickly. He didn't want to be around Chris anymore.

"Hey, man," Chris said, catching up to him. "Why so fast?"

Jaidee didn't answer. His dorm wasn't far. It'd take maybe twenty minutes to walk. He walked faster.

"Hey," Chris said, grabbing Jaidee's arm, turning him around. Chris looked at Jaidee and laughed. "Holy shit, dude," he said. "Your fuckin' face. I didn't really take a good look till now but holy shit. You're like—"

Jaidee pulled his arm out of Chris's grasp and continued walking. The exercise was helping him think. He'd get home, drink four big glasses of water. That should sober him up. Then he'd sleep. Hopefully, the room would stay in one place.

"Man," Chris said, "like you're in a hurry to get somewhere? We could go somewhere else. Night's still young, right?"

Jaidee shook his head, kept walking. He didn't like college binge drinking in America. It seemed so silly; it was what everyone seemed to look forward to, and Jaidee found that obnoxious. It was very common that late on a Friday or Saturday night, he'd hear retching in the bathroom. One night, he even caught a guy on his floor peeing in the hallway. What was it that Americans were trying to erase? he wondered. That they needed to binge so much to feel anything. That they needed to make themselves so sick all the time, and that they looked forward to this sickness, that they were *proud* of this sickness, saying, the next day, "Man, I was so drunk. I was puking everywhere," as if it were a badge of honor to make your stomach revolt.

He was in his dorm now, checking in, and to his surprise, Chris was still next to him.

"Yeah, I'm his guest, you got a problem with that?" Chris said to the front-desk guy, a pale, small-boned sophomore.

Minutes later, they were in Jaidee's room.

"Not bad," Chris said, looking around. "But really, it's better to live off campus. But I get it. It's, like, your first year, right?"

With Chris in his room, Jaidee felt suddenly less tired. He went to the mini-fridge, pulled out two bottles of water, offered one to Chris, who just stared at it. "Water?" he said. "It's pretty early for that shit, right?"

Jaidee shrugged, uncapped the bottle, took a long swig. His roommate wasn't there—lately, he'd been spending weekends at Simone's and his mother's apartment. Jaidee didn't mind. He liked having the place to himself.

"What else you got here?" Chris said. "I'm sure you got something stashed away, right? Some vodka, maybe?"

Jaidee shook his head. "Just water and Coke," he said.

"Nah. That's not true. Who doesn't have alcohol in his dorm room?"

"I don't."

"Well, I bet your roommate does. This his desk?" Chris opened the top drawer, rifled through some papers. "He Asian too? Or is he hot?"

"I don't think you should do that," Jaidee said. He lay down on the bed. Though he knew it'd be good to sleep, something else snaked inside him: a warm, syrupy desire. He was a virgin, had masturbated constantly to the slow-loading pictures of naked men he could sometimes get on his computer, but had never touched a guy, had never dared. But now—drunk and safe in his dorm room—he felt like it was time, and Chris had come up for a reason, right? He hadn't just wanted to hang out. Guys weren't like that.

"Bingo," Chris said, pulling out a bottle of Jim Beam from Bryan's file drawer. He unscrewed the cap, drank, exhaled loudly. "That's good shit," he said, his voice more gravelly than normal.

Jaidee looked at Chris's stubble, imagined it prickling his face. He thought the contrast of that prickle with the thinness of his lips would be remarkable. It'd be right.

"You want some?" Chris said, looking over at Jaidee.

Jaidee shook his head. He moved his hand to his inner thigh.

"You guys could spruce it up a bit in here," Chris said. "You know, decorate. It's a little too plain. I mean, it's okay, but I'm just of the mind that you shouldn't have a bare wall, that's all. You should always be looking at something."

Jaidee sat up. All he could do was stare. He didn't know the mating ritual for gay men. Should he go over to Chris? Put his hands on his shoulders? Should he just ask him if he wanted to have sex? Should he pretend it was hot and take off his shirt? He'd seen all of this done in movies before, but in real life it seemed strange and awkward. But still. He needed to try something.

"Are you hot?" Jaidee said. "I'm hot." He pulled his shirt over his head and realized, even in his state, that the room was certainly *not* hot. Goose bumps bubbled his arms.

Chris stared at Jaidee, took another swig. "Hmm. Serious?" Chris said.

"You could get more comfortable." This was also a line he'd heard many times on television. *Getting comfortable* always required removing some article of clothing.

"Your chest, man, it's like *sunken*," Chris said.

"Sunken?"

"Yeah. You gotta hit the gym. Seriously."

"I hate the gym."

"Well, it shows." Chris took another swig, looked

away. "Look, I thought we could hang, but I gotta get going, okay? This, this isn't—"

"It isn't . . . ?"

"Dude, I'm not at *all* attracted to you, okay? Sorry, just being honest."

"I was just too warm—"

"Fuck, man. It's like I can't just be *friends* with gay guys. They always want more, like to jump my bones. Sometimes I just wanna chill, you know?"

Jaidee put his shirt back on. He felt small, inconsequential, embarrassed. He wanted Chris to leave, but he just sat there, talking, berating.

"It's, like, the worst from ethnic dudes, you know? Like, they're all over me, like, all the time. My friends too. We're not racist or anything—I mean, that's why I wanted to hang tonight with you—but man, it's like they just don't get that we don't wanna screw, you know? We all got our preferences and that's not ours, but they just keep coming at us like we're just gonna give in one day. And no offense, Jaidee, but Asians are, like, the *worst.* Like, they come over here from China or wherever and just don't get that we're not into them like that. I mean, we could definitely be friends, but they're like *falling all over us.* What's up with that? It's like they don't even like each other, just us white dudes.

What's up with that?" He took another swig, exhaled. "Like I said before, there are guys who're totally into Asian guys. That's cool. But, well, me and my friends, we're just not, and that should be cool too."

Jaidee climbed under the covers, pulled the blanket up. He closed his eyes, tried to sleep, but Chris's voice kept droning on and on in the background like an insect's buzz.

"I just want to reiterate that I'm not a racist guy, you know? But not being racist doesn't mean we wanna fuck any ethnic person that shows us interest, right?"

"Why are you talking in the plural?" Jaidee mumbled.

"The plural? Like 'we'? Well, because it's my friends too. I already established that."

"So you have the same thoughts?"

"On this, yeah. Are you being bitchy now? Just 'cause I said I didn't wanna jump your bones? Sheesh. I thought you were different, Jaidee. Seriously. I thought you'd be cool. But you're just like all the rest of them."

"I'm tired," Jaidee said.

"I wouldn't even pity-fuck you," Chris said, wobbling. "Like, what, did you think taking off your shirt was gonna fucking *impress* me? That tiny little thing? Christ."

"Please go."

"Oh, I'll go. I'll go now. Such a fucking shame, man. Here I am, reaching out, and this is how you respond. Well, if that's how you're gonna be, you're gonna have a tough time in America, I'll tell you that."

Jaidee didn't say anything, just closed his eyes tighter. He felt the cold sting of tears in his sinuses and tried his best to keep them at bay.

"See ya, loser," Chris said, and left.

Jaidee rolled over in his bed. Before he closed his eyes, he looked at Bryan's desk. The Jim Beam bottle was gone.

Cell Three

A dank gray classroom with twelve desks, all neatly aligned, three rows of four. The desks are old-fashioned: they flip from the top—Pac-Mans. *Who knows what's beneath,* Jaidee says.

A chalkboard. A map of the world. A globe. Above: soft whirring; otherwise, quiet. The scoreboard reads:

- # Envelopes Total: 8
- # Envelopes Needed to Proceed: 5
- CONTESTANTS WHO ATTACK WILL BE DISQUALIFIED
- FIRST-AID KIT BEHIND CLOCK

The time clock counts down from 7 minutes.

Sitting upright in row three, desk two, her eyes enormous and glowing, is an oversized doll, scratched black and red with makeup, smiling, hands folded in front of her, her teeth and mouth painted black, her hair a series of limp, greasy strings running down her cheeks. She wears a schoolgirl's uniform—plaid skirt, short, button-down white shirt tied at the navel, exposing a tiny stomach. She doesn't move.

Let's just get this done, Bryan says. He's bleeding real blood from Cell Two. He breaks from the group, goes to the clock, reaches behind, pulls out the small white first-aid kit. Inside: gauze, tape, bandages, cotton balls, cotton swabs, antibiotic ointment, gloves, a towel. He takes the gauze, wraps it around his forearm, his hand, pulls the tape around, affixes. Jane offers to help. He declines. When he finishes, he hands the materials to Victor. Jane helps him apply the gauze.

We're insane, she says.

I've got the girl, Bryan says.

What? Jane says.

I'll open the girl's desk.

But you've done so much, Jane says, her hand on his arm. Bryan thinks of Leslie Hemming, pulls away.

Challenges are good, Bryan says. *And I feel fine.*

Just be careful, Jaidee says.

Bryan looks at his roommate, registers a small but potent respect. He nods.

We don't have much time here, Victor says, motioning to the clock.

6 min, 15 sec.

Bryan walks over to the desk containing the doll woman. He inspects her, leans in. She's breathing; she's real. Even with him hovering, though, she doesn't move, continues to smile. He grabs the edge of the desk. Her breathing quickens. *Whatcha got, sweetheart?* he says. He flips the top open, finds confetti. *What is it with this place and confetti?* he says. He digs through it—it's endless. He looks down; the desktop extends to the floor. The doll girl's breath—heated, arrhythmic, fraught—mists his arm. He wipes it off, makes a face. He pulls the confetti out in clumps, throws it on the floor. The third time he reaches in, she grabs his arm, her eyes still staring at the chalkboard. *Oh yeah?* he says. He keeps digging, brushing off her fingers. The fourth time he digs, she reaches into her skirt, brings out a chef's knife. She raises it above her head, brings it down a few inches from his arm. *You're gonna get it,* he says, evening out his breathing. *You're gonna fucking get it.* She raises the knife again. It slices the air, misses him by an inch. *I told you!* he says. She opens her mouth, laughs, lifts her knife again.

Around him, his fellow contestants dig through the other desks, revealing similar reservoirs of confetti. No envelopes.

Nothing! Victor says.

Nothing! Jaidee says.

Nothing! Jane says.

4 min, 22 sec.

Bryan is suddenly stuck in the desk. His hands have reached the bottom, are clamped down. He can't feel his fingers. His wrists are covered in cold goo. He breathes hard. Why am I always stuck somewhere? he thinks. He groans; a small terror inches toward his eyeballs. Not afraid, not afraid, not afraid, he thinks. When he pulls up, his shoulders scream. *You gonna stab me?* he says, glaring at the girl. *I dare you, you dumb bitch. I dare you.*

The knife comes down, a half inch from Bryan's armpit. Brian flinches.

Too close, he says. *You're getting too close.*

She raises her arm again, smiles.

Just know, Bryan says, *if you hurt me, I have a whole slew of women who'll be more than happy to tear you apart. You heard of my mom? Rae Douglas? She'll hunt you down, cut your lips off. She'll gouge your eyes out. No mercy. Just sayin'.*

He thinks of his mom then and feels a bitter grinding in the bottom of his stomach. He'd never told her what he was doing, of course. He'd figured if the tour got a lot of publicity, if he got outed, so to speak, he'd tell her that he'd done it because of the money. He'd say that he'd planned on getting her a new car: she had a 1985 Mercury Topaz that made strange coughing noises every time she braked, and since she refused to get it checked out, the noises grew worse, and were now accompanied by a slight jerking motion.

She'd kill me, he thinks, pulling his arms some more, looking up at the demonic doll woman. If she knew what I was doing, she'd take one look at this doll woman and say, *Go on, finish it. That's right. Just do it. Slice him up.*

He thinks about the day she'd first heard of the Quigley House. He'd been just a kid at the time, a teenager, and she'd come barreling into the living room, waving around a newspaper, slamming it on the coffee table as if it were a bad report card.

What? he'd said, thinking immediately of his principal.

If I ever see you anywhere near this place . . . She pointed at the paper. The headline read HAUNT TAKES IT TEN STEPS FURTHER.

Quigley House? Bryan said, looking at the article.

Things are not *well in the state of Nebraska when*

this filth is allowed in our town, she said, putting her hands on her hips, breathing dramatically through her nose. *I'm telling you, Bryan, I know that your age group likes to take risks and do this sort of thing, but I have such a negative feeling about this. I can't even tell you how bad it's settling with me.*

It says you can win money, he said.

In place of your soul? she said.

Well, he said, *you don't need to get worked up about it. That's not really my thing.*

She scoffed, looked up at the ceiling. *Your thing. Ha. You don't know what your thing is. How could you? You're so young. But I'll tell you this. Your daddy's thing was numbers but seems he couldn't count past two 'cause as soon as you were born, he got confused, didn't understand that a child made three.*

But I thought you threw him out? Bryan said.

That doesn't mean he should've accepted it.

Bryan shook his head. He had trouble keeping up with his mother's logic. On the subject of his father, whom he didn't know, she'd told conflicting stories. One minute he was the sweetest, kindest, most generous man who'd only had difficulty keeping up with her strong personality, the next he was a filthy abandoner who should've begged her to reconsider her decision to leave *him.* In all cases, she never volunteered any concrete information, and after a while, Bryan stopped caring.

Just be careful in this world, Rae said, looking down at the paper. *Things are changing for the worse, I swear.*

In the classroom, Jaidee, Victor, and Jane are at the perimeter of the room. They search the walls, the map, the chalkboard, the globe. Bryan watches them, thinking that maybe it wasn't so bad, being stuck here. It wasn't the most comfortable position, but at least he wasn't scrambling, at least he could breathe. He watches Jane put her hands all over the map; he wonders what she thinks she's going to find on a flat, vertical surface. Not too smart, that one. But he sees the allure. It's the same thing Leslie Hemming had, the thing that'd made him forget, momentarily, that he'd been in a committed relationship.

The doll woman drops her knife on the floor, gets up from the desk, brushes her skirt, stares down at Bryan. Bryan thinks she's going to stop tormenting him. He breathes. *That's right,* he says. *Go away.* But she doesn't. Instead, she opens the desktop fully and brings it down on his arms. His shoulders flare. He shouts, *That what you got? Really?* Doll woman repeats. Bryan braces for a blow, squints, and sees a desk at the front of the room—a teacher's desk. It'd materialized, as if out of nothing. A simple illusion, an opening that only became visible from a lower vantage point. Sort of stupid.

He shouts, *There's a desk!*

We've checked them all! Jaidee says.

No, the front desk!

WHAP! The desktop comes down. Bryan groans.

In the corner! Bryan says. *That wall, there's an opening. An illusion or something. Come here!* She slams the desktop down harder. His shoulders burn. Sweat rains down his back. The others run to him. And just then, ten people—five men, five women, all in school uniforms—enter. Their faces are painted similarly to doll woman's: exaggerated lips, exaggerated eyes, exaggerated ears. They skip in single file. Three of them have blue wands. Above, children's voices sing a song. *Old MacDonald.*

For fuck's sake, Victor says.

Doll woman leaves Bryan and the desk and joins her skipping classmates. She giggles and hums. *EE-I-EE-I-OH!*

What're you seeing? Victor says, crouching down. Sweat drips from his nose.

You see? Bryan says, breathing hard. *Look. There. You see? Where that wall juts out?*

EE-I-EE-I-OH!

The conga line passes. The blue wands come out, shocking Victor, Jane, Jaidee.

Jane screams. Her arms shake.

I see it! Victor says, shaking off the shock. *I see it!*

Jaidee and Jane follow Victor to the corner of the room. The conga line passes a dazed Bryan. He braces for a shock but nothing comes. Instead, they conga right back out of the room, and everything is quiet. In the corner, Victor, Jaidee, and Jane are coated in a brown haze. They've gone through the fake wall; they're searching the front desk.

1 min, 22 sec.

Warmth returns to Bryan's hands. He's now free. He limps to the wall illusion. Standing straight, it looks like regular plaster, but bent down, as he was, it'd revealed clear plastic flaps, a large office desk behind it. Low budget, Bryan thinks. Anything in the dark can be made to look magical.

1 min, 0 sec.

He puts his arms out, goes through the wall, and is immediately met by his three scrambling co-contestants, throwing open drawers, rifling through stacks of blood-spattered papers.

Guys, I got three! Victor says, holding out his envelopes. *We just need two more.*

Only one more! Jaidee says, waving an envelope.

Okay, only one more!

They sort swiftly through stacks and stacks. Some of the papers contain pictures—childish drawings of murders. Here's a stick figure with a knife in his eye. Here's a family represented with crayon and blood. Here's a black demon with red eyes devouring an entire village. Farther in the stacks are photographs: mangled women, mangled men, cannibals feasting, eyeballs punctured, a woman performing oral sex on a man with five needles in his face.

Who thinks up this shit? Bryan says.

32 sec.

It's gotta be here! Jane cries.

Keep going! Victor says.

They keep going.

22 sec.

It's Jaidee who spots it, a beautiful square of red paper-clipped inside a file folder. He opens the folder. The black-and-white photo beneath the envelope is of a young woman, dressed scantily—short black skirt, low-cut, revealing augmented breasts—looking into the camera seductively—eyes sleepy, head tilted, lips open slightly, covered in gloss. She's sitting on a dentist chair, her legs wide open, and instead of looking inside her mouth, the dentist, a short bald man with warts all over his hands and face, peers up her dress, his drill and scraper aimed directly at her crotch. Around them are pools of blood.

I got it! Jaidee screams.

Bryan comes up behind him. He looks down at the picture in the file folder, frowns. *These people are truly, truly sick,* he says.

Jane and Victor crowd around Jaidee, inspect the envelope. Jaidee throws the picture in the desk drawer. They all look at the screen, expectant.

YOU MAY PROCEED appears. They all cheer.

Leonard

In the Bangkok airport—groggy and anxious, waiting for his luggage—Leonard's heart pressed insistently against his chest. *What if I have a heart attack around all these foreigners? Will they even know how to help? I shouldn't have come. I shouldn't have come. I shouldn't have come. What was I thinking?* His luggage came. He picked it up. He went to his hotel. He slept for twenty-four hours.

When he awoke, everything seemed outlined in gold. In the lobby—a sleek, modern, refined atrium with shiny marble floors and white leather chairs, one hundred times more glamorous than the Claymont's—he passed groups of dapperly dressed visitors speaking various languages. At the front desk, a smiling, thin-faced woman in a smart business suit greeted him.

"Well, look at me," he said. "Talking to a hotel clerk in Bangkok."

"Excuse me?" she said.

"I'm in the hotel business myself."

"Welcome," she said.

"I'm impressed," he said. "You speak English so *well.*"

Her smile remained. "How can I help you today?" she said.

"Oh," he said. "I'm famished."

Her smile grew. "There are many restaurants," she said. "Mostly Thai, but many international as well. What are you looking for?"

"Well, I'm in Thailand, right?"

"That's right," she said. She reached beneath her, brought out a brochure, opened it, pointed. "You're here," she said. "Khao San Road is here. You can take a tuk-tuk there—see some of the city. Very good street food. Very nice environment."

"Khao San Road," he said.

"It's very popular."

"I've heard."

He walked outside, squeezing by throngs of people. Vendors crowded him. This one sold purses. This one, sarongs. This one sold lamps, and this one, bootlegged American VHS tapes. He stopped at a tent to let a few people pass. An ancient woman stood up, wrinkled her eyes in welcome, and said, "Real poo. Yes."

"Excuse me?" he said.

"Real poo!" She pointed to a stack of books in front of Leonard, chuckled. "You want?"

He looked down, saw that she was pointing to a series of paper pads. *Made with real elephant dung*, they said. He picked one up. "How does *that* happen?" he said.

"Real poo!" she said.

He put the real poo down and kept walking.

He wandered around a temple grounds (*wat*, his guidebook had said, that's what they were called), saw spires—red, gold, twisting, some dragon-shaped, others curled like smoke—people bent in supplication before an enormous golden Buddha, shelves lined with golden statues, marble gatekeeping monsters, their jaws open, revealing rows of sharp teeth. The guidebook told him that temples were open to the public, and that they were certainly sights to behold, but Leonard felt like an intruder walking around like that, gawking. If random people had roamed around First Presbyterian in Omaha, the church his parents had taken him to on Christmas and Easter, he was certain a confrontation would've ensued. At the very least, the ushers would've told them to take a seat, to not disrupt the sermon. But here, the monks and worshippers didn't even notice the crowds. They just knelt and bent and prayed while tourists stared and pointed and took pictures. Weird, Leonard thought. But then, it's a different culture, so maybe not so weird. Who knows.

As he exited the *wat*, a man leaned out of his tuk-tuk, yelled, "Ride?" Leonard stared at him for a moment. All around him, Bangkok whizzed by, some people in tuk-tuks but most on motorcycle taxis—the locals dangled off the backs, unconcerned with amputation. There were hardly any "car" taxis around, and the tuk-tuk looked sturdy enough, but still: what if a car crashed into it?

"Ride?" the tuk-tuk driver said. He smiled broadly. "I take you. Only seventy-five baht. Anywhere you want. Great deal."

"Oh, fine," Leonard said. He hobbled in, paid. The driver, a short, frail-looking middle-aged man with a thin mustache, turned around, nodded, laughed. "Welcome to Bangkok, sir! Khao San Road? Or Patpong? No too early Patpong. Khao San Road?"

"I think, yeah," Leonard said. "Khao San Road."

"Khao San Road! I take you. Yes, yes!"

Leonard held on tight.

After a few moments, realizing he most likely wouldn't be hurled from the vehicle, he leaned out, allowed the air, moist and thick, to race through his scalp. He smelled oil, fish, dirt, exhaust. He saw buildings stretched higher and farther than any of the buildings he'd seen in Omaha. Crowds of Thai people and smaller groups of white people walked everywhere, everyone comfortable, the foreignness unforeign. Signs for various establishments crawled up the sides of buildings, written in both Thai and English. Massage. Food. Girls. Temple. Bank.

"You from America?" the driver said.

"Yes," Leonard said. "Nebraska."

"Nebraska!" he said.

"You know it?"

"I don't know. But very good, I'm sure!"

The tuk-tuk driver dropped him off at the foot of Khao San Road. He looked back at Leonard, smiled. "You will have great time. I wait if want ride later?"

Leonard shook his head. "No. I'm okay."

"Okay, sir! Okay! Thank you thank you." He put his hands together, bowed.

Leonard walked down the road and noticed, to his enormous comfort, that many of the people around him were white. If he needed help, he thought, he'd be able to talk to someone. It'd all be okay. He walked more. Around him were open-walled restaurants, just like he'd seen in the photos in the guidebook John had given him. Attractive men and women beckoned him from the sides of the street, always smiling. It was dusk: the lights of the establishments blinked on. Stray dogs, matted and flea-ridden, strolled around him. He gave them a wide berth.

He stopped at a café that boasted "Pad Thai for Days!" along with a picture of a heaping plate of steaming noodles. He sat outside. The waiter, a young man in a white shirt, black slacks, looking much too formal for a place with pictures on the menu, asked if he wanted any alcohol. He looked over the menu. Yes, yes, he would like some alcohol. Gin, perhaps? Gin went good on a night like tonight, the waiter said; it offset the steamy weather. Leonard ordered a small bottle of Tanqueray. Then he pointed to the picture that'd lured him in.

"Pad thai," he said, "for days."

When the food and drink came, he guzzled, shoveled, chomped, swallowed. Soon he was drunk and full, and the sun had completely fallen, and everything around him was dazzling, electric, smothered in intrigue. A group of young white American men passed him, all red-faced, drunk, bellowing, looking straight out of a Greek-life advertisement from some major land-grant university. They leaned on one another, laughing. One of them said, "We're in fucking *Thailand.*"

Leonard stood up, found himself wobbly. He paid the bill, left a hefty tip. He felt emboldened. He hadn't thought of Mary once, at least not in a significant way. He walked.

He went up to a coconut cart, lingered, stared. The woman behind the cart was mesmerizing, her skin clear, her body willowy, lithe. She wore little makeup, just some pale lipstick, and she moved behind her cart softly, gracefully. Leonard thought of what John had told him before he'd left. *Every woman's for sale over there,* he'd said. *Even if they're married. Even if they're young. Every woman. Just name your price.*

"Hey, you," Leonard said, winking. "You're the most gorgeous thing I've ever seen."

She laughed. "You want coconut?"

"I want your number."

She shook her head. "Coconut only fifty baht. Special."

"I want *your* coconuts."

She frowned. "More customer behind. Please hurry."

There was something off about her voice—it was grating, nasal, it didn't match her exterior grace. He'd expected some lilt, a soothing rush of feminine calm.

"I gotta see you again, beautiful," he said, thinking, *If only Mary could see me now.*

"No coconut, please keep move."

"I'll be back."

"May I help you?" she said to the man behind him.

He took a few steps back. The people behind him—two middle-aged men and one woman, all of them Asian—stepped forward. The woman ordered three coconuts in broken English. The vendor smiled, took their money. "Isn't she beautiful?" Leonard said. The three Asians looked at him. One of the men frowned, whispered something to his male friend. "This is paradise, right?" Leonard said. The group left, not looking back.

Leonard approached the cart again. The woman sighed. "You want coconut?" she said.

"This is my first night here. Well, not exactly. I slept, but I mean, out, this is my first night out here. I would love to take you for some delicious pad thai tomorrow, right down the street? I was just there and they were very nice, so if you want, we could . . ."

She swatted away a fly. A bone-thin dog came up to Leonard. Leonard jumped back. The dog walked by, unamused.

"It would be nice to have a local show me around here," Leonard said. "So if you're free tomorrow I can come meet you here and we could have dinner and walk around and you could tell me about this fascinating place. You could—I'm an honest, sincere man. Just so you know. And I'm single."

"Sorry," she said. "I too busy. And I have boyfriend. Sorry."

"But it's not like that. I don't have to be, we can be friends, right? We could just be friends. We could go eat pad thai, then you could show me around maybe, just as friends."

"I am not one you want," she said. "Please. Customers behind."

"I will come here tomorrow just to see if you're free. Then maybe we could get some pad thai . . ."

"May I help you?"

He made note of her stand, noticed the picture of the big fuzzy coconut on the front of it, committed it to his drunken memory, and kept walking. It was very busy now, so much so that in many parts, large groups of people brushed against him just to get by. Sometimes, when an attractive Thai woman passed, he reached out his hand, let it linger, and one time, a woman shouted at him in Thai, batted at his hand before stomping away.

"Oh, don't be like that!" he said. "I've got money."

She scoffed, continued walking.

He was feeling good, he was feeling great, and the only thing that could make him feel better, he thought, was some company, and so, like a pro, like a *local*, he flagged down a tuk-tuk driver and shouted, "*Patpong!*" The driver, a young guy, much less animated than his previous driver, snorted and said, "Yes."

It was a Tuesday, but in any place in the States, it would've looked like a Saturday night. Men clumped together in twos and threes, many of them stumbling. From the establishments on either side of the alley, women in slinky skirts smiled, shouted, grabbed. One of them, sitting outside a bar called Pleasure Dome, shouted, "I love you. You! You! I love you!" The air fulminated neon—pinks, purples, reds—and some of the more aggressive women danced in the alley, pulling at their hair, sliding their hands up their thighs, sucking their fingers. "Come see!" one said. "Many, many beautiful girls. Come see!"

Leonard walked in a daze, his drunken contentment giving way to awe. A thick, mustached white man passed him with a girl on his arm. The girl looked fifteen, maybe sixteen. The man's considerable chest puffed. The girl tried to match his long strides.

He'd break her, Leonard thought as they passed. Just a slight shove and she'd be across the room.

He passed a row of outdoor vendors beneath a large white tent. The tents looked misplaced among all the sex. People—mostly Thai—roamed among the goods, browsing. Why would you come *here* to shop? he wondered.

He walked down the length of the alley, which ended at Silom Road, a main artery that seemed wholesome and bright. He thought, I'm not sure about this.

His initial desire for company dissipated. Though he'd known Patpong would be seedy, he hadn't really realized how seediness would shape itself. One of the seediest places he'd ever been—besides a smattering of strip clubs—was a bar called Lucky's in west Lincoln. It was a singles bar, and often, before the lights came on, men and women drunkenly groped each other in shadowy corners. He'd never participated in the groping but had secretly wondered what it'd be like to show such sexual ferocity in a public place.

But that place is nothing compared to this, he thought. Nothing.

He walked. Two women flashed their breasts at him, one fingered herself, moaning, and another reached out, grabbed his crotch, said, "I like so much please!" He couldn't determine whether this aroused or deflated him—perhaps a bit of both. But there's a better area, according to John, he thought. A more interesting area. He flagged down a taxi.

Nana Plaza was much brighter, less seedy. It was in a giant mall-like structure: four floors, the first dedicated to food and drink, the other three to sex. It was a big rectangle, awash in pink light, and because it was contained in a single building, it didn't seem as destitute as the places on Patpong. Perhaps it was his middle-American mall-going upbringing that made him appreciate it more: he felt instantly comfortable there, even amid the tremendous crowds of shouting men and women.

He decided, after walking around, after dodging gropings and ignoring catcalls, that he would go into one of the "stores." They all seemed similar—bikini-and-thong-clad girls sitting outside on stools, beckoning, smiling coyly—but one in particular looked different, the entrance a series of black rubber flaps, the girls outside less aggressive, almost bored, their makeup darker than the rest, more creative. It was called "The Spider."

At the door, the girls on the stools hardly raised their eyes from the floor.

"Yes, go in. Very nice," one said. She smiled weakly; she might as well have shrugged. Leonard went in.

It was dark inside—too dark. He put his hands out in front of him. Someone grabbed his arm, a soft touch.

"It's okay," the girl said. "Hard adjusting. Just stand for seven seconds. Next show delayed but will be on soon."

She let go of his arm. He stood, and slowly, the place filled in around him. To his right: stadium seating, fifteen steps high. He counted eighteen men, some with girls on their laps. To his left: a series of raised platforms, each containing a pole. They were spread out in an arc, the center platform larger than the rest. Spider-shaped, he thought. Above: music, some sort of American rock. It was loud; his entire body shivered with the beats. He shuffled toward the seats, walked up to the top, sat down.

A minute later, the show started.

The women, predictably, were topless, listless, bored. They each wore a thong with a number pinned to it. White, purple, and red light shot down from above, crisscrossing frantically over each platform. Def Leppard's "Pour Some Sugar on Me" started the set. The girls danced, some jerkily, some smoothly, some using the pole, most just swaying their hips back and forth, looking drugged. A few touched their breasts suggestively, licked their fingers, grabbed their crotch—very rehearsed, very disingenuous. They've done this night after night, he thought. What actual desire do they have left? He sat back. A man in the row in front of him had unzipped his pants and was rubbing himself. Leonard felt queasy. Was this what he wanted?

It'll be weird at first, John had said. *But you need to go with it. It's a vacation, a release, and you deserve it after what you've gone through.*

A girl with a tray clomped up the stairs, sat next to Leonard.

"Whiskey or beer?" she said.

He said nothing.

"Where are you from?" the girl said. She put a hand on his forearm. He moved his forearm away.

"America," he mumbled.

"Oh, you're so handsome," the girl said.

"Thanks," he said.

"I wonder if everyone in America is so handsome."

She smelled nice, like berries. He kept his eyes on the stage. She touched his arm again. They were silent. Slowly, carefully, desire crept its way back into his blood.

"So hot in here," she said, fanning herself. "I dance someday, but not yet. Not train. You watch me someday?"

He breathed deep. The woman's voice was soft, naïve. He sensed something not yet broken in her. He turned, saw her face. She was young. Her eyes drooped slightly at the edges, spreading melancholy through her temples. Her lips were full, her cheeks angular, and when she smiled, a small wrinkle formed at the top of her forehead. Beautiful, he thought. And then: *What is someone like you doing here?* And then: If Mary could see me now. And then: Fuck Mary.

"This is my first time here," he said.

"I understand," she said, her hand still attached to his arm. "I hope you like?"

"Oh," he said, leaning closer to her. "Yes. Yes, you're very pretty."

She turned away, blinked. "You buy drink for me?"

"Sure," he said. "What'll you have?"

"I go get. You wait." She removed her hand from his arm, stood up, smiled down at him, and walked down the steps to the bar. He watched her go, enjoying the way she swayed as she clomped downward. He sat back in his seat and wondered if he was really about to do this.

She returned with two drinks. On the stage, the dancers were switching platforms, the strobe lights flashing around them like lightning. The girl sat down. She said, "I am Boonsri."

"I am Leonard," he said.

"Nice to meet you, Leonard." She giggled, gave him a glass of whiskey and ice. She wrapped her lips around a straw, looked up at him. "Spider many beautiful girl," she said, setting her drink on the floor, running her hand through her hair.

"Yes," he said.

"You like?" she asked.

"Oh," he said, "they're not as pretty as you." He smiled. She put a hand on his leg. "You're something else completely."

"Hmm."

They sat for a while, drinking, watching. Boonsri drank fast, looking up at him often, blinking rapidly. Soon: the slurry, bubble sounds of a straw sucking on an empty cocktail glass. Leonard looked at his own drink. It was still half-full. He downed it in one swig. Down at the bar, men were transacting, taking girls from the stage, paying the bartender. Leonard leaned in to Boonsri, the weight of drink pressing hard against his temples.

"Hey," he said.

"Yes?" she said.

"You wanna come to my hotel?"

She didn't answer. She took his hand and led him down the steps.

In the hotel room, she immediately went to the window, looked out on the city. Her eyes scanned the buildings, the horizon, the roads; she followed the traffic as it sped past a busy intersection. He put his hands on her shoulders. They were cold.

"Would you like something to drink?" he said, standing back, realizing too late that he had nothing, that he'd have to go down to the hotel bar if she said yes.

She turned around, smiled. She wore a small white dress—it barely covered her upper thighs. "Good tip?" she said. "I do many thing."

She started easing out of her dress, but Leonard stopped her.

"No," he said.

"No?" she said.

"Can we just talk for a bit?"

"My English."

"It's okay. I'll pay a good tip."

She replaced her dress strap.

He sat on the bed, motioned her to join him. She sat close. He put a hand on her leg. "I suppose you're used to doofuses like me getting all nervous," he said. "I'm sure they come out of the woodwork for you." He turned to her. She blinked. "I've never done this before."

"I begin mouth," she said. "You like?"

"Yes, I like," he said. She got off the bed, positioned herself between his knees. "Wait," he said. "No—not yet."

"No?" she said.

"Just—can you just sit here for a while? Or maybe—here, let's do this. Lie down. On your side. I'm gonna put my arms around you, okay?"

"My dress."

"Just leave it on for now."

"Okay."

Fully clothed, he held her. She felt small, his arms completely encircling her body. Mary had never liked cuddling, had pushed him off when he'd tried, citing his inflated body temperature, so he'd stopped trying, just rolled over and slept after their perfunctory love-making. But he missed it, had loved running his hands against her slick abdomen as he drifted off. That first year—the year things had been good—he'd fallen asleep thinking how his life was as he'd wanted it, how this woman, Mary, in such a short time, had shown him a limitless possibility.

"You have a beautiful country," he told Boonsri.

"Mmm," Boonsri said.

"This is my first time outside America."

"We have thirty minute," she said.

"It's okay," he said. He held her tighter. "If we don't . . . it's okay." He sniffed her hair, smelled lemon. "This is my first time doing this."

"You say already."

His hands wandered around her abdomen, up to her breasts, down to her hips. He kissed the back of her head. “You’re a good girl,” he said. “I can tell.”

“Mmm,” she said.

“There’s a sense I get here in Thailand,” he said. “A different sense. A respectful sense. Everyone’s been kind. Everyone smiles. It’s great.” He paused. “It’s like the hospitality industry here really understands how to cater.”

“I will go back in twenty minute.”

“I saw you and thought, Man, why is someone as gorgeous as you doing this? Like, surely you can do other things, right? But that’s just it. This country. I’ve only been here one day, and I get it, I think. I think I get it. You have this very practical approach to everything, right? You see that people have needs, but still, it’s not *all* practical because the temples, all that history and all that gold.”

She turned around, looked at him, smashed her lips against his, running her hand down to his crotch. He responded by tearing off his clothes, running his hand up her leg, kissing, thrusting. He raised her dress, climbed on top of her. She moaned, closed her eyes. It was over in five minutes.

Afterward, she rose from the bed, went to the bathroom. He lay on his back, panting. The faucet came on.

"You don't have to go so quick," he called out. "I'll pay a higher tip."

She came out of the bathroom, her hair combed, her makeup reapplied. She leaned against the wall, a hand on her hip.

"I'm serious," he said. "You don't have to go so soon."

She remained still.

He sighed, stood up, took his wallet from his pants, removed the first bill he touched. It was 1,000 baht, or roughly $30 U.S., definitely more than he'd planned on tipping. He looked up at her, saw her eyes light, understood that anything less now would be a testament to her "performance," so grudgingly handed it over. She placed it in her purse. "This is good," he said. "I'd like, if you're free, to see you again."

"Spider," she said. "Every day not Tuesday."

"Oh, so I can just meet you there," he said.

"If long day, cost more."

"I am good with that."

She smiled, turned to the door. "Bye-bye," she said. "See you again."

"Yes," he said. "Most definitely."

The next day, midmorning, he went to the Spider, found Boonsri sitting at the bar, bored, her head resting in her hand, her eyes half-open. He paid 5,000 baht for a full day.

They took a bus to Pattaya, then a taxi to Koh Larn Beach, where they sipped rum from a coconut and watched people navigate the waves. He continued his conversation from the previous night, regaling her with compliments about her country, her food, her looks, and then—buzzed and happy—he talked to her about his own life: Nebraska, hotel, Mary, the breakup. She nodded, sipped, stared out at the waves, smiled. Once in a while, she attempted to converse, but her syntax was jumbled, so he often misunderstood her, but still, he loved that she tried, and he loved that once in a while, when a child wandered too far out in the ocean, she grabbed at his wrist and squeezed.

"You want to swim?" he said. They sat in red-and-white reclining chairs. Above, the sky was a spectacular pane of blue, only a few cottony wisps interrupting its stride, and the sun struck the sand with soft insistence, allowing for momentary glints of sparkle.

"Oh no, no, no," she said. "Not swim."

"But you love the beach so much, I can tell," he said. "I'd think you'd love to swim as well."

She turned to the ocean. He put his hand on her shoulder. "You're a bit warm," he said. "Let me put some lotion on you." He dug through his bag, found some sunblock, squeezed it into his hand, kneaded it in. "You know," he said, "last night after you left, I got to thinking. I mean, it makes absolutely no sense that I never took a vacation. People need to recharge, right? And here we are, relaxing. How could anyone not want to do this?" He massaged the lotion into her arm. "And now I'm thinking of my life in Nebraska and all I can think of is how dreary it is. Why would anyone pick that life when this exists? John was right."

"John?" she said.

"But then I also think that it's America, that's why. It's the land of the free, you understand? It's the best country in the world. People from everywhere want to be there. People from *here* want to be there. Imagine that. People from paradise want to be in a place that gets below zero and is flat and has a whole bunch of stuck-up people who think they're better than everyone else just because of their job, or their house, or their looks. People in America aren't *friendly*, Boonsri," he said. "But I guess that doesn't matter when you live in a superpower."

She wiggled her shoulder, removed his hand.

"Too much?" he said.

"It's okay," she said.

"Anyway, what I'm saying is that maybe someday you'd want to come over there. You know, just to see it. To visit me. I have room. It would be nice. Fall is an especially good time. The trees are real pretty."

He put the sunblock back in his bag, looked down at his belly—it humped slightly over his blue trunks.

"You know," he said, "I don't have much. But that doesn't matter, ultimately, right? What matters is that people care for each other. That's it." He sipped his drink.

Boonsri touched his forearm, smiled, grabbed her coconut from the small table, took a sip. On the inside of her left thigh, a small bruise blossomed: oval, the center a dark purple, its outer rings yellow-green. On the top of her right knee was a crusting scab. Her arms, he noticed, were flecked with small cuts, what he'd first thought were mosquito bites. He touched one, rubbed it. It was crescent-shaped: a fingernail.

"Boonsri," he said. She turned to him. "Are you hurt? Is someone hurting you?"

She stared out at the ocean. "Not hurt," she said.

"You should stop this," he said. "You understand? You can't keep working at the Spider forever. You have to stop."

"Not hurt," she repeated, taking another sip.

"This isn't a life for someone like you."

"Mmm," she said.

They had lunch, dinner, sex—frenzied this time,

acrobatic—and when he dropped her back at the Spider, he said he wanted to spend the week with her if possible—he'd pay extra. She said, "Okay," then waved goodbye.

The next day, and the next day, and the next day, and all the days until he left, he picked her up from the Spider and they did tourist things together—caves, trails, temples, massages. She showed him the landmarks of the city—Chinatown, Wat Arun, the Grand Palace—though to Leonard, everything looked similar—gold, red, spired, dense, foreign. When they visited MBK Center, the enormous mall in the middle of the city, he felt, finally, that he could breathe: the mega-commerce behind air-conditioned walls, the familiarity of it all, served as a welcome reprieve from everything he didn't understand. They roamed, bought unnecessary things, stuck their feet in an aquarium full of flesh-eating fish, and though she didn't speak much except to the Thai people around her, she laughed at his jokes and looked at him with bright, fawning eyes.

"You understand me," he said. They sat in a mall café, sipping iced tea with condensed milk. The walls were a hazy yellow, punctuated with pictures of rural Thai landscapes. Somewhere nearby was the sound of gently running water. "I've had the best time of my life with you," he said. "I mean it. It's like all that shit with Mary's just gone, poof."

She ran a hand through her hair, grabbed her straw delicately with thumb and index finger, leaned over, sipped.

"I know we've only known each other a little while, but there's a connection here, right? There's a *real* connection."

She didn't respond but looked out at the people roaming the halls.

"I'm telling you—and I know you understand me, I see it all in your expressions—I'm telling you that you're completely different from my ex. Not that you're my girlfriend, I know. But you know. You just have more to offer. You've shown me around. You're always upbeat. You smile so easily. You're so, I don't know, *pleasant.* I'm really learning things out here. I'm learning how *unpleasant* Mary was. It took that distance, you know? But man, she was a raging bitch. Anyway. I understand there's a language barrier, I get that, but I'm telling you, even if you *did* speak English fluently, I'm positive we'd still have this connection."

She blinked, said, "Leonard, you are good, good man."

"You can see that, huh. I knew it. I knew you could

see deeper into me. It's a Thai thing, an Asian thing. They see souls and not all the meaningless surface bullshit. And you embody that. I swear."

She breathed in deep, rummaged through her purse, brought out some lip gloss, applied it.

"And you're so, so gorgeous. Did I tell you how gorgeous you are? God, everyone at the Spider, all those men, they can't stop staring at you, and that makes me feel proud, because you picked me, well sort of." He sipped his iced tea. "I'm sure you get asked out by guys all the time there, I mean, really asked out, because you're not like the other girls there. You're a totally different breed. You're not some random slut. You just see this as a job, right?"

He thought again of Mary. If he'd ever said the words "random slut" around her, she would've pounced, telling him how degrading it was to label a woman that way, how derogatory. Why can't a woman just enjoy sex? she'd ask. Why is it wrong for a woman to have multiple partners? Why should *men* be seen as studs when they slept around? Why was sexism and misogyny so embedded in our language? Everything, he thought, had been so *difficult* with her. He hadn't been able to share a meal with her without watching every damn word he'd said, and what had all that resulted in? It wasn't that he hadn't wanted to talk to her; it's just that everything he'd said seemed so aggressively infused with wrongness.

"You're like a person I want to know everything about," he said. "And I'm telling you, Boonsri, I haven't felt that way in a long, long time."

And yet, given this declaration, he never asked her a single personal question. If he had, he would've discovered, through rickety but decipherable English, that she was from a village north of Chiang Mai, that her mother and father owned a small farm and some livestock, that one year, the monsoon season had left a hole on top of their cottage where rain and wind swirled and caused her father to cough. He'd discover that she'd left her village at sixteen to work at the Spider, that she sent most of her money home, that she'd been a virgin when she'd arrived, that the manager, a smoky, wrinkled woman named Intira Kurusattra, had taught her the art of pleasure through various pornographic videos, that the first time she'd had sex she'd felt her body crack in two. If he'd been particularly interested in her life—and if she'd eventually felt comfortable enough around him—she'd have told him of the New Yorker Andre Rule, a hairy, sweaty man who'd jumped on her stomach and batted her head and gouged her thigh with his teeth and who had, afterward, cried and cried while she lay helpless and bleeding and swollen, telling her he was sorry, that he couldn't help these impulses, that it all stemmed from his childhood—his mother had abused him, see: he had all this rage.

But really: Leonard wasn't interested in any of this. He was still hurt, and Boonsri, through her sex, her quiet, her paid-for agreeableness, calmed this hurt, made him think, momentarily, that happiness and contentment could exist, and that he didn't have to be so alone.

In bed that evening, after sex, Leonard leaned over to her and whispered, "I can't stop thinking about you." He'd bought her for the entire night, had assured her a good tip. She lay on her side, away from him. He ran his hands through her hair. "This is what I've been missing out on my entire life. You."

"Sleep now," she said.

"Oh, I will."

"Sleep now, yes," she said.

"Yes. Yes, sleep well. In the morning, I'll make you breakfast. Or I'll take you to breakfast. No way to make it here, I guess."

"I sleep now," she said.

"Good night, Boonsri," he said, circling her waist with his arms. "Sweet dreams." He closed his eyes.

Before Mary, he hadn't felt this particular feeling. He'd certainly had moments of joy, thrilling snippets of life that culminated in some endorphin-rich experience, but these moments were ephemeral, quickly replaced by despair, gloom, tedium, ennui. Even his childhood seemed defined by these small bursts, occasions when, for a quick second, he understood that a future existed, that what lay before him could, in fact, be awesome, that his suffocating cloud of dejection wouldn't last. Then Mary had happened, and love had risen. But with that love had been an endless stream of doubt—*Why me, why me, why me?* And then everything had died. But this: This was perhaps less severe, but more whole; it coursed through him, pacified his stubborn ailments. Boonsri was satisfaction, comfort, safety. Lying with her, watching her breathe (small wheezes on the exhale, a slight snort on the inhale), he felt protective, strong, masculine; he felt in control, something he'd never experienced with Mary.

Boonsri stirred, turned on her back, opened her eyes. "No sleep?" she said.

"Shhh. I'm fine."

"Sleep time," she said, and closed her eyes again, her mouth, for a moment, twitching into a half smile.

"Yeah," he said. "It's sleep time."

On the final day of his visit, Leonard kissed Boonsri's forehead at the train station. She was on her way back to her village to see her family.

He wrapped his arms around her. She bristled.

"Is this okay?" he said. "I know I didn't buy today, but . . . do you need money? I just wanted to be here to say goodbye." He stood back, looked at her. "I'm going to ask for more time off," he said. "I'm going to come back in a couple months. I have a bunch of vacation they want me to take."

She pushed at him. He let go. She brushed her hair away from her face. She looked inordinately tired, her face drawn and creased, her shoulders rolled forward. She forced a lopsided smile. "Leonard," she said.

"Maybe I'll just *live* out here for a bit," he said. "I could get a job. All these English teachers. I could teach just as well as them, right? I don't have a degree, but that shouldn't matter. I know what a noun and verb and all that jazz is. I could do a good job."

The train screeched into the station. Leonard reached for Boonsri again, grabbed her hand.

"I'll write you as soon as I'm back," he said. "Or. If you can do email. I have one now. America Online. It's simple, but, never mind. It's okay. I'll write."

Boonsri picked up her bag, walked to the train door marked 2.

"And what I said earlier," Leonard said, shouting over the train's noise, "about coming to the U.S. You should think about it."

Boonsri, on the train steps, turned to Leonard, put her hands together, and bowed. She said, "Goodbye, Leonard. Good luck." She waved, then walked up the steps.

"Talk to you soon!" Leonard said. He watched her through the train window. She looked for her seat. She sat. "I love you," he said.

Soon, the train left, and he stood there, wondering what to do next.

Cell Four

Those aren't real, Jane says, holding her nose. *There's no way.*

Sure as fuck look real, Bryan says. *And smell . . .*

Dangling upside down—arms reaching for the floor, legs crisscrossed, feet bound together by rope—are corpses, fifty of them, men and women, all drenched in blood. A single green light roves madly across the bodies, illuminating the room like a strobe, and from everywhere, long, tortured moans rise up and down, up and down.

But where would the envelopes be? Jane asks.

Jaidee motions to his right, where, attached to the wall, are four carving knives: long and thin, with red wooden handles.

Inside? Jane says.

Jaidee nods.

But they look so real, Jane says.

The scoreboard reads:

- # Envelopes Total: 12
- # Envelopes Needed to Proceed: 10
- CONTESTANTS WHO ATTACK WILL BE DISQUALIFIED
- FIRST-AID KIT BEHIND CLOCK

The time clock counts down from 30 minutes.

But how can we be sure none of them are real? Jane says.

Nobody answers. Bryan thinks Jane is done. She has the wide-eyed, frenzied look of someone who's on the brink.

We only have two more cells left before Martha, Bryan says, staring hard at Jane. *Only two more.*

He's not concerned about Jaidee anymore; he's proven surprisingly resilient. Bryan hasn't talked much with him, but he thinks something is changing: this experience, fucked as it is, has kindled some sort of admiration on both their parts. The guy hasn't complained, has hardly said *anything* though he's been hit as many times as the others. He just gets through each cell, moves on to the next. There's something awe-inspiring about that level of focus.

Bryan walks over to an inverted woman. He shakes her. Her eyes flick open. He jumps back, crouches down, looks at her face. *They're big dolls!* he says, motioning for Jane to come near. He touches the woman's cheek. He closes her eyes. They flick back open. *They don't look real up close.*

But do we know if they're all *dolls?* Jane says, crouching next to Bryan.

Come on, Jaidee says, heading for the knives. *We're wasting time.*

28 min, 22 sec.

Okay, Jane says, breathing in through her nose, out through her mouth. *I can do this.*

Just don't think too hard, Bryan says. *This is all a joke, you know? This is all make-believe.*

Okay, Jane says. *Okay.*

They begin.

Bryan starts with a man in the fourth row. The man is wearing a sailor outfit. His eyes are closed. A hat is on the ground, collecting blood. Bryan inhales a nose full of rot, takes the knife, raises it, thrusts it deep into the man's abdomen. The man's eyes open. Blood spurts from the wound, covering Bryan's face.

More fucking blood, he thinks, wiping the goop from his eyes.

The entire room fills suddenly with screams. Bryan looks over at Jane, who's holding her knife by her ear, ready to strike. She stands in front of an inverted elderly woman, her floral-print dress flowing over her torso and face, exposing a pair of light-green panties. Jane drops the knife, kneels down, covers her ears.

It's not real! Victor shouts to her. *Just remember what Bryan said!*

Jane shakes her head. *I can't.*

Okay. Just hold tight, then!

Bryan refocuses. He stabs the doll again, cuts from the sternum to the abdomen, pulls the chest cavity open, inspects. Inside, affixed to the outer shell, are a series of plastic tubes meant to look like intestines. But they're too big. They look more like swollen sausages or vacuum hoses. He cuts into one. Blood spurts out, collects beneath his collar bone. He cuts until the blood stops squirting. Then he reaches inside the tube, searches, finds nothing.

Got one! he hears Victor shout. He looks over at his teammate. He's waving a red envelope proudly, his face a spiderweb of gore.

Bryan inspects his doll again; her "innards" now

dangle loosely from her body. Whoever formed these representations had no concept of actual internal structures, he thinks. For one, the heart is the size of a grape. For another, the "stomach" is above the lungs, which themselves look like two bunched-up pieces of steel wool. Everything is tied together with rope and tape and looks so shoddily done that for a moment Bryan is embarrassed for the Quigley House, wonders how such careless work could ever be labeled "terrifying."

A high school kid could've done a better job, he mumbles, thinking of his anatomy class during his senior year. There he'd dissected a cat, and he and his partner, William Flaten, a curly-haired mouth-breathing white boy, had, after cutting away all the yellow, sopping fat, revealed a beautiful, intricate network that until then had been alive only in his textbook.

This is nuts, he'd told William. *All these connected pieces.*

Look at its butt, William had said.

20 min, 44 sec.

Bryan eviscerates six corpses, finds no envelopes. Victor finds one, Jaidee none, and Jane is out of commission, sitting on the sidelines, holding her knees, rocking back and forth. Bryan glances over: she looks so distraught and small. Victor runs to her, kneels down, puts his arm around her, returns to his cutting. Once Victor's back to his corpse, Bryan goes to her. He kneels down.

Too intense, huh, he says.

She smiles noncommittally.

Jane, we need you. We need your help.

Her smile fades. She shakes her head. *The smell,* she says.

You'll forget it someday, Bryan says. *But you can't quit now. We're close. We're very close.*

17 min, 12 sec.

I wanted to be here, Jane says, her eyes pleading. Overhead, the green light races across her scalp, turning her, for a second, into a monster. *I made Victor do it.*

Get up, Bryan says. He extends his hand. *Now, Jane.*

But—

You wanna tell people we failed because you couldn't cut up some dolls? Is that what you want?

No, but—

Then get up. He stands, stares down at her, thinks how dumb the dolls' insides look, how uniformly unreal. That anyone should actually be *scared* of them seems ridiculous.

Bryan, she says. *I can't.*

You don't have a choice.

But I can't!

Get up or I'll yell the word, Bryan says, feeling heat steam from behind his back. *We're a team. Remember? That's how the Four got through this. Always a team.*

But—

No more excuses. We're wasting time.

She stares up at him, her eyes vicious and cold, and he thinks this is the end, that it's all over, but then her hand is in his, and she's on her feet.

There ya go, Bryan says, smiling through cracked blood.

Fuck off, Jane says.

Sure, he says, and goes back to his corpse.

13 min, 8 sec.

Bryan stabs a man in a suit.

What's the count? he shouts. He has yet to get an envelope. He rips, pulls.

I have four! Jaidee says.

Jaidee's on fire! Bryan says.

Three here! says Victor.

Only three left? Bryan says. *Jane, whaddya say? You and me? Two and one? One and two?*

Jane doesn't respond.

11 min, 35 sec.

Bryan feels electric. He feels unyielding energy. The malaise that'd shot through him in the last cell has evaporated. In its place: vibrant, colorful anticipation.

He designs a dance around each fake corpse: knife back, elbow out, wrist flicked, shoulders back, hip turned, arm extended—pirouette, switch hands—knife deeper, downward cut, grab skin, *pull.* The dance becomes meditative, incantatory, and even during the last few minutes, when the ghouls with shock wands once again enter the room, he finds himself immune to their assaults. With five minutes left, he has eviscerated ten dolls, and he wants more. Because:

Yes, he'll buy his mother that car. He'll finance something nice, something with power-everything, red and sleek and shiny, a car that she'll be proud to drive around town. Every time someone comments on it, she'll sigh, smile sideways, and say, *My son got me this, can you believe it?* She deserves it, he thinks. Because: Look at him! He's getting good grades! In *college,* no less. There's a future for him now. A future devoid of smoky bus fumes and crowding vagrants and drunk college kids telling him he's one of the coolest Black bus drivers they've ever met. There's real hope at real betterment now: a tangible, buoyant, luminous beyond. And:

Yes, he'll make up with Simone. He'll beg and plead if he needs to. He'll confess that what happened happened and say there's no going back, but that if she'll have him, if she'll take one more chance, she'll see that the past is always the past, written without possible modification, but the future contains infinite possibility, and that he wants more than anything to experience those possibilities with her.

Who knows? He might even propose.

He imagines his mother's face. *My baby!* she'll say. He imagines Aunt Lynette, crying. He imagines Kendra with her spiderweb earrings saying, *I did this. I made this happen, you know.* She'll grin so wide he'll see her molars.

Bryan! Victor shouts. *Bryan, how many do you have?*

Bryan looks at Victor, breathes deep. He stuffs his hands in his pockets, brings out five red envelopes. He hadn't even known he'd collected them.

Holy shit, Victor says. *We have all of them!*

But we still have time, Bryan says, looking at the doll he's half carved.

It doesn't matter! We're done!

But—

We're done! You get that? Only one fucking cell left! Only one fucking cell left!

Indeed, for below the clock are these words: YOU MAY PROCEED.

PART III
Cell Five

Kendra

Kendra spent her first week of school in a fog. Lincoln High, while not as white as she'd imagined, was still pretty white, and she felt entirely conspicuous: suspicious eyes judged her wherever she went, and in class, it seemed that everyone already had solid, impenetrable friend groups. So she roamed the halls alone, head down, shuffling from room to room, sitting in the back, focusing on her feet. In her American history class, when the teacher—a stocky, balding man named Mr. Swenson—called her name, she vomited in her mouth and swallowed, the hot, acidic gruel burning her throat.

"It's customary," the teacher said, "for students to say 'here' when called for roll."

Kendra slunk in her seat.

At lunch, instead of eating by herself, she used her mom's calling card to call Camille, who started school a week later than her. Her friend picked up on the second ring.

"You're calling from *school*?" Camille said. "Like, a pay phone?"

"Yeah," Kendra said.

"But you should be making friends," Camille said. "Like, white Nebraska friends, or, I don't know—*can you*? Is it *possible*? Like, what do people *think* of you?"

"There are some Black kids—"

"So, D and I were at the library because he's thinking of going back to school, you know? He wanted to look up some books on colleges and stuff, like which ones had high rates of success for psychology, because that's what he's interested in. Anyway. We were looking at this thing called microfiche and he found this article that said that people who are minorities in their towns have higher rates of depression and mental things like that. So do you have depression now? Like, do you feel upset? Sad? Angry? Confused? This study said that people in your situation feel that way, and I got mad and I said, 'D! We can't let her get depressed! We've gotta help somehow!' But he was like, 'What the fuck can we do?' so we left it at that because we can't do shit being out here, you know?"

Kendra sat on the floor, held the phone tight to her ear. An ant scurried by. She squashed it. "My history teacher eats cheese at his desk," she said, wiping her hand on the floor. "Like, that string-cheese shit."

"I told D that you'd be just fine and that you only have, like, two years left and then you'll be done anyway, and you can come back here. We could be roommates, Kendra! You'll get into Georgetown, I'm sure of it. You're so smart and you read all those books so I know you can do it."

A boy cleared his throat a few feet away. Kendra looked up at him. His face was pudgy and stern and covered in acne. He stared down at her. She rolled her eyes.

"I guess someone else needs to use the phone," Kendra said.

"What?" Camille said. "You just got on. Fuck 'em."

"I start my job this week," Kendra said. "Thursday night. My first shift."

"You talk to Shawn about that?" Camille said. "I'm sure he's having wet dreams thinking of you at that haunted whatever. I'm sure he's—"

"He's excited."

"You two are so *weird*," she said. "I mean, you've always been weird, but you two together are like Elvira and Fester. He's Uncle Fester, of course. You're Elvira 'cause your boobs are nice."

"Thanks."

"So you're Elvira and he's Fester but what am I? What *am* I? And what is D? We're definitely not freaky like you and Shawn but we're something, right? We're *something*. I'll have to think. I'll have to—"

The boy cleared his throat again. Kendra said, "Hey, I gotta go. This kid keeps clearing his throat like I can't fuckin' see him standing right in front of me."

"Is he cute?" Camille said. "If not, don't bother."

"I gotta go anyway," Kendra said, feeling her chest sink into her stomach. "But I'll call you this week. Like, after my first shift, tell you all about it."

"Yes! Kendra! I'm really fucking sorry that you called me instead of eating lunch with friends but this job will probably introduce you to some of your kind, you know, freaks, so . . . and you don't need to make friends at school anyway, you know? You don't need that shit."

"Talk to you later," Kendra said, glaring at the boy.

"Hey, do you want me to—"

Kendra hung up.

She spent the rest of the day floating through her

afternoon classes, a sea of khaki and chalkboards and textbooks and paper, and when it was over, when the final bell rang, she thought: I did it. I made it through okay. But then: at her locker, a brown-haired, mouse-faced girl. She knocked on the metal as if Kendra were behind an actual door. Kendra looked at her, then turned around, expecting that this girl in floral-print jean shorts had mistaken her for someone else.

"You're Kendra?" the girl said.

"Yeah?" Kendra said.

"I'm Sarah!" she said, extending her hand. "So happy to meet you."

"Okay?" Kendra said, frustrated, thinking that she *wasn't* done, that she'd somehow missed something—but what? A meeting? An orientation? An actual class?

"I'm your coworker? I work at Quigley?" She smiled, leaned against the locker next to Kendra's.

"Oh," Kendra said, relaxing.

"We're gonna have a *great* season!" Sarah said. She giggled, covered her mouth, turned, looked down the hall, then back at Kendra, lowered her voice, widened her eyes. "Hey, John said you don't have a car?"

"I can find a way," Kendra said. "Is it, like, a *secret*?"

"I'll give you a ride, of course!" Sarah said, slapping Kendra's shoulder. "It's really no problem."

Kendra grabbed where she'd been slapped. "We start at eight?" she said, kneading her shoulder.

"What? No. I mean, yeah, that's when we have to be in the lot, but there's a bunch of stuff before, you know, costumes, makeup, all that. I usually get there at seven. I can't believe nobody told you any of this." She paused. "John said you live way out past Seventieth? Sort of weird that you're going to school here, but that's really no big deal for me. I can still come and get you."

Kendra slung her backpack over her shoulder, closed her locker, walked toward the front door. Sarah followed her. "John is completely in love with you and your cousin, you know that?" Sarah said, matching Kendra's steps. "Like, he told us all about you two and he was seriously *glowing*. Like, he thinks you guys are gonna change things up."

"Huh?" Kendra said. "Bryan's not working there."

"You never know! Maybe John'll hire him for something else."

Kendra shook her head. "He's definitely not interested."

"But you!" Sarah said. "John adores you too! Couldn't stop smiling when he talked about you. I swear."

"That's weird."

"John's got a sense about these things. He only hires the best, you know?"

"Didn't Cory hire me?" Kendra said.

"No way," Sarah said. "John is the only person who hires. Cory can refer people, but John always has the last say."

"Hmm," Kendra said. They opened the doors to blazing sun and near-suffocating humidity. Kendra pulled her backpack tighter on her shoulder, squinted against the heat.

"I'm serious," Sarah said, brushing her hair off her shoulder. "He *loves* you." They walked down the steps, paused. Blue sky pressed down overhead. Students whizzed by, yelling at one another, free. Kendra thought about the day she'd rushed out of her geometry class at Dunbar. It seemed like ages ago.

"It's gonna be great," Sarah said. "You'll have a blast." A breeze pushed Sarah's hair into her face. She grabbed it, wrapped it up, reached into a pocket, and pulled out a red scrunchie. Toward the top of her neck, right underneath her chin, Kendra noticed a fading hickey. "I haven't heard him talk about anyone like that," Sarah said, tying her hair.

"He talks to you about new employees?" Kendra said.

"We had a meeting. Your paperwork hadn't gone through yet, that's why you weren't there. But you'll be at all of them from now on."

"Okay," Kendra said, grabbing her backpack strap. "Hey, I gotta catch the bus," she said.

"The bus?" Sarah said. "No, I'll give you a ride. We're *coworkers* now!"

"Coworkers," Kendra said.

"And I'd be *honored* to have the newest, most prized employee in my car." She grinned, touched Kendra's shoulder, led her to the parking lot. Kendra hesitated. She wanted badly to get away from this chirpy, creepy girl, but Sarah's touch was insistent, and Kendra hated the bus, so she relented. She eased into Sarah's Pontiac, which smelled like old coffee, and hugged her backpack close to her lap. Once on the road, to calm herself down, she pictured Shawn's face, his large eyes tapered slightly at the ends, the mole by the right side of his nose, his sharp chin, his soft lip fuzz, and of course his forehead, that long, beautiful expanse that would undoubtedly happy-crease the moment she told him how much of an impression she'd made with just one appearance.

She turned to Sarah and said, "So how long are the shifts?"

On Thursday, before Sarah picked her up, Kendra told her aunt and mother that she was going out, that she'd made a friend. In the living room, Lynette and Rae stared down at her, their brows furrowed.

"A boy?" Rae said.

"No," Kendra said. "Her name is Sarah."

"Sarah who?" Lynette said.

"Sarah Luchs," Kendra said. "Why, do you *know* her or something?"

"Luchs," Lynette said. "What kind of name is that?"

"I think it's wonderful," Rae said. "Best to be moving on from D.C."

"She doesn't need to *move on* from D.C.," Lynette said, staring hard at her daughter. "She's hardly been gone a few months."

"I suppose she can just be alone and mopey," Rae said.

"Please," Lynette said.

"Just saying," Rae said.

"You don't just move on from these types of things," Lynette said.

"This is what people do," Rae said.

Her mother shook her head.

As it happened, Rae and Lynette had been embroiled in a personal conflict for the last month. Rae thought it best, a year after Greg's death, that Lynette try dating again, go back on the market. "You have so much more life to live," Rae said. "And you're not getting any younger."

Lynette lashed back by pointing out that Rae certainly hadn't "gone back on the market," that it'd been *way* more than a year since Bryan's father had left.

"There's a difference, Lynette," Rae said. "I don't *want* a man. I don't *need* a man. But you—you're not like me. You know this."

"Please," Lynette said, shaking her head. "I don't *need* anything."

"Hmm," Rae said. "If that's what you say."

Rae persisted, widening an increasingly hostile chasm, sending the sisters into a maelstrom of back-and-forth until finally, one day they stopped speaking directly to each other. At dinner, when they all sat down together, Rae and Lynette talked through Kendra, making comments like "Kendra, I know you use your aunt's bathroom sometimes, and I'm sorry it's so filthy, but what can you do?" and "Kendra, you might be wondering why the refrigerator is so empty. Maybe you should ask your mother about that?" When Bryan came to visit—which was often—lines were drawn: Kendra and Lynette versus Bryan and Rae, and though Bryan clearly wanted nothing to do with the escalations, he told Kendra that family required him to side with his mother.

"Family?" Kendra said. "But we're *all* family."

"Yeah," he said. "But you know what I mean."

In Sarah's passenger seat, thinking about her mother with another man, trying to fathom the idea of a *stepfa-*

ther, Kendra sat rigid while her new colleague weaved through O Street traffic. Hootie & the Blowfish—a band Kendra had sworn was fake until Camille had shown her the CD cover in CD Warehouse (*Wait, he's Black?* she'd said)—blared from the speakers. *Just let her cryyyyyy . . .*

"So you're from Washington, D.C., huh?" Sarah said, turning onto the freeway, adjusting the radio volume.

"Yeah," Kendra said.

"That's so cool! I've never left Nebraska, unless you count the time I went to Disney World when I was, like, eight."

"Mmm," Kendra said.

Sarah exited the freeway, took a few turns, and suddenly, impossibly, they were surrounded by cornfields.

"So did you leave a boyfriend or anything?" Sarah said. "You don't have to tell me. Just wondering."

"No," Kendra said, and thought of Shawn. "No boyfriend."

"There are some cool guys here," Sarah said. "At the haunt? Maybe not. Probably wanna stay away from the actors and the crew and stuff, but at Lincoln High, there are a few."

"You have a boyfriend?" Kendra said, thinking of her hickey.

"Ha, me? No way, man. I'm *waaaay* too busy."

They sat for a while, listened to Hootie.

Kendra asked about the other employees. Sarah told her about Christy Bladensburg, the third parking-lot attendant.

"You just have to get used to her," Sarah said. "But deep down, she's really great."

Christy, Sarah said, was a senior at North Star High School, and her modus operandi, it seemed, was to publicize the fact that when she was a freshman, her school had cast her as Fastrada in *Pippin*. She had blond, curly hair that floated past her shoulders, crystal-green eyes, and tan, toned arms that seemed unusually long: standing straight, her hands hovered just above her kneecaps. And though the parking-lot attendants were free to choose any costume from John Forrester's massive collection, Christy stuck to the ostentatious and suggestive. On any given day, she'd be a sexy, gory nurse; a sexy, gory cheerleader; a sexy, gory businesswoman; a sexy, gory nun. Sarah found it odd that Christy chose these smaller outfits since the weather was cold and the nights were long, but she never said anything: Christy was Christy was Christy.

"She can be real sweet," Sarah said. "And she's got so much talent. She's gonna go far. Everyone knows it."

"Is she, like, bitchy?" Kendra said.

Sarah laughed, tossing her head back, spilling her hair down her shoulders. "You'll meet her soon enough."

Kendra crossed her arms over her chest. "Looking forward to it," she said.

"We all have our things," Sarah said.

They drove down streets that all looked the same—flanked by cornstalks, peppered with roadkill—until they turned onto Quigley Road, which was just John Forrester's long, winding driveway. The house slowly came into view, and Kendra, expecting the same nervous awe she'd experienced the first time she'd been there, felt momentarily disappointed. Daylight stripped the mansion of its horror: the dilapidation became simple laziness, the belfry turned odd and cheesy, and the fifteen-foot bleeding baby reconfigured itself into a series of painted plywood boards and ripped cloth. Additionally, there were *people* around. Grizzled men in jeans and T-shirts walked in and out of the front and haunt entrances while a cloud of curly-haired middle-aged women scuttled out of the west entrance. Everyone was glaringly white.

"Yeah," Sarah said, waving a line of women past, "all the admin people are like prototypes of each other. Just look at them." She pulled behind the house to a gravel parking lot marked EMPLOYEES ONLY and killed the engine. They sat silent in the car for a while. On the radio, Alanis Morissette screeched. Kendra reached over, turned the music all the way down. She let out a long, raspy breath.

"Are you okay?" Sarah said.

"Yeah," Kendra said.

"No need to be nervous," Sarah said. "We're family here. You're family now."

"Family," Kendra said.

"Yeah," Sarah said. "Family. You're stuck with us, no matter what." She winked, opened her door, stepped out.

On the porch, one hand on his hip, the other holding a cup of coffee, wearing an oversized wool sweater though it was nearly seventy degrees, John Forrester stood surveying the men and women coming and going. Once in a while, someone asked him a question, and he would answer softly, keeping his gaze focused on his long, wooded driveway. When Sarah approached him, he brightened. She threw her arms around his neck, kissed his cheek, said, "Happy season!" He grabbed her by the waist, lifted her up, said, "Sarah, Sarah, Sarah." She pulled away, giggled, then looked back at Kendra. "Here's the newbie," she said.

Kendra looked up at them from the bottom of the stairs, felt small. A broad-shouldered man in blue flannel walked past her, nodded at John. He was carrying a twelve-inch monitor.

"See you soon!" Sarah said, racing into the house.

John looked down at Kendra, smiled so wide his eyes nearly shut.

"Kendra," he said, extending the *n* and the *a*, effecting a satisfied exhalation. "It's so great to see you."

Kendra shrugged, palms up. Here I am, she thought.

"Well, come on in," he said. "Let's get you started."

She walked up the porch stairs, stood next to him. He put his arm around her shoulders, and she instinctively pulled away, but he brought her tighter to his chest. He smelled like autumn, like leaves and smoke and apples, and it reminded her for a second of how her father, toward Thanksgiving break, would take over the kitchen and cook strudel—cherry, apple, raspberry—for two days straight. After Thanksgiving, he'd retreat to his office, but for those few days, the house would smell sweet and autumnal and he'd be there, physically there, and he'd always be happy.

"Say cheese!"

A camera flashed in her face. The whine of a Polaroid exiting.

Kendra blinked and saw Cory, the scraggly man who'd invited her to his apartment. He looked down at the picture. "This'll be good," he said. He gave the picture to John, who waved it in the air. "Welcome aboard, Kendra," Cory said. "Good to have you here."

John removed his arm from Kendra's shoulders, stared down at the square in his hands. "He does this every time," he said, shaking his head. "Takes these pictures of new staff, catches us off guard. He says it's more authentic that way, captures some sort of true emotion, but the only emotion he ever captures is surprise." He chuckled. "Well," he said. "Shall we?"

John led her inside, up the stairs, past two men in overalls, and walked to the first door on the left. He showed her the time clock (*Easy, standard stuff,* he said, *just line things up right*), and the wall behind the clock where everyone's first-day pictures hung. In the photos, each employee, in various states of surprise, stood next to John.

"As you can see, we're a bit of a ragtag group," John said.

Kendra didn't understand what he meant by "ragtag," but she found it unnerving that he hadn't hired a single non-white person before. Certainly Black people were *available,* right? Lincoln and the surrounding areas weren't *all* white. And since, as he'd said earlier, people came from everywhere to be a part of his attraction, wouldn't he at least *try* to diversify? Her stomach rumbled. Nebraska sucked.

"I've grown close to every single person up here," John said, waving his hand around the pictures. "We really are one big family."

Kendra searched for Sarah, found her toward the middle. Her face was partially shielded by her hands, her mouth fixed in a startled O. She looked like she was dodging a blow. John, however, looked directly at the camera, serene and placid, his eyes relaxed, arms loose by his sides.

His arm's not around her, Kendra thought. I wonder what that means.

John pinned Kendra's picture to the top of the wall, said, "Look at that. You're starting a row all your own."

The picture, still hazy, showed Kendra with small eyes, one eyebrow cocked. Her mouth was slightly open, and her right hand pressed against John's chest. John, conversely, looked like he did in Sarah's picture—relaxed, unsurprised, mildly amused. His left arm held tightly to Kendra's left shoulder.

"Do we get to keep those pictures?" Kendra said.

"You want to keep yours?" John said.

"Well, not now, but maybe after the season?"

"Tell you what," John said. "I'll take another one, a better one, and you can have that."

Kendra nodded. She knew that if she sent that picture to Shawn, he'd put it on his wall and look at it every day.

John led her farther down the hall, past the control room, to the costume room. She expected to see it like she'd remembered: a glittering, empty department store with rack upon rack of intricate disguises. Instead, however, the room was havoc: men and women tore furiously through the clothes, some shouting, others smoking. One young woman said, "It's not *here*! Where's Cory? It's not *here*!" People zoomed past, most in various states of gore, and in the corner with the dentist chairs, a line eight deep waited to be made up by one of seven makeup artists—all women, all bone thin, all sporting tattoos. The masks that'd lined the perimeter of the room were now jumbled in a single box, and people scavenged through them, trying on one then another then another.

"Here's the thing," John said. "You can make anything scary in the dark. But look around. Look at everything in the light. It's not so scary, is it?"

The reason it wasn't scary, Kendra thought, was because everything there—every person, prop, costume—was a secret revealed. A magician's trick inspired no awe once you knew how it worked, and there, in that room, watching people paint themselves with blood and guts, apply fake appendages, scramble and be human, the magic died. Shawn would *love* this, she thought. He could stay and watch this room forever and ever.

"Usually, you'd pick out whatever you wanted, get made up, be on your way to the lot," John said. "But today I'm afraid it's a bit of a mess. First days always are. So you see that girl over there, the pretty one with the long legs? I want you to go to her, tell her who you are, let her pick something out for you. It'll be better for today, okay? She'll take you to the lot. She'll fill you in on everything. She's great. Her name's Christy."

"Christy," Kendra said.

"Yeah, and look. There's Sarah. She can help too. But Christy's been here a little longer. So any questions? You ask her."

John turned and left. Kendra felt suddenly exposed. She breathed in deep, inched her way toward the girl John had pointed to, a tan blonde who grabbed costume after costume, held them up to the light, threw them onto the floor.

"Cory *told* me it'd be here," Christy mumbled, grabbing what looked like a werewolf suit. "He *told* me it'd come yesterday."

Kendra cleared her throat. Christy looked up, froze, stared, then looked back at the rack. "It's here somewhere," she said. "It's gotta be."

"I'm Kendra," Kendra said.

"I know who you are," Christy said, her eyes still on the rack. "Welcome, and stuff."

"John told me that you'd pick something out for me?"

"We pick out our own stuff."

"Yeah, but he said just this time."

Christy looked up, let out a long, irritated breath. "I'm sorta busy," she said. She looked at her watch. "Fuck."

"So should I just—"

"Oh Christ, here. Come here." She picked up one of the costumes off the floor, held it against Kendra's body, shoved it into her hands. "For your first day it doesn't matter. You'll get used to everything. Put this on."

Kendra looked down at the costume. "Dorothy? Like *Wizard of Oz*?"

"Go to makeup. They'll gore it up for you."

"But is this the best, I mean, I definitely don't look like—didn't she wear pigtails?"

"Just put it on, okay? I don't have time for this."

So on Kendra's first day on the job she wore a blood-splattered blue-checkered dress (a size too big) and ruby slippers (a size too small). Her toes pinched against the shoes as she walked down the dark driveway, and though she didn't complain out loud, she silently cursed each step, thinking it would've been much easier if she'd just picked her outfit herself. Christy, in a low-cut vampire costume, and Sarah, in a black wedding dress and veil, directed her to the lot, where they stood beside a strangely tall lamppost. Christy checked her watch, said, "Okay, Sarah, let's train quick," and Sarah, smiling under her veil, said, "Okay, listen up, newbie."

During the season, they told her, two sets of teams arrived each night Quigley was open—Thursday, Friday, and Saturday evenings. Many came via the Quigley Quester, the van that picked up contestants from the Claymont Hotel, but others wanted to drive themselves, untrusting of the department-store spook ride. The attendants' job was to direct those arriving via personal car with green glow sticks, ushering the vehicles around the lot to their designated spots. The lot was small, and three girls was really two too many for the position, but John liked having that many: a young, spooky welcome committee was nice, he said, even if they *didn't* speak, which he instructed them not to.

After cars were parked, the girls batted on windows, growled, made other nonsense noises, and while this was supposed to unnerve the contestants, give them a small taste of what was to come, the contestants mostly greeted the girls with anticipatory grins. Once out of their cars, they said things like: *What's it like? You think we'll make it through? What should we be looking for? Is it gonna hurt? You look great, man. Makeup's perfect.* The girls didn't respond, just pointed dumbly with their green glowing sticks.

The busy times in the lot were, of course, eight P.M. and ten P.M., the designated Quigley start times being eight thirty and ten thirty, but the girls couldn't just slack off in between: they each had a walkie-talkie, and when the contestants were finished, someone would CB them to make sure their costumes were minimal (they didn't need to wipe off their makeup between sets, but they needed to be in street clothes). It was the girls' responsibility, once the house guide got to the lot with the contestants, to point out whose car belonged to whom. (The girls tagged each car once the contestant arrived and gave the contestant a slip with a number to make sure nobody forgot.) Many people didn't need this close ushering—they knew their cars and could identify them easily—but some were still in shock from the experience and required extra help. If someone was too upset to drive, the Quigley Quester would take them to their hotel, and an actor from the house would return their car that evening.

"That's it!" Sarah said. "That's all we do."

"It can be boring," Christy said, looking around. "But mostly, time goes by pretty quick."

The first night went spectacularly. Kendra directed,

pointed, even startled a couple when she banged on their window, and though some people looked at her strangely (*A bloody Black Dorothy?* one guy said. *Okay, whatever*), she experienced intermittent spurts of real power: These people, these *contestants,* thought she had information—they thought she knew the intricate details of Quigley. And by being silent, by simply pointing with her glow stick and looking evil, she didn't reveal otherwise. These people were nervous, and they thought she, a sixteen-year-old girl, could help quiet some of their anxieties. And maybe she could! But she wouldn't! She definitely wouldn't!

She'd started her shift with enormous reservations, thinking the job itself would be exceedingly stupid, but by the end of the night, understanding that she really *was* the face of the organization, or at least the first and last person that many contestants saw, she found herself flooded with pride and excitement. She thought, then, that perhaps Nebraska wouldn't be such a bad place after all. The night air was crisp and the *autumn* night air so cleansing. She loved witnessing the giant tapestry of stars above (in D.C., she'd hardly noticed the sky), and her coworkers, for the most part, seemed pleasant enough. (She even caught Christy smiling at her once.) Things wouldn't be as awful as she'd imagined. Just as long as she had this place.

After she punched out, after Sarah dropped her off (*You have a good time?* Sarah asked. *Incredible,* Kendra said), Kendra grabbed the cordless and dialed Shawn, her heart pounding in her throat.

"I've been waiting here all night," Shawn said. "Tell me everything."

"Shawn," she said. "It's all amazing. Where do I even begin . . ."

They talked until two A.M.

After that first night, Kendra quickly fell into a rhythm: She'd drive in with Sarah, arrive by seven P.M., punch in immediately, sift through the costumes, splatter herself with blood, go through makeup if needed, and walk with Christy and Sarah down to the lot. She wasn't as picky about her costumes as Christy or Sarah, and was drawn, interestingly, to life-sized insects and demonic inhabitants of the underworld, and since these outfits weren't very involved, she often found that she had extra time. On these days she'd sit on the front porch swing, reading a horror novel, waiting for the others to finish.

One evening in early October, the sun an orange strip atop the trees, John joined Kendra on the swing, sipping his coffee. He leaned back, swung hard, nearly toppling Kendra over.

“King fan, huh?” John said, nodding toward her book, *Needful Things.*

“Some of ’em are great,” she said.

“And that one?” he said.

“Okay so far,” she said, thinking about the poor haunted town of Castle Rock.

He smiled, looked down at his mug. “I’ll tell you a secret,” John said, abruptly stopping the swing. “This coffee is mostly Bailey’s.” He chuckled.

“Really,” she said, closing her book.

“Gets me through the season,” he said.

They sat, swung gently. Around them, actors and crew raced in and out. Chaos was always the norm an hour before each tour.

“I hope you’ve had a good time here,” John said, his face half-hidden in the dying light. “I know we sort of threw you into everything. But I had a feeling, the moment we met, I had a feeling. You were going to be just fine.”

She nodded, swung. This night, she was a demon, orange-red fire painted outside her eyes. She wore a skintight red suit, and a black prosthetic over her tongue, forking it. The prosthetic felt large and plastic in her mouth, making speech somewhat tiresome.

“So you and Bryan,” John said, staring out at the

darkening driveway. "How did you find out about us? I mean, Bryan probably knew because he lives here, right? But you? How did you find out?"

"Oh," Kendra said, sliding her tongue against the roof of her mouth. "A friend from D.C. told me."

"A friend?"

"Yeah. I guess he'd read about you in *Fangoria* or something? He's a big fan."

"Is this *just* a friend?"

Kendra looked at him, then looked away. She closed her mouth.

"I'm sorry," he said. "I don't mean to pry like that."

"No, it's okay," she said. "It's just sort of complicated."

"I understand," he said. "It's a wonder how any of us manage to be with any other person. We're all so complicated."

"I'm not *with* him," she said.

"But you want to be?"

She shrugged. "I don't know."

Though she *absolutely* knew; she knew without a doubt. She knew at night when she talked to him, told him about her shift. The changes in his breathing, the acceleration of his sentences, the increases and decreases in his vocal volume—she lived for these things. Once she was old enough, once she graduated and moved back home, once Nebraska was behind her for good, they'd be together; they'd finally stop this strange dance they were doing and consummate their attraction.

"He'd be stupid not to be with you," he said.

Her skin tingled. She looked at John and repressed an urge to embrace him. "He just doesn't know what he wants yet," she said. "But he'll eventually figure it out."

John's eyebrows arched. "But he likes us, huh. He likes Quigley."

"Oh yeah. He *loves* Quigley. Obsessed, probably."

"Well, that's good," John said.

"I guess," Kendra said.

John patted her leg, got up, went inside.

After this conversation, these pre-tour chats with John happened regularly. Kendra looked forward to them, so much so that she'd often choose the first costume that fit her just so she could get on the porch. John would bring her a cup of coffee or cocoa, and they'd swing, the chains creaking, the wood biting into her thighs. He'd ask her about school, about her Nebraska adjustment, about her family life, and she'd spill, telling him about her cousin, her aunt, her mother, her father, his death, the move. As time went on, John asked more and more questions about Bryan: *Is he an athlete? Is he very competitive? Does he like challenges?* And Kendra, thinking nothing of it, responded truthfully: *He ran track, yes he's competitive, of course he likes challenges, we all like challenges, apparently right now his roommate is his biggest challenge ha-ha.* John asked if he'd ever be interested in a job at Quigley. (*With his size, his build . . .*) and Kendra said no, he had no interest in it whatsoever.

"Ah well," John said. "Maybe that'll change."

Out in the lot, the girls spent their downtime in a twenty-square-foot storage shed that John had converted into a homey respite from weather and boredom. He provided hot chocolate, cider, pastries, sometimes pizza, and allowed the attendants to use it whenever they weren't mandated outside. On one Friday night in mid-October, drizzly and cool, after they'd just sent the ten thirty group up to the house, they congregated inside.

"Nobody'll ever win this," Christy said. Her left eye was painted black, dripping red. From a distance, she looked like she'd been shot. She stood next to the snack table, eyeing a glazed doughnut. "It's a scam."

"People *have* won it," Sarah said. She sat next

to Kendra on the purple couch. "What did they call themselves again?"

"Those four Asian kids?" Christy said. "They were plants."

"That's what everyone says," Sarah said. "But I don't believe it."

Christy shrugged. Kendra thought she tried too hard to look aloof. Something about the way she curled her top lip and stood at a small angle from whomever she spoke with—it seemed much too performed. Christy picked up the doughnut, took a big bite. The sides oozed jelly. "God, I'm gonna get fat here," she said, wiping her mouth.

"You know," Sarah said, "we should feel pretty lucky we're even getting to do this. I hear it's rare that John ever hires people from the community. All the actors? They're, like, professionals. They've done commercials and everything."

"Right," Christy said. "They're professionals. They're so famous that they came to Nebraska to work at the Quigley House."

"I've talked to a bunch of the actors," Sarah said. "They have impressive résumés." She was wearing her black veil again this evening, a widow this time. She'd pulled it up to expose her face; some of the nylon tulle drooped over her left cheek, mixing with her dark hair, making her look like a girl with a terrible haircut. "I think I'm gonna see if I can be an actor next year. I'll be eighteen next August."

Christy shook her head. "I'm eighteen *now.* You think I applied to be a parking-lot attendant?"

Outside, rain bleated against the windows. The wind bent the tops of trees.

"I don't think I'd want to be an actor here," Kendra said. "It sounds too physical."

"All acting is *physical,* Kendra," Christy said.

"Well, this seems more."

Christy rolled her eyes. "God, this rain," she said, moving from the snack table to the window. "Why is it such a wet fall? El Niño?"

"Makes for a good tour," Sarah said. "Everything's spookier in the rain."

Christy shook her head. "Not if there's no thunder and lightning."

Sarah shrugged. "I guess."

Christy turned to the couch, pulled up a folding chair, sat opposite Sarah and Kendra. Kendra instinctively turned away. It was difficult, she'd noticed, to look Christy in the eye. "Hey, so what do you guys think of John?" she said.

"John Forrester?" Kendra said.

"Duh."

"He's okay, I guess," Kendra said.

"Well, I think he likes me."

"What?" Kendra said, feeling suddenly hot.

"Yeah. I mean, this was last weekend when I was a little late. When I clocked in, there he was, just standing in front of the time clock, and he says, sort of snidely, 'Running late?' and I thought I was in trouble even though seriously it was only, like, *two minutes,* but anyway, I'm nervous, but then I see that he's smiling, and I chuckle, say some dumb shit like traffic or something, and he starts making small talk about traffic, talking about how Lincoln wasn't laid out very well, that there should be a freeway that goes east-west so people don't have to hit all the lights on O or Cornhusker or Highway 2 or whatever, and I'm just inching to the costume room thinking, *If he doesn't shut up I'll* actually *be late,* but he keeps talking and then it dawns on me: he's hitting on me!"

"He was probably just being friendly," Kendra said.

"At first I'm like, *ew,* because he sort of looks skeezy, right? But then I look at his eyes and did you know that they're gray? Like *gray,* gray, not gray flecks or anything. Well anyway, they're also very kind eyes, small but kind, and they sag a little—not puppy-dog, but maybe halfway—and I'll be honest, I thought then, Why not? I mean, he's the owner. And if I'm staying in

Lincoln after I graduate, might as well try for a real job here, right? So."

"So?" Kendra said. "You *slept* with him?"

"What? No, Jesus, Kendra," Christy said. "I just thought about it. But it can't hurt, you know, to have him like you like that."

"Gross," Kendra said.

"Jealous?" Christy said.

"Huh?" She found her way to Christy's eyes, saw that they were cold and hard. She looked away.

Christy sniffed. "Please," she said. "We've seen you sitting with him on the porch. Having your talks. We know what you're doing."

Kendra looked at Sarah. Sarah shrugged. Kendra's whole body tensed.

"I don't spend a lot of time getting dressed," Kendra said, still looking at Sarah. "I sit on the porch, waiting for you guys. He talks to me. I don't *ask* him to."

"Of course," Christy said.

"You think I'm into John Forrester?" Kendra said, turning to Christy. "Are you fucking crazy? He's *old*."

Christy tossed her hair over her shoulder. "What do you talk about then? School?"

"Sometimes."

"You sit on the porch of the Quigley House with John Forrester and talk about school."

"Yes."

"Pshh." Christy leaned back. "Right."

They fell silent. Kendra stood, went to the snack table, put a piece of cheddar on a Ritz, chomped loudly. Sarah stood next to her, played with her veil. Kendra resisted the urge to slap her for her silence. She took a long swig from a bottled water, tried to breathe slowly.

"So you're friends now, buddies," Christy said.

"I guess," Kendra said.

"Pshh," Christy said.

"Is that so hard to believe?" Kendra said, feeling her chest tighten.

"Just saying," Christy said, "he picked you out of the bunch. That's—interesting."

"Interesting?" Kendra said.

Christy didn't respond. She looked out the window.

Kendra's insides tangled. Though Christy had never said it outright, Kendra knew that she thought of her as a diversity hire: all the actors and crew were white; in fact, the only Black person she'd seen roaming around was an electrical guy named Richard, and he was contracted out. It made sense, then, that Christy and others would see her as a means to infuse color into the aggressively bleached staff. And yet: seeing herself this way in relation to Quigley felt desperately wrong. Sure, Kendra felt violently conspicuous there—she felt violently conspicuous *everywhere* in Nebraska—but because of John, and because of the costumes and the blood and the masks and the strong, almost unbearable, desire everyone had to be something else, the conspicuousness leveled out; it didn't suffocate her as much as it did at school. It was manageable, sometimes even invisible.

"I just sit there and wait for you guys," Kendra said. "He talks to me. That's it. He'd talk to you too if you were there."

Christy inhaled deeply, exhaled through her mouth, forming a gray oval of condensation on the glass. "Listen," she said to the window. "No big deal, okay?"

Kendra closed her mouth.

"I shouldn't have said anything," Christy said.

Kendra shook her head. "I don't get it," she said, wondering if Christy was racist or just power-hungry. Maybe a little of both?

"You don't get what?" Christy said.

"Nothing," Kendra said. "Never mind."

For the rest of the evening, nobody talked. They just drank, ate, sat in different parts of the shack. Sarah bit her nails, pretended to be busy at the food table. Kendra sat on the couch, her knees pulled up, her head in her arms. Christy stood by the window, examining the rain, her arms crossed, her face pinched.

At 10:59 P.M., Kendra's walkie-talkie beeped. On the other end: Marcus Lonetree, that night's floor manager.

"Contestants returning," he said. "ETA five minutes. Arriving via Quester. Confirm."

Kendra held the walkie-talkie to her mouth. "Roger," she said.

"Roger," Sarah said.

"Roger," Christy said.

They walked outside.

Five minutes later, the Quigley Quester pulled into the lot. The rain had petered back to a drizzle, but it was still cold. The door of the big van slid open. Out stepped four contestants: two young men and two young women, college students from Virginia who'd played competitive sports since early childhood. One man had bandages on his face. The other walked with a limp. The women seemed unhurt but edgy, their eyes darting around the parking lot, suspicious. A fifth man—the chaperone—appeared at the van door once the contestants were out. "They're all yours, girls," he said. He handed Christy a clipboard. She signed the paper on top. This was how it ended.

The contestants had driven together, so there was only one set of keys. Sarah said, "Who's driving?" The man with the limp grunted. "Are you okay to drive?"

Sarah said. The man grunted again. Christy passed the clipboard to Sarah, who handed it to the limping, grunting man. "Please sign at the bottom," Sarah said. The man did as told. Sarah gave him the keys.

"We hope you had a good time at the Quigley House!" Kendra said, her rehearsed lines. "Please drive carefully."

"You people are freaks," one of the women said.

"Yes, please drive carefully," Christy said.

"You'll hear from our fucking lawyers," the woman said.

From the front seat, the other woman said, "Connie, come on. Get in."

"Please drive carefully," Sarah said.

The three girls backed away from the vehicle, stood under the orange streetlamp. In unison, they raised their right hands, waved. "Goodbye!" they said. "Goodbye, goodbye, goodbye!"

As soon as the contestants were gone, Kendra, wanting to be as far away from Christy as possible, went into the cabin, grabbed her things, and ran alone down the driveway, in the dark, racing toward John Forrester's infernal house of horrors.

Cell Five

They enter. The screen reads: 18 minutes, 5 envelopes.

It also reads: CONTESTANTS MAY ATTACK.

The light from the screen flickers, striping the room momentarily with thin lines of white. The screen goes dark. They can't see the clock. They can't see anything.

Be on guard, Bryan says. *They can come from anywhere.*

The room is cold. Somewhere distant, a faucet drips. They reach for one another. They huddle.

We only need five, Bryan says, his voice echoing. *Five in eighteen minutes.*

We just crawl around? Jane says. *Like, on the floor?*

Nobody's been here before, Victor says.

Don't be a bitch, Jane says.

Timbre and cadence take on a rough salience in the dark. Each letter of each word sounds careful, enunciated.

Do we have a plan? Bryan says. He closes his eyes, tries to remember Kendra's description. Four jail cells, she'd said. In each corner.

Maybe we should look around in pairs, Jaidee says. *Maybe Victor and me, and you and—*

What, no, Jane says. *Victor and* me. *You and Bryan.*

Okay. Bryan pats around, searches, finds Jaidee, engulfs his hand in his own. *Good idea.*

So we just walk around? Victor says.

For now, Bryan says.

The two groups separate. Bryan hears retreating footsteps, distant. He doesn't know if they belong to Victor and Jane or someone else.

It's so dark, Jaidee says.

Madness, huh, Bryan says.

They shuffle around, decide on a direction, sync their footsteps. Jaidee's hand is bony, slim, smooth.

Tell me something, Jaidee, Bryan says to the dark. *Did you ever think that one day we'd be walking around in the dark holding hands?* He laughs.

Jaidee doesn't say anything. They continue to take slow, measured steps. Nothing happens.

How're we supposed to find anything? Jaidee says.

Don't worry. Something's gonna happen, Bryan says. *We have eighteen minutes.*

From somewhere, Bryan hears a groan. From somewhere else, Bryan hears panting. He hears creaking, clanging, slow, subtle moaning.

You think we'll finish? Jaidee says.

We've gotten this far, Bryan says. *We better.* They walk. Left foot, right. Right foot, left. *Since we're waiting,* Bryan says, *why don't you tell me something. Anything. Something about you.*

Huh? Jaidee says.

Just tell me something.

I'm from Thailand, Jaidee says.

I know that. Tell me something else.

I don't know, Jaidee says.

Sure you do. What about when you were a kid? What did you do for fun?

Silence.

Jaidee?

I wrote a play with my friends.

A play, huh. What was it called?

It was called Belly-Kos.

Belly-Kos. What's that mean?

It was about a superhero and a villain. It was stupid.

Was it? Or was it brilliant?

It wasn't brilliant. It was really—

ZZZZ-ZAP! A blue light, followed by a shout, followed by swift retreating footsteps. Jaidee lets go of Bryan's hand.

Jaidee? Bryan said. *Hey, man. Where'd you go?*

I'm here. Jaidee coughs.

I can't—

ZZZZZZZAP!

Fuck no, Bryan says, feeling heat course up his legs. He falls to the floor, scrapes his knees. He scrambles to his feet, whirls around, sees nothing. *Jaidee!* he says. *You there? Follow my voice.* He tilts his head, shouts to the big black nothing above: *Whatever happens, everyone, don't say it! Don't say it!*

Bryan.

Jaidee?

My shins, Jaidee says from somewhere distant. *They're burning.*

I know. I know. But keep cool. Just follow my voice. Bryan takes a few hesitant steps, stretches his arms out in front of him. *Victor! Jane!* he shouts. *You good?*

Nothing.

God that hurts, Jaidee says.

My voice, Bryan says. *I'm going to stay put. Just follow my voice.*

Okay, I'm coming.

I'm over here. Follow my—

Hands on Bryan's chest, pressing hard, pushing him through the void, farther and farther and farther away. *FOLLOW MY VOICE, JAIDEE! JUST FOLLOW MY VOICE! FOLLOW MY—* Then there's tape, and his mouth is shut. He claws at it, but hands hold his hands, hands hold his arms, and though he's strong, these people are *also* strong. He hears footsteps everywhere—scurrying, anxious. He tries to open his mouth, rip his lips from the adhesive, but nothing gives, and he's still moving. He braces for impact. When it comes, it feels like every breath he's ever taken exits. He can't breathe in. There is oxygen all around him, but he can't access it.

What if I actually died in here? he thinks. What would it have been for? Would it have been noble? Would I have been dying for love?

He puts his hands on his knees, bends over. The footsteps withdraw after a loud clang. He's in one of the jail cells. He must be. He breathes deeply through his nose, tears at the tape, pulls it off. Tears slide down his cheeks. He walks around. His hands meet cold metal bars. He grabs them, shakes them.

Jaidee! he shouts, his voice hoarse. *Jaidee!*

I punched him! comes a tiny voice to his left. *I punched him!*

Jaidee? Bryan says.

I tore his mask off and punched him! I tore his mask off and—

From Jaidee's corner, Bryan sees a flicker of blue. Jaidee shouts.

The envelopes! Bryan shouts as loud as he can. *They're on the actors. Get 'em, Jaidee! Find 'em! Find 'em! Find 'em!*

WITNESS:
Jane Roth

Cross-Examination Excerpt
September 17, 1997

Q. It's not a stretch to say that you're a fan of these types of attractions, is it, Ms. Roth?

A. Not a stretch. I love everything Halloween. I've been to so many mediocre haunts in my life and that's why Quigley means so much to me. It's considered the best.

Q. Some people say that you have to be sort of masochistic to like things like this. How do you respond to that?

A. These haunts are therapeutic, actually; all the research says this. We have all this pent-up energy that goes wasted every day because we have to be nice, we have to be polite, we can't be too loud or too physical when we're feeling negative feelings. At these places, you get startled, and scared, and your adrenaline is sky high, and all that pent-up energy releases itself every time you scream. Ask anyone: people feel extremely *calm* after they've done an extreme haunt. They feel *focused.* They feel *centered.* It's the most *incredible* experience.

Q. Ms. Roth, when Leonard was standing behind Bryan with a knife in Cell Five, did you think it was all an act? Did you think it was part of the game?

A. Yes. I mean, it seemed like that was the end, almost like someone had shouted the safe word, but nobody had, so yeah, I assumed we were still in it. I assumed they were trying to trick us.

Q. Did you want to rush at Leonard? Did you want to find the envelopes you presumably thought were on him?

A. At that point, to be honest, no. I was finished with the game.

Q. But why? If you were so sure that both Leonard and Bryan were deceiving you?

A. I was tired. And honestly? There was a part of me, a small part, that thought it could be real. I'd just been in a jail cell with a bunch of rats and some big demonic gnome. I'd been shocked. I'd had *tape* around my mouth. My hands were cuffed. Everything was *insane.* So yeah, I thought that what was happening could be actually happening. I mean, I had real bruises.

Q. Did you tell Victor this?

A. That I thought it might be real? No.

Q. Did you try to stop him from rushing Leonard?

A. Not directly, I guess. I did tell them it was over. I told them we were done, that we should stop.

Q. Did they listen to you?

A. No.

Q. Ms. Roth, what's your degree in?

A. My degree?

Q. Yes, your college degree.

A. Marketing.

Q. Marketing? Not psychology?

A. No.

Q. Do you have any graduate degrees in psychology?

A. No.

Q. Have you taken any graduate courses in psychology?

A. No.

Q. Interesting. Now, earlier you mentioned studies, or research, right? On the benefits of attractions like Quigley? Where did you read these studies?

A. I dunno, various magazines.

Q. Can you name a few?

A. *The Horror Monthly*, for one.

Q. *The Horror Monthly*? Is that a scholarly journal I'm not aware of?

A. It's a magazine.

Q. What kind of magazine?

A. They conduct real studies.

Q. Yes, I'm sure they do. Can you discuss how they go about their research?

A. I don't know the specifics right off-hand.

Q. But you're certain they're a credible resource.

A. Yes.

Q. Interestingly, Ms. Roth, I have a copy of *The Horror Monthly* right here. Could you turn to page twenty-five, read the first paragraph?

A. I mean, this isn't really representative . . .

Q. Can you just read?

A. "It's a known fact: most children between the ages of nine and thirteen are possessed by a demonic spirit. Nobody knows exactly how this happens, but investigations have shown higher levels of paranormal activity in households that contain children within this age range. It's widely accepted that the hormonal changes that come with adolescence thrust these demons out of the child's body, and that demonic control is at its peak right before this occurs."

Q. Ms. Roth, do you believe the assertion in this article?

A. No.

Q. But it says right here that it's a "known fact."

A. I don't believe *everything* I read.

Q. But you just cited this as a valid source. A source that does "studies."

A. That doesn't mean that they don't mess up.

Q. But a minute ago, you called them credible.

A. Overall, but not everything in a credible source is always true.

Q. Well, what would make it credible, then? If only a few things are true, how can it be credible?

A. Most of the things are true. Just not all.

Q. Interesting. Okay. Can you please tell us about your time in Cell Four?

A. Cell Four?

Q. That would be the butchery, yes?

A. Yes.

Q. Please tell the court about your time in that cell.

A. Um. That one was different from the others.

Q. Different? Different how? Different good? Different bad?

A. Just different.

Q. Can you explain, please?

A. There were all these hanging people. They looked real. The envelopes . . . were inside.

Q. Inside where?

A. Inside the people.

Q. But the people weren't real?

A. No. But they looked real. They were dangling.

Q. So you were supposed to eviscerate these dangling people?

A. Yes.

Q. And what happened? Did you do it?

A. I couldn't, not at first.

Q. Even though they weren't real? Even though you knew that they weren't real?

A. They looked so real. And the only sound in the room was screams, like from some record player or something.

Q. But you knew they weren't real?

A. Yes.

Q. So why couldn't you do it? Why couldn't you cut into these mannequins to find the envelopes?

A. I don't know. I just couldn't.

Q. Is it safe to say that this cell manipulated you emotionally? So much so that you couldn't go through with something you knew would harm absolutely nobody?

A. I don't know.

Q. But you couldn't do it. You made everyone else in the group do it while you sat in the corner and cowered. Victor came over to you, right? Tried to coax you, but you wouldn't budge, is that right?

A. No, I mean. I eventually—

Q. No?

A. I mean, yes. That happened, but I eventually got up. Bryan helped me up.

Q. But it's safe to say that you'd been consumed by emotion, emotion elicited by the house itself.

A. I was just taken aback. I didn't expect to see that.

Q. What you're saying is that the house startled you? Isn't that what it's supposed to do? Isn't that what you said results in *calm* and *focus*?

A. Well, yes, but—

Q. But in you, in that room, it resulted in the opposite, didn't it? It resulted in disorientation, in terror, in paralysis?

A. The calm and focus happens *after* the haunt's over.

Q. I see. So inside the haunt you're anything *but* calm and focused?

A. I guess.

Q. And who designs the haunt, creates that sense of disorientation, terror, and paralysis?

A. The owner? I don't know.

Q. The owner. Okay. Ms. Roth, in Cell Four, there's a lot of fake blood, isn't there?

A. Yes.

Q. Every time you had to cut through one of those fake bodies you got doused, right?

A. Yes.

Q. Cory Stout has already told us the components of the fake blood, but I want to hear a few things from you. Can you describe what it feels like?

A. I'm sorry?

Q. What does the blood feel like on your body?

A. I don't know. Wet.

Q. And when it eventually dries, what does it feel like?

A. Sorta waxy, I guess.

Q. You mean it leaves a film?

A. Yeah, a little bit.

Q. So if someone were to touch your skin after the blood dried, it's conceivable that they'd think it wasn't actually your skin, that it was some sort of covering, maybe even a molding?

A. I don't really think so. I mean, it's not *that* thick.

Q. But wouldn't that depend on how *much* was on you?

A. Yeah, I guess.

Q. And in Cell Four, who'd found the most envelopes?

A. Bryan.

Q. So he'd have the most fake blood on him.

A. Yes, I suppose.

Q. He must've been *completely* covered in that fake gore by the time he got to Cell Five.

A. He was. We all sorta were. But yeah, he was the most.

Q. And if we rewind all the way back to Cell One, he'd been in a cage with someone who basically hosed him down with that stuff, right?

A. Yes.

Q. So there was plenty of time for it to dry.

A. I mean, I think he wiped some of it off between cells, but yes, he got the brunt of the fake blood.

Q. Was the fake blood coating his neck?

A. It was everywhere.

Q. Everywhere including his neck?

A. Yes.

Q. And you said when the fake blood dries, it leaves a waxy coating.

A. Yes.

Q. So when Leonard had the knife to Bryan's throat, he was touching this waxy coating.

A. Well, yeah.

Q. Ms. Roth, let's switch gears a bit now. When you saw

my client standing behind Bryan Douglas with a knife, you said that you thought he was one of the actors.

A. Yes.

Q. So you thought he had some envelopes on him. Maybe hidden in a pocket or something?

A. Yes, I did.

Q. But you didn't rush at him, not like your fiancé, or Jaidee afterward?

A. No.

Q. Did you think that Bryan Douglas was in danger?

A. No.

Q. So you thought the knife was fake?

A. Yes.

Q. Ms. Roth, in your deposition you said that you saw something in Leonard, something that made you think he *could* be a killer.

A. Yes.

Q. Can you describe that again? What you saw?

A. Desperation. Like he was capable of doing something terrible.

Q. Thank you. When Victor rushed the defendant, what did you do?

A. I didn't do anything.

Q. But you thought you'd seen the shimmer of a real killer in Leonard, a desperation.

A. Yes, but I didn't actually think he was going to hurt Bryan.

Q. But you saw the potential. You said so yourself, Leonard was capable of doing something terrible. So why didn't you try to stop them, even if there was a chance that Bryan might be hurt? Why didn't you try to hold your fiancé back?

A. It happened fast. I don't know. And then Cory came over, and then Jaidee . . .

Q. Ms. Roth, how many haunted attractions have you visited?

A. A lot.

Q. More than ten?

A. Yes.

Q. More than twenty?

A. Yes.

Q. More than thirty?

A. Maybe.

Q. And in those thirty haunted attractions, have you ever witnessed this shimmer before? Like on an actor that you thought was capable of committing a grisly murder?

A. I don't know.

Q. Oh, come on. I'd think if you'd seen it it'd be memorable, right?

A. I don't know.

Q. Maybe because you never *actually* saw that shimmer? Maybe because you were confident that Leonard was acting?

A. I saw it.

Q. But yet you didn't do anything.

A. I already said! It happened so fast. I didn't know. How could I have known? How could anyone have known?

Q. Did you feel manipulated and confused? After it was all over?

A. Yes! Of course!

Q. And once again, Ms. Roth, who was the mastermind behind this manipulation? Who led you to question the reality of a man standing behind another man, holding a knife to his throat? Who's in the very business of making you question reality?

A. John Forrester, I guess.

Q. John Forrester, yes. A man who keeps coming up in these testimonies. A man who orchestrates horror shows for a living. And a man who might just have orchestrated his best show yet.

Witness:
John Forrester

Direct-Examination Excerpt
September 17, 1997

Q. Can you tell the jury what compelled you to start the Quigley House?

A. The house is a family house, passed down to me from my parents, passed down to them from their parents, passed down to my grandparents from their parents. I grew up there. My family grew up there. The house means everything to me. But I have no children. My siblings are estranged. I'm not married. The house essentially ends with me, and I knew this ten years ago—I understood that I would be the last Forrester to own it.

Q. Is it fair to say that your siblings are estranged because they didn't approve of what you did with the house?

A. It's fair to say that, yes.

Q. Why did you transform the house into Quigley?

A. It was my way of carrying on a legacy.

Q. But why a full-contact haunt? Why not something more innocent, like a small museum or a gift shop?

A. I wanted people to *interact* with the house, or to at least interact with how I'd fashioned the house.

Q. But again, why a full-contact haunt? Why not just a regular haunted house?

A. This is *legacy* we're talking about. A regular haunt is fine, but boring. There would be no memory of the house after Halloween. I wanted to give visitors an immersive, memorable experience, and the only way to do that, I knew, was to differentiate myself from the rest of the haunted-house attractions.

Q. Do you hurt people?

A. No. People might leave with cuts and bruises and minor shocks, nothing major. Everything is timed, everything is staged, everything is choreographed, but people don't necessarily know that—they think there's a chance they can be hurt, and because of this, something in them changes, they become entirely new people, primitive.

Q. Do you want your contestants to succeed?

A. More than anything.

Q. Mr. Forrester, do you know the defendant?

A. Yes.

Q. In what capacity?

A. The Quigley House works with the Claymont Hotel. He works—or rather, *worked*—at the Claymont.

Q. Would you consider yourself a friend of the defendant?

A. At one time I did.

Q. At one time? Meaning you don't anymore?

A. I'm afraid he wanted more than I could give as far as friendship. I'm a busy guy. He and I hung out when I had the chance, and that was good for me. Most of the time, my mind is wrapped up in the house, but these social outings with him got me out of that headspace for a while.

Q. And what would you do during these social outings?

A. Just drink a bit. Unwind.

Q. And during these outings, did you ever talk about the Quigley House?

A. Unfortunately, yes.

Q. And did you ever show the defendant the inside?

A. Yes. One day in January. It was cold. We were closed. It was one of those rare days I was alone in the house. I knew he had the day off, so I called him up. We met at the house, drank some bourbon. He asked if he could see the haunt. I said no at first. Nobody's allowed down there that doesn't work there. But he kept asking, kept saying that we were friends so why not? I guess I felt some sort of camaraderie, and nobody was around, so I opened it up, gave him a bit of a tour.

Q. And this was in January. The incident with Bryan Douglas happened in April. Was the house set up already?

A. You mean the cells?

Q. Yes. Were the cells set up just like they were in April?

A. Yes.

Q. So the defendant, when he came into the house on April twenty-seventh, would've known the layout.

A. Yes.

Q. Did the defendant ask questions during the tour?

A. A lot of questions.

Q. Such as?

A. He asked about all the pulleys and levers. He asked if there were alternative ways to get into each cell. He was trying to figure everything out.

Q. You said that you no longer consider the defendant a friend. Why is that, exactly?

A. He became hostile.

Q. How so?

A. He was seeing this woman in Thailand.

Q. Boonsri Pitsuwana?

A. Yes. But before that, he'd broken up with Mary Kenilworth and was very depressed about it. I told him to go on vacation.

Q. A vacation that you helped arrange?

A. Yes. We were friends. I knew Bangkok, had contacts, could get him some deals. He needed rest. So he went to Thailand, and apparently fell in love with this woman. And he became obsessed with her. When he got back, he told me all about her, wouldn't shut up about it, and I was getting busy, so I distanced myself, anyone would. But he kept calling. It got to be too much. I blocked his number. These things have happened to me, you know? People like Leonard idolize my success.

Q. Did he ever threaten you?

A. Yes.

Q. Please explain.

A. Like I said, he wouldn't stop calling, so I agreed to meet with him in person, at Pete's.

Q. The bar in Havelock?

A. Yes.

Q. Go on.

A. Leonard told me that he was extremely lonely, that things were falling apart, that he didn't know if he could keep it together. I told him that I was busy, that I was trying to put together this spring competition, and it was taking up a ton of my time. I apologized for being out of touch. I told him I wished him well. And that's when he got angry.

Q. What did he say?

A. He said he'd ruin me. He said that he would do everything he could to take me down.

Q. Why do you think he was so angry with you?

A. I really don't know. He'd had some bad luck. The woman in Thailand wasn't really working out, it seemed. I guess I was an easy scapegoat.

Q. Did you feel threatened?

A. Not at the moment. My mind was elsewhere. But I should've felt threatened, because it was a threat. I shouldn't have underestimated him because now, well, you know.

Kendra

One particularly warm November evening on the Quigley House porch swing, John asked Kendra how she'd liked her first season. Had Halloween week—a week they'd been open seven days—been too much for her?

"No," she said, looking out at the growing dark. "It was fun."

This night she was a giant cockroach, the abdominal portion of the costume cut open, oozing green and red and black strings. Her hands ended in large fuzzy pincers. She cut at the air with them, wondering if they'd make a sound on car windows.

"Good," John said. He put his coffee mug on the ground, folded his hands on his stomach. "I'm glad it was fun for you."

They rocked for a bit. Kendra stared at the cup on the floor.

"I've noticed you're a bit quieter lately," John said.

Kendra shrugged. "Preoccupied, I guess," she said.

"Is your friend still doing okay? Still a fan?"

"Who, Shawn?"

"I believe that's his name."

She sighed. "Who knows," she said.

"You mean he hasn't been asking about us? About you?"

"I don't really wanna talk about it," she said.

"Okay," John said, pushing the swing with his feet.

Shawn, lately, had become distant, cutting their calls short, citing schoolwork or fatigue or parental problems. Sometimes, he simply didn't answer at night, no matter how many times she rang. His absence clawed at her, filled her head with a pounding, relentless dread. In late October, she'd called Camille, had asked about him, whether he seemed different, whether he was with anyone. Camille said that she hardly saw him—they shared no classes and only crossed paths fleetingly in the hall.

"He looks the same as ever," Camille had said. "Thinner than shit, but really, I don't pay attention."

On the porch, John picked up his mug, sipped. He

blinked, said, "This is the first year we've been down applicants."

"What?" Kendra said.

He sighed. "Halloween week isn't usually this difficult."

"What do you mean?" she said. "We were full every night."

He scratched his chin, looked out at one particularly odd-shaped tree. Its thin trunk curved to the west side of the house, and its branches drooped downward, creating a small arc of wood. "We were," he said.

"And you have a *waitlist.*"

"Mmm," he said.

Kendra leaned into him, put her hand on his shoulder. "I think lots of businesses go through ups and downs," she said. "No biggie."

"Of course," he said. He turned to her, and she saw, for the first time, how tired he was: his face, usually bathed in a crinkly excitement, was drawn and dark. "We close next week," he said.

"Oh my god," she said.

"Not *close,* close," he said. "Close for the season. You know that."

"Oh," she said. "Okay."

"We open again March through May, but sometimes those months people back out. Fall's really the only haunt season, and October's really the only haunt month. Spring, summer, people aren't wanting scares as much." He paused, sipped his coffee. "But I want to change that. What do you think, Kendra? What do you think of changing our entire idea of haunts?"

"Sounds great," she said.

"So you'd help me. You'd be willing to do what it takes."

"Sure," she said.

He cleared his throat. "I'm doing a series of promotions," he said. "And I might need you to, well, I'd have to talk to you about it when things are more certain."

Kendra's heart raced, imagining a job promotion. To see the look on Christy's face! "What do you need me to do?"

"Not yet," he said. "I'll tell you in the spring if I need anything. Now, let's just get through this week, take our break, get through the winter, then talk in March."

"Will I get to see the cells?" she said.

He stood up. The yellow porch light cast a truncated shadow across the wood. "Someday," he said.

"Just a peek?"

He smiled, wanly, and walked back into the house.

On the final night of the season, John hosted a wrap-up party for all non-administrative employees. He bought beer, wine, catered in food from five different restaurants: one Chinese, one Italian, two pubs, and one sandwich shop. In his front living and dining area, he cleared out tables and replaced them with chairs and couches, hooked up five speakers to his personal CD player, and hung two ornate chandeliers above each room, effecting a sort of trashy opulence. There was no theme to this party—most of his staff was sick of all things horror—but rather, he decorated generically: yellow, red, and green streamers, a few balloons (one that shouted, in bold lettering, THANK YOU!), and a few sprinkles of star-shaped glitter on the food table. On this evening, only one group of contestants went through the house: a group of four brothers from Erie, Pennsylvania. They only lasted until nine P.M., the second-youngest yelling reprieve during Cell Two, so the party started early, and Kendra, once she and Christy and Sarah waved goodbye to the brothers, raced up to the house, flung open the door, and said, "We're done! They're gone!" A few sound guys were already fixing plates at the food table, and Cory sat spread on the couch, drinking a bottle of beer, smiling.

"Well, congrats on your first season," Cory said, as Kendra sat next to him. "Wasn't so bad, was it?"

"Nope," Kendra said.

The music started—mid-'90s alternative. Stone Temple Pilots. Alice in Chains. Pearl Jam. Kendra said, "God, these songs are so *terrible*."

"Terrible?" he said. "What, you want some rap?"

She frowned. "Because I'm Black?"

"No," he said, turning red. "No, I mean. It's what the younger kids listen to. It's—"

"Just stop," she said, looking away.

He put his hand behind his head, scratched. "You did good," he said. "John sure likes you."

"I can't believe it's already over," she said.

"We start up again in March," Cory said. "But it's a lot less hectic."

"I've heard," Kendra said.

They sat for a while, drank their drinks. Cory offered her half his sandwich. She shook her head.

"Hey," Cory said. He paused, turned toward her, leaned in, lowered his voice. "You play your cards right, you could be an actor here. I swear. That's how much he thinks of you."

"An actor," Kendra said.

Cory leaned back, nodded. His scruff seemed especially messy this evening, stopping and starting at random places along his jawline. "Play your cards right," he repeated.

"He *did* say something about me helping out, doing more. Do you think he meant that? Like, being an actor?"

Cory shook his head. "You're still underage. I doubt it. But then, with him? Who knows."

"Yeah, he asked me if I'd be willing to do what it takes."

"That could mean a lot of things," Cory said. "Just stay tuned. You're on the up-and-up." He smiled, fashioned his left hand into an ascending airplane.

They sat for a bit longer, then got up, walked around, mingled, laughed. She hadn't interacted much with anyone besides Sarah, Christy, John, and Cory, so most of the people she encountered she knew only from the costume room or via CB or from the Quester. All of them seemed much more integral to the operations, so assured and confident and knowledgeable. When she saw or talked to them in the hall before a tour, she usually cut it short, certain they thought of her as some low-level fringe employee.

But there, at the party, she felt immensely seen. As she floated from conversation to conversation, many of the employees, lips loose from alcohol, revealed a secret fondness for her. She was better than Christy, they whispered. Christy could be a bit *much*.

"Not that she's not good at what she does," said Seth Hinkerman, a Cell One actor with muscles everywhere. "But you're the chillest parking-lot girl we've ever had. Like, I've had comments from some of the contestants. They really like you."

"But I just stand there," she said, feeling sparkly and warm.

"Don't matter," he said. "You got a *presence*."

At ten thirty, Kendra found herself on the couch again, this time with Christy. She felt uncomfortable sitting next to her, especially after the barrage of hate her coworkers had thrown at the blonde, but Christy seemed unusually approachable right then, all smiles and laughs and easy-flowing gestures.

"You're so pretty," Christy said, her eyes slitting. "I mean, I usually see you in makeup."

"Thank you," Kendra said, though she didn't know if Christy meant it. It was hard to tell with her. "You know you're gorgeous, so."

Christy shook her head. "It's not like that," she said, pushing her hair from her shoulder. She took a swig of beer. "I'm always showcasing, you know," she said.

"Showcasing?"

She took another swig. "Yeah," she said. "But hey, I know things have been tense between us. I said some things I shouldn't have. I'm a theater person, you know." She winked.

"Yeah," Kendra said, unsure what "theater person" meant.

Christy played with her fingers, looked into her palms. "I hope you don't think I'm intruding or anything," she said, "but I heard about your dad."

Kendra choked. The only people she'd told about her dad were Sarah and John, and though it made sense that word would've gotten around, she hadn't expected anyone to bring it up, especially not Christy. She looked away, started to get up.

"Wait," Christy said, extending her arm. "I just want to say I get it. Like, grief, or whatever. My mom died a couple years ago. Breast cancer. She was sick a long time."

"Oh," Kendra said, sitting back down. "I'm sorry."

"It still hits me, like rushes over me sometimes. It's stupid. I'll be doing something normal, like driving, listening to music, and I'll hear some old song from the seventies and I'll be like, 'I need to ask my mom if she liked that band,' totally forgetting that she's gone. And when I realize, it's like no time has passed at all. I'll just be crushed for hours." She sniffed, rubbed her nose. "Anyway, I just thought I'd share."

Kendra leaned back, folded her hands over her stomach. She, too, had experienced that forgetfulness. The other day, folding her clothes in the laundry room, she'd thought: When's the last time Dad *ever* folded his own clothes? only realizing later that for a moment she'd thought of him as alive, as a figure to be detested. It'd been almost reflexive, thinking that thought, and in her bedroom, daylight streaming through the red curtains, burning her eyes, she'd cursed herself, wondered if things would've been different if she'd been a little kinder to him.

"What I mean to say," Christy said, "is I'm sorry, okay? We shouldn't be arguing. We shouldn't be enemies. We're all family here, as they say. And you and me, we should be even closer because we're stuck out there all night."

"Right," Kendra said, feeling suddenly regretful. Over the last few weeks, she hadn't talked much to Christy, and Sarah had followed suit. At school, she ate lunch with Sarah, met her at Sarah's locker, talked about Quigley, and when the subject of Christy came up, they'd take turns mocking her, brushing their hair from their shoulders dramatically and saying things like "Oh my *gawd,* Cory forgot to special-order my costume *again*" and "When I played Fastrada in *Pippin* I seriously got a *standing ovation*" and "I *seriously* can't help it if guys *want* me. I mean, really, it's not *my* fault." Afterward, they'd burst into tearful laughter.

"So what do you think of all this?" Christy said, gesturing to the party. "I mean. Crazy, huh?"

"It's been good," Kendra said.

Christy looked at her watch. "But it's sorta boring, right? Just sitting here and drinking?" Christy said.

"No," Kendra said, wishing Christy would talk to someone else. "I'm not bored."

"But hey," Christy said, sitting up. Her beer breath warmed Kendra's eyes.

"What?"

Christy inhaled deeply, smiled. "Listen," she said, looking furtively around the room, "I just thought of something. There's another way to the cells. Not just from the main haunt entrance."

"What're you talking about?" Kendra said.

"Just . . . there's another way. More than one way in and out, you know."

"I don't understand."

"To *downstairs,*" Christy said, and Kendra's heart fluttered. "Marcus showed me. I think he thought he might get lucky." She scoffed. "But we went down there after everyone left. Even John was gone—can't remember where. But I saw it." She looked around. "Hey," she whispered. "Let me take you down there. We could go now."

"What?" Kendra said, goose bumps covering her arms.

"I wanna make it up to you," Christy said. "And anyway. Look around, Kendra. Nobody's paying attention! I mean, the only person I'd be worried about is Sarah, and look at her, she's busy talking to what's-his-face. We could sneak. The door's just off the kitchen hall. Come on."

"You're serious?" Kendra said.

"You wanna see," Christy said. "I know you do."

"Yes, of course, but aren't they still cleaning up? Aren't they—"

"Kendra. They're all up here. Everyone. Look around you."

"But John. He's—"

"He's probably in bed. Seriously, last year? He made an appearance and then left. Cory cleaned everything up." She scanned the room. "I mean, he's *old,* Kendra, just like you said."

"He's not *that* old."

"Come *on.* Look. Everyone's turned away. Hurry."

Before Kendra could object further, Christy grabbed

her hand and pulled her through the kitchen into the adjoining hall, where she was suddenly surrounded by dark, the hall lit only by seeping moonlight. Her airways constricted. She concentrated on her breath. Two doors on the west wall stood ajar: one led to a storage room, one to a closet. Christy, her smile gleaming, chose the door to the storage room.

"Careful," Christy said. Her voice came from below. She was kneeling. "Watch your step.

Kendra heard a creak. "I can't see," she said. "Isn't there a light?"

"No," Christy said. "Here. Take my hand. It's a trapdoor. Be careful."

Kendra descended a series of metal steps, each footfall unsteady, clanging.

"Grab the rail," Christy said.

"If we can't see anything, what's the point?" she said, grabbing the rail.

"We'll see things," Christy said. "Once we're down there. I'll find the light. Marcus showed me."

Once they both stood on solid ground, Christy said into the dark, "Just wait here. Don't move." Kendra waited by the stairs, holding on to the rail, ready to bolt. The air was damp. She felt, suddenly, that she was violating an important trust.

"I'm going back up," she called to the darkness.

"Wait. Kendra," Christy said from somewhere remote.

A long wheeze sounded above. And then: white light. Kendra shielded her eyes.

"Aha!" Christy said. "There we go!"

Kendra blinked, looked around, her hand still firmly wrapped around the handrail. The room was impossibly large, empty, and gray. A scoreboard was mounted on one wall, turned off. Around her, she felt movement—Rats? Mice? Snakes? In each corner sat a miniature jail cell, iron bars connected to concrete. In the northeast cell was a shadowy human figure seated in a red folding chair, its face obscured by a green gas mask.

"Holy shit," Kendra said.

"Don't worry," Christy said, standing a few feet from the cell. "It's just a prop."

Christy walked into the cell. Her steps echoed. She became small. "Well, hello there Mr. Mask!" she shouted. "Aren't you a scary, scary thing!" She giggled, patted the top of the figure's mask. "Very, very scary."

Kendra shook her head. She knew from movies that this was the point where they were supposed to play around with the monster in the chair. Christy, the pretty blonde, would talk to it suggestively, maybe give it a lap dance, while Kendra, the no-nonsense Black character, would say, "I wouldn't do that. Please don't." Minutes later, the monster-slash-killer would disappear, only to reappear behind them with a weapon, slashing to pieces the Black character who'd ultimately been deemed inessential to the storyline.

Christy looked out at Kendra, put her hands on her hips. "Jesus, Kendra," she said. "Are you just gonna stand by the stairs? I mean, you wanted to see, so look around! It's a little ridiculous, isn't it? Look how low-budget everything is! Just a room with four little jail cells. But this is, what, Cell Five? If anyone gets here, they're pretty beaten up already. And it's pitch-black, and everyone goes mad in pitch-black."

The figure stood up. Kendra screamed. Then she laughed. "Lonetree?" she said. "Is that you?"

The figure towered over Christy. It wore bib overalls, a flannel shirt, work boots, all streaked with blood. Christy turned around. The figure stretched out his arms, lifted Christy by the shoulders. Christy squirmed, her feet jerking in the air.

"Yes, very impressive," Kendra said. She looked up the stairs, chuckled. "But don't worry, Christy. You and I both know that the Black one always dies first."

She thought, then, of *The Shining,* the movie she forever associated with this sort of tokenism. It'd been the biggest disappointment of her entire movie-watching career to see Dick Hallorann axed by Jack Torrance. Hallorann, a Black man who'd had the gift of the "shining," who'd communicated cosmically with Danny Torrance, who'd been en route to enacting full-fledged heroism, had met his demise not *five minutes* after he'd arrived at the Overlook. *Five minutes.* His single line inside the hotel had been: *Hello? Anybody here?*

"Kendra!" Christy shouted. "Help!"

"I'll get right on that!" Kendra said, grinning. "Hold tight!"

Shawn had turned angry at the Hallorann murder scene. He'd said, "I'd rather they just not put a Black person in the movie than have them *die* so meaninglessly every time."

"But *everyone* dies meaninglessly," Kendra had said, though she, too, felt gutted.

"You know it's different," he'd said, his face long and fuming. "You know it's not the same thing at all."

In the jail cell, the killer-man's masked face was inches from Christy's, peering thoughtfully. Christy screamed. Kendra felt momentarily unsettled.

"*Kendra!*" Christy said. "*Please!*"

The man in the mask whipped Christy against the bars. Kendra flinched. "Just take off his mask!"

Kendra said, mentally inventorying everyone she'd seen at the party.

"*Kendra!*" Christy said. She was on the floor now, having somehow gotten free from the monster's clutches. She was crawling away, slowly. "*Help!*"

"Christy," Kendra said, her stomach knotting. "Really, this isn't funny. This isn't—"

"*Just help!*" she said. "*My leg. I can't move . . .*"

Christy edged out of the cell, tried to stand up, but fell. The masked man looked at her, cocked his head.

"Jesus," Kendra said. She looked at the stairs, then back at Christy. "I guess we're playing this game." She ran to her coworker, bent down, put her arm around her shoulders. When they were halfway across the room, wheezing, grunting, sweating, the stairs folded up into the ceiling. *WHAP!* Kendra turned around. The masked man moved slowly, and in his hand, Kendra now saw a weapon: a glistening silver hatchet.

"No," Kendra said. "Seriously?" Sweat ran down her forehead. Christy was heavy on her arm.

"Kendra," Christy whispered. "My leg. I think it's broken."

The masked man stomped closer. Kendra's hands shook. *What the fuck?* she thought. Next to her, Christy's breathing became labored, moistening her neck.

Kendra surveyed the room. About fifty feet away was a door. "Is that where we go?" she said.

"Kendra," Christy said.

Kendra pulled on her coworker, but her weight was too much. "Come *on,*" Kendra said, thinking again of Shawn. Would she ever see him again? Or would she die down here a pathetic virgin? Would she— No. None of this was real. It couldn't be. This was a game. From behind her, she heard grunts, the slow-moving gait of a bloodied man in a mask.

Everyone in horror movies should always err on the side of caution, Shawn had said during one of their early horror club meetings. *It's their disbelief that gets them killed in the end.*

"Christy," Kendra said, panting. "Did he actually hurt you?"

Christy didn't answer, just let out a terrific scream. "Oh *fuck,* my leg! Oh *fuck*!"

"I can't hold you up much more," Kendra said.

"You have to!" she said.

"You need to be honest with me here!" Kendra said.

"Oh god, we're gonna die!" Christy said. "We're gonna die!"

Kendra stopped. Now she knew. There'd been no need to err on the side of caution. Disbelief wouldn't get her killed. She (probably) wouldn't die a virgin. She looked down at Christy's face, and saw, through the mess of tangled hair, a monstrous grin.

"Just save yourself!" Christy said, draping a hand over her forehead. "Save yourself!"

"I knew it," Kendra said, and dropped Christy, who stood up perfectly fine on her own.

The monster took off his mask.

"Yep," Kendra said. "Of course."

John Forrester shrugged, smiled. "You like the night-vision mask? Military-grade. And this hatchet looks *so real,* doesn't it?" He ran a finger across the edge: plastic. "All an illusion, Kendra," he said. "Everything."

The stairs dropped back down. Kendra ran to them, looked up and saw Sarah peering down at her, grinning. "Take off his mask!" Sarah chided. "Just take off his mask!"

"I'll give you a proper tour soon," John said, walking over to her. "You've definitely earned that."

Kendra shook her head. "I never thought any of it was real," she said.

"Take off his mask!" Sarah repeated. "Take off his mask!"

Soon the rest of the crew stood around Sarah, joining the chant. "Take off his mask! Take off his mask!"

Kendra climbed the steps, still shaking her head. Dark heat swirled around her cheeks and ears, but when she reached the hallway and saw Sarah's pointy face smiling into hers, scratchy embarrassment immediately reverted to cool, easy friendship. Who'd have thought? she wondered. Me with a white girl, feeling mushy. Who'd have thought? She hugged Sarah. Sarah hugged back.

"I'm so glad to have met you," Sarah said.

"I'm glad too," Kendra said.

Christy and John joined them in the hall, both of them beaming. John put his hand on Kendra's shoulder and said, "You're family."

"I know," Kendra said. "I get it."

"You're *family*," John repeated.

And she felt, in that moment, like she could possibly leave her entire D.C. life behind her. If she had this, if she had Quigley, she could maybe fashion an existence for herself here. She could maybe survive.

Jaidee

Jaidee was miserable in Nebraska: it was the start of spring semester, and the cold and snow were merciless, a constant, confining freeze that burrowed deep into his skin. At the library, huddled in a puffy coat, he entered computer chat rooms—"Nebraska m4m" "Midwest m4m" "men seeking fun"—and posted every day, asking if anyone knew of a man named Victor Dunlap. Only one person responded via private message. He said: DUDE, STOP IT.

STOP WHAT? Jaidee typed back.

The man closed his window.

At the group on campus, Jaidee avoided Chris Driscoll and waded out to some of the other, less caustic members, starting a small friendship with Katie, the Pride float ruiner, the woman who'd called Chris a douche that awful night last semester. At first, Jaidee found the friendship slightly disappointing—he'd wanted to meet men, not women—but as winter pounced and searing subzero winds carved into his face, he realized that loneliness took on deeper, more profound dimensions in the winter, that with each howling gust, each numb appendage, he slipped into a greater state of despair, and the only way to scale his way out was to talk to those sharing the winter with him.

"You never get used to this cold," Katie said. "It's just . . . insane." They were eating lunch in the student union. Around them, students walked sluggishly, hiding behind parkas, their backpacks small against their swollen outerwear. She'd just finished a math exam and was noticeably relaxed. *I don't even know why we're required to take math,* she'd once said to Jaidee. *It's not like I'll ever use the Pythagorean theorem in my life.*

"It's not so bad," Jaidee said.

"Are you kidding?" she said. "It must be *horrible* for you, coming from a tropical climate and all."

He shrugged. "It's different, that's all," he said.

Katie laughed. "You're funny," she said. "You say the best things." She wore a Metallica T-shirt that flopped over her large breasts and hung down to her thighs. It was the album cover with the crosses: *Master of Puppets.* Her face was stout, her hair burnt reddish-orange, and she had a habit of crowding other people's spaces. In fact, the first time Jaidee had ever hung out with her, she'd grabbed his hand, laced his fingers with her own, swung their arms back and forth. She told Jaidee that she expressed herself through touch, and that this sometimes got her into trouble.

"So how was your mall trip?" she asked.

"It was fine," he said.

"It seems like such a hassle, to take the bus in this weather. Waiting in the cold. If I didn't have class, I'd probably just stay in my dorm and sleep," she said. "Seriously."

"I can't do that," he said. "I need to get out."

"I hear you."

The previous week, feeling restless, he'd bundled up and bused over to Gateway Mall, a place he'd come to think of as his second home. Usually, he felt good there, surrounded by advertisements and soft music and potential fashion statements, but on that day, all of it discomfited him: everything, then, had seemed overly synthetic and manicured. Orderly, yes, but *too* orderly, like a beautifully landscaped hedge maze that came complete with instructions for escape. Standing in the food court, slurping his Orange Julius, he wondered: Had America become powerful *because* it lacked character? Had this massively wealthy country somehow convinced everyone else that higher degrees of regularity determined overall success? And had his fascination with this country—a country that now seemed a bit robotic—stemmed from his own desire to lack character? To be part of some powerful mainstream?

He threw his Orange Julius cup away, wandered down the east spoke of the mall, and stopped outside a shoe store containing a poster of a very ordinary-looking blue sneaker. The words below the shoe read: BE DIFFERENT. He thought about this. What did it mean, exactly, to "be different"? Didn't the company want people to buy this blue shoe? And if everybody bought this blue shoe, how would they be different? It seemed like a major problem in America, this hypocrisy. The only way to be truly individual was to conform as rigidly as possible. For example: Chris Driscoll and his friends. They certainly thought of themselves as different, as exceptional, irreplaceable, distinctive. But they'd all buy this shoe, he knew. They'd be the first in line.

And also: wasn't Jaidee himself *actually* different?

Yes. People went to lengths to remind him of it.

But did anyone want to "be" him?

No, no, no, no, no.

So what did it all mean? What was the answer to the riddle?

Who knew?

After staring at the poster for five more minutes, contemplating its pretense, Jaidee went inside and bought the blue shoes.

"So what's it like having Bryan Douglas as your roommate?" Katie said, munching on a french fry.

Jaidee bit into his pizza crust, chewed. He shrugged. "He's fine."

"We went to high school together," Katie said. "I mean, he was older than me, but I knew of him—everyone did. He was mucho popularo." She grinned, bunching the skin around her eyes.

"What?"

"He's got charisma."

Jaidee shook his head. "He's not home very much. I don't even know why he decided to move to the dorms. He always goes to his mom's house."

"Doesn't he have a new girlfriend? I'm not sure."

"I think he's homophobic."

She frowned. "Could be, I guess. Lots of people are. But you wanna watch that."

"Watch what?"

"Saying a Black man is homophobic just 'cause he's Black. That's racist."

"Racist? I didn't say anything about race," Jaidee said, suddenly perturbed. One thing he disliked about Katie was her unyielding propriety, her inability to simply gossip. She'd even semi-defended Chris Driscoll, whom she purportedly hated. She said that Chris's awfulness stemmed from the deep-seated insecurities that accompanied being a gay man in the Midwest, and that he'd have to live with these insecurities for the rest of his life. *Not that that excuses his behavior,* she'd said, *but he's dealing with his own demons. Just remember that.*

She sighed. "You can't just say those stereotypes about races."

"I'm not saying stereotypes. I didn't even mention his race."

"Black people have had to deal with injustices, Jaidee, a ton of them. And it all stems from these assumptions we make."

"But I don't think that way. I just said—"

"I'm just saying to watch it, okay? That's all."

Jaidee prickled. "Racist" sounded so vile, especially since he knew enough about American history to understand the roots of American prejudice. And yet:

His interactions with Bryan lately hadn't been great. At times, Jaidee had wanted to study in his room, and thinking that Bryan would be out, he'd come home to a room full of Bryan's friends, conspicuously smoking weed and blowing the smoke out the window. Bryan would welcome Jaidee in, tell him to grab a drink if he wanted, but Jaidee, feeling a well of anger in his stomach, would stomp over to his desk, find his books, throw them in his backpack, and go to the library. Upon leaving, he'd hear some of Bryan's friends chuckling. One time he heard one say, "Man, how'd you get paired with *that*?"

He didn't confront Bryan about the impromptu parties because he knew, even in his rage, that it would be silly—it wasn't as if Bryan was doing it all the time, Bryan was hardly ever *home*—but he couldn't help but think that after he—Jaidee—was out of earshot, they all talked about his gayness: he was certain they threw around words like "fag" and "queer" and "homo."

"I'm only saying that because his friends . . ." Jaidee said. He was no longer hungry. Talking about his roommate made him uneasy. "But whatever. Forget it."

"His friends what?"

He shook his head. "I met them the first day I moved in. They were nice. But now, it's just different, and I think they all know."

"Know you're gay?"

"I think they all know. I think I've overheard them talking. And I think, I think they're not good with it."

"You should just talk to him." She sipped her drink. "Maybe, I don't know, you need to have one of those counseling sessions, you know, the ones where they bring both you and your roommate in and you just discuss all this?"

Jaidee looked at his watch. "I don't know about that."

"Just something to consider."

"Well. I'll consider," he said, looking at his watch again.

After lunch, he went to his dorm room and saw in his mailbox a copy of the phone book he'd sent for a week prior. He grabbed it and traced the words "Des Moines" with his fingers, feeling his heart in his throat. He'd already examined the Lincoln and Omaha books to no avail, but now . . .

In the Lincoln book, he'd found three Dunlaps: Roger, Ethel, and "B." With Roger and "B," he only got an answering machine, and Ethel, a crackly, snarling woman, said, "Who? Who? Who?" He'd put the phone book aside. A semester passed. He became busy. During semester break, he sent for the Omaha phone book, found twelve entries for "Dunlap," one simply named "V." He dialed the number.

A man picked up. He said, "Victor? No. But I've gotten confused with a Victor before. Try Des Moines. Last person said he thought he might've moved there, so I'm just referring everyone else."

So he'd sent for a Des Moines phone book, and now, here it was, on his desk. He thought, Third time's a charm. The phone book glistened up at him. Isn't that what they say?

He stared at it for a while, heart thumping, hands clammy, forehead hot. Inside that book he knew he'd find Victor's name, that his address would be on the flimsy white paper, that everything would be okay—his entire journey out to this vast, green open country would make sense once he actually spoke to his former teacher. Calm warmth tickled his legs. My life, he thought. The rest of my life.

The door opened. His roommate's luggish footsteps followed. Jaidee opened his eyes.

"What's up," Bryan said.

Jaidee's chest fell, his face heated. In his head: rage, rage, rage.

"You okay?" Bryan said.

Jaidee breathed in deep. "I'm fine."

"Okay," Bryan said.

"Will you be here long?" Jaidee asked.

"Excuse me?"

"Will you be here a long time?"

"In my dorm room? Will I be in *my* dorm room a long time? That's what you're asking?"

"Yes."

Bryan shook his head. "You're unbelievable, Jaidee."

"I was just wondering."

"Dude, you're the rudest fuck. Seriously." Bryan shrugged off his backpack, flopped on his bed. "Don't know what it's like in your country, but here you don't ask questions like that."

"You're not around much, so it's not rude."

"It *is* rude. Even if I were here for one hour a month, it's still *my* dorm room."

"Not just yours."

"Christ."

Bryan sat up, rummaged through his backpack, brought out a green textbook, a notebook, a pencil, went to his desk, opened the book, started scribbling. "I got a quiz in a couple hours, so leave me alone."

"So you're staying here a couple hours? Like just two?"

Bryan closed his eyes, breathed loudly. He clenched his teeth.

“A couple hours?” Jaidee repeated.

“Jaidee.”

“I’m just trying to plan.”

Bryan sat for a while, put his pencil down, turned to Jaidee. He said, “Look, how difficult is it for you to just leave me alone right now? How difficult is that?”

“I just asked a simple question.”

“I have a *test,* Jaidee. I’m studying in *my* dorm room, a dorm room that *I’m* paying for. Don’t you get anything? Don’t you get how rude you are? How rude you’ve been? Doesn’t that even register?”

“I’m not rude. I’m just asking questions.”

“Since the very start, you’ve been rude. To me. To my friends.”

“What?”

“Yeah. Every time I try to introduce you, you—what? Scoff? Yeah, you *scoff.* Like you’re *better* or something.”

“No, that’s not what I did.”

“See, that’s it. You don’t get it. I’m giving you some room ’cause you’re from Thailand, but Jesus. I mean, I can’t.” He shook his head.

“You can’t what?”

Bryan picked up his pencil again, gripped it hard, turned to Jaidee. His face warped with frustration.

Jaidee braced himself. "Look at you!" Bryan said. "Seriously! All dressed in Abercrombie and Fitch. That shirt! Jesus. *Look* at yourself. It's pathetic."

"What's pathetic?" Jaidee said. The rage surged from his head to his neck to his shoulders to his chest. Everything internal expanded and pressed against his skin. He couldn't move his fingers; they dug violently into his palms. How many times had Bryan interrupted his studying? How many times had he had to leave the room because Bryan refused to get off the phone? The hypocrisy! The absolute nerve!

"You. Trying so hard," Bryan said. "*That's* pathetic. It's so transparent, dude. Look. Your haircut. Those clothes. News flash, Jaidee: You're not white. You'll never be white. Your reverence for whiteness is fucking *embarrassing*."

"What? What is wrong with you?"

"I'm just saying."

"What are you saying?"

"Listen," Bryan said, his eyes dancing, "I see you, trying to hang out with white dudes on campus, ignoring your own. I see that. And I've held it in, because you're different, trying to assimilate I guess, and maybe that's your idea of being American, you know, to be this bland Abercrombie and Fitch drone, but that's not America, dude! It's just one representation. And anyone who's receptive to that dominant representation, well, they're weak, because that shit is boring as fuck. But you, look at you, you don't even see how pathetic you are. None of those fratty white dudes *like* you, Jaidee. And yeah, I know you're gay. I've known forever. You think I care about that shit? You think I'm . . . Listen. They make fun of you and you don't know it. They make the chinky eyes behind your back. They do! But you. You just play into it because of this weird reverential bullshit. What do they call your type of people—Twinkie? Yellow on the outside, except that's not you, you're not *even* a Twinkie, because you aren't white anywhere, you're a *wannabe* white, and that's so much worse."

"You don't know anything about my life."

"I know enough. I observe, Jaidee. I see with my eyes. The world. I see it." He paused, scratched his chin. His eyes were large.

"You see it? Oh, you don't see anything." Jaidee stood up. "If you saw anything, you'd see how rude *you* are, to invite people to this place, my place, when *I* need to study, when *I* have an exam, and now you have the gall to get upset when I ask you a simple question? And I am not a racist person, I'm not, but I do think that your type . . . your type . . ."

"My type? Jaidee. Jesus."

"I think that your friends, your type, oh, but what I'm saying is that maybe your type is not studious—"

"Jaidee! Do you understand the words coming from your mouth?"

"I am only observing, just like you. In my composition class, there are two Black people and they sit in the back and they don't listen to the professor, and you—"

"We need different roommates."

"Why can you say things about me, and the minute I say things about you—"

"I'm saying things about you *specifically*, Jaidee."

"Oh really? Just me specifically? Oh, what did you say? *Twinkie? My type of people?* You see what this is? It's hypocrisy!"

"Saying Twinkie isn't racist."

"Oh, it isn't? Grouping people by race with negative connotation? That's not racist?"

Bryan shook his head. "It's totally different."

"It's only different when it benefits you."

"No, dude. I'm talking *observation.* I'm talking . . . I'm trying to help you look less pathetic. I'm trying to stop you from, well, whatever it is you like."

"You're homophobic."

"That's me! Yep. What did I just say? I've *known* forever. I've never cared." He turned back to his book, lowered his voice. "What else, Jaidee? Anti-Semitic? Sexist? What else am I?"

Instead of answering, Jaidee left, slamming the door, hating himself for his spotty articulation. He stomped through the halls, down the stairs, and out into the spikes of winter. He hadn't put on a coat, which was fine at first, the wind and snow and cold hovering just outside his body, his anger a protective shield. He held on to his collar and walked past faceless students behind bulky scarves and wool hats. *Hypocrite!* he screamed inside. *He's a goddamn hypocrite!* He walked downtown. The anger-warmth faded. Suddenly, the sting of the season attacked. He shouted, brought his shirt up across his nose, ducked into the first building he could.

Shoulders covered in snow, he passed through the lobby, sat on one of the couches, brushed off his shirt, shivered, crossed his arms over his chest. He didn't know where he was, and he didn't care; though the initial rage had worn off, Bryan's words rang through his head. *Wannabe white, wannabe white, wannabe white.* That wasn't right, right? He wasn't wanting to *be* anything but Thai.

He lay down. He wanted to rest, to nap somewhere other than his room, and this room with the scratchy green couch and clean, oxidized smell, and fluorescent warmth and auditory numbing from above—Muzak?—seemed the perfect place to clear his head, so he did, and that was that.

He was awoken, however, only a few minutes later by a man in oversized khakis. "Up and at 'em," the man said. "This isn't a shelter, bud."

The man's face—long, clean-shaven—took up the entirety of Jaidee's line of sight. Jaidee looked down at the man's shirt. A silver name tag blinked up at him. *Leonard Grandton, Manager.* Jaidee scrambled to his feet, noticed his soaking clothes, the wet couch.

"I'm sorry," he mumbled.

"You don't have a coat?" Leonard said. "It's freezing out."

"I forgot it."

"You forgot your coat?"

"I'm sorry. I'll leave now."

"No, now, wait. Where you heading? You can't go out there without a coat. I mean, you a student? You heading to campus? Here. I'll give you a ride. To a dorm, maybe? Listen. I can't let you walk out there. Look at it!"

"I don't know. I'm sorry."

"I'll take you, okay? I have four-wheel drive, so this snow? Simple. Just give me a minute. Have to tell my staff I'll be right back, okay? Just hang on."

So Jaidee stood in the lobby, feeling miserable, wet, cold, wondering how it'd come to this, how everything that had seemed so promising had blown up into this pathetic, distressing moment: falling asleep in a hotel lobby, waiting for some random man to plow through snow with his four-wheel drive so Jaidee could get back to his hateful roommate.

"Ready, bud?"

The man with the name tag smiled at him. He was wearing an immense parka, the hood like an unruly lion's mane. He was tall, though his body seemed not to have grown into its height: he hunched over, his shoulders pushed down by some heavenly force.

"Well, come on," Leonard said. "Car should be warm by now."

In the car, blasted by artificial heat, Jaidee felt itchy all over.

"Can you turn down the heat?" he said.

"Serious?" Leonard said.

Jaidee looked out the window. The snow was still falling, but gentler now, coming down in large crystal puffs.

"What're you doing walking around in this, anyway?" Leonard said. They were less than a mile away from his dorm, but some of the roads had been closed off, left unplowed, making Leonard take a longer, more circuitous route. "Seriously dangerous. But I'm sure you know that."

Jaidee thought again of his roommate's words: *wannabe white.* He looked over at Leonard and thought, No. That's not me.

"So," the hotel manager said, turning slowly onto Eleventh, "where you from?"

"I live in the dorms," Jaidee said.

"Yeah, well I know that. I'm driving, right? But where are you *from*?"

"Oh," Jaidee said. "I'm from Thailand."

"No shit, really?" Leonard said. "My girlfriend's Thai."

"Okay," Jaidee said.

"She wants to come over here, to the States," Leonard said. "She's desperate to, but we've gotta get everything lined up, you know? We've gotta get things perfect because, as you know, it's difficult to come from an Oriental country to ours. It's all pretty scary, I imagine."

"Not that scary," Jaidee said.

"And I've been learning some Thai, like *sawatdee-krap!* and all that. Gonna learn recipes, too, make her feel at home."

Jaidee looked out the window at all the swirling white. The man was annoying; he reminded Jaidee of the lady who worked at the student cafeteria who'd shouted, *Ni hao!* at him, then smiled and waved and told him that her adopted niece was Chinese and had adjusted really nicely. Jaidee tuned the man out. When he dropped him off at his dorm, Jaidee didn't say thank you, just raced off.

In his dorm room, he half expected Bryan to fly at him from the shadows, to descend on him with further indictment. But the room was empty. On his desk was the Des Moines phone book, full of promise. He thought, then, of how Xavier Klein on *American Blademan* had once traveled all the way to Siberia for Becky Thatcher. She'd been held hostage by Electro in a purple ice cave that only became visible twice per year, and since Klein didn't know the specific whereabouts of the cave, he'd had to journey from village to village, gathering information from the locals and securing maps and supplies from an assortment of seedy characters.

Sort of like me, Jaidee thought, his hand on the phone book's cover. Lots of seedy characters on my route to you, Victor. But that's love.

He sat, opened the phone book, looked for the name, found it. (Found it! Found it! Found it!) Here it was: DUNLAP, VICTOR R. His heart pounded. He put his finger on the name, traced it over to the address, the phone number. This was it, he thought. It'd been so easy! Just look the name up in a book, and there it was! Travel halfway around the globe to try to find one person, and all you had to do was order a book, look for the name, and it was all given, right there, the most personal information—destiny!

He wrote the address and phone number down in his history notebook. *Hey, it's Jaidee,* he imagined himself saying. *I came so far.* And Victor: *Jaidee. You can't believe how great it is to hear your voice.* And Jaidee: *I'm here now. I'm here just for you.* And Victor: *I'm so happy.*

Cell Five

Someone has entered Bryan's jail cell. It's a hard-breathing man. The man's voice is a devious whisper, sometimes close, sometimes far. Mostly, he makes unintelligible noises—suckling, clucking, chirping—but sometimes he whispers enraging missives. Bryan lashes out against the blackness.

Hello, Bryan, the man says.

Bryan punches into the dark, but the whisperer is quick on his feet, and Bryan can never pinpoint his location.

I've heard so much about you, the man says.

You're all fucking freaks, Bryan says.

The man clucks by Bryan's right ear. Bryan lunges, hits something hard. He punches the air again: nothing.

What did your cousin say to get you into this mess?

the man says. *"Please, Bryan, be the alternate. They just need one." She pleaded and begged. And you said yes?*

Bryan races around the cell, punching at everything. His fist hits the wall. Pain scatters up his forearm, his shoulder. He runs back the way he came, trips, falls, scrapes himself, pinwheels his arms into nothing. He feels something skitter up his leg. He shouts, shakes it off. It's furry.

Not much time left, the whisper says.

Bryan lunges, makes contact. The man, surprisingly small, grunts as Bryan tackles. Bryan finds the man's masked face with his hand. He cocks his fist back, punches. His fist hits concrete. Bryan screams. The man is on top of him now, his arm around his throat.

Was it worth it? the man pants.

Bryan chokes. But the man on top of him is small. Bryan bucks his hips back, throws his fist up, makes contact with something fleshy. The man howls, falls back—*thunk.* Bryan reaches out, finds the bars. He jiggles them hard. Harder. Harder. They open. He runs out into darkness.

He stops, breathes, closes his eyes. He knows there are four jail cells, one in each corner of the room. He just ran straight out of one. If he keeps walking in one direction, he'll reach another.

He walks, hands outstretched, until he hits a slimy wall. He inches his way along it. Around him, rodents skitter. He imagines the floor crawling with them. He hears bangs, thumps, crashes, grunts, shouts, all amplified, all hideous. Darkness, he thinks, is torture.

Jaidee! he shouts. *Do you have any envelopes?*

Bryan! Jaidee shouts faintly from his corner. *Over here!*

I'm going to get Victor and Jane, Bryan says.

CLUNK. BANG. ZZZZ.

Suddenly: muffled screaming—shattering, curling, impaling.

Jane! Bryan says. *Jane!*

The screaming doesn't relent. Bryan races along the edge of the wall. He hears a snap, then his fingers are screaming. *Motherfucker!* he shouts, pulling his index and middle finger out of a mousetrap. He takes his hands off the wall, walks without its aid. Just go straight, he tells himself. Keep going straight. His hands hit metal bars. He relaxes. *Hey,* he says. *I'm here. Who's in there?*

Mmmmmfffff, someone says. *Mmmmmfffff!!*

Blue light punctures his eyes. His fingers, throbbing already from the mousetrap, are suddenly aflame.

Fuck! he says, wringing his hands.

Mmmmmfffff!

Victor, is that you? Bryan says, panting. *If you can, come to the bars. I'll rip the tape off.*

Some shuffling. Then Victor's at the bars. Bryan reaches for his face, finds the lip of the tape, pulls down.

Victor screams, then regains composure, says, *Here, I'm gonna turn around. My hands are tied. Can you—*

ZZZZZZZAP!

Goddammit! Victor, briefly illuminated, falls to his knees. *There are two of them in here with me,* he says, his voice coming out in harsh rasps. *I can never tell where they are—they keep moving, and one's a fucking clown. Sometimes they get up—*

Beat 'em, Bryan says. *Just punch into the air. That's what I did. You're gonna hit something.*

And then?

Find the envelopes. They're on them. They have to be.

Okay, Victor says. *Okay, okay, okay.*

I'm gonna find Jane, Bryan says.

Wait, Victor says. *How did you get out?*

Rattle the door as hard as you can. Mine eventually gave.

But I've tried . . .

Try harder. And get those fuckin' envelopes. We're almost there.

I'll try.

Bryan leaves Victor, heads back into the abyss. He waves his arms up and down in the dark, braces for more electricity. *Jane!* he says. *Jane!*

And then: a door opens, yellow light tumbles onto the floor. Bryan shields his eyes. In the doorway, suddenly, is the shadow of a man. *Hello?* Bryan says. Behind him, Bryan hears footsteps. He walks toward the open door, toward the man.

Where is John Forrester? the man says.

What? Bryan says.

I need to talk to John Forrester.

Bryan continues walking: closer, closer, closer.

John Forrester, the man says.

Wrong room, Bryan says.

The lights come on. Bryan shields his eyes.

The man grabs him, turns him around in a bear hug. Something cold and hard is by his throat. He can't breathe. White light stabs at his retinas. He blinks hard. Hot breath comes in dark waves down his face. *Where is John Forrester?* the man says.

Bryan's eyes adjust. He looks around.

The jail cells unlock. The actors stop their assaults, remove their masks. Everyone looks at Bryan. Everyone is silent.

Jaidee

Jaidee knew, from his years watching Thai soap operas and American movies, that in order for a man to win over the love of his life, he needed to relentlessly pursue. Even if the partner rejected the man's advances at first (they always did), persistence won in the end, and the love interest—usually a beautiful woman—eventually realized just how awesome the pursuer truly was. This was how things were.

Sometimes, love was founded on deception, as in: *Falcon Crest, Dallas, Overboard.* Other times, people realized weirdos were beauties: *The Breakfast Club, Pretty in Pink, The Goonies.* Sometimes, love was based on a growing friendship: *Sleepless in Seattle, When Harry Met Sally.* And other times, love arose out of unusual circumstances: *Splash, Big, The Princess*

Bride. Jaidee thought his love would be more of a *Say Anything* sort: Jaidee, coming from a separate culture, would face obstacles to his love based on difference, causing him to continue pursuing until those obstacles dissipated and he'd proven himself worthy. Love would always win in the end, he knew. That's what everyone said.

So he would go to the address in the book. He wouldn't call first (calling isolated voice, and Victor needed to see Jaidee to understand his grand gesture)—he would just go. Before he went, though, he would prepare.

He got a haircut—Caesar-style, he told the hairdresser, pointing to the white boys in the magazine. The stylist, a curly-haired woman with smoker's breath, told him that with his hair it wouldn't quite look like the pictures, but she'd do her best. *Get it as close as you can,* he said. She did her best. In the end, he was left with a lop of poofy, thick hair atop skin-shaved temples. He used lots of gel.

He bought a henley sweater from the Gap, some chinos from Abercrombie, gray-and-white hybrid shoes from Skechers. He stored these clothes in his closet, saving them from wrinkle until the day of the reunion.

He wrote fictional dialogue, predicted retorts—*Yes, I've changed a bit, America has widened my waist!*—and practiced conversations in the mirror, noting his most flattering expressions, angles, and movements. In class, instead of taking notes, he wrote down memories, developing them into full-fledged anecdotes—adding humor, poignancy—reminding himself that once upon a time, many years past, he'd developed the life of a fictional superhero, and that that life had moved at least one person, Aran, his childhood friend.

He practiced slang. He used the word "man." He watched MTV, practiced intonations.

People always say that I don't have an accent like other Asian people, he'd say. *You taught me the best English—thank you for that.*

While he prepared, he did his best to avoid Bryan: his roommate's words still stung, and instead of thinking about them, processing them, analyzing them, he grew resentful of them. As time passed, this resentment transformed into an overwhelming, encompassing spite. In classes, if he was paired with a Black person for an assignment, he would make offhand remarks—sometimes callous, often offensive—implying that the Black person would not do his or her fair share of the work, or that the Black person obviously was not that smart, or that the Black person cared more about sports, or partying, or the opposite sex than the actual task at hand. Some of these Black students brushed the comments off as the naïve words of an international student, but once in a while, there would be an argument, and a meeting with a professor, and a switching of partners and/or groups. Jaidee, through his hatred, alienated large swaths of the student community, gaining, over just a few weeks, the moniker of "Small Man," though he was oblivious, unnoticing of the revulsion he evoked in others.

At the group, his one friend, Katie, stopped sitting by him, and at outings, she threw him only the most cursory of smiles, and this bothered him, for it was still cold outside, and though he had a renewed sense of purpose now with Victor's address in hand, he still needed to live this life on campus, and he'd thought that they'd connected in a singular, strident way. So one night after the group, he confronted her outside of the student union. It was early March—damp, windy, cloudy—and she wore a black hoodie and ripped jeans, exposing a cut on her left knee. When he came up to her, she quickened her pace, but he was fast, and before she could get far, he stood in front of her, frowning.

"Yes?" she said, stopping, looking at a call box attached to a lamppost. It was nine P.M., dark.

"Katie," he said. "What's going on?"

"I'm going home, that's what's going on," she said.

"No," he said, wishing she'd reach for his hand, wishing she'd touch him and then apologize for touching him. "I'm not good at confrontation, as you know. But I want to know why you stopped answering my calls."

"Jaidee," she said, "I've been busy. I told you."

"That's an excuse. I know better."

She shook her head. "It's true."

"There's something else."

She shrugged. "I mean, we don't really know each other that well, right? We just hung out a few times."

"Just a few times? Like every day during break? Like all the beginning of the semester? What do you mean just a few times?"

She sighed. "Jaidee, listen. I gotta go, okay?"

"I miss you," he said, feeling something catch in his throat.

She looked away. "I really *am* very busy." She blinked hard.

"Okay," he said.

"I'll see you next week?" she said, stepping away.

"Yeah," he said. "Next week."

"Bye, Jaidee."

He felt an ache in his clavicle. He wondered, as he watched the night swallow her, if perhaps friendship was something for other people, if his stubbornness, and his ego, and his drive, intimidated and ultimately repelled people like Katie, like Bryan, like Aran. In

Thailand he'd always been more forthright than his classmates—quicker to judge, earlier to evaluate—and he knew that sometimes this had turned people off. But with all of them he'd simply stated what he'd deemed obvious, so he'd attributed their negative responses to oversensitivity. With Katie, however, he couldn't pinpoint an altercation that would've resulted in such banishment, so it bothered him more than the others, and at home, he began making wild assumptions about how she perceived him.

Then one day, the very next week in fact, at Brewsky's, sitting at a table that entirely ignored him, two of his roommate's friends, the friends he'd met on move-in day, one tall, one short—Eli and Terrence—approached him, asked if they could talk to him outside. The table fell silent. Jaidee looked up at them, said, "I don't know where Bryan is."

"We're not looking for Bryan," Eli said. "We want to talk to you."

"But why?"

"Come on," Eli said. "Just for a second."

Jaidee's stomach tightened. He suddenly remembered talking to Eli outside the party house in the Bottoms. *You'll be more than okay!* Eli had shouted as he'd walked off. Hadn't he liked him back then? Hadn't he felt some sort of kinship with the tall, gregarious biology major? He had. Eli had told him about a time when he'd shoplifted, when Bryan had saved him from a predicament, and Jaidee had felt warm all over: he'd felt a sort of belonging only felt when a person opens up about a past indiscretion. But now? No warmth. Eli's eyes drilled through him. Jaidee didn't move.

"We'll hold your spot," Katie said, as if it were an issue, as if anyone in that sports bar wanted to be associated with the table of weirdos.

"I'm not going outside," Jaidee said.

"If you don't," Terrence said, "we'll talk right here, in front of your friends, and I don't think you want that."

"Seriously, Jaidee," Katie said. "It's okay."

"What do you mean it's okay?"

"I mean, we'll be here when you come back."

"I didn't expect otherwise."

"Just—"

"Come on," Eli said. "Just a second, okay? Just a second."

And slowly, his face hot, eyes everywhere burning his skin, Jaidee stood up, walked to the door, let the cool night air smash into him. Before he exited, he said a short prayer, for he knew, somewhere, that he'd done something wrong, and that whatever he'd done, he was going to pay now.

Outside, the sky was wispy, jovial. A thin pink line

stretched across the horizon. It was earlier than he'd thought.

"I don't want any trouble," Jaidee said. Small puffs of vapor flew from his mouth.

"Nobody wants trouble," Eli said. They stood on the sidewalk, Eli and Terrence with their backs to the wall, Jaidee closer to the street.

"Well, what do you want, then?" Jaidee said.

Eli looked at Terrence. Terrence nodded.

"Listen," Terrence said, his eyes icy, "right now everyone thinks you're a piece of shit. That includes Eli and me."

"What?" Jaidee said, stepping back.

"You're being called a racist," Terrence said. "It's all over the place. You're the Small Man."

"What?" Jaidee repeated, his heart in his throat.

"You haven't noticed?" Terrence said, crossing his arms over his chest. "Seriously?"

"Just tell us you'll stop," Eli said. "Just tell us that. You tell us that, we're good to go."

"Stop what?" Jaidee said, thinking of Katie's coolness. Did *she* think he was racist too? Was *that* why she'd been so distant?

Eli sighed. "We gave you the benefit of the doubt, you being an international student and all. But the comments you make, like the one you told Todd Wilder, telling him, and only him, that you expected to do most of the group work, assuming he wouldn't do his share—that's why people don't like you, Jaidee."

"No," Jaidee said. "He sits in the back. I didn't want to be in his group, but the professor—"

"Listen to yourself," Eli said. "Take a deep breath and just hear the words you say."

"But it's true! He sits there and sometimes daydreams and the professor doesn't call on him ever."

"He's a straight-A student," Terrence said. "But that doesn't even matter."

"I worry about my grades," Jaidee said.

"Didn't you hear me?" Terrence said.

Jaidee crossed his arms over his chest. "Are you gonna beat me up?"

"We should," Terrence said. "We should beat you right here and now."

Jaidee took another step back. "In front of all these people?"

"Who would care?" Terrence said.

Jaidee took another step back. He had one foot on the street now. "I haven't done anything to you."

"Just say that you'll cut it out, okay?" Eli said.

"I'm not racist!"

"We're trying here," Eli said. "We're trying."

"Is this about that fight I had with Bryan? When he called me a Twinkie? Like an Asian wannabe white?"

Terrence chuckled.

"Oh, that's funny?" Jaidee said.

"In fact, it is," Terrence said.

"I don't understand you," Jaidee said, balling his fists. "I don't get it. You all talk about racism all the time—never-ending! Is that what you're wanting me to 'cut out'? My talk about *your* race? But then you talk about mine like that? It's incredible. A double standard."

Terrence closed his eyes, shook his head. "You know," he said, "we should be on the same side. It's such a shame."

"The same side of what?"

"None of us is white," Terrence said. He took two steps closer to Jaidee. Even though he was shorter, he still radiated menace. "What happens when we have these confrontations, huh? What happens? What happens when we splinter like this?" He dug his finger into Jaidee's chest. "This is what they want, you see? They want this friction. If we're doing this, they can continue their domination. I mean, look at us, look at me, here I am, the angry Black man, picking on you, the helpless pawn, and that's really all people see, that's what people *want* to see. But it's not truth, right? It's not—listen, if you and me, if you and Eli here, if we're not brothers, then we're enemies. But we're *not* enemies. And nobody here *wants* us to be enemies. But if you continue on with your ignorant shit, we don't have a choice. And then they win."

"I don't—"

"If you want to be them, they have the power; how can you not understand that? If you want to *be* them, they can *use* you. And who do you think they'll use you against? Huh? Who the fuck do you think they'll use you against?"

"I don't understand," Jaidee said, his eyes misting. "I'm not racist!"

"It's seductive, right?" Terrence said, clearing his throat. "That world, their power, the proximity to whiteness. They say, *Try to be us, wear our clothes, listen to our music, watch our movies, read our books, speak our language because we're good, we're sexy, we're successful, everyone sees it, look around you, billboards, commercials, we own it all, right? We control the world, so strive as hard as you can to join us, our ranks.* They say this knowing full well that you can *never* be them, and that as long as you stay in line, keep up that *desire* to be them, you're no real threat. Next thing you know, you're indoctrinated into their way of thinking. Black people are subhuman, Black people are animals, Black people are angry thugs. Always, Jaidee, this is what it comes down to. Always. Don't you see?"

"I'm not against you," Jaidee whispered. "I'm not against anyone."

Terrence groaned. "Maybe I should've just beat you and be done with it," he said.

"But it's true!" Jaidee said. "I'm not against anyone!"

Terrence stepped back, joined his friend on the sidewalk. "Come on," he said. "Let's go."

"Eli," Jaidee pleaded. "I'm not against anyone. You know that! I'm an international student. Everyone's against *me* here."

"Think about what we said," Eli said, walking away. "Just think about that a bit, okay?"

"But I'm not the villain here!" Jaidee called out. "I'm not the villain!"

"Watch yourself, Jaidee," Terrence called out, not looking back. "Not everyone around here is as gracious as us."

"I'm not the villain!" Jaidee said. "I'm not the villain! I'm not the villain!"

After this interaction, Jaidee expedited his trip to Des Moines. He needed no more preparation. What he needed was a reprieve from all the nonsense he'd endured over the last few months. His first winter in America had been nearly unraveling: to stay mentally intact, he'd require a reminder of what his purpose had been in coming here.

Three hours passed quickly. The bus dropped him off in downtown Des Moines. Jaidee disembarked, got in a cab, gave the cabbie the address.

On his way to the house, he rummaged through his backpack, ensured that he had everything he needed to show Victor. He'd brought all his vocabulary exams, circling words that had summed up his feelings—*joyous, anticipatory, iridescent, adoration*—and had highlighted, in pink, the word *affection.* He'd also brought all the worksheets that contained the heart-shaped smudges, and the three short papers he'd written containing Victor's encouraging annotation. He'd brought a change of clothes (just in case), a box of Twinkies (nostalgia; and now, irony), and, as a gift, a small globe piggybank with Thailand outlined in a heart.

"Hey, buddy," the cabbie said. "This is when you get out."

Jaidee hadn't realized they'd stopped. He zipped up his backpack, paid the driver, and climbed out. The cab zoomed off.

Victor's house was larger than Jaidee imagined—dark yellow with a wraparound porch, two stories, black shutters flanking large, boxy windows on the first floor. Toward the top, the paint peeled, revealing small gray puzzle pieces of wood, and the sizable deck contained only one rocking chair and one round glass-top table. On the table was an ashtray overflowing with cigarette butts. He smokes? Jaidee thought. He couldn't recall Victor ever outside with the other teachers, quickly inhaling nicotine between class hours, but perhaps Jaidee hadn't paid close enough attention, or maybe Victor had picked up the habit later. No matter—it was a minor indiscretion, something that would bother his mother more than him.

The street Victor lived on was quiet, tree-lined. In the driveway was a green Jeep with a single orange stripe. Jaidee imagined living there, walking down that street, driving that car, waking up each morning to the sounds of birds and light traffic. He could do it, he thought. It could be fun, or at least comfortable. It certainly would be an improvement over his current living situation—anything would be. He drew in a deep breath, walked up the porch steps to the front door, knocked.

No answer.

He knocked again.

Still nothing. His heart fell. I should've called first, he thought. I'm so dumb. Why would he be home on a beautiful Saturday? He tried once more, waited. After a while, he heard footsteps.

At a messy, stained kitchen table, drinking coffee, they stared at each other, Jaidee grinning, Victor squinting. Every few moments, Victor slid his tongue to his molars and bit.

"Sorry," Victor said. "I, um, just woke up." He was in flannel pajama pants, a white T-shirt. His hair clumped over his head in oblong misshapes. Jaidee looked at his watch. It was almost noon.

"I understand it has been some time," Jaidee said. "But you have to remember, right?"

They'd stood at the front door for three whole minutes, Victor behind the screen door, rubbing his eyes. *It's me,* Jaidee had said, over and over. *It's Jaidee. Jaidee Charoensuk from Thailand. I've come back. I've come to see you.*

At the table, Victor said, "You're here to sell me something? Like, are you some ambassador to try to recruit me to go back there?"

"Recruit you?" Jaidee said. "No. No, of course not. I came to see you."

"But why?" he said. "I don't get it."

Jaidee unzipped his bag. "You smoke now?" he said.

"Huh?"

"I saw, outside. Cigarette butts."

"Dude, it's too early for this. Could you just tell me what you're needing?"

Jaidee brought out his exams, his papers, his exercises. He laid them in front of Victor. Victor leafed through them. "Okay," he said. "Yeah, so you were my student."

"You remember, certainly," Jaidee said, his voice fluttering.

"Yeah," Victor said, his eyes resting on the highlighted *affection*. "Yeah, starting to come back to me. It's been a few years—sorry, that whole time's a bit of a blur."

"A blur?"

"Yeah," he said. "I was—never mind. But—Jaidee, is it? You're in Des Moines now?"

"I am a student at the University of Nebraska," Jaidee said.

"Okay," Victor said. "And you're passing through or something. I get it. Well, cool." He sipped his coffee. "We'll actually be in Lincoln soon."

"We?" Jaidee asked.

"Yeah, my fiancée and I."

"Your fiancée?"

"We won a free pass to Quigley House. Crazy, huh?"

"You have a fiancée?"

"Yeah. But anyway. What I should say is that I *hope* to be in Lincoln soon." He shifted in his seat, leaned forward. "They require a team of four, and so far *nobody* but me and Jane wants to do it. I mean, I've asked *everyone*. Crazy, right? It's sixty thousand dollars. You'd think a bunch of people who work in a bank would be all up to try for some free money and, you know, international fame. But nope. They're all too chickenshit. Anyway."

Jaidee sat silently, looked at the pile of papers he'd put on the table. They seemed absurd now. Had he really thought Victor had drawn him hearts? Had he really lugged those hearts across the globe to show Victor what he should've remembered?

"None of my friends and none of her friends are game either," Victor said. "Can you believe that?"

Jaidee shook his head.

"Jane's pretty fired up about it, so I'll make it happen," Victor said. He looked out the window. Outside, the branches of a silver maple tree batted lightly against the window.

"Where is Jane?" Jaidee said, his voice barely above a whisper.

"Oh, she's at work now."

"I see."

Victor picked up the pile of papers, looked through

them again. “I think I’m starting to remember, Jaidee. You were a good student. A really good student. Your reading proficiency—it was higher than most. You sat—oh shit.” Victor’s eyes flickered. “Now I remember. My best student. You were my *best* student! Sorry, so sorry! How could I, but yeah, I remember now. Sorry again, everything then was so hazy because . . . but yes! How could I forget. Please. I’m sorry, Jaidee. It’s just been a while and I’ve been preoccupied and I’m tired.”

Jaidee filled with hope. He sat up straight, forced a smile. “Thank you, Teacher,” he said.

“Ha-ha,” Victor said. “You were upset that last day. I remember now. Well, how about that.”

“You were my best teacher,” Jaidee said.

“Thanks. Appreciate it. People there, they were good to me. I was a bit immature, I think, but I still appreciated how well I was treated.”

“You were not immature. At least to me.”

“You were a kid then, right? Like, seventeen or so? Of course you didn’t think I was immature. But I’m nearly thirty now. Things are different. Priorities.”

“Things are different for me too.”

“I’m sure they are. UNL is a good school. I’m sure you’re doing very well.”

They sat for a while longer in silence. Outside,

the wind had picked up; it howled against the side of the house. Jaidee reached into his mental reservoir of memories, sifted through them, tried to pick one that would resonate with Victor, but everything, sitting there, was colored with love, and he knew, then, that if he went that route, that explicit route, he would lose Victor's interest. Victor was engaged! To a woman named Jane! Had Jaidee's entire life post–high school been pointless? Had he come to America for no reason? But no. He'd known that something like this might've occurred, that years had passed and that a man as striking as Victor was bound to attract someone—male or female—whom he'd find suitable enough. Though he'd wanted to believe in the clarity and depth of their love, a love that crossed oceans, cultures, and races, he knew, pragmatically, that Victor was an American living an American life, and that he'd eventually want to settle down. Jaidee cursed himself for not contacting Victor earlier. If he'd secured Victor's address before he'd come to America, he could've written him letters, could've stoked the interest over time—for that's what he needed, Jaidee thought: he needed time. Victor still didn't quite understand his desire, and he certainly didn't understand his destiny. In movies, all the time, the protagonists, the lovelorn, they needed time.

"So you will get married soon?" Jaidee said, holding his breath.

"Eh. We haven't set a date. I'm in no rush."

"You aren't?"

"We're basically married now. But all the wedding crap—neither of us is looking forward to that."

"Probably good to wait a little longer, then," Jaidee said.

"Yeah, but not forever."

Jaidee crossed his arms over his chest, thought about this woman, this Jane. It didn't really matter that she *was* a woman. Love was love; it knew no boundaries, especially in the West. On an American talk show called *The Bryanna Folger Show*, he'd witnessed two women, both claiming to be attracted to men, engage in a long-term monogamous relationship with each other, citing that they'd fallen in love with the human and not the sex. The audience had booed and cried and jeered (both women had left husbands to be with each other), and one audience member said, in a rage, "You should be *ashamed* of yourselves! You guys are *sick, sick, sick*!" But Jaidee understood, and he knew, as soon as he'd seen the show, that his envisioned future with Victor was not only possible but ordained; he'd seen that particular show for a reason—all his efforts would eventually be rewarded.

"Hey, man," Victor said, his eyes suddenly alert. "I don't suppose, I mean, nah, but . . ."

"You don't suppose what?"

"Well, we're scheduled at the Quigley House on April twenty-seventh. Not much time, you know? And we have to have everything in by April fourteenth."

"Not long."

"Yeah. And I called them, told them my situation, and they said that because of the circumstances, meaning because we'd won this thing and there'd been press and everything, that if I could get a group of three, they could possibly supply a fourth, like, they have reserve people or something, I don't know. Sorta fishy. But they said it'd just be someone from their list, and I guess I trust them, though who knows." He moved in his seat. "And I was gonna go around the bank, ask again, and Jane was gonna call everyone she ever knew, though she's done that already, but . . ."

"But?"

"I mean. Is it weird if I ask you? I mean, sort of nuts, huh? You already live in Lincoln. And you're my former *student*, which is simultaneously nuts and awesome, and it'd be a bonding experience for sure. I know we haven't talked much, but I get a good feeling from you. You seem levelheaded, and you know that the only group to win was Asian, not to stereotype or anything." He paused, shook his head. "Sorry, dude. That's too weird, isn't it. It's just that we've really been asking *everyone,* and here you just show up and—"

"Yes, of course I'll do it."

"What?"

"If you want me to do it, I'll do it."

"I mean. Really? Like, *really*?"

"Yes. It could be fun. And like you say—a bonding experience."

"Oh man. Oh man. If you're serious. If you're really fucking serious, you've made my day. You've made my *month.* You know how long I've been stressing about this? And here, you just plop down out of nowhere, like, from heaven."

"What will I need to do? Will I need to stay with you to prepare?"

"Stay with me? No. Nothing like that. But we should probably exchange numbers. Dude, you're unbeliev-able."

"I have yours," Jaidee said.

"My what?"

"Your number."

"You do? How— Oh yeah. You found me in the phone book."

"I'll give you mine." He scratched his dorm number down on a napkin. "Here."

"Oh man. It's like a weight has lifted. I'm serious."

"We should talk regularly. Every day?"

"Every day? No, I think that's overkill, but yeah, regularly. Holy shit. Jane's gonna flip."

"Maybe every other day?"

"Like once per week, okay? We have, what, a month? A little more. I'll mail you the paperwork—it's at my office. Be warned, it's long. You have to get a physical, include the results in the paperwork. And don't be freaked out by the waiver. It's just to cover their asses. But really, they've assured me, in all its history, nobody has ever been seriously hurt. I think it's all part of the scare factor, make you think you're signing over more than you actually are. I mean, I don't think it's even legal to waive away your right to not get killed."

"Killed?"

"They say that shit, you know? It's hype. I'm sure you've seen the testimonials in the magazines, right?"

"I'm not that familiar—"

"Just don't worry. You can fill out everything, and get your physical, and, well, I'd suggest between now and then, maybe exercising a bit? You're not gonna get seriously hurt, but it might wind you. That's what they say, anyway." He sipped his coffee. "Holy shit. We're going to the Quigley House. We're going to the fucking Quigley House!"

He sat back, beamed, and Jaidee felt momentarily happy.

EXHIBIT 10:

Letter Written by Leonard Grandton (Defendant) to Boonsri Pitsuwana

Summary:

- Letter dated March 13, 1997, addressed to Boonsri Pitsuwana c/o The Spider, Bangkok, Thailand.
- Letter returned to sender.

Content of Letter:

Dear Boonsri,

I'm suffering suffering suffering. I have bad bad dreams, and sometimes there's violence and I wake up and I don't know where I am and I won't know where I am for a long time even though it's my own house and I've lived here for years. Sometimes I look around this house and I imagine you sitting there, at my table on my couch in my bed and I swear to god sometimes I actually see you there with your smile and your hair and your beautiful skin and in those moments I feel happier than I've ever felt. It's like I understand all the secrets of the world when I see you, it's like it's all there laid out for me.

What I'm saying is that it's not just love but worthiness that you make me feel and I'll say I've felt so unworthy for so much of my life and I don't know what it is but being with you makes everything right so please answer please please please please I'm begging you. This is my life we're talking about.

I love you more than anything in the world.

Love,
Leonard

EXHIBIT 11:

Email Written by Leonard Grandton (Defendant) to John Forrester

Summary:

- Email dated April 27, 1997, 9:16 P.M. from hotelguy789789@aol.com to quigleyhouse666@aol.com.
- Subject: ?

Content:

You gonna call me?

LG

Leonard

Leonard wrote Boonsri letters. In them, he expounded on the tedium of his life back home, about how he couldn't stop thinking about her, how—as grossly premature as it was—he couldn't help but see a future together, perhaps in the States, but perhaps in Thailand. The sooner he could get things arranged the better, he said, since his life in Nebraska—alone, alone, alone—was not a life that any man should have to endure, especially after having met someone with whom he so fiercely connected.

I don't know if you heard me on the platform that last day, he wrote. *But if you did, I meant it.*

He'd taken pictures of her, and in his bedroom, above his small desk, he taped her face to the wall. Every time he passed the picture, he flooded with pride, because:

Look at her! What pristine beauty! What remarkable joy! Those slim cheeks, those almond eyes, that smooth brown skin—any man would be *proud* to be seen with such an exotic enchantress. He imagined people seeing the pictures and saying, *Leonard, who* is *that?* to which he'd reply, *Oh, she's my girlfriend. We're doing a long-distance thing for now.* Nobody, of course, came over, so he was the only one to see her there, smiling out at him from his wall, and that was fine.

He started his weekly binge-drinking again with John Forrester. When he told John about Boonsri, John's eyebrows shot up.

"Oh?" he said. "You're staying in *contact*?"

"I know what you're thinking," Leonard said. "It's different than that."

"I'm not thinking anything," John said.

"I understand the situation," Leonard said, shaking his head. "I understand how it looks."

"I'm sure it's fine."

"And you?" Leonard said. "I read somewhere that there've been declines in visitors at Quigley?"

"Ridiculous," John said. "We're doing the best we've ever done."

"Well," Leonard said. "I'm sure you'll be fine."

"Of course I'll be fine. I've *been* fine this whole time. The press is just showing its petty evils right now.

But we're good. Everything's golden." John swigged his whiskey. "And you," he said. "It seems like you're *also* golden. A long-distance Thai girlfriend. Isn't that something. This trip was good for you. Didn't I tell you? Didn't I call it?"

"You did," Leonard said, red-faced, beaming. "Yep, you sure did."

Winter descended. Leonard wrote and wrote and wrote. A couple times, he even called the Spider. The woman on the other end, speaking over the blare of the music, shouted something in Thai. He replied, slowly, "Boonsri. Boonsri. I would like to speak to Boonsri." But she continued yelling in Thai, and finally hung up. When he called again, nobody answered.

So he wrote. Every day he constructed a letter, all of them at least five pages.

Are you there? he wrote. *Ha-ha. Just kidding. I know you're there. I just wish you'd reply.*

And: *You'll leave there soon. I'll get you out. The Spider is no place for someone like you.*

And: *It's so hard to picture you with other men. I know it's happening, but you have to know that it kills me to think about it.*

His grocery store had an Asian section, and he took pictures of the shelves, asking if there was everything she needed here to make her food (*but don't expect me to cook that stuff ha-ha I can barely make a sandwich!*) and he took pictures of his neighborhood, his car, the Claymont Hotel, and various other parts of Lincoln. He even took a picture of a group of Asian people he saw downtown. *I live in a very diverse place,* he wrote. *You will feel at home I am sure of it.*

Every day after work he ran to his mailbox, hoping to see a blue envelope with a red stamp bearing the words "Air Mail," a response of some sort, perhaps something in Thai, something he could get translated, but day after day, week after week, his mailbox overflowed only with inanity: bills, reminders, advertisements.

He took more vacation, went to Thailand again, this time at the end of January, and sat with Boonsri in his hotel room, a cheaper, smaller place three blocks from Nana Plaza. It was the end of Thailand's cool season, and the air was lighter, crisper, but still quite warm. They sat on the bed, facing each other, clothed. The comforter was damp from the air-conditioning. The room itself was dim and gray, the sun outside refusing to retreat. She brushed her hair from her shoulder.

"I respond soon yes," she said, breathing deeply.

"All you need to do is tell me you received the photos," he said. "That's it. Just a simple note saying you received the photos. And you should really get an email account. It's free."

"Email?" she said.

"Yes, email! It'd all be so much easier if you just got email!"

She shook her head.

He put his hand on her shoulder. "Hey," he said. "Don't get upset. I'm just trying to make this as easy for you as possible."

"Make it easy?" she asked, and he saw something hard in her eyes.

"The transition?" he said. "Your move? Everything I've written in my letters? Everything you seem to agree with?"

"My English," she said. "Not good."

He stood up. "Your English is fine. It's way better than you think. Are you taking lessons? Someone's paying for that, I suppose, right? Someone else? You can tell me. I'm an adult. I know what you do," he said.

"What?" she said.

He shook his head. "Nothing. I just need you to respond to my letters, okay? I need to start making arrangements."

She folded her hands in her lap, drew in a deep breath. Then she went to him, dropped to her knees, unbuttoned his shorts.

He returned from that trip confident in their renewed vows. At the beach, at the mall, at the markets, in bed, he'd asked her, over and over, if she was serious about visiting—he would make arrangements, he said, but she needed to assure him that she was sincere about it all. She'd said yes, yes, yes, and he'd taken her words at face value, so he rearranged his apartment, learned Thai recipes, bought a Thai-English dictionary, studied it. He told her, through letter, that sooner was better: it was still cold and snowy, yes, but wouldn't she want to experience that? She'd never seen snow, and she'd never experienced cold, so what better introduction to America than an American winter! He sent the letter off, FedEx. She'd receive it within a few days.

A week passed. Then two. Then three. No letter, so Leonard wrote more. Winter deleted visibility, reddened faces, chapped skin. A young Thai man, covered in snow, came into his hotel, slept on his couch. Leonard took this as a sign.

Corporate, during this time, called and called. Leonard, it seemed, had spent more time writing letters and making plans than managing his hotel, and when housekeeping or kitchen or front-desk staff came in to inquire about supplies, or schedules, or technical problems, Leonard would shoo them away, tell them he'd take care of whatever it was later. The problem, of course, was that he didn't take care of anything until it was too late—until a customer complained, or an employee quit, or the computer system crashed—and so the Claymont lost more business. Leonard received a warning. Then another warning. Then a threat of dismissal should another warning occur.

"This is on you," Corporate said. "We've seen what you can do, so we're not losing hope yet, but if you don't turn this around . . ."

He asked for a raise. They laughed.

"How do you expect me to turn this place around on my salary?" he said. "I deserve this!"

"Leonard," Corporate said. "Are you for real?"

He grew despondent. Boonsri had fallen for another man—he knew this.

What if this won't work? he thought. What if none of this works?

His meetings with John became more frenzied, more animated. He ranted, informed John of the inherent unfairness of the entire corporate system, how he felt like a stupid cog in some giant, malevolent machine, how there was no empathy in the hospitality business—*You know this, right, John? You know this business*—how all those corporate know-nothings sounded the same: clipped, robotic, big-haired blowhards. And John sat back and listened to Leonard, stroking the stubble on his chin. Sometimes he'd ask follow-up questions, most of them pertaining to Boonsri. *She hasn't responded? You should keep trying. She'll come through. It's just difficult, the language barrier and everything.* One time, he asked about Mary. Leonard turned red.

"Mary can suck my fucking nut," Leonard said.

"You're over her?" John said. He sipped his whiskey.

"Of course I am. I've moved way beyond that."

"Because of Boonsri."

"No. I mean, sort of. But—listen, even if Boonsri hadn't come into the picture, I would've gotten over that hateful bitch. This distance from her has made everything clear. She was fucking toxic."

"And it sounds like you might *love* Boonsri?"

"I know it's fast. I know we haven't spent much time together."

"I suppose love is weird that way."

They sat silently for a while, listened to Molly Hatchet, sipped their drinks. Someone on an end stool grunted.

"Listen, Leonard," John said, shooting the rest of his drink, "I'm gonna be out of town for a bit."

"Yeah?" he said. "Where ya going?"

"Work things," John said.

"Okay," Leonard said.

"I'll contact you when I'm back. We'll hang again."

"Sounds good," Leonard said.

John stood up, looked down at Leonard, furrowed his brow. He opened his mouth, closed it again. Then he reached over, patted Leonard's shoulder, and left.

John had been different lately—more subdued, reserved. Leonard attributed this to the press, which hadn't been kind to him. The papers sported headlines like END OF AN ERA? and THE EMPEROR WEARS NO CLOTHES with pictures of John and the Quigley House, looking bleak and murky. The articles focused on lower sales, potential lawsuits, angry customer testimonials. One said that the "experiment" of full-contact haunts was over, that while people wanted to be startled, they didn't want to be touched—personal space was actually a thing, it read. Even in such close, terrifying quarters.

Leonard figured it'd all iron itself out—people like John Forrester, just because of the nature of his business, had to endure these types of attacks. He'd come out of it soon. And who knew? Maybe when he did, he'd want some sort of business partner. Maybe that's what he'd wanted all along. Maybe *that's* why he'd been meeting with Leonard this whole time. Maybe he saw potential, promise. Stranger things had happened.

March came swiftly, and Boonsri had yet to respond. He'd written and written, called and called, but it seemed, then, that she'd never even existed: she'd become a spectral conjuring from an exhausted brain. Thailand itself seemed like a fantasy, a recurring dream in which he spent hours cramped on a plane—attempting sleep but failing, suffocating under human proximity—only to land in an over-humid third world, surrounded by the fetid smell of fish and sweat. In this dream, he was forever uncomfortable—sticky, sweaty, claustrophobic—until he saw Boonsri, at which point the unease of foreignness evaporated, and he felt once again solid and robust.

Because Boonsri wasn't responding to his communication, his Thai dream remained trapped in a state of perpetual ugliness, and he began to find everything about the country disgusting, backward, and ignorant. Why were there areas of such destitution? he wondered, walking around alone in his dream. Why all this gold, why a goddamn *palace* for a *king* when, down the street, women and men smiled with black, rotted teeth? Why such lavish temples when the roads were too narrow, the restaurants too dirty, the strays too ubiquitous? Why have filth displayed so openly, the air in Nana Plaza and Patpong saturated with disease and abuse? This place was a cesspool with beaches, he thought. He considered canceling all future trips.

At the Claymont, Leonard's professional life dangled by a small, crusty thread. The Claymont was hosting a conference for area business entrepreneurs—the Excellence in Ownership (EO) Conference—something they hosted every year, and usually it was easy, just set up the rooms, prepare the meals, direct the traffic, but this year, for the first time in the conference's history, some members were electing to stay elsewhere and commute to the hotel during the day. The number of commuters wasn't large—most still wanted the convenience—but that *any* customers weren't staying there testified to the hotel's spirited decline.

On the first day of the conference, he ran into his ex, Mary Kenilworth, just outside the women's restroom.

"Mary," he said, his breath catching in his throat.

She looked stunning. Her hair was shoulder-length, shiny, and straightened, and her skin, previously pale and ruddy, looked beautifully fortified: it emitted a slick healthiness that he usually equated with airbrushing. She was trim, bright, confident in pose and expression, and suddenly, inexplicably, brutally, he wanted to be with her again.

"I wondered if I'd see you," she said, clutching her purse close to her chest.

"You're part of the conference?" he said.

"Yes," she said. She looked down the hall.

"I didn't see you on the guest list. Are you—"

"I'm not staying here."

"I see." He bit his lip. "Well, how are you? How've you been?"

Mary shook her head. "I'm not going to do this," she said.

"You're here for the conference," he said. "You own a business?"

She ran a hand through her hair. "In Omaha. It's called Nebraska Fresh."

"That's great," he said, his gut churning. "Congratulations."

"I gotta get back. Just a ten-minute break."

"But wait. Maybe, I mean, can we get a drink or something? Dinner?"

She sighed. "No," she said.

"It'd just be as friends," he said. "I've been in a bad place. I could use someone to talk to."

"Do you even listen to yourself?" she said.

He closed his mouth.

She hooked her purse around her shoulder. "What you need," she said, "I don't want to give you."

"Okay," he said, looking at the floor.

"And please don't make these next three days awkward, okay? Just stay away from me."

He looked up at her, his throat tingling. "But we weren't all that bad together, right? We were good."

"Please," she said. "Just stay away." She sniffed, turned, and walked down the hall. Leonard watched her go, biting his lip till it bled and thinking how unbearably unlucky he'd been in life, how the world had piled upon him one enormous sack of mistreatment.

On the final day of the conference, he received a call from Corporate. Brittany Grace, that ever-present whine-drone, told him that she'd spoken to numerous people in the office, that she'd reviewed all of his reports, interviewed his employees, evaluated comment cards, and had concluded, after thorough examination, that his final chance had expired eons ago, and that everyone had decided he was to be terminated, effective the end of the week.

"We've appreciated all you've done," she said. "But really, Leonard, you had to have seen this coming."

He pleaded, choked, cried, promised he would do better, that he was just going through a rough patch and things would turn around, but Brittany remained silent, and when he was finished, she said, simply, "Your desk needs to be emptied out by six P.M. on Sunday."

"You're making a big mistake," Leonard said.

"Goodbye, Leonard," Brittany said. She hung up.

The conference ended. Polished men and women in suits milled about the hall outside the main conference room. Leonard waded through them until he found Mary, who was talking earnestly with a white-haired woman with a cane.

"Excuse me," Leonard said.

The white-haired woman looked at him, smiled. "Oh, you're the manager here," she said. "It's been a great conference." Her voice was throaty, uneven. He couldn't imagine what sort of business she ran.

"Mary," he said.

Mary turned to him, frowned. "I'll call the police."

"The police?" the woman said.

"They're gonna fire me," he said.

"*Fire* you?" the old woman said. "What for? You're doing such a terrific job!"

"I just got off with Corporate. I have till the end of the week."

Mary sighed. "Christ, Leonard." She turned to the old woman. "I'm so sorry, Leah," she said.

"Whyever would they fire you?" Leah said, staring at Leonard. "This has been so lovely."

"I think I can get them to change their minds. After all I've done. I'd just need to bounce some ideas around, you know? Just a few ideas. So maybe we could just hang out for a bit? Maybe we could go over some ideas together? Please? Just one cup of coffee?"

Mary shook her head. "What about your best friend, John? Can't you talk to him? I'm sure he could give you a lot of good guidance."

"John Forrester's a fuckwad idiot," Leonard said, surprised by the energy behind his performance. "I don't need him. He's ruined my life, you know?" He thought of Boonsri. He thought, If I'd never met her . . .

"You know *John Forrester*?" the old woman said.

"Just an hour!" Leonard said. "Come on! Just one hour! It's my life here!"

"Goodbye, Leonard," Mary said, putting a hand on his shoulder. "I hope you can get things worked out. But I'm not going to spend any more time with you."

And once again, he watched her walk away, his chest tight, his throat dry. He breathed, remembering Sausalito, her hair damp against his chest, his fingers gripping her left shoulder, her breath released in small, raspy gasps. He remembered the black sky crashing down on the Pacific, the waves foaming and raging against the rocks, the rain pelting from above, weighting his hair to his scalp. He thought: I'll never experience another moment like that again in my life. He thought: It's over. It's over. It's over.

"I just remembered!" the old woman said. Leonard had forgotten she was still there. "The Claymont hosts Quigley House contestants. *That's* how you know John Forrester!"

Leonard looked at her, scoffed, shook his head, and walked away.

"Well, I think you're doing a great job!" the woman said. "Everything here was so lovely!"

He didn't reply.

On Thursday, two days after seeing Mary, he wrote another letter to Boonsri. It started:

> I'm suffering suffering suffering.

He sent the letter. He cried.

He called Corporate. He yelled, told them how ethically decrepit their organization was. *This is my life,* he said. Brittany Grace listened to him, offered a few words of encouragement—*someone with your skills and talent*—but in the end, things remained the same; he would be jobless soon. Sixteen years down the drain. He'd have to start over.

"I'll sue you for wrongful termination," he said, defeated. "Don't think I won't."

"Threats aren't good, Leonard," she said.

"Don't tell me about threats," he said.

He met John Forrester that night. The haunt owner was back, and had called, sounding relaxed, perhaps even happy, on the phone. He'd said, "Let's meet," and Leonard had said yes.

Pete's, that night, was unusually empty. Only a couple men sat on the stools, grudgingly sipping their Bud Lights. The music, Leonard noticed, was subdued, the usual classic rock replaced by brooding alternative, the kind with deep male voices and minor chords. At their booth, Leonard fidgeted with the buttons on his shirt. He'd come to Pete's directly from work.

"Sort of dead today," Leonard said, looking around.

"It's early still," John said.

John looked fresh, well rested. He rapped his fingers against the table and smiled. Leonard smiled back.

"You were gone for a while, huh?" Leonard said.

"Just to clear my head," John said. "And it worked."

"Where'd you go?"

John sipped his whiskey. "Leonard, I heard the news."

"What?"

"About the Claymont. I'm sorry to hear that. Very sorry."

"I'm still talking to them. Nothing's for sure yet."

"I heard earlier on."

"You heard what?"

"About what might happen. To you, your job."

"You knew?"

"The Claymont relies on me for a lot of its business. You think Corporate doesn't talk to me?"

"Jesus." Leonard shook his head. "You should've told me."

"It seemed inevitable. I didn't want to talk about it. Would've been unprofessional."

They sat for a while. John shot the rest of his drink, went to the bar, brought back another round. "Listen," he said, leaning in, elbows propped atop the table. "Leonard. I need to talk to you."

"Okay?"

"It's good. Don't worry. It's very good. I think it'll make this situation better for you."

"What?"

"Just listen. This will all be good in the end. I promise."

John told Leonard that he'd gone to Thailand, to Bangkok, that he'd needed space from the American media, which, he said, had pummeled him unfairly. Sitting beneath a green awning with blinking white lights, sipping a specialty martini (chocolate, he said, Godiva), he'd thought hard about Leonard's troubles—

Leonard's life, he'd thought, had sweltered in that certain pit of unfairness that went hand in hand with relations with the opposite sex, and the trip that John had arranged for him had gone somewhat awry, insofar as love itself, particularly long-distance love, was a case for abundantly complicated awry happenstances, so he felt, right then, as a soft, wet breeze lapped at his cheek, that he must correct the wrong, since Leonard had proven himself John's only real friend. Certainly, other people *wanted* to be his friend, John said, laid *claim* to his friendship, but they all, in the end, wanted something else—money, fame, or, at the very least, proximity to money and fame. But Leonard hadn't wanted any of those things. Leonard had, like him, only wanted companionship. And so, feeling selfless and warm and kindly, but most of all obligated, John had gone to the Spider. He found Boonsri quickly—Leonard's description had been on-point, simple. He bought her. He brought her to his hotel, but he didn't have sex. *I'd never,* he told Leonard. *Never ever ever.* Instead, he told her who he was, what his resources were, and how he was a good friend of Leonard Grandton's. *He loves you,* he'd told her. *He loves you truly and purely and your life in America would be exceptional.* He told her how he could make things happen, how he had clout, and how because he had clout he could get things done;

he could expedite processes, influence bureaucracies, and if she was willing, if she'd just take this one chance on love, he could take care of her passage to America, at least for a while. *Think about it,* he'd said. *Think about a new life. Think about a caring, loving husband. Think about being surrounded by opportunity every day. Think about it.*

"You talked to Boonsri?" Leonard said, his mouth open. "You *talked* to her?"

"Listen, Leonard," John said. "You're my friend. I hated seeing you so miserable without her."

"You talked to her?" Leonard repeated. "What did she say? You didn't—"

"No, I told you. I didn't fuck her."

"But what did she say?" Leonard said, leaning forward. "You offered to bring her here? You really offered that?"

"I knew your situation," John said. "I knew what you were dealing with."

"But John! What did she say?"

John sighed. "It took some convincing. Her family—she's very close."

"She *told* you that? About her family?"

"Leonard, quieter, okay?" He paused. "She said yes."

"She said yes?"

"She said yes. I'm filing paperwork soon. It's going to happen."

"She's coming here? She's actually *coming* here?"

"You'll need to get your place ready. It'll be culture shock for her. You'll need to help her ease into American life. She's never left Thailand before. She'll need your guidance the moment she gets here."

"But when?" Leonard's heart raced. "When? Is this real? Are you for real?"

John chuckled. "You've been a friend. It's the least I can do."

"But when? When will it happen? Oh my god. John. This changes everything."

"Leonard," John said, still rapping his fingers against the table. He glanced at the men at the bar, turned back to Leonard, lowered his voice. "Now, I'm happy to do this for you, but I'd like you to do me a favor, okay? Just a small favor. Nothing huge. I'm getting the paperwork situated as we speak—talked to a few people already about visas and all that. She'll be fine. But I'd like you to do me a favor. Something small."

"But when will she be here? Holy shit. I've got so much to do."

"We can talk about specifics soon. It might be a while. These things take time."

"I've already bought a few things for the apartment, but it's not enough."

"Leonard," John said. "This favor."

"Sure," Leonard said. "Yeah, of course."

"I'm going to be straight with you and only you, okay?"

"Okay?"

John leaned back, crossed his arms. "Those media hounds, they're rabid beasts, you know, but, well, I'll be honest, some of what they're saying is true. Tours have gone down. Nothing dramatic, but yeah, it's happened. People are just going through a phase—you know how it goes. This country is getting too soft. But anyway. I'm doing a special contest, regional, nothing huge, but something to drum up publicity. Anyway, I want to do something different this time." He lowered his voice further, leaned in. "I want to bring in someone in street clothes. I want to scare my actors *and* the contestants. It'll be big, something no other haunt has done. It'll be closely monitored, of course. Nothing dangerous. But I was wondering, if you're willing, if you'd be the guy. I'd tell you everything you need to know, where you need to go, who you need to target."

"Target?"

"It's a show, Leonard. The people who need to be in on it will be in on it, you get it? I'll give you specific instructions. It'll be very easy. You just have to channel your inner actor."

"The inner actor? John. I'm not really like that."

"This isn't some Oscar-worthy performance. Just have to come off a bit crazy. That's it. Not difficult to do. My cast does it all the time, and really, they're the most normal people you'd ever meet outside the haunt. One of them used to be an *accountant,* for Chrissake."

"Don't you want someone with experience?"

"Keep it down. This has to stay top secret. It's a totally new innovation. But no. My cast needs to really think something is happening."

"I don't understand."

"I'll explain."

John explained. And as he did, Leonard found himself becoming excited. He'd never been one for John's business, had secretly agreed with Mary that it was a rotten, perverse place, but now, thinking of being inside, of being a part of it, he couldn't help but think that this involvement, an involvement that John described as *professionally pivotal,* would serve as a giant fuck-you to Mary. *Look at me!* he'd shout from the headlines. *Look at me, you ungrateful cunt!*

More important, however: Boonsri was coming! Boonsri was coming! He would do anything. He would lick the Quigley House floor if he had to! Who cared?

John was a stand-up guy. John was a true friend. He sat back, beamed.

"My involvement will be publicized?"

John leaned back, smiled, and said, "After the fact? Oh yeah. For a minute, you'll be famous."

"I'm in," he said.

"One other thing," John said.

"Okay?"

"You have to call me. You have to call me a lot. We have to set this up perfectly, okay? I'm not going to answer, but you need to call. Constantly."

"Call you?"

"This is acting."

"Okay?"

"So here's the plan."

John smiled, drank, told him the plan.

A month later—jobless but uncaring—Leonard sat in his dining room, waiting and drinking. He'd followed all of John's directives, had gotten into character; he'd called, written, made scenes. A few days before he was to "perform," the Quigley House blocked his number. This was how things were supposed to go.

On this day, April 27, he stayed at home, waited for a call.

He sat alone, sipped whiskey, imagined cooking

dinner for his beloved. He was no chef, but that didn't matter. Everything would be new to Boonsri, everything, to her, would be *exotic.* He figured he'd start her off with an exceptionally American meal: cheeseburgers, fries, potato salad, Coke. He'd get a pie for dessert: apple. He'd top it off with ice cream and watch as she squirmed and squealed. When she finished, he'd lift her from her chair, carry her to the bedroom, kiss every inch. They'd have sex all night, and this time, he wouldn't pay.

He looked at his watch—9:01 P.M.

Leonard stood up. His head felt light. But good. Everything was fine.

John had said the paperwork for Boonsri was nearly complete, that soon she'd be there. *Before summer,* he'd said. Summer was only a month away.

Lovely Boonsri, he thought. Lovely, lovely Boonsri.

He went to the kitchen.

The knife, he thought. TLB. The Lovely Boonsri. Ha. Ha.

He removed TLB from the block, inspected it. Fate was right there, he thought, engraved on the side of that stupid knife, the knife that he'd discussed so often with Mary. He looked at the letters. They were jagged, scribbled, unprofessional. They reminded him of tree-trunk carvings, hearts stabbed with arrows containing rough, shaky initials. The lovely Boonsri, he thought. The lovely, lovely Boonsri.

John had wanted him to bring an actual knife, a real knife, and he'd said, *What? No.* Because real knives harmed, real knives killed, and this was all a show, wasn't it? But John had told him that his actors inventoried all the props, knew where they were at all times, and that they needed to think he was a madman, they needed to think he was legit—that was the whole point.

I need their reactions to be as real as possible, John said. *This is gonna be legendary.*

At the house, John had shown him the prosthetic, had cut into it an inch deep.

See? John had said. *You're not gonna hurt anyone. You couldn't even if you wanted to.*

But what if the actors rush at me? Leonard had said. *What if they try—*

Relax, John had said. *I'll be there the whole time. One misstep and I call it quits.*

Leonard checked his watch—9:16 P.M. He went to his computer, logged onto his AOL account. Though he'd been instructed not to email, he wrote a message to John. You gonna call me? He logged out.

Ten minutes later he got a call. Caller ID said "Unknown." He picked up. A scrambled voice said, "Go now." Leonard grabbed the knife, left his apartment.

Kendra

One wet March day, Cory called Kendra and told her that John wanted to see her alone: he, Cory, would be over to her apartment in a half hour to pick her up.

"Alone?" Kendra said.

"I told you, you're on the up-and-up," he replied.

At the Quigley House, she swung on the porch swing with John. Instead of looking out into dying light as per usual, they now looked out onto bright-gray sky, puddles, gravel, green, green trees. A woman passed by, headed for the west entrance. John waved, said, "Hi, Stacey." She hurried off.

"Kendra," he said, turning toward her. "I've got some great news."

Her head filled with light. Earlier that week, she'd spoken to Shawn, who'd apologized for being so absent.

He said he'd needed time to think about things. He said he'd been confused. There was a girl at school who liked him, and he thought he liked her, but recently all he could think about was Kendra. Kendra, playing cool but burning inside, asked if he'd done anything with this other girl, if he'd *kissed* her, and when he'd said no, she'd thought: I need to see him. I need to see him now before he just disappears and I have to start over.

"I'm doing this great promotion," John said, rapping his fingers against his thighs, "partnering with this bank in Iowa. It's going to up our press tenfold, I know it. I mean, everyone banks, right? And now we're part of that system." He paused, scratched his leg. "It's gonna blow up, make Quigley go completely mainstream," he said. "You're in for a real treat."

"Sounds great," Kendra said.

"I only have one problem," he said.

"Okay?"

"The bank hasn't been able to get a full team. They have three, but they need one more person."

"You want *me* to be a contestant?" Kendra said, thinking of her time down in Cell Five, John chasing her with a hatchet, Christy leaning into her full-force. She'd let everything overwhelm her then, had run away, but now, with what she knew, she thought she could do it. She thought she could last.

"Oh no, no, *no*," he said. "You're underage, for one. And you're an employee."

"Oh," she said, looking at the ground. "Okay."

"I was thinking maybe Bryan?"

"My *cousin* Bryan?"

"I was thinking that," he said.

She scanned his face, searching for some sign of insincerity. She found none. "I don't think he'd be into it," Kendra said.

"He might," John said. "If I told you . . ."

"Huh?" she said.

He leaned in, whispered, "I need a winning team."

She gasped, pulled back, stared at him. "You mean—"

"Shhh," he said, smiling. "But yes."

"But how would that work? What if they yell the safe word? How does that even work?"

"I can't control everything," he said. "If they yell the safe word, it's over, but certain things could be made, well, how do I say, simpler."

"You're serious," she said, imagining Bryan shaking John's hand, accepting an oversized check, cameras everywhere, people cheering.

"For starters: your tour."

"My tour?"

"Last season. When I showed you around. I showed you the layout. I showed you the cells. And who's to say that you wouldn't pass that important information on? Who's to say?"

"So the cells are the same?"

"I won't say one way or the other. I'll say that they're not much *different,* though."

"Holy shit," she said.

"Indeed," he said.

She shook her head. "But even then, I don't know. I don't know if he would. He's not a fan of all this, not like me. He's—"

"He just needs *convincing* by someone like you," he said. "I think he'd be perfect. He's athletic. He's charismatic. He seems like a natural leader. And if you did that for me, convinced him to compete, that is, for a *cash prize,* mind you, a cash prize that he'd have a *very good* chance of winning, I might be feeling generous in other regards."

"Huh?"

"A little business deal, perhaps? You get Bryan here. I get Shawn here."

"What?" she said, her chest tight.

"That *is* his name, right? Shawn? Your friend back in D.C.? The Quigley House superfan?"

"Well yeah. But what do you mean, *get* him here?"

"Exactly that. I fly him out here. He actually stays here, with me, in one of my guest rooms, and I, his humble servant, give him a grand tour of the place, show him some of our neatest tricks. Of course, he'll have to sign an NDA, but if he's as big of a fan as you say he is . . ."

"Wow," Kendra said, thinking how perfect his arrangement was, how stunningly flawless. "Wow."

"Pretty sweet, huh?" he said.

"And Shawn would stay here? With you?"

"Or at the Claymont. Or with you." John grinned. "It doesn't really matter. Wherever he stays, I'll make sure to show him a whole hell of a lot. Can't have too many superfans." He winked.

"Wow," Kendra said.

"What you're saying with these wows is that he'd be happy to come out here?"

"Over the moon," she said.

"It's settled, then?" John said, running a hand over his scalp. "You'll ask Bryan?"

"I'll ask Bryan. I can't guarantee—"

"Here," he said, pulling out a folded sheet of paper, "I have all the info Bryan needs right here. People, dates, times . . . looks like the eight thirty tour on April twenty-seventh."

Kendra took the paper, perused it. On the first page, in caps, were three names—Victor Dunlap, Jane Roth, Jaidee Charoensuk—followed by a blank line under which was the word "alternate." Kendra read over the names again. "Jaidee Charoensuk?" she said. Her mouth went dry.

"Yeah?" John said.

"Is he from Des Moines as well?"

"He's actually from Thailand, of all places," John said, grinning. "But he's a student at UNL."

"A student," she said, biting her lip. "I mean, is Jaidee a common Thailand name?"

John shrugged. "How should I know?"

"Bryan has a roommate," Kendra said, feeling her insides bunch up.

"Yeah?" John said, staring at the driveway.

"His roommate is named Jaidee."

"I don't make the teams," he said.

"They're not the best of friends," she said.

John exhaled. "Be persuasive," he said, leaning close to her, drilling holes into her head with his sharp gray stare. "I know you can be. I know you've got skills."

"I'll try," Kendra said.

"You do that, Kendra Brown," he said. "You do that, and we'll all be A-okay."

A week later, after Bryan and she had dinner with Rae and Lynette, Kendra told him about John's proposal.

They sat in her room on her bed while she rehashed John's plan. The further she got into it, however, the more his face squirmed, and when she finally finished, showing him the papers that contained Jaidee's name, he said, "No. Fuck no."

"But why not?" Kendra said. She leaned back on her pillow, crossed her arms. It was a Tuesday, after school; the dying sunlight drew long orange lines across the white carpet. Bryan sat at the foot, one leg tucked in, one dangling over the side. Kendra thought he looked uncomfortable.

"You know my take on that shitshow," he said.

"But you don't *get* it," she said. "It's almost certain that you'll get the money! John himself told me as much."

Bryan shook his head. "He's gonna rig it?"

"It's a business decision," she said. "All the major attractions do it. And no, he's not gonna *rig* it. You'd still have to go through it. But you'd have advantages. Major ones. And think about it, Bryan. You'd make fifteen grand just for an hour or so of running around."

"But why me?" Bryan said. "Why would he single me out?"

"He knows you're athletic," she said. "He knows

you'd have a good chance of actually getting through. He knows that it wouldn't look weird if you got through, *because* you're athletic."

"And how do you know what he's thinking?" Bryan said. He stood up.

"We talk," she said. "Like, all the time."

He paced the length of the bed. "Fifteen grand, huh?" he said.

"Think what you could use that money for," Kendra said, her heart in her throat. "You could get your car fixed. You could help Rae out. You could pay off your credit card. You could take Simone on a vacation or something. You two are back together, right?" she said. "I mean, you're over there—"

"It's complicated," he said. "But Jesus. Quigley House?"

"Who knows," Kendra said. "It could be fun."

"But Jaidee?" he said. "Is that some sick fucking joke? Did you arrange it? Some sort of demented bonding exercise?"

"Think of it this way," she said, breathing deep, "you *know* him: that's a big deal in the game. Plus, he complements your height—there's bound to be challenges that require a range of sizes. And really, when else will you ever get to watch him get bruised?"

Bryan smiled, sat back down. "You've been practicing that," he said.

She shrugged. "Maybe, maybe not."

"Why do you even care so much?" he said. "You think I'm gonna share the money?"

"Well, I can't keep riding Rae's Schwinn all over town," she said.

"That's it?" he said.

"No," she said, shaking her head, picking at some fluff on her comforter. "No, that's not all of it. There's something bigger, I guess. Weird to say, but Quigley means something to me now."

"Well, damn. Kendra Brown!" Bryan said, laughing. "Are you getting sentimental about a part-time job? You with all your sullen counterculture ways? You're having strong *feelings* about something?"

"Oh, fuck off," she said, smiling. "I have plenty of feelings."

"Is there a boy?" he said. "Or a girl? I don't judge. But don't tell me it's one of those carny-lookin' white dudes from Quigley."

"No," she said, thinking of Shawn, thinking of him on top of her, pressing down, his hot breath on her neck, telling her he thought of her all the time. Camille had told her it would hurt, but that it'd be a good hurt, a *necessary* hurt. *Just make sure he knows how to put on a fucking condom,* she'd said. *My first got it backwards and we had, you know, that scare, which completely dampens the magic.*

"Well," Bryan said, "I don't know."

"I need to know," Kendra said.

"I know, I know," Bryan said. "It's just that—"

"You don't have to do it," she said, feeling suddenly somber. "You don't *have* to. I mean, I keep thinking about my dad, what he'd say. He'd think it was all a big joke. He'd probably think *I* was a big joke, doing this, caring about this."

"Hey," Bryan said. "Hey now."

Kendra looked at Bryan, realizing, with a flutter in her chest, that the mention of her father had instantly turned him serious. She wiped her eyes, sniffled, hugged her pillow, tried to drum up more explicit emotion. Bryan grabbed her foot, massaged it. "You're fine," he said. "You'll be fine."

"He would've, though," she said, leaning into the drama. "He would've thought this was a big stupid joke."

Bryan bit his lip, sighed. He leaned forward, rested his elbows on his legs. "Hey," he said. "Remember when we first went to Quigley? After we talked to John and saw the costume room and everything?"

Kendra nodded.

"Well, you asked me if I thought your dad was a good person, and I've been meaning to get back to you on that." He stretched his arms to the sides, breathed in deep. "I couldn't answer that right then because I didn't know, you know? I mean, on the one hand, he was sort of a shit to you and your mom. But on the other hand . . ." He paused, looked at Kendra with glassy eyes. "You know right after the acquittal of those four cops in the Rodney King beating, he called me? Yeah. The riots were starting. He was nervous. But he called me. I was like, what, seventeen? Everything sucked—school, friends, everything. I didn't know what was going on with my life. But that call, that call changed me."

"What did he say?" Kendra said, wiping her nose.

"He said a lot of things, most of which went over my head, to be honest. But what stuck with me was when he started crying—like, *sobbing,* Kendra—and he said, 'I do what I do because someday you'll be him, and someday Kendra'll be him, and I can't stop that, but I can try as hard as I can to make people hate it. That's what I can do.'"

"Wow," Kendra said.

"And I thought about that for weeks and weeks, about being Rodney King, about making people hate it, and it depressed the shit out of me, because how the *fuck* would anyone have to *make someone hate that shit*? How the fuck could a human being watch that video and not feel anything but fucking revulsion? Why would an *attorney* have to dedicate his life to making people hate something that is the embodiment of hate? What kind of world is that, Kendra, where that happens?"

Kendra shook her head. She really *was* thinking of her father now. She really *was* missing him. She felt a pang of regret for what she'd done, using him like she had. She said, "Bryan, listen, you don't have to—"

"Your dad wasn't a good man," Bryan said. "He was a complicated man. He was a principled man. He was a fucking brilliant man. But good? How can anyone be *good* when *good* and *bad* are defined by people who've categorized you as *bad* since the dawn of time? What I'm saying is fuck that question about goodness, okay? Just fuck that question."

They sat silently for a while. It had gotten dark, but they remained in the room, only a small band of light seeping in from beneath the door. Bryan stretched out his legs.

"But Quigley House," Bryan said, standing up. He let out a long breath. "Sure. Why not."

"Bryan—" Kendra said.

"You probably shouldn't say anything now, otherwise I might change my mind. Just get me the application, okay? And get me all the information you have. I'll talk to Jaidee. It'll be okay. Fifteen grand is fifteen grand."

He smiled against the dark, walked over to the door, and left the room.

* * *

In the Quigley House parking lot a few weeks later, dressed as a giant fly, Kendra guided her cousin and his roommate into the parking lot. The moment they parked, Christy rapped on the window, waved coyly.

"I know you," she said. She was in a black-and-red cheerleader outfit, the skirt ending just below her pubic bone. She'd painted blood on her legs. "You know my sister, Alicia."

"Alicia?" Bryan said. He stepped out of the car.

"Alicia Bladensburg."

"Oh. Yeah, I know her sorta."

Christy smiled, patted his arm. "I can't believe you're gonna do this. It's *crazy* in there."

"He's gonna win," Kendra said. She looked skeptically at Jaidee, who climbed out of the car. The guy was exactly as she'd pictured him: small, smug, distant.

He was dressed in khaki shorts and a red Abercrombie T-shirt, and he didn't introduce himself, just looked out toward the road. "He's gonna be famous," Kendra said, keeping her eyes on her cousin's roommate.

"So this is what you do," Bryan said. "Just stand out here in a costume."

"Yep," Kendra said. "We're not supposed to talk."

"At least he's paying you."

"It's not so bad."

They stood for a while longer. Jaidee rocked back and forth. Kendra thought he had an impatient face, creases joining at erratic angles. She wanted to go to him, sit him down, tell him that the world would be easier to navigate if he just stopped trying so hard.

"Be careful," Kendra said, embracing her cousin. The fly-hair on her arms scratched his neck, and the eyes, which took up half her face, bumped into his cheek as he knelt down to hug her.

"Positive thoughts," Bryan said, thrusting his fist victoriously in the air. "Win, win, win!" He looked at his cousin, grinned, said, "You know, I'm *excited* for this shit now. Never thought I'd be in this position, but why the fuck not? We're gonna win some money. We're gonna go *earn* that dough."

Christy laughed. "Just remember that no matter how intense it gets, everyone survives."

"Well, *that's* a good pep talk," Bryan said. "Hey, Jaidee, you hear that? Everyone survives!"

Jaidee turned around, looked at the group, frowned, turned back to the road.

"He's preparing," he said, tapping his temple. "He doesn't rev up like me. He's more, how do you call it, cerebral?"

"Well, good luck," Sarah said. She'd been standing a bit behind the group. Her outfit—a vampire in a black veil—leaked blood, and she didn't want anyone to get dirty prematurely.

"Thanks," Bryan said. "But we don't need the luck. We got the *skill.* Jaidee and me, we're gonna *obliterate* this shit."

"The others are already here," Kendra said. "They came a little early. They should be up at the house already."

"Well, okay then," Bryan said, drawing in a deep breath. He looked over at Jaidee. "You ready?"

"Yeah," Jaidee said, his voice small. "Let's get this over with."

"That's the spirit right there," Bryan said, winking at Kendra. He bent down, hugged her again. "I got this," he whispered into her ear. "Don't worry. I got this." Kendra pulled back, touched her cousin's cheek, then pushed him on down the road, smiling.

"Don't you dare come back without that fifteen grand," she called to him as he walked with Jaidee. "Don't even *think* about it!"

The shed smelled strongly of cinnamon that day—Cory had made a fresh pot of cider, and along with the scented candles, it infused the room with the feeling of autumn though it was late spring. Kendra poured herself a cup, sat on the couch, sipped, thought about her cousin and Jaidee racing around the cells, trying to avoid traps, shock wands, dowels. It seemed impossible that the people with whom she'd danced during the end-of-season party would now be responsible for a family member's wounds. It seemed ludicrous. *They'd better take it easy. They still have to work with me here.*

She thought about the money. Fifteen thousand dollars was a lot. It could certainly buy a round-trip plane ticket from D.C. to Lincoln. Maybe she wouldn't even *have* to take John up on his offer. Maybe it'd be better that way, if Bryan just gave her a cut. Of course, she'd have to then tell him about Shawn (if her mother hadn't already), and he'd tease her endlessly about having a horror-loving boyfriend (*He's* perfect *for you,* Bryan would say. *You can slice your wrists together and mix your blood in a pentagram and shit*), and that'd be annoying, but it felt better than having John in control.

Not that she didn't trust John (who'd, strangely, had to make an emergency run up to Omaha and would miss her cousin's tour), but something about the transaction seemed off to her. Something didn't settle right.

She inhaled the cider's steam, relishing the herbs. Sarah and Christy were out in the lot, talking about something or other. She didn't care. She liked being alone. She closed her eyes, envisioned the conversation she'd have with Shawn.

Bryan won, she'd say.

No fucking way, he'd respond.

Yep, she'd say. *And he's giving me some of the prize.*

Are you serious?

Guess what I'm doing with my share?

What?

Well, that depends. Do you mind coach?

Of course, Rae wouldn't like it, would tell her that there were better things to spend her money on, more helpful things, but fuck her. There wouldn't have *been* this money without Kendra, so if she wanted to spend it on a boy, she would spend it on a boy. Bryan would certainly give Rae some of it anyway. Her aunt didn't have to worry about her.

She set her cider on the table. She was tired. Maybe she'd take a short nap. Just a few minutes. Nobody would care. Nothing was happening anyway. Everything would be fine. This was a good day. And it was about to get even better, she just knew it.

She awoke to the sounds of screaming. She sat up, thinking, for a moment, that she was back in the apartment. "Mom?" she said. She looked around, saw the chairs, the food table, the pot of cider, remembered. "Shit," she said, heart thumping, thinking she'd missed the contestants' return. "Bryan," she said. She leaped off the couch, ran out of the shack, and found Christy on the ground, grabbing her leg. Sarah was crouched next to her.

"Should I call 911?" Sarah shouted.

"What?" Kendra said. Sarah looked up at her, pleading. On the ground, Christy writhed.

"I can't move it!" Christy shouted. "I can't move my fucking foot!"

Kendra breathed in the night air. Did they think they were going to get her again? This soon? It'd only been a few months since the last time. "Your foot, huh?" Kendra said. "Might want to try your upper body next time, mix it up."

"I'm gonna go get ice," Sarah said.

"Ice?" Kendra said, smiling. "She'll get frostbite."

"*Kendra,*" Sarah said, throwing her a deep, penetrating stare. "We're not fucking around."

Kendra's mouth dried. She thought it was a bit messed up that they were staging this in the middle of her cousin's tour. It seemed very rude.

"Okay, fine," Kendra said, rolling her eyes. "What happened?"

"Just stay with her, okay?" Sarah raced to the shack.

Kendra knelt down. "Where are you *hurt,* Christy?" she said.

"I twisted my ankle, I think," she said, panting. "Kendra, you gotta CB the house."

"Your right ankle? This ankle here?" Kendra touched it, pressed down hard. Christy howled.

"What the *fuck,* Kendra?"

Kendra stepped back. She hadn't expected such an ear-splitting reaction.

"Kendra!" Christy said. Her hair obscured half of her face. "Get on your CB! You need to warn them!"

"What?"

"You need to call up there!"

"Call up where?" Kendra said. She looked where she'd pressed on Christy's ankle. It was swollen, puffy, at an odd angle from her shin. There were prosthetics in the costume room, but she hadn't seen Christy put one on, and usually those took time. She would've noticed. "You're fucking with me, right?" she said.

"Hurry up!" Christy said.

Kendra pulled out her CB from the fly costume's left leg compartment. She pushed the orange button, said, "Hello?"

Static.

"Hello?" Kendra said. "Hello? Hey, you guys. Don't you have things to do? My cousin is up there."

"Kendra!" Christy screamed.

Kendra's chest tightened. Something wasn't right. That ankle. That bruising. And something in Christy's voice. Her head spun. "We need help here?" Kendra said into the CB. "Christy's . . . hurt?"

"Kendra?" It was Cory. "Kendra. What's happening?"

Kendra didn't respond, just handed the CB to Christy.

"Cory," Christy said, breathless. "There's a blue pickup. It just raced down the street. I tried to wave it down, but it didn't stop. I jumped out of the way, must've landed wrong."

"A blue pickup?" Kendra said.

"He's up there now," Christy said. "He wouldn't stop."

"Shit," Cory said. "I'll send medical down."

"Some lunatic," Christy said. "Just watch out." She handed the CB back to Kendra.

Sarah returned, her breath coming out in short rasps. She knelt down, held an ice pack to Christy's ankle. "It'll be okay," she said.

"Cory?" Kendra said into the CB. Something below

her stomach was scratching at her. It was the same scratch she'd felt right after the police had come to their house, told her about her dad's accident. "I don't think this is funny," Kendra said. "Tell John that I don't think this is fucking funny at all."

"Stay put," Cory said. "Just stay put."

"I'm coming up there," Kendra said, thinking once again about Bryan whipping through the cells, dodging her coworkers, getting shocked, punched, struck. "Sarah's here," she said. "I'm coming up there."

"Just stay put!" Cory said.

"Sorry," Kendra said.

She threw the CB next to Christy, tore off the fly costume, and ran.

Outside the house was the pickup truck, glossy and smooth against the early night stars. Breathless, sweaty, she shouted, "*Cory!*" Kendra rushed inside the main house, shouted again. Nobody answered. The house was deathly quiet; it looked strangely hollow without people, the tables and chairs and lamps and rugs all seeming to fade into one empty yellow-red dome. She ran upstairs to the control room. The door was wide open. Nobody was inside. She walked in, heard all her exhalations, all her footfalls. Thirty black-and-white screens blinked back at her, the top row snowed-out.

She looked.

Each screen with images was uninhabited except for screens 21–24. These screens were marked CELL 5.

"Shit," Kendra said, looking at a center monitor.

A tall, long-faced man stood in the center of the cell, pressing the blade of a knife to Bryan's neck. Around him were actors in various stages of costume along with crew members and the other contestants. It looked, Kendra thought, like a Halloween party.

"Just punch him or something," Kendra said, staring at Bryan. "Can't you tell that the knife is plastic?"

But was it? She thought of Christy's ankle, twisted and swollen. She thought of Sarah's eyes, crazed and panicked, and the blue pickup, shining bright against the moonlight. She thought of Cory's voice: *Stay put.*

Kendra searched for an intercom button. None was marked. She pushed random buttons and screens 4, 5, and 6 turned to snow. "Fuck," she said.

"Listen, sir." Cory's voice came from the center monitor, number 22. Kendra raced to it, put her hands all over the screen. "We've called John. He's on his way. But in the meantime, what can I do for you?"

"I need John!" the man said, his voice rough. He pulled Bryan closer, choking him.

"He's coming," Cory said. He inched closer to the man.

"Stay back," the man said.

"Okay, okay," Cory said, stopping. "But I need to know what you want."

The man spat. Kendra thought it looked strange, like he'd practiced spitting in front of a mirror or something. He was a bad actor. He rested on melodrama. Her shoulders relaxed.

"Please," Cory said. "If you could just put down the knife."

Maybe this was all for her? she thought. This big, elaborate show? But it didn't seem like John to waste so many resources just to trick her. And how would he have known that she'd run up to the control room, that she wouldn't listen to Cory and stay put?

On screen 22 was a zoom button and a small joystick. Kendra pushed the button and angled the joystick toward her cousin's face. It was a gory mess, blood splashed everywhere but his eyes and mouth. Sweat rained down his cheeks. He breathed in chunks, every inhalation pressing the knife blade closer to his throat. "Christ, Bryan," she whispered. "Just kick him or something. Just elbow him in the gut. He's harmless. Look at him. You can take him." But maybe he wasn't allowed to attack? John had told her that in most cells an attack by a contestant meant immediate disqualification. But then: What was he supposed to do? Just stand there while his teammates gawked? It didn't seem fair.

She looked at his lips. They were moving. She couldn't make out what he said.

She angled the camera around to the crowd, found Jaidee and the other two contestants, all slimy and panting. They stood a few feet from Cory, whispering. She zoomed in.

"It's part of it?" the white guy, Victor, said. "It seems pretty real."

The woman, Jane, shook her head. "Maybe?"

Victor looked at Bryan, squinted. "Where would the envelopes be? On the dude with the knife?"

Yes, Kendra thought. *Obviously he has the envelopes.*

"It makes sense," Jaidee said. "They couldn't expect us to find them in the dark like that, right?"

"But time's been up for a while."

"No," Jaidee said, gesturing to the west wall. "Look."

Kendra looked at monitor 25, the scoreboard with the countdown clock. It said 3 min, 22 sec. She looked back at Bryan, saw that the drops rolling down his cheeks weren't sweat—they were tears. He's afraid? she thought. Like, genuinely? She zoomed the camera onto the blade at his neck. The knife, now just a gray, pixelated blob on the screen, pressed at the surface of a large, dark mass. It was difficult to determine if it was doing any damage: the camera image was too grainy, and Bryan was covered in so much fake blood that all the darker spots looked the same. She squinted, put her face up to the monitor. The knife-blob wobbled; one end looked slightly darker than the other. She got closer. There was something happening. From the one edge of the gray mass, a thin stretch of dark now streaked. It wasn't clumpy like the rest of the patches, but tiny and narrow, like a crack on the screen. She zoomed out, looked at Bryan's face, gasped.

"Oh my god," she said, feeling dizzy, unsteady, short of breath. "Oh my god."

"This is the *last cell* before the final," Victor was saying. "Isn't it a little convenient that this happens when we're so close?"

"Guys." It was Bryan this time. "Guys. Please. Don't do anything dumb. I think this is real. I feel—"

"Are you a part of it, Bryan?" Victor said, his nostrils flaring. "You're the alternate. You were picked *by* Quigley. Are you a part of all of it? Getting us this far and making us lose?"

"Stop talking!" the knife guy said. With his left hand, he felt along Bryan's neck—pinching, scratching—before resuming his bear hug.

"This was all planned?" Jane said.

"Guys," Cory said. "This isn't part of the game. Please. Trust me."

Kendra stood paralyzed, her hand stuck to the joystick, her eyes fastened to the blade and the blood. She knew she needed to do something. She needed to shout, run down to the cell, save her cousin, but right then, she couldn't move, could hardly breathe.

"Of course you'd say that now," Victor said. "But the clock is still running."

Cory looked at the clock, shook his head. "We forgot to turn it off," he said.

"Convenient," Victor said.

Kendra concentrated. She slowly peeled her fingers from the joystick. If she could just focus on small things, one at a time, she could make it down to the main stairs. She could call the police. She could CB Sarah and Christy. She could get help. Then she could run to Cell Five, maybe sneak behind the guy. Maybe—

"I'm not buying it," Victor said, his voice low. "This guy's a lousy actor and it doesn't add up. We're right there. *Right there*. Just through that door. The envelopes *have* to be on him."

"Guys," Bryan said, his voice hollow. "Guys, no."

"Everyone, shut up!" the knife guy said.

"Just put the knife down," Cory said. "Everything will be fine. We'll get you money. We'll get you whatever you need."

"This is hokey bullshit," Victor said, looking at the clock. It read 1 min, 3 sec. He turned to Jaidee, bent down close. "Listen," he said. "We can still do this. We'll do it together."

No! Kendra thought, regaining her breath. *No!*

"No," Jane said. "Listen, we're done. Let's not. We can't—"

"What do you want me to do?" Jaidee said.

"I rush the back, grab the knife. You check his pockets," Victor said. "The guy doesn't look that strong."

"Guys," Jane said.

"But all these people," Jaidee said.

"They're not doing anything," Victor said. "It's a game. They're actors. Enough talk. We're almost out of time."

"*NO!*" Kendra shouted, her limbs fully animated now. She pushed every button she could, trying to find an intercom. "*NO, NO, NO!*"

Victor rushed forward. Cory raced over to him, stood in his way, pushed him back.

"What the fuck are you doing?" Cory said.

"Jaidee, *RUN!*" Victor said.

Jaidee weaved around Victor and Cory, ran toward the man with the knife. Cory turned, shouted, "Hey!"

Jane said, "Jaidee! Wait!"

"*JAIDEE, NO!*" Kendra cried. "*NO, NO, NO, NO, NO!*"

Victor shoved Cory as hard as he could. Cory lost his balance, fell to the ground.

"REPRIEVE!" Bryan shouted. "REPRIEVE!"

The knife man smiled down at Jaidee right as he made contact. "Gotcha," he said, and sliced.

The world went mute. On the screen, Kendra saw Jaidee run toward her cousin. She saw Cory's mouth become a long, horrified O. She saw the actors' and crew members' eyes distend, the knife man's face contort into a long bundle of creases, his mouth open. The knife man smiled, and Jaidee's face, suddenly, was dotted with black specks. He stopped running. His jaw fell.

Kendra's paralysis returned. Around her, more monitors had turned to snow, all shouting *Shhhhhhhhhhhhh.*

On monitor 22, her cousin choked, hitched, sputtered. His neck oozed, the black torrent falling carelessly to the floor. He extended his arms. Jaidee shouted and stepped back. The knife man released Bryan. Bryan took a step. Then another. Then another. He reached for Jaidee. Jaidee grabbed him as he collapsed.

Kendra screamed. Her legs gave out. She fell to the floor, shivering. Her arms slid to her sides. Not happening, she thought. Not happening not happening not happening. She thought about Bryan at Holmes Lake, turning to her, his face etched with concern, saying, *We're always gonna be here, no matter what.* She thought, Not happening not happening not happening.

Behind her, from the screen, she heard the knife man say, "Welcome to show business!" She looked up at the monitor, saw him run out the door.

Next to Bryan's bleeding body, everyone hovered. Cory knelt down. Victor knelt down. Jane knelt down. Jaidee knelt down. They touched his face. "Bryan," Cory said, "just hold on." Victor touched his wound; Jane batted his hand away. Blood poured onto the concrete in black streams.

"It's not real," Victor said. "It's not real."

Jaidee put his hands on his roommate's chest.

And Kendra, finally mustering some strength, stood, raced out of the room, down the stairs, outside to the haunt entrance, past the giant bleeding baby, down more stairs, and on to Cell Five, where she fell instantly once again into paralysis, watching as the contestants, the crew, the actors, hovered around her cousin. Her body cold and numb, she slunk into the wall by the outer door, the door she'd nearly rushed to with a fake-injured Christy. From somewhere distant she heard Cory's voice: *Kendra! Kendra, go back up-*

stairs! She closed her eyes, exhaled, thought of Bryan in her bedroom, telling her that her father wasn't a good man but a complicated, principled, brilliant man. She thought of Bryan at her dad's funeral, telling her that goth shit was for white losers, that she needed to be there more for Lynette. She thought of Bryan at home, sitting at the dinner table, twinkling his eyes at her as her mother and Rae fought about something ridiculous, something trivial. These thoughts, in their aggregate, broke her stupor, opened her eyes, propelled her forward through the mess of people she'd come to know as friends, who now represented foreignness and unfamiliarity, and with each step, the illusion of Quigley House cracked and crumbled, encircling her with years and years of immutable treachery. When she got to Bryan, on the ground, flanked by Jaidee, Victor, Jane, Cory, her entire body filled with a twisted, tangled, writhing horror, and she let out a terrific scream, finally understanding what her father had meant all those years ago when he'd pointed so intensely at the television.

You watch this, Kendra, he'd said. *This is the world we live in.*

Witness
John Forrester

Cross-Examination Excerpt
September 17, 1997

Q. Mr. Forrester, where were you the night of the incident?

A. I was in Omaha. My mother hadn't been feeling well.

Q. Is it common for you to be away during business hours?

A. Business hours? We don't have things like that. But during a tour, is it common? No. But it does happen from time to time. I have a competent management team.

Q. Did you communicate with your management team that night?

A. Yes, regularly.

Q. Right. Phone records indicate that Cory Stout called you at 8:42 P.M., 8:57 P.M., 9:05 P.M., and 9:25 P.M. All these times coincide with the times contestants completed a cell, right?

A. Yes.

Q. Mr. Forrester, were you aware that my client received a call from an anonymous number at 9:26 P.M.?

A. Only after the cops told me.

Q. Was this call from you?

A. No.

Q. But you have to admit, it's a little coincidental. You'd been updated on the contestants' progress throughout the night, and Leonard then gets a call as soon as they hit Cell Five.

A. Is it coincidental? I don't know. I was just doing my job.

Q. And Leonard knew about the hidden hall flanking the side of the basement, right? The one the actors use to go between cells?

A. Yes. As I said, I'd given him a tour in January.

Q. And according to the video footage, Leonard went right for the door to Cell Five.

A. That seems to be what happened.

Q. So how is it that he got tipped off that the contestants were in that cell? Who would even know that but you?

A. Everyone in the control room knew it. All the actors knew it. But that's irrelevant too. Nobody from Quigley made that call. I really can't answer that question because I just don't know.

Q. Leonard also sent an email to you at 9:16 P.M. Were you aware of this?

A. Not until the cops brought it up. I'm afraid I don't check my email as often as I should.

Q. Here's a copy of the email. Can you read it, please?

A. Sure. It says, "You gonna call me?"

Q. Right. He sent this message ten minutes before he received the anonymous call. Fifteen minutes later he was in your house.

A. Yes. But as I've said before, Leonard had been obsessing about me for a while. He'd been calling the house nonstop. We had to block him. It makes sense that he'd email me too.

Q. But that's the only email on record we have between you two.

A. We usually spoke by phone. When that got cut off, he moved to email. It's not that difficult to figure out.

Q. Mr. Forrester, you said that at one point you and the defendant were close.

A. We were friendly, yes.

Q. So friendly that you helped organize a trip for him to Thailand.

A. I did that as a favor, yes. He was stressed, as I've said. It wasn't overly burdensome. Just a few calls.

Q. And there he met and fell in love with a Thai prostitute.

A. Yes.

Q. Did you at some point tell him that you could bring this woman, this Boonsri Pitsuwana, to the United States?

A. I did not.

Q. So in a conversation at Pete's Bar and Grill on March thirteenth you did not tell him that you'd met up with her in Bangkok, that you'd promised to bring her over if he'd do you a favor?

A. That's ludicrous. I haven't been to Thailand in five years.

Q. But you *were* at Pete's on March thirteenth, with Leonard?

A. Yeah. That's the last time we talked.

Q. And do you remember what you talked about?

A. I told him that I thought we should stop hanging out. He wasn't too happy about that. I've already discussed this.

Q. So you didn't *tell* him to storm out of the bar that night?

You didn't *tell* him to make a scene? You didn't *tell* him a plan that included him calling the Quigley House, acting obsessed, all in exchange for bringing his new girlfriend to America?

A. No. Do you realize how insane that sounds?

Q. Mr. Forrester, you spend hours choreographing each cell, is that right?

A. I do. Along with my team.

Q. And how often do your actors practice?

A. It depends on our schedule. During the season, every day, for at least a couple hours.

Q. But this was an off-season tour.

A. Yes.

Q. So how often did the actors practice?

A. I treated it like regular season. They practiced every day, for at least a couple hours beforehand.

Q. In fact, they practiced more than that. In fact, they practiced for this particular tour for three hours, five days per week for two weeks. Is that right? I'm going by your own payroll hours.

A. If that's what payroll says.

Q. But why would they have to practice *more* than regular season? What was so important about this *off-season* tour?

A. Every tour is important. We practice for safety reasons. It's important. One slip-up can be bad.

Q. But again, why was this *particular* tour so important?

A. It wasn't. I mean, not any more important than the others.

Q. And yet the actors were required to practice longer hours.

A. We had some hiccups. Really, you're reading into something that's not there.

Q. I see. Mr. Forrester, can you describe how you and your staff choreographed Cell Five?

A. Of course. Cell Five is our largest cell. It has four individual jail cells with iron bars. It's completely dark. The actors wear night-vision masks and guide the contestants away from the walls, making sure they don't hit their heads.

Q. And how do they guide them?

A. Shock wands.

Q. So if a contestant gets too close to the wall, they get shocked?

A. Essentially, yes. It's for safety.

Q. But what's so unsafe about walls, Mr. Forrester?

A. We don't want them running into them.

Q. I see. Go on.

A. After three minutes, the actors grab the individual contestants and drag them to one of the four jail cells.

Q. And how large is each jail cell?

A. Ten by twenty.

Q. Feet.

A. Yes, of course.

Q. Enclosed on all four sides?

A. One side is metal bars.

Q. And yet you were afraid of contestants running into walls?

A. It's a more enclosed space. Less damage if they do.

Q. Strange logic, but go on.

A. We have two actors per jail cell. They split duties: one taunts, one observes. The observer makes sure nothing gets too out of hand.

Q. And yet, on April 27, Jaidee Charoensuk gave Craig Sanford a black eye.

A. Yes, that was unfortunate.

Q. Okay, Mr. Forrester. So all four contestants are in their jail cell getting *taunted,* as you say. How long does this go on?

A. It goes on for as long as it goes on, until time runs out or one person yells reprieve.

Q. So they're just getting shocked and hit and terrorized in these cells?

A. I suppose. The contestants can fight back in this scenario. They sort of have to. The envelopes are in the actors' pockets.

Q. So actors can expect things like black eyes here.

A. It happens. It happened. Everyone knows what they're getting into.

Q. So you said that it goes on until time runs out or someone yells the safe word. Why, then, did Bryan Douglas's jail cell unlock prematurely?

A. I don't know. I told you, we'd been having technical glitches.

Q. But during your planning, you'd arranged for Bryan to be in the southwest jail cell, the cell with the "technical glitches."

A. Yes. But it wasn't purposeful in the way you're suggesting.

Q. And my client, heading straight for Cell Five after he broke in, knew somehow that one person would be free from their jail cell.

A. I don't know what Leonard Grandton was thinking.

Q. Well, let's take a look again at the footage. Here's the cell. Jaidee's in the northeast jail, Jane's in the northwest, Victor's in the southeast, and Bryan's in the southwest. Let's fast-forward a bit. Okay. There. Bryan's now out. He's the only one. And your actors, Mitch Slattery and Corbin Quick, they're checking the jail locks instead of rushing after him.

A. They were puzzled. You've already heard from them.

Q. And then the door opens. And look, Mr. Forrester. Leonard just stands there, as if waiting for someone to come to *him*.

A. I have no idea what was going through Leonard's mind.

Q. And almost as soon as Bryan gets to Leonard, the lights come on, and Bryan's momentarily blinded.

A. It looks that way.

Q. Talk about choreography!

A. Yeah. Okay.

Q. But Leonard's not blinded, because he hasn't been in the dark all that time. So he can overpower someone who he clearly wouldn't be able to overpower if things had been equal.

A. I know what you're implying. It's absurd. And you know it.

Q. Do I?

A. I wasn't there.

Q. And it looks like you didn't have to be.

A. You're really grasping for straws here, aren't you?

Q. Mr. Forrester, I'm going to ask you a series of questions now, and all you have to do is answer yes or no. Okay?

A. Fine.

Q. Does the Quigley House have prosthetic necks, moldings that go over someone's real neck?

A. Yes. We have prosthetic everything.

Q. And are these prosthetics filled with fake blood?

A. Yes. Usually.

Q. Do the prosthetics feel like real skin?

A. Yes.

Q. And did you tell Leonard Grandton that Bryan would be wearing one of these necks?

A. Of course not. I never told Leonard anything.

Q. Was Bryan wearing one of these necks?

A. No.

Q. Okay. Do you know how long it takes to get from Leonard's apartment to your house?

A. No.

Q. Have you ever been to Leonard Grandton's apartment?

A. No.

Q. Have you ever driven from Leonard Grandton's apartment to the Quigley House?

A. No.

Q. Do you know where Leonard Grandton lives?

A. No.

Q. Please look at this photo. Do you see your car in it?

A. Yes.

Q. And where is your car?

A. It looks like the corner of Fifty-Third and Orchard.

Q. Can you read the date on the photo?

A. Looks like March thirtieth.

Q. And once again, you aren't aware of where Leonard Grandton lives.

A. No.

Q. Interesting, since he lives at Fifty-First and Orchard, just two blocks away, and we have no record of your car anywhere near that vicinity on any days before March thirteenth, the day you met him at Pete's. We also don't have any record of your car near that vicinity on any days after April twentieth. Why is that?

A. I have no idea. I drive a lot around Lincoln, obviously.

Q. So you're saying it's just coincidence.

A. I guess.

Q. So many coincidences, don't you think?

A. Life is a big coincidence, isn't it?

Q. Mr. Forrester, what's the future of Quigley House look like?

A. Unfortunately, we're closing.

Q. Why?

A. Really? You have to ask?

Q. Oh, because of what happened?

A. Yes.

Q. But weren't you considering closing before?

A. No. Not sure where you heard that, but it's false.

Q. Right here, in this *Fright Night* article dated December 12, 1995. Can you read the highlighted lines?

A. Of this cheap trash tabloid?

Q. Please, Mr. Forrester.

A. Fine. "The Quigley House had their worst season yet, and John Forrester, the proprietor, has decided that if next season doesn't bring in major revenue, he may shutter his doors forever." I never said this. These media hounds twist every damn word.

Q. But it's true: the Quigley House was struggling, right?

A. "Struggling" is harsh. We were going through a small

slump. Not a big deal. We remained successful by industry standards.

Q. But according to your quarterly earnings statements, you'd been losing money steadily for the past three years.

A. As I said, a small slump. Three years is nothing in the grand scheme of things.

Q. Mr. Forrester, you'd mentioned earlier that you were concerned with legacy, that because you had no children to bequeath the house to, you decided to develop this attraction, to make the legacy the house.

A. Yeah, I said that.

Q. And isn't infamy a way to continue on a legacy?

A. This house was my life. You don't understand what you're talking about.

Q. So you must have some strong feelings about closing.

A. It tears me apart to leave it like this. But how can I continue? How can I run a business knowing that it was the scene of a horrific injustice? A white man killing a Black man in cold blood.

Q. So you think this was racially motivated?

A. I have no idea what was going through Leonard's sick head. But anyway. Yes. I'm leaving the business. I'm not heartless. I think of the Douglas family every day, and Kendra. Kendra was family. It's not right. I can't stay open. And I'm offended that you'd suggest that any of this is for personal gain. You don't know what I'm leaving behind.

Q. You've announced that you're donating money. You've announced it very publicly—newspaper, radio, everywhere.

A. Yes, because I'm proud of it. The money that these four contestants would've earned, the money they would've received had Leonard not done what he'd done, it's going directly to the NAACP.

Q. And why the NAACP, Mr. Forrester?

A. Do I really need to answer that? It's not obvious? All of this isn't obvious?

Q. Let's say it's not obvious to me. Could you please answer the question?

A. I'm done. Finished.

Q. Mr. Forrester?

A. You're acting like a fool, questioning my integrity like that. You think because they let someone like you into a fancy law school that you somehow *deserve* to question me like this? I refuse—

Q. Someone like me, huh?

A. Yes, someone like you.

Q. Mr. Forrester, can you please just answer the question?

A. I've got nothing more to say. Really. You don't have a clue what you're talking about. You haven't this whole time.

Q. Interesting. Someone like me doesn't have a clue. A *woman* like me doesn't have a clue, is that what you meant to say?

A. Are we done here?

Q. Oh, Mr. Forrester. We're a long way from done. A very, very long way from done.

PART IV

2019

Jaidee

I ran.

I ran.

I moved around Victor and Cory, and I ran.

Jaidee is sitting in a restaurant in North Beach in San Francisco, a subdued Italian place on Columbus called Arpeggio. He's in the United States on business, will be meeting the next day with potential investors on a land deal. He's become an architect of some renown, though his team here cares nothing about his input: he's only here as a face, a creator, someone to lend legitimacy to the business ventures of his colleagues; he is, in other words, the talent.

Around him, sips and coughs and clinks and wisping conversation emanate, and above, lulling piano music streams, pacifying and elegant. His waiter, a young white man with a close-cropped red beard, has refilled his water three times, not because he's particularly good at his job but because the restaurant isn't that busy, and the young man seems bored, and Jaidee downs each glass in a couple gulps.

"Are you sure you wouldn't like some wine while you wait?" the waiter asks, head cocked, concerned.

Jaidee shakes his head.

He wishes he were back at his hotel, sitting in silence, or reading a book, or video-chatting with Kiet. He nearly hadn't come here, to this meeting, because Kendra Brown and he have never actually spoken face-to-face. At the trial, they hadn't made eye contact, and as soon as the verdict had been read—*guilty, guilty, guilty*—Kendra and her family had silently and swiftly exited the building. Jaidee had looked for them outside, but had only found a still parking lot, a bright-blue sky, the thrumming yawn of early-fall cicadas.

"Here's a wine menu, just in case," the bored waiter says, setting a leather-bound book on the white tablecloth. Jaidee opens it, sees a bunch of words, closes it again. From a distance, he feels the waiter's frown. He puts his elbows on the table, closes his eyes.

I ran, he thinks. I moved around Victor and Cory, and I ran.

For the last few days, the Cell Five scene has played

out every time he's closed his eyes: Leonard pressing a knife—a *real* knife—into Bryan's throat. Everyone bewildered, whispering. Bryan pleading, crying, sweating, bleeding.

Are you a part of all of it? Victor shouted. *Getting us this far and making us lose?*

Jaidee shakes his head, beckons the waiter over, opens the wine book, points to a random pinot noir, orders the bottle. The waiter says, "Good choice."

He closes his eyes again. The scene repeats. Over and over, just like it had for months after the incident, after the trial.

I ran, he thinks. I made a choice. I ran.

The moment before the running, the moment Cory steps in front of Victor, blocks his way, pushes him, and says, *What the fuck are you doing?*, the moment right after Victor's shout but before Jaidee's right foot pushes his left foot forward: that moment is a blank.

Cause and effect, he thinks. Cause. Effect. Victor. Run. Cause. Effect.

He'd told the jury that the cells had gotten to him, that all the crazy, creepy chaos had affected his thinking, his logic: by that time in the game, he'd said, he was so used to running, dodging, racing, that when he saw an opportunity, he took it, more as a reflex than anything.

The cells got to you? the defense attorney asked.

Yes, Jaidee replied. *I wasn't in my right mind.*

The wine comes; the waiter presents it, opens it, offers Jaidee a taste. It burns his throat, warms his chest. Jaidee nods. The waiter fills his glass, leaves the bottle, departs. Jaidee checks his phone.

Maybe she's not coming, he thinks, noting that it's now twenty minutes past the time they'd agreed on. Maybe she backed out.

He checks his messages. Two from Kiet. The first wishes him good luck in the meeting tomorrow. The second says, I love you.

He takes a sip of wine and thinks about his boyfriend's face—his chubby cheeks, his thin goatee, his quick, generous smile. After the trial, Jaidee hadn't wanted to stay another minute in Nebraska, so he'd bought a ticket, flown home, and enrolled in Chulalongkorn's architecture program. While there, he'd met his future boyfriend, a physical-therapy student named Kiet, and the first time they'd slept together, anxiety, dread, fear, apprehension, and all of the inadequacies he'd felt since adolescence slid smoothly off him: he slipped out of an old, dusty skin and tumbled into Kiet a new person, one who no longer felt unwanted, one who understood that while power determined the world, the world did not dictate his own personal power.

During a series of dinners, he'd told Kiet about Victor, about Lincoln, about Bryan, about the Quigley House, and Kiet listened sympathetically, sometimes nodding, sometimes shaking his head. Kiet couldn't believe that such a place as the Quigley House existed, let alone that his boyfriend had gone through it, and in the dark trenches of night, when Jaidee shivered and shook, shouting to an apparition in the dark, Kiet held Jaidee tight, cursing America for producing something that had caused his love so much trauma.

You're always safe here, Kiet told him one night, his right arm firmly grasping Jaidee's left pectoral. *Remember, always.*

Jaidee smiles at Kiet's text, sends back five heart emojis, puts his phone back in his pocket. He pours himself another glass of wine.

Cause and effect, he thinks. Victor, love. Run, Bryan: death. Cause. Effect.

But no. What had Malee said all those years back? What had she wrongly thought must come before an effect?

A command.

Yes, a command. Not love. Command. Meaning: Victor, command. Run, Bryan: death.

He shakes his head, sips his wine. Ten minutes pass.

Jaidee considers getting the check, heading back to his hotel. It'd be morning in Bangkok. He could video-chat with Kiet before Kiet starts his shift at the hospital. Jaidee flags the waiter, and right as he does, she appears, scanning the room thoughtfully. He hasn't seen her in over twenty years, but she looks the same—the spray of freckles across her cheeks, the kind but suspicious brown eyes, the short, meaty legs. She crosses her arms, heaves a long sigh, tucks her hair behind her ears. He lifts his hand in a half wave. Her face lights. She smiles. Then, as if realizing the inappropriateness of her smile, she looks away, tightens her lips.

"Yes?" the waiter says.

Jaidee has forgotten that he'd signaled him over. He shakes his head, says, "No, we'll be a bit."

"Another glass?" the waiter says.

"Yes, please," Jaidee says.

Kendra takes the seat opposite him, rests her hands on the table. They sit for a while in silence, looking at each other. Close up, Jaidee sees that she has indeed aged: two curved lines fall from the corners of her lips and purple crescents ring the bottoms of her eyes. She wears a red floral-print dress that puffs at her forearms and, on her face, a pair of smart round glasses, brown and yellow and unfailingly hip.

"It's good to see you," Jaidee says.

Kendra's face bunches up, and for a moment Jaidee fears she'll cry. Instead, however, she says, "I'm sorry I'm late. I'm such a cliché. CPT and all."

"CPT?" Jaidee says.

She shakes her head. "Truth be known, I nearly didn't come."

"I wondered if you might not," he says.

"But here I am," she says. "And here we are."

"Yeah," Jaidee says, feeling an ache in his chest. "Here we are."

He'd found her online—it hadn't been hard. She was a senior financial analyst at Maddox Bank, and her promotions had been very public, very celebrated. She wasn't on social media, but her husband was, and he was an avid poster, sharing album after album of them in various tropical locations—Cabo, Jamaica, Tahiti, Hawaii. In all the pictures, she looked cautiously happy, her smile tentative, her eyes skirting, and if Jaidee hadn't known better, he'd have thought that she harbored misgivings about her spouse, a tall, muscular Black man who'd founded a music school for underprivileged youth. In no pictures did they define the visual caricature of happy coupledom: mainly, she looked away, smiling that sensible smile while he angled the camera above, trying to get a decent shot.

Come on, babe, Jaidee imagined him saying. *Just look at the camera. Just this once.*

But she never did, and Jaidee, after a while, concluded that this had nothing to do with her husband. Jaidee himself had experienced the lingering effects of trauma: it'd become nearly impossible to confidently look anyone directly in the eye for more than a second, and it made sense that Kendra might share this condition.

Jaidee emailed. Kendra didn't respond. Jaidee emailed again. Kendra still didn't respond. Jaidee emailed a total of twenty-three times before receiving a curt, three-word response: Leave me alone. Jaidee felt encouraged by the message: it meant that she hadn't filtered him out, nor had she blocked him. He continued emailing. Finally, he told her that he had a business trip coming up in San Francisco, and knowing that she lived there with her husband, asked if she'd be willing to meet, just for a single dinner, nothing more than that—perhaps at a place called Arpeggio in North Beach? Say, 7:15 P.M. on the fifth? He'd make the reservations.

She replied: Fine. Okay.

"It's way too easy to find people nowadays," Kendra says, pouring herself a glass of wine. "Even if you don't put anything out there, other people do it for you. It's almost impossible to be left alone."

"Yeah," Jaidee says, taking the jab.

"I tell my husband this all the time, to stop being so *online,* but he won't listen, says it opens up a broader community that he needs." She shrugs, sips. "Whatever."

They sit for a while. The waiter returns, takes their order. They both get the special: ravioli. Jaidee orders another bottle of wine, thinks about his meeting the next day. It'll be good to be hungover, useless. Nobody will care. In fact, they'll like seeing him sitting there, quiet and demure. He takes a long gulp of wine, feels his face flush.

"So, what is this?" Kendra says, resting her hands in her lap. "What is this reunion about?"

"I don't know," Jaidee says. "I just thought, we were in the same city, so—"

"No," Kendra says. "Don't minimize it. Don't do that. You dredged up a bunch of shit, so don't make it seem like a pleasant and friendly hello."

"Dredged up?" he says. "Did it ever go away for you?"

She blinks, bites her lip. "That's a dumb question," she says. "You know that."

The waiter returns, shows them the bottle, gives them a taste. He pours. They drink. A handsome white couple is shown to a table a few feet away from them. *Enjoy your meals,* the host says.

"I suppose you've heard about Leonard Grandton's release," Kendra says.

"Yes," Jaidee says.

"I'll be honest," she says. "When I heard, I was okay with it. I hate him, I'll always hate him, but I also feel a little sorry for him. For someone to be so easily used . . ."

"Yeah," Jaidee says. "I know."

They fall silent. A few tables away, a phone rings. Jaidee looks over, sees a pudgy man in a dark suit gritting his teeth. *Are you gonna get that?* he says to his table mate, a young brown-haired woman in a dark-green dress. *Don't be bitchy, Dad,* the woman says, digging through her purse.

"I suppose you've also heard of John's death," Kendra says, filling her glass, sipping.

"Yes, that too," Jaidee says.

"Fitting, huh?" she says. "Stories like that really make me think there's some cosmic meaning to all this shit."

Jaidee nods. Apparently, John hadn't ever been able to recoup his losses from his haunt and had wound up working as a prep cook at a strip club in Reno. One day, as luck would have it, he'd slipped in the dry storage room, hitting his head on the moving steel cart, and toppled over a five-gallon tub of ketchup. The tub hurtled directly onto his upturned face, snapping his neck, and he'd died, the article put it, surrounded by synthetic red paste, as appropriate a death as anyone could've expected for a man like him.

"I laughed when I found out," Kendra says. "I've never laughed at anyone's misfortune in my life, but I laughed for days about that one. I mean, the guy got off, right? Nobody even investigated him. So him dying like that? Yeah. I laughed."

Jaidee nods again. He hadn't laughed, per se, but he'd felt, upon hearing the news, a sort of feathery levity. Though he'd only ever seen John from afar in the courtroom, he'd known that the man was, in some large way, the source of his constant, wretched heartache, and he couldn't have wished a more ridiculous death on anyone.

"So whatever happened to everyone else?" Kendra says. "Jane? Victor? You contact them too?"

Jaidee shakes his head. "I haven't spoken to them since the trial. I have no idea."

She fidgets with her purse, checks her phone, looks up. "Talking about this again, after all this time," she says. "My god." She pauses, looks around the room. "I'll say this: For the last two decades, I've blamed everyone. I've blamed you. I've blamed Victor. I've definitely blamed Leonard and John. I even blamed my aunt and mother. Can you believe that? They didn't even know I *worked* there, but still, I blamed my mom for dragging me out to Nebraska and Rae, well, I blamed her for just being Rae." She chuckles. "You know neither of them would talk to me for, like, six months afterward? Even now, twenty years later, there's this hesitation around me. Neither of them has been out here to visit. They barely call. They're old and all, but still." She sighs. "Anyway, I guess I blamed all of them, but the person I blamed most was myself."

"Yourself?" Jaidee says. "Why would you blame yourself?"

"I asked Bryan to go," she says, her lips broadening to a sad smile. "I begged him to go. I used my dead father to make him more *likely* to go. Isn't that terrible?"

"But that doesn't make any of it your fault," Jaidee says.

"I wanted him to win the money. I was interested in flying some stupid boy to Nebraska. It was all so silly."

"But again, that doesn't make it your fault."

"I know," she says. "I know that now. I know that

it's nobody's fault but John and Leonard's. I just have these thoughts, you know?" She pauses, runs her finger along the edge of her wineglass. "I think about what I've learned through all of this, Jaidee, through these years of piecing things together," she says. "I think of myself back then and cringe. All that horror nonsense that I loved. Thinking that those stories *meant* something, tested the limits of love. It's ridiculous that I thought that way. Love isn't meant to be wrung through all that treachery. It's not supposed to be as *hard* as we make it."

"Yes," Jaidee says, thinking of Kiet.

"I hate it now," she says. "Halloween makes me sick. Every year, I get a bellyache in October. It lasts all the way until Thanksgiving."

"I understand," Jaidee says.

She sighs. "I mean, life is the real horror, isn't it? A president who looks at guys like John and Leonard and says, 'Good guys, both of them.' Half the country defending him, and other people, well-meaning people, so shocked and horrified, thinking this is new, like this hasn't always been the reality for Black people in this country. This is the true nightmare." She looks toward the window. It's drizzling; raindrops zigzag purposefully down the glass. "You know, I went back." she says. "After I graduated high school, I went to UNL for college. It's like I'd decided I couldn't avoid the tragedy in my head, so why not get physically closer to it? Anyway. When I was in college, I took long study breaks, went to Holmes Lake and biked around alone. Bryan used to take me there, and it felt good, to be reminded of him. But it also felt awful. Because every time I went, I kept wondering what he would've become, you know? Every time I went, I thought, *Where would you be, right now, if that hadn't happened?* And it's the worst thing to think that. Really, it is."

Jaidee fidgets. He'd thought, at first, that he'd wanted to see her to reiterate his innocence, to confirm for her, in person, that he hadn't known that it was real, that he'd rushed Leonard because he'd firmly believed he was still in the game. The clock had been running. Leonard's acting had been terrible. Nobody could blame him, right? That's what everyone had thought, anyway. But over the last few years, as the scene played and replayed in his mind, he'd begun questioning what he'd known, how he'd felt, what his role had really been. Cory had blocked Victor, and Victor had said—no, had *commanded* Jaidee to run. And Jaidee had made a choice. It hadn't all been adrenaline. It hadn't all been reflex.

"You know," he says, "Bryan's friends once threatened to beat me up. Eli and Terrence? You know them?

They took me outside, gave me a sermon. They said that we should be brothers, we should be on the same team, me and them."

"The same team," Kendra says, her voice distant.

"Because we weren't white," he says. "They called me a racist. They said I wasn't white but wanted to be white. They said my desire to be white inflicted its own type of harm. They went on and on, and it was all really tough to hear, so I ignored it; I shrugged it off as nonsense. I mean, I was angry and stupid then. I didn't understand what they were saying. But I get it now. I really do. And this meeting—our meeting, you and me—it was supposed to be about one thing, a different thing, but now, even as I'm talking, that thing is changing. As I'm gathering my thoughts, I'm realizing that the purpose of this, the purpose of me pestering you, of seeing you like this, the purpose of all of this is to apologize."

"Apologize?" she says, finally looking at him. Her eyes are dark and hard. Many people have apologized to her over the years. Jaidee knows this because many people have apologized to *him* over the years. But nothing has helped. Nothing has erased Bryan from his mind or his heart, so for her, he can only imagine.

"I feel ashamed," he says, bowing his head.

"Ashamed," she says, leaning forward, her hands fastened to the table.

"Yes," he says. "But more than that. I feel responsible."

"But you didn't back then?" she says, her voice quavering. "You didn't feel responsible then?"

Jaidee shakes his head. "I don't know."

She breaks off a piece of bread, dips it, eats. "Okay, fine," she says. "Tell me why you feel responsible now."

Jaidee fumbles. Thoughts tear through him, new thoughts, thoughts that needed Kendra's presence to crystallize. He thinks of Terrence digging his finger into his chest. *What happens?* he'd said. *What happens when we splinter like this?* He thinks of sitting in his dorm room, suggesting to Bryan that Black people weren't studious. He thinks of Chris Driscoll, the blond douche who'd told Jaidee he wouldn't even pity-fuck him. And he thinks of Cell Five. Of that moment: Victor shouts, *Jaidee, RUN!* Jaidee runs.

At the table, Jaidee hitches. He's going to cry. He can feel it in his nose. But he needs to say this. He needs a release. He looks away, says: "I thought I loved Victor. I thought we were going to be together. I'd come to *Nebraska* for him. I thought that if I just did this one last thing, this Quigley thing, that he'd see my devotion. He'd see *me.* But he didn't. He'd never seen me.

He didn't even recognize me when I showed up on his doorstep. I was nothing to him." Jaidee stops, calms his rapid breaths. "I have a partner now, Kendra. We've been together a long time. He's Thai. It's easy, you know? So much easier. With Victor, I'd sacrificed—and for what? I was *invisible* to him. I didn't *matter.* But still, I continued because all I thought I ever wanted was an American boyfriend. A *white* American boyfriend. You see?" He chokes, bows his head even further. "And that's how I made my choice to run at Leonard. That's what informed it. It wasn't adrenaline. It wasn't confusion. It was a choice made under the assumption that Victor mattered and Bryan didn't." He let out a long, deflating breath. "There," he said. "That's it. That's what I had to say."

He looks at Kendra. Her face is rigid, the lines beside her mouth deep and severe. She sits silently for a moment, looking at the couple next to them, then she draws in a long, wheezing breath, and says, blinking fast, "My *god* that hurt, Jaidee. *My god.*"

"Kendra—"

She gets up, leaves the table, heads for the bathroom, and Jaidee sits alone with a half-drunk bottle of wine and a basket of bread. When the entrees arrive, Kendra's seat remains empty, and when the waiter asks if they'd like anything else, Jaidee shakes his head.

She returns ten minutes later. She stands next to the table, hovering over the steaming plate of pasta. She looks down at Jaidee, her face drawn and cheerless. "I can't do this," she says, pulling two twenties from her purse, laying them on the table. "I thought I could, but I can't."

"Okay," Jaidee says, staring down at the money.

"I can't sit here and pretend," she says. "I just can't."

"I understand," he says. The garlic from his dish pinches his nose.

"What you said . . ." She wobbles back and forth. "What you said . . ."

"I know."

She closes her eyes, clasps her hands in front of her. When she opens them, she looks resolute, determined. "Maybe someday we can finish this conversation," she says, looking down at her plate. "Maybe someday. Who knows. But not today, okay? Not today."

She pulls her purse strap over her shoulder, throws him one last glance, then leaves Arpeggio. Jaidee watches her through the window. She hurries, pulling her bag close to her. A couple blocks down, she turns, and then she's out of sight.

At the table, alone, an immense sorrow rips through Jaidee's chest. His heart beats double-time, and he thinks, for a moment, that he's going to fall forward, that his neck and shoulders will simply give out and he'll splat face-first into his plate of pasta, drowning in herbs and tomato and garlic. His hands shake; he puts them on the table. It takes him a few seconds to regain his breath.

At his hotel, Jaidee considers video-chatting Kiet, but decides against it. Kiet will be starting his shift and won't be able to talk. Feeling buzzed and crushingly sad, Jaidee pours himself another glass of wine from a bottle he bought earlier that day. He takes it to his bed, sips, allows himself to get drowsy. He thinks about Kendra, about that last meaningful glance, how her face had flamed with heartache, weariness. She'd said, *Maybe someday we can finish this conversation. Maybe someday.* He hadn't paid much attention then; he'd been too distraught. But now, in bed, near sleep, he repeats her words aloud.

"Maybe someday."

In his stomach, in his chest, a small but significant hope blooms: if she wants to speak to him, if she wants to continue, she might be able to forgive.

He sits up, adjusts his pillow. When he gets home, he determines, he'll email her. If she doesn't answer right away, he'll wait. Perhaps a month, perhaps a year.

However long, it doesn't matter—he'll continue emailing. He won't give up.

His head nods. He puts the half-drunk glass on the nightstand, lies down, hugs his pillow, closes his eyes.

In his dream, Cell One spreads out before him. Jaidee's there with Bryan, Victor, and Jane, scrambling through the cages, digging through the confetti, searching for envelopes, fending off the actors with low-throated howls. Jaidee finds every red square, much to the consternation of his fellow contestants—*Come on, J,* Victor whines, *we're a team.* Jaidee ignores him. He knows, in this world, that if he doesn't find them all, if he lets any of them discover even one, Leonard will come, and Bryan will die, so even after he's found the number the scoreboard says, he continues digging. At one point, looking outside the cage with the bleeding baby, he catches Bryan's eye. There's a knowing there, a deliberate glint that tells Jaidee that no matter what he does, no matter how many envelopes he finds, Leonard will come. Jaidee is no savior; Jaidee is no hero.

Bryan! Jaidee screams through the bars.

Bryan looks directly at him, and his face crumbles into years of blinding torment from which there's been no reprieve, and from inside the cage, Jaidee grabs the bars, shakes them, and shouts, *I'm sorry! I'm sorry!*

Acknowledgments

I am indebted to my brilliant editor, Jessica Williams, whose tireless dedication to this book moved me in ways I'll never forget. Also, Marya Spence, agent extraordinaire: Thank you for your passion, your heart, your devotion, and your friendship. I feel so lucky to know you.

Thank you to Julia Elliott and the entire team at William Morrow, particularly Eliza Rosenberry, Angela Craft, and Ploy Siripant. Thanks also to Nat Edwards, Hellie Ogden, and the team at Janklow & Nesbit, and Alexis Kirschbaum and the team at Bloomsbury UK. I'm grateful for all the work you've done to usher this novel into public life.

Thank you to Sarai Schulz, Katie Axt, Edward

Helfers, and Kevin Elliott for reading earlier versions of this book and offering such insightful feedback.

For the many conversations about haunts and special effects, and for giving me a tour of your new spectacle, thank you to Billy Livingston and Mike Gemeny. Thanks also to Amanda Orr for introducing me to dorm life at the University of Nebraska–Lincoln.

For friendship, support, and advice throughout the writing of this novel, thank you to Akemi Johnson, Rei Onishi, Jung Yun, Richard Cochnar, Christopher Allen Franklin, Bernard Welt, Samantha Chang, Andrew Malan Milward, Beth Randklev, Darrel Randklev, Kate Sachs, Jennifer duBois, T. Geronimo Johnson, Benjamin Hale, Angela Richerson, Kevin Richerson, Carol Downey, Jeff Downey, Mike Gray, Gerry Stover, Barry Nelson, John Mahon, Richard Golding, Dale Ray Phillips, Ann Neelon, Carrie Jerrell, Andy Black, Julie Cyzewski, Allen Wier, Erik Rodriquez, and Viet Le.

Thank you to the creative writing program at Murray State University, the professional writing program at the University of Maryland, the creative writing program at the George Washington University, and Humanities North Dakota for financial and institutional support.

Thank you to Chloe Salmon and everyone at *The*

Moth for allowing me to tell a story onstage and giving me one of the best nights of my adult life.

Finally, to my family, thank you for your faith, your guidance, and your steadfast encouragement. I'm grateful for everything you've done.

About the Author

JAMES HAN MATTSON is the acclaimed author of *The Lost Prayers of Ricky Graves.* A graduate of the Iowa Writers' Workshop, he is the recipient of awards from the Michener-Copernicus Society of America and Humanities North Dakota. He was a featured storyteller on *The Moth* and has taught writing at the University of Iowa, the University of Cape Town, the George Washington University, the University of Maryland, Murray State University, and the University of California–Berkeley. He is currently the fiction editor of *Hyphen* magazine. He was born in Seoul, Korea, and raised in North Dakota.